SELFISH

By

LAYER MOORE

Table of Contents

Dedication

To my daughter – dreams come true. x

Acknowledgements

To everyone who encouraged me (as if I needed it)!!! You believed in me, and my hope is this: you will relax and enjoy the ride and come back for more.

He knows who he is. Thank you for your constant support and encouragement. The process was so much more enjoyable with you.

A Big Thank you to the publishing team -- you are all amazing

About the Author

Layer has always dreamed of creating a series of books that take the reader on a journey. A journey that excites and intrigues the reader, who is left wondering what happens next.

It was after having some serious health issues that Layer decided to put her dream to reality, so she started her own journey, not knowing where it would take her.

Introduction

Thank you for purchasing this novel. This is my first and I hope you enjoy it.

I imagine you relaxing on a sunbed or a couch. You will be warm and comfortable, maybe a drink by your side, immersing yourself in the book. Time will go quickly, and when you take a break, you will think about the characters. I wonder who you relate to the most!

Chapter One: The Country Manor Hotel

The Country Manor Hotel is an opulent hotel set in its own grounds. The Country Manor Hotel has only 34 rooms (well, it has 35 rooms, but one room belongs to the Arlington's). All rooms are luxurious, with king-size beds made up of Egyptian linen and mulberry silk for the pillowcases. Each room feature's a power shower, a wet room, and a deep jet bath. They provide a minibar and a fridge stocked daily with goodies. The facilities include a spa, indoor and outdoor pool, a sauna and steam room, and, best of all, a woo-woo room, which is the most relaxing experience. It was this that brought people from miles away to the hotel. The food is five-star quality, all organic and from the local farms. The luxury comes at a high cost, but the hotel remains in high demand, with guests booking a year ahead.

"How about staying overnight? It's late, and we are all pissed! Are you sure you can drive? Let's sleep it off?"

"Shhhh, I'm not pissed," shouted Jo. "I've only had two, or was it three? Anyhow I'm driving, get in the car, it's bloody freezing!"

"Yes, bottles, Jo, two or three bottles!" laughed Helen.

Allow me to introduce ourselves.

I'm Mandy Cane, 26, a single nurse looking to mingle. My preference is men, and my interests, well, I don't have many except dating men. I don't really like to be alone, so picking up men suits me. I get a good meal, a few drinks, and usually a good snog, maybe more! I know my family would be outraged, but since they are back in New Zealand, I believe what they don't know won't hurt them.

These girls are my family, and even though they moan at me for picking up men all the time, I love them dearly. Jo, short for Joanna, 30, single, drives trucks, loves it, always on the road. A different woman in every town! Everyone in the group sees her as the tough one. When things get rough, she's the one you want by your side. She is a superb woman. Then we have Cindy, who is 25, engaged, and due to marry soon. Cindy is the reason we were at the Country Manor Hotel. She's the spoilt one; she doesn't work. Lives off mummy and daddy. She wants for nothing. The bloke she is marrying is a real snooty twit; that's why we call him Lord Snooty! His real name is Terrance. Well, it's Lord Arlington Jr. Their wedding seems to be a secret. I'm not even sure the bride knows when it will be. The Arlingtons seem in control of everything, and Lord Snooty, well, he seems oblivious to most things, including Cindy!! A strange family, but I am sure they will look after Cindy once she marries Lord Snooty. Cindy's mother was beside herself with excitement when Cindy announced she was to marry Terrance. According to Cindy, her mother is an overbearing snob who can't wait to get herself in the big house. She is so excited about meeting the Lord and Lady. So, I'm guessing they should all fit in well! Then lastly, Helen 31, the rational one, a personal trainer, keeps us all in shape, although tonight she's wasted! After getting divorced, Helen found herself in a messy situation, and alcohol seemed to help blot it out. She's a strong woman and will overcome anything! (eventually)

So, there you have it: four girls on a day out to the country manor tasting wine and posh food, having a swim, a massage, and anything else we could get as Lord Snooty was paying, apparently!

"Get in the bloody car," shouted Jo. "What are you dreaming about? Men, I imagine; that's all you think about these days. Now get in. I'm bloody freezing."

"I was just thinking about how lovely it is to spend time with my friends. Our day has been lovely, I mean. I'm so lucky to have you girls."

"Save the sloppy stuff! It's bloody raining, and these country lanes are pitch black," Jo shouted, "Let's get going. Strap yourselves in, girls."

Cindy and Helen snuggled together in the back. Jo had been driving for about 30 minutes; the rain was coming down heavily, and visibility was poor. "There's something in the bloody road!" shouts Jo. "What the fuck!" Despite Jo's grip on the steering wheel, the car skidded. "HELP Girls HELP!! Nothing's happening. HELP!" Jo shouted as the car started to swerve out of control, colliding with a cut-down tree, flipping onto its roof, and gliding down the road before hitting another felled tree trunk, which flipped it again, turning it back onto its wheels as it hit another tree bringing it to an abrupt halt. The Screams that had filled the air had stopped, and Silence took over.

MERRYFIELD 31st OCTOBER 8. 30 PM

"Who's driving? We should have left a long time ago."

"Rich is bringing the transport."

"So where is he? And who the fuck invited him?" asked Cruz.

"I did," said Dazer. "He's Ok. I felt sorry for him; he never goes out!"

"Oh, my god, you have fallen for his bullshit. He's a complete wanker, a waste of time. Lazy bastard!"

"Hey, don't be that way. Get to know him!" said Dazer.

"It's fuckin'' nine o'clock; it's freezing. We're standing here waiting for that daft prick, and you tell me not to be like that. He's a waste of time. Why is he even a friend of yours?" demanded Cruz.

"Here he is!" Shouts Dazer. The group looks up to see a white van speeding towards them.

"Evening Lads. Get in."

"I'm not getting in that heap of shit."

"Get in," laughed Rich. "Beggars can't be choosers; besides, I got you something to make it all better!"

"That's it! That's it! I'm not getting in," shouts Cruz

"Come on, man, don't spoil my weekend. It means a lot to me to have you all here. Come on, man, we may be a bit late, but we'll be Okay,"

"Well, I'm driving, not this prat. He's drunk or something!" exclaimed Cruz

"Hey man, chill. You wanna drive? I'm Okay in the back. It's nice and comfortable, and to show how much I care, I left water for all of ya at the front. Ya can thank me later," laughed Rich.

"Anyway, why are you so fuckin'' late?" asked Cruz

"Busy," Rich muttered, winking and stumbling towards the van's rear.

So here I am driving, the sensible one, the organised one, the MR. Nice Guy, 27, single. I am a model, and my name is Cruz. Yes, I know a handsome name!! I have one of those faces that everyone wants to look at. I have my dad to thank for my skin colour. He originated from Turkey, and he met my mum when she was modelling swimwear in Scotland! They have been together ever since, not that I see them. They travel a lot, promoting self-help courses and books! I moved to London a few years ago. All the big modelling contracts were in London, and the airports were better connected to hop over to Paris or Milan. So that's me, I'm a nice decent guy, I enjoy the best of everything, which is why I agreed to come to the Country Manor with my mates Dazer and Mike, what I didn't know was they had invited the bad boy.

Rich (Richard) 29 is rough, doesn't give a fuck about anything or anybody. Works when he wants to. He messes around with women and the local drug dealer. He's married to Tanya, poor cow, and I am told his confidence is what women find attractive, although his jawline, bright blue eyes, beautiful smile, and enormous cock could have something to do with it! Anyway, I think he's a twat, and I'm not sure how we are in the same friendship group the bloke gets on my nerves.

Then we have Mike, 32, who is a soft and caring person. He is getting married soon. That's why we're heading to the Country Manor Hotel for the weekend to sample the food, wine, and beds! His wife-to-be is a demanding cow. Poor Mike works so hard to please her; he works non-stop; he sorts everything out while she lazes about. We have told him, but he won't listen. He loves her. He's a mechanic, a very good one, a handy person to know he can tackle anything.

Then Dazer, 27, my best mate. He's a lovely chap. We have been mates since we were in school together. He's a PE teacher who despises his job and children. He gets away with doing very little because he's attractive and gay. Everyone adores him. He takes good care of his appearance and hates getting dirty. Even the slightest amount of dust on his shoes stresses him out and sends him into a paddy!

So that's us four guys, posh hotel, weekend break.

"This van is a heap of shit. It's dangerous!" shouted Cruz

Rich felt comfortable in the back, although it lacked heating. He had made the back of the van into a travelling bedroom, for those times he got lucky, which was quite often. He could hear everything the boys were saying, but his mind felt empty. Rich had stolen a bag of powder from his friend and decanted it into twelve water bottles. Rich had no idea what the powder was but guessed cocaine. He thought it would be fun to get everyone high for the weekend! But the water was making him feel strange. Whatever the powder was, it was working! He thought!

Mike and Dazer were in the front. "Come on, Cruz, get us going. I'm thirsty!"

Mike grabbed the water and took a big sip. "Want some?"

The weather was bad; the rain was coming down heavily, and it was freezing cold.

"Put ya foot down, pretty boy. It's fuckin' freezing in the back," shouted Rich.

"Fuck off."

"Now, now, play nice, you two. Rich, just shut up, and Cruz, just drive."

Visibility was poor, and the van's lights were not the brightest!

"This bloody van is dangerous. The steering wheel has its own will. The brakes are almost non-existent, and the bloody indicators don't work. I can't believe I am driving this heap of shit in a dark country lane! Pass me some water, please," asked Cruz. "My throat is dry cus I'm so fuckin'' nervous driving this heap of shit!"

Suddenly, the van swerved. "What the fuck!" Gripping the wheel, Cruz lost control as the van hit something! Initially, the van veered left, then right. The steering wheel had locked. All Cruz could do was hold on as the van continued to spin out of control. Aqua gliding along the road until it came to an abrupt halt, causing everyone to launch forward.

The men who had been shouting and swearing had stopped, and everything was quiet as a hush fell in the van!

Chapter Two: The Cottage

"Where am I? Who are you?" "You've a beautiful body, babe. I've helped myself several times when you were sleeping! I hope you don't mind?" Agonising pain shot through Mandy's head and fanny, making it nearly impossible for her to move. My Fanny! Why on earth would that be painful? She tried to think, but her mind was blank. "Please, can I have some water?!" "You're so polite, babe, don't struggle. It will only make it hurt more. Try anything and. Well, you don't want to know! You got me? Oh, and I forgot to say don't shout. Everyone thinks you're dead, and no one is looking for you!" Mandy could not make sense of this. Her head was throbbing; her fanny was throbbing. She had woken up in a cold, damp bed with a man who claimed people thought she was dead. Rich came over with water in a plastic cup. Mandy looked up at him. "Where am I? Who are you?" She asked, "Shhh," hissed Rich, "too many questions," as he cradled her head to let her sip the water. "Once you're better, we can get to know one another. Now, go back to sleep. I like it better when you're sleeping. I can fuck you, and you don't complain! You're one lucky girl. You're getting a lot of action, babe; now sleep." A thud struck her head. Rich looked down at her, smiling. She is mine, all mine. At last, I have a woman who is quiet, beautiful, maybe a bit thin, but I'll fatten her up, he thought, kissing her forehead.

Rich, a regular seasonal worker for the farmer, had settled into one of the farm hand cottages. The cottages were basic, especially in the winter. They were cold but dry, and what Rich really liked was that they were silent. The cottages had running cold water and electricity. When Rich didn't feel like going home, he would often opt to stay in the cottage. No one came to the top fields in winter. The farmers had a few crops remaining in the lower fields. This allowed the farm to shut down, giving the farmer a winter rest. Rich knew the area well. He knew all the secret cut-throughs. Rich knew how to hide. His ability to get himself out of situations was impressive! All his previous women had called him selfish (among other names), but he didn't care. Rich did what he wanted when he wanted and with whom he wanted. These days, he never gets turned down by anyone.

Chapter Three: 5th November

LIVINGSTONE HOSPITAL

"Hello Cruz!"

Cruz opened his eyes. "Where the fuck am I?" he thought. Cruz tried to speak, but his mouth and lips were so dry that it was difficult to speak.

The Nurse smiled, "Hello, you are in the hospital. Now let me give you some water, just a sip to start." Cruz tried to move, but everything hurt. Then he realised he had something attached to him.

"Hey, it's Ok. Don't worry said the nurse. It's great you have woken up, "we can get you on the mend." The nurse cradled his head so he could sip more water. Cruz tried to move again, but His legs felt numb! "Nurse! Nurse, I can't feel my legs," shouted Cruz.

"Hey, don't fret now. We think you have spinal damage from your fall. You have lots of swelling. We need to get you stronger. Now relax, I will get the Doctor."

Cruz looked around and tried to think how he got here, but his mind was blank, like someone had erased his memory. His arms were sore. In fact, he was sore all over. He had tubes going into each arm and a frame around his bed. "WHAT ON EARTH HAPPENED?"

"Hello Cruz"

Cruz looked towards the man speaking.

"Hello Cruz, I am Dr. Lavery. You're a lucky lucky man."

"I am'

"Yes, lucky to be alive. We are unsure of the duration of your time on the roadside, but perhaps a few days? What happened?" The doctor paused and waited for a response! Cruz stared at the Doctor. "We are deeply concerned about the swelling on your spinal cord, as it poses a significant risk to your health. We are unsure at the moment about potential permanent damage. With reduced swelling, the picture will become clear. That's why it's important you rest, and we will monitor you closely. Did you fall? Fall from a tree? What were you doing climbing a tree on your own? Or were you attacked?" Asked the Doctor."

"What the fuck. Too many questions. I can't remember a thing," thought Cruz.

"Never mind," sighed the doctor. "Over time, it may return to you. Now rest, Cruz. Oh, by the way, you had no phone with you or anything, no wallet, nothing! Strange for a young man nowadays. We only got your name from your necklace. Do you have a family?"

Cruz stared at the doctor. He didn't know what to say.

"Ok, Cruz, let's not worry right now."

Dr. Lavery exited the room. "Nurse monitored him; I have prescribed some medication for the pain. Start more oral fluids and see how he goes. I will be back later."

"Yes, Doctor," said the nurse

5th November The cottage

"Hello Babe, you're coming round! Sorry about your lips. We had some rough sex last night; I think I got carried away! Sorry, I forced your mouth open too much! But at least ya got fed!" laughed Rich. "You're looking skinny, ya gotta eat, babe. I don't like me women skinny! I like more meat on me, women, babe. I have decided you can stay awake now, and I will feed ya, ya know, fatten ya up a bit. Ya, a beautiful girl, especially now your bruises are fading away! But remember, try anything and, well, it will upset me, and you don't want to do that! I choose ya, babe, so ya are lucky. Not sure what happened to the others! I can't remember. Never mind, it's me and you now. Just relax, eat when and what I tell ya, talk when I tell ya, and, oh ya, open those legs for me when I tell ya. How is your pussy? Sore, I bet! You have had some real good sessions, babe. I'VE FUCKED THE LIFE OUT OF YOU. You were getting dry, though, babe. I used some olive oil to help me cock slip in! Hope you don't mind. I know it's selfish!

Fuck, just talking about it makes me want ya again, but I'll wait. It will be different now that you're awake," Rich smiled at her.

Mandy looked at him. Taking it all in was a struggle for her. Tears rolled down her face as she sat in silence. "Where am I? Who is this man? Why me? How?" she thought as she closed her eyes in the hope that it was all a dream. Questions swirled around in her head. It's a bad dream. Surely, this is not happening; it's not real. Things like this only happen in films; pull yourself together, Mandy. But it was real; she felt his presence near her. His breathing seemed heavy. Mandy opened her eyes slowly. He was next to her, pleasuring himself.

"Look at me! Look at me," he panted. "I said bitch, look at me, Look me in the eye." Mandy's gaze went from his cock to his eyes!

"Yeah, that's it; now watch me. Watch me how I pleasure myself. Watch and learn, babe, 'cus this should be your job! Now open ya mouth. I said open ya fuckin'' mouth, bitch, that's it, that's it, babe." Rich grabbed her head and forced her down onto him. His juices shot into her mouth. "Swallow, bitch, swallow."

Despite wanting to be sick, Mandy swallowed as much as possible. She opened her mouth to allow the rest to run out. "You ungrateful bitch, you're losing some!" Rich started licking her face. "Yum, tastes good! Leave it to me to tidy ya up! You're an ungrateful bitch, after everything I have done for ya!" Rich pulled her hair. Making Mandy scream, "Hey, babe, no need to be scared," said Rich soothingly. "We love each other, babe, and you are the kinda woman of me dreams, well nearly, maybe if ya was a bit more er... Oh, never mind, babe. Now I'm gonna wash you, cus you're smelling a bit, babe, and I like me women clean!"

Mandy said nothing. She was empty; her mind was blank.

Rich stroked her hair, "Don't worry, babe, I will look after yoa." The water was icy, but it was refreshing to her face and shocking to her body. She was naked, freezing cold in a strange place, being washed with cold water by a stranger. Nothing made sense. Her body trembled with shivers. "Hey, hey, you're trembling, poor baby. It is cold, but you needed a wash, babe. Come on, let me wrap you up." Rich wrapped her in towels and a blanket and held her tight. "I've dreamt of this moment," said Rich. "Being somewhere quiet with a beautiful woman, with a beautiful body, a woman who knows her place, a woman who only wants to please me. Oh, babe, you make me so happy." Rich picked Mandy up and made his way to the bed. He laid her down and started removing the towels. Mandy grabbed the towel, "No, please don't take the towel. I am too cold." "Hey, I say what goes on, and right now it's me! Look what ya do to me, babe! LOOK!" His erect cock caught Mandy's attention; it was one of the biggest she had ever seen. His arousal was clear, and he had only one desire in mind. "You'll soon be warm, babe," hissed Rich.

"No, no, please don't. I'm too cold. Please don't," pleaded Mandy. "Please let me get warm first."

Rich had a problem; he had turned into a sexual monster once he got aroused and had an erect penis. He would kill anything and anyone that stood in the way of him finding relief, and right now, it was her, the woman he loved, his babe. She had turned into a fuckin' cold bitch!

"No one tells me what to do, do ya hear me? NO ONE, especially when I'm ready to fuck. Now open your fuckin'' legs, or do I have to force them open?"

Mandy lay still, holding onto the towel. With one quick swoop, Rich pulled the towel away, pinned her arms above her head, spreading her legs with his knee; he started teasing her with his cock. "Yes, that's it. Pretend you don't want me, but I know you do. You want this inside you, don't you? I said don't ya? I can't hear ya. Your man can't hear ya. Louder! What ya say? Tell me, tell me LOUDER," Rich shouted. The tip of his cock was teasing her, and despite being cold, scared, and hungry, Mandy felt herself getting turned on by this handsome, strong stranger. "TELL ME!" Rich shouted, "Tell me you want me."

"I want you, I want you," shouted Mandy. With one push, Rich was inside her. "That's it, babe. I knew you wanted me. You're a fuckin' bitch, but you're all mine." His rhythm was getting quicker, the force harder. "That's it, babe. I'm all yours. Oh my god, babe, you make me so happy. Oh My God, babe, take that! And that! And that!" Rich shouted as he pounded into her harder and harder. Eventually, he collapsed on top of her. Mandy felt warm, desired and strangely safe in these strangers' powerful arms!

Chapter Four: 6th November
The Police Station

"Serg! Serg! Sir! Sir!"

"What? What the fuck do you want? I'm busy enjoying my tea and biscuits."

"But, Sir, it's a murder!"

"Calm down, lad, calm down."

Jessie was a bright young officer who was very enthusiastic and very active. He dreamt of working in the city on big cases. He was always doing something and always wanted to be first on the scene; not that he had a lot of scenes to attend, but Serg would always send him first to everything. These young ones have far too much energy. He will make a great detective one day, thought Serg.

"Sir, Sir, we have two people in the front office. They were walking in the woods and found a body, a woman's body, in Castle Woods! They could not get a phone signal, so they came straight here. What we gonna do, Serg?"

"Calm down, kid, get them tea, take a statement, and it's probably all and nothing!"

"But Serg, we have a body to find!"

"Ok, Ok, lad, get them in the car, get them to take you to the body, let me know what you find. I might have finished my tea and biscuits by then! And kid, it won't be a body. Nothing like this happens here, but if by some chance you find anything, don't fuckin' touch anything."

"Yes, Sir." Jessie rushed out of the office, "At last, something exciting."

"Mr. and Mrs. Taylor, please come with me. Can you show me where you discovered the body?" They all piled into the car and headed off with Mr. Taylor directing, they had been driving for about thirty minutes. "Pull in! Pull in!" shouted Mr. Taylor. "Do you think it was here, Mr. Taylor?" asked Jessie. "Yes, officer, we need to go through that gap," replied Mr. Taylor, pointing to a gap in the hedge.

Mr. and Mrs. Taylor had been married for fifteen years. Hoping for more excitement, they had joined a group of naked ramblers. The Taylors hadn't met up with the group yet. They wanted to practice feeling comfortable walking outdoors with no clothes on before they met up. Today was a practice run for them. Just as they were about to undress, they stumbled upon the body.

"This way, officer," the group walked for another ten minutes. Mr. Taylor stopped and surveyed the area. "Ah, yes, this way."

Jessie wondered if they knew where they were going.

Mrs. Taylor had been quiet, then she shrieked, "My knickers! I've found my knickers!" Mr. Taylor and Jessie looked at her. "I took them off by the tree, then we saw her."

"Your knickers?" questions Jessie. "I had just taken them off, hoping for a quick moment to spice things up with Mr. Taylor." Mrs. Taylor glanced at Jessie, who shook his head. Despite having many questions, Jessie asked none.

Jessie turned to Mr. Taylor just as he was smelling the knickers. "You naughty girl, I will have to deal with you later,"

"Ok, Ok, you two, get a room," said Jessie, who was getting impatient with the pair.

"So where now?" asked Jessie

"Oh yes, it must be back down this way."

Jessie sighed. He started walking back when he spotted a girl slumped by a tree.

"There, over there!" Jessie pointed.

"Yes, there she is! She's dead, I know it! She's dead!" Mrs. Taylor started to scream and wail.

Jessie approached the body. He was careful not to touch anything,

The Taylors were both hysterical.

"Shhh! Shut the fuck up!" Jessie shouted.

The body was slumped by a tree. Jessie thought she looked dead. He touched her skin. It was cold. He felt for a pulse, but nothing. He lifted her head. 30s, maybe, he thought.

Jessie got out his phone. "Fuck! No signal."

"Hey, you two, do ya think you could wait here? I'm just gonna walk down the hill to get a signal." Jessie looked at the couple, who were red and wet in the face from crying and screaming.

"Yes. Yes, sir, we will wait right here," sniffed Mrs Taylor

"Don't go touching anything," warned Jessie.

"No, no, sir."

Jessie marched down the hill.

"Serg, it's Jessie. You better get out here. Bring a team. We have a body, a white female, maybe 30." Jessie gave Serg the directions and went back to the scene.

Jessie stopped in his tracks. "What the fuck!?" Mr. Taylor's bare arse was pumping away at a tree!! Jessie shook his head, not quite believing what he was seeing. As he got closer, he could see it was Mr. Taylor vigorously thrusting into Mrs. Taylor, who had her legs spread around the tree, causing her large breasts to bounce. "Fuck me," thought Jessie. "He is going for it." Jessie could not take his eyes off the pair. She was moaning quietly at first, but she was getting louder as Mr. Taylor banged her harder.

Jessie felt his cock twitching in his pants. He knew he was about to watch them both orgasm. Jessie found his hand down his pants. "It's been a long time," he thought. As He started massaging his cock up and down as he watched the Taylors. Jessie felt himself get into the rhythm, which was getting quicker and quicker and quicker, then it happened; she screamed, "I'm—I'm cumming, Mr. Taylor!"

"Hold on, baby, I'll be right with you," shouted Mr. Taylor.

Jessie was with them, pulling every drop out. Oh My God, he sighed! I needed that, but it was so wrong. Jessie had always had strange sexual desires. That's why he struggled to find a woman who would go along with them. Jessie was deep in thought as he heard the sirens approaching. He got himself back together and walked towards the Taylors. They were both flushed and looked extremely coy!

"Get some clothes on," hissed Jessie, "Before I arrest you."

"We will be on our way now, Sir," said Mr. Taylor.

"No, you're witnesses. You stay here for now. I will get you to the station for statements soon, and then you can go home. Ok?"

Serg made his way up the hill, followed by his team.

Serg was 59, a well-respected senior detective just waiting to retire. After spending years in London, he had endured years of drama that came with working in the city. He now wanted a quiet life in a quiet village full of sleepy people. His days were mostly uneventful, with sporadic involvement in petty theft, car burglaries, minor neighbourhood incidents, and the occasional accident. But oh no, not today; someone found a bloody body!!

Serg stood over the body. Something felt wrong. A young woman slumped against a tree in the woods. Why? No obvious signs of a struggle! Serg's sense of wrongdoing had kicked in.

"What's up, Serg?"

Serg glanced around, spotting Jake, the coroner approaching.

"Dun know lad looks like she dead a young white female with no obvious injuries." Jake approached the body and asked permission to lay the body down flat.

Serg nodded, "Yes. Go ahead."

Jessie knelt down with Jake. They put a hand around the back of the body.

"Serg, she's warm," shouted Jessie.

Jake nodded in confirmation, "Yeah, warm."

"Find a pulse," ordered Serg. Jake got out his stethoscope and started moving it down the body.

"I've got one. Faint, very faint, but I think I have one. I think she's alive, but only just."

"Fuckin' hell, get the paramedics," ordered Serg. Jessie ran down to the road. The paramedics had automatically been called and were on standby.

"Oh, Mr. and Mrs. Taylor, I need you at the station for statements. Young Jake will take you to the station, and a constable will take the statements. That said, Mr. and Mrs. Taylor, I don't want you to leave the country, not planning on leaving, are you?"

"No, no, we are home birds. We only ventured out today to try something new.

Serg looked at the couple but decided not to ask.

"Ok."

The paramedics were making their way up the hill.

"What we got?" shouted one of them.

"We got a fuckin' woman who needs your urgent help; now hurry."

The paramedics acted quickly. They established her oxygen levels, stabilised her with fluids, wrapped her up, and set off down the hill to the ambulance. "Jessie, go with them," Serg ordered.

"What you gonna do?" asked Jessie.

"Have a fuckin' party, what do you think? Now piss off!" Serg snapped.

Jessie looked at Serg. He had never seen him so annoyed. Jessie did not understand this was the most excitement they had had in years. Well, in the last year since Jessie got his placement in this sleepy station. Jessie had heard great things about Serg. He wanted to learn from him. But Serg had done it all and wanted a quiet life. Yes, he had tales to tell, and they were exciting. Jessie would listen and pick up tips, but this, well, was exciting for Jessie. It was something different. Jessie was ready for something big, and this felt like something big.

Livingstone Hospital 6th Nov

The emergency room was prepared and awaiting the unknown female.

"Here they come." The medical team acted with speed and care, all knowing what each other was doing and all having a job. It was like a well-oiled machine.

All Jessie could do was stare in both admiration and horror.

"Sir, you will need to leave the cubicle now. You can wait down the corridor. We will call you. Are you related?" Asked the nurse.

"No, No, I'm a police officer, Jessie Warrington."

"Jessie, I'm sorry, but you'll need to wait in the waiting room. The condition of this girl is critical. We'll keep you updated when there's any news."

Jessie walked to the coffee machine, got himself a coffee, and waited.

Two hours later, the nurse came to find Jessie.

"Hello, Jessie?"

"Yes, how is she?"

"We have stabilised the girl, said the nurse. She was hyperthermic and severely dehydrated. Her oxygen levels were low. We have ventilated her. This way, her body will be resting whilst getting oxygen and fluids, and the good news is that her temperature has already come up slightly. Also, the x-ray does not show us anything broken, so it's just time now. Oh, what's her name?" Questioned the nurse

"I don't know; she had nothing on her."

"What, no phone?" Exclaimed the nurse.

"No. Nothing."

"Oh, I will let the Dr. know."

"Will she be Ok? "asked Jessie?"

"It's touch and go. but you probably got to her just in time; you may well have saved her, so let's wait and see." The nurse smiled and headed off.

Jessie headed out of the ward. He walked past the nurses station and they were discussing the events of the day.

"Sorry, I'm inspector Warrington. I couldn't help but overhear you discussing someone else who had been admitted who had no ID or phone."

"Yes, a young man was brought in yesterday."

"Where is he?"

"Ward 1B, but no point talking to him. His memory hasn't returned yet; bless him," said the nurse. "He's so handsome. she laughed."

"Ok, thanks. I will be back tomorrow."

Chapter Five: The Gilberts

"Calm down, calm down," said George.

"My daughter has not come home, and you're telling me to calm down?"

"She's with friends, and it's our daughter, snapped George.

"What friends, George, what friends tell me? Why is there no phone call, and why doesn't she answer her bloody phone?" Tell me that.

"Maybe she is having fun away from her overbearing mother!!"

"Why are you calling me overbearing when my daughter is missing? I'm going to the police, and then I will deal with you!!"

George and Susan had one daughter; she was their princess and always had been. Susan fussed over her and gave her everything. Of course, George loved his daughter, but he thought Susan spoiled her far too much, and now that she was getting married, well, it was over bearing. In particular, Susan's obsession with the posh family Mandy was marrying into. George believed Susan had a strong desire to become part of the posh group and valued this marriage more than Cindy did.! He simply went along with everything to avoid conflict. Fishing provided George with peace, not that she allowed him much of that. "I'm going to the police, George, our girl is missing!!" snapped Susan. "Ok," sighed George. "They will want to know things like what she was wearing, where she was going, and with who!" "I don't know," cried Susan. "I don't know any bloody thing!! But I know something is wrong. Why hasn't she called? I'm calling Terrance." "If you must," murmured George, "he's a total waste of time, not that I have met him. I'm not important enough. I mean, I'm only the father!" sighed George.

"Terrance, it is Susan, Cindy's mother. Is she with you?"

Terrance was a lord and heir to a lot of land owned by his parents, Lord and Lady Arlington. They rented most of the land to farmers. The land also included lots of woodland and private, well-maintained grounds around their manor house. Terrance believed he worked, but he only wandered the estate, preening like a peacock. The farmers would laugh at him, and he was often the butt of their jokes. His parents were very popular. They did a lot for the farmers, for charity, and for the local community. The Arlingtons always organised a special Christmas ball and extended invitations to everyone. This year, Terrance was tasked with organising the Christmas ball. His Dad, the lord, was not interested in anything outside of shooting with his old mates and lying in bed. His mother (lady Stephanie Arlington) always organised everything, but she was busy doing other stuff, apparently. Terrance was unsure what other stuff his mother had on, but he had big plans for this year's Christmas ball. He envisioned the biggest and best one yet, featuring a masquerade theme, an abundance of food and drink, dancing, and pure joy.

Despite Lady Arlington's desire for her son to be more responsible, she couldn't relinquish her beloved annual event, and as Terrance was not used to taking on responsibility, organising the ball consumed him and turned him into a bigger nightmare than usual. Unknown to Terrance, his mother was overseeing everything in the background. Every decision he made, she would agree or change. Terrance was so caught up in himself that he was oblivious to any changes.

"Oh, Susan! Good morning! How the devil are you?" asked Terrence.

"Cut the crap. Where's my daughter?"

Terrance was taken aback by her abruptness.

"Susan, I haven't seen or heard from my soon-to-be wife in a few days. She went off with her feral friends. She chooses them above me. I mean, can I say how disappointed I was!! I mean, I told her not to go. Only trouble will come from those common tarts. I told her! I'm surprised you allowed her to go off with them. Now, let me update you on the Christmas ball.

"Let me stop you," shouted Susan. "I am sure everything is coming along just fine, but my daughter, who is your wife-to-be, is missing, and you haven't seen her?"

"No, I swear to you, Susan, I thought she was ignoring me because I called her friends feral, and I shouted at her because she wanted to be with them and not me. Hang on, so you haven't seen her since?" questioned Terrance as his voice trailed off.

"What if something has happened to her?" cried Susan.

Terrance was silent. He had been praying for this nightmare to end, something to stop this marriage. God, awful woman, and now she's missing. I imagine she has done this on purpose for attention, or have his prayers come true? He thought to himself.

"Terrance Terrance shouted Susan. You still there?"

"Yes, yes, sorry, I was just thinking!"

"Where is she, Terrance, my baby? Where is she?

Susan cried as she threw down the phone.

Terrance hung on the other end, wondering what on earth was happening. "Terrance, it's George. The wife's upset; she can't talk now, but our girl is missing. Please help us find her."

The phone line went dead.

After the call ended, Terrance pondered over the conversation. What could he do? He had the Christmas ball to plan, but now she is missing. This better not impede the ball arrangements, thought Terrance, the selfish cow going off with her ferral friends, drinking and laughing at him. Terrance ran toward his mother. "Mummy, mummy, something has happened!" "What is it, sweetie? Is it the caterers or the decorators? "No, no, it's that woman I'm marrying Cinderella." "Oh, I'm sorry, sweetie, she changed her mind." "NO, NO, mother, she's disappeared." Terrance sat down, poured himself a brandy, and explained everything to his mother. "Terrance, you need to go to the Gilberts and offer support, and you need to go now."

"But I am in shock, Mummy. I cannot go, you go!"

"Terrance, stop acting like such a bloody baby. Man up and go. You are or were supposed to be getting married; for goodness sake, you need to stop this nonsense, Terrance. Now offer support. I will hear no more, Terrance."

"Damn it!" shouted Terrance "I will have to go around to the Gilberts and show support or something!" The idea of entering a tiny house was as repulsive to Terrance as the thought of touching Cindy. It was his parents pushing him to marry. "She will do you well," said his father. "She's pretty, has good hips for children, went to private school, and is a local girl." Terrance loved his parents, so to keep them happy, he had agreed to marry but had not agreed on a date, and as far as he was concerned, it would be sometime never.

When Terrance arrived at the Gilberts, the police were already in attendance. "Calm down, Mrs. Gilbert, we will find your daughter. I am sure it's a simple explanation. Now, I am going to need some details. We can then put a search out for her,"

"So, let's start with her name."

"Cindy Marie Gilbert,"

"Age?"

"25."

"Description?"

"5ft 4in, medium build. Long black hair and blue eyes."

"Any birthmarks, piercings, tattoos?"

"No, No, nothing like that."

"What was she wearing?"

"A dress, pink or pinkish, I think, and boots."

"Type?"

"Black leather, knee high."

"Anything else?" asked Taz. "Coat, Handbag?"

"Yes, she had a fur coat, the cream one, I think."

"So, when was the last time you saw her?"

"It was on the 1st of November, about 9 am. She was going to meet friends."

"So, who are these friends?"

"I don't know." Susan stared at the officer. "I don't know her friends!"

"So, did she get picked up?"

"No, no, she was driving to her friends."

"Ok. Registration number, make, and model, please."

"CMG21 BMW 1. 8 in Black."

"Nice car!"

"Yes, it was a birthday present a few years ago.

"And you say you don't know her friends? Any names? Addresses? Workplaces? Where does Cindy work?"

"She doesn't. We look after her, and no, I don't know her friends. She never brought them home or told me anything about them. Terrance, do you know them?" asked Susan.

The Police officer Taz turned around to Terrance, "And you are?"

"I am Lord Arlington, Terrance of Arlington Manor."

"So, do you know Cindy?

"Yes, I am to marry her!"

"I see. So when was the last time you saw her?" asked Taz.

"She was at the manor house on Halloween. We had a splendid party, and it was such fun. Of course, I organised it, and we had a rum butler and…"

"Ok, I'm not interested," snapped TAZ. "You were saying about Cindy. She was at your party. Did she seem Ok? Did she stay over?

"Oh no, officer, our driver returned her home."

"So, how was she? Did she say anything to you about going somewhere?" Everyone looked at Terrance.

"Well, we actually had a tiff. Cindy told me she was going out with her girlfriends. She loves them! Ferral tarts, that's all they are, and I told her so. I told her not to go, but she got mad. She defended them and told me to poke my eyes out and stick them somewhere that I would rather not repeat; she told me I was so rude; I mean, I never heard her so mad. Then she said I was a bore, and she was going out with her friends to the Country Manor Hotel, and I was paying!"

"Country Manor Hotel? You mean the one on your estate?"

"Yes"

"You stupid idiot," screamed Susan. "WHY didn't you say? I could have been up there by now."

"Calm Down, Mrs. Gilbert, we will check it out. I need you to stay here in case Cindy calls, Ok?

Taz sighed at Terrance. "If you remember anything else, call me; here's my number. Oh, and don't go far. I'll be off now."

Taz returned to the station just as Jessie was clocking off. "Long day?" "Yeah, it's been a long day for someone like me," he laughed.

"And how about you?" "Yeah, not finished yet; a few more hours. I need to ring around. I've got a missing girl."

"A young girl?" asked Jessie. "Sort of 25. Why?" "Well, we found someone in the woods with no ID. I would guess she was in her 30s, but I don't know for sure. She is in the city hospital in a critical condition."

"RTA?" asked Taz. "No, don't think so," replied Jessie. "At the moment, we have no clue about the circumstances, but it's strange, so it may be worth checking, anyway. Have a good one. I'm off home. I'm knackered."

"Cheers, Jess, see ya, oh Jessie."

"Yes."

"What colour hair did she have?"

"Black or brown, dark anyway."

"Ok, thanks, babe."

Taz looked at her notes. She had little to go on, but the girl in the hospital sort of fit the description. It was worth following up. Eventually, after 35 minutes, Taz was through to intensive care. TAZ explained for the tenth time who she was, why she was calling, and who she was looking for. Eventually, she found a Nurse who was helpful. "It looks like the description fits, but the poor girl is still in a critical state. However, we believe she has made slight improvement since being admitted." The nurse explained the next few hours would establish if the girl would pull through and if she had any lasting damage to her organs. The Hospital was keen to identify the girl for many reasons, one major one being Allergies. Something Taz had never really thought about, but it made sense.

Taz put down the phone and thought about what to do. What if it is Cindy? What if she doesn't make it? Serg would hate me calling him at this hour, but I can't wait until tomorrow, thought Taz as she decided to call the Gilberts.

"Hello, Constable Hind here, Mr. Gilbert. We discovered a female in the woods who potentially matches Cindy's description. Look, Mr. Gilbert, I don't know if it is Cindy, and the girl is in a critical state, but I would like to rule it."

"Yes, yes, I'm on my way."

"No, no, Mr. Gilbert, wait, I will pick you up, be about 15!"

Mr. Gilbert dropped the phone and dropped to his knees. "My girl, my girl," he sobbed. Susan came running down the stairs. "What is it, George? What's wrong?" George, containing himself, explained to Susan. For once, Susan showed compassion towards her husband. "Come on, dear, let's get ready. We need to be strong, we need to know, and if it is her, we need to be with her. Come on, let's get ready."

The drive to the hospital seemed a long one. Taz tried to make conversation, but the Gilberts were numb. Bless them, she thought. She wasn't sure if she wanted this to be Cindy or not!

A nurse escorted the three of them into a room in intensive care. The Doctor explained they would hear lots of machine bleeps and noise and not to be alarmed. If it was Cindy, he would talk through the treatment plan in more detail. "Now, please put on theses gowns and masks. Please be quiet and touch nothing. Remember, you are here to establish if this is your daughter!" The Gilberts nodded and followed the Doctor. Susan looked up to see her beautiful daughter wired up to machines with tubes everywhere. Susan let out a scream and fell to the floor. "Please don't die, no, no! My daughter, my baby, don't die! Don't let her die, Doctor! She's all I have. Save her, save her!" Susan wailed.

Taz and the nurses assisted Susan off the floor and guided her to a private room. Mr. Gilbert remained calm, fighting back the tears. "Yes, Doctor, that's our daughter, Cindy Marie Gilbert, age 25." "Any allergies you know of?" "No, no allergies, doctor." The doctor nodded has he ushered Mr. Gilbert into the private room.

"I'm going to be honest: stated the Doctor. Your daughter is in a critical state. She has organ damage, a dislocated shoulder, head trauma, and extensive bruising, all consistent with a car accident. Let's focus on getting her through the next 24 hours. We are doing all we can. It is early days, but I have seen a slight improvement already, so that should give you some hope. However, it's time and rest she needs. We will monitor her continually. Any Questions?" asked the Doctor.

"Not at the moment. Thank you, Doctor."

Taz listened to everything. Poor girl, what on earth happened? She thought, "I will take you back home now," said Taz. "I'm not going anywhere, I'm not leaving her; you go, George, make sure you inform Terrance and bring me back clean clothes, something to wash with, and some money, we will take it in turns to stay, or I will just stay, but I am not leaving her," said Susan. Mr. Gilbert nodded. "Ok, love, I will be back tomorrow," George leant in to kiss her goodnight. Susan moved. "This is all your fault. You were never strong enough, never strict enough. You let her do as she wanted, and you never cared what she was up to. It has been me that's got her to settle down. It's been me that's got her to this point of marrying into a decent family, not you," Susan exploded. "Susan, enough. This is not helping," exclaimed George as he marched off. Taz wasn't sure what she had witnessed, but it didn't feel harmonious.

Taz felt awkward as she drove Mr. Gilbert home in silence. Mr. Gilbert felt embarrassed and annoyed at his wife and heartbroken over his daughter. All he wanted was to go back home and weep.

Taz wrote her report. Tomorrow, she would start establishing the facts. Serg is going to hate this, she thought. He will have work to do. However, she felt excited, as nothing like this happened in Merryfield. Taz closed down her workstation when she noticed an alert from the Hospital.

Man found at the roadside in Castlewoods. No ID, thought to be climbing trees, critical state, help required to identify!

Wow, thought Taz, "This is turning into something exciting. Can't wait until tomorrow. Serg will go crazy," she laughed to herself.

Chapter Six: November 6th
The Farm

Dazer began to come around slowly. Despite knowing he was alive, he felt numb, heavy, cold, and weak. He was struggling to move and frightened to open his eyes. Dazer moved his fingertips and felt around. It was cold, wet, and sticky like mud! MUD! Dazer opened his eyes in horror. He hated dirt; he hated dust and defiantly hated mud. Dazer was always the very smart, clean one. He looked around. It was dark, but it looked like a piece of tin above him. What was this heavy object on top of him? He tried to move, but he was stuck. He felt around the object on top of him. Shit, It was a person! A Person! Dazer screamed, "HELP! HELP! Somebody, help, please help me!" Dazer was stuck; he had no strength, and whoever this was had some weight on them. Dazer cried. Is this how it ends? Alone in the mud cold and with someone on top of me, what on earth happened? Dazer took a deep breath and, with all his strength, attempted to push the person off him, but it was no good; he was too weak. All he could do now was pray. He wished he was a tough man's man, but he wasn't. He was someone who liked the finer things in life. He liked fancy cocktails, fancy chocolate, fancy food, and coordinated outfits. He liked his hair to be just so, not a hair out of place. He liked Zen, not agitation. "Help me, Lord, help me, please. I am cold and hungry and really frightened. Please help me, please." The tears rolled down Dazer's face. He had never felt so hopeless. He had no clue where he was, how he got here, or how, if at all, he would get out. As Dazer thought about his life, he fell into a deep sleep.

November 7ᵗʰ, Farmer John.

"You taking a flask, John?" asked Martha.

"Yes, my love, I will stay and prepare all the pig huts for the new arrivals. If you could pack me some of your delicious sandwiches made with strong cheese and your homemade chutney, and maybe some of your wonderful sponge cake, that would keep me going, my love."

John had been a farmer all his life. He had wheat, beet, corn, and potatoes growing in various fields, along with a dedicated strawberry field in the summer and an apple orchard. But his passion was pigs. He sold the last lot a few months ago, and he had no intention of getting more this side of Christmas, but Lord Arlington had made a deal with someone, so 25 Piglets were arriving this week. Lord Arlington owned the land, and although he left all the farmers alone most of the time, sometimes he did strange things like this, buying stuff without checking. It's not right; it never works out well. John had told Lord Arlington, "It's too bloody cold for the little pigs. Who bred the sow this side of Christmas?" asked John, but Lord Arlington was not for sharing his source. "Do as I ask John, or I will start charging you Rent!" he had snapped. So John had no choice. "Martha, my love, I be off now. There is lots to do, and I won't be back until dark." "Ok, my love, I will have something nice and tasty waiting for you—a delicious homemade pie with your favourite vegetables and potatoes."

John set out on his tractor, thinking about what he needed to do: clean the pens, fill them with clean straw, check all the fences, fill the troughs with fresh water. The pig field was the furthest away. Luckily, it was a nice, dry day. The weather's been good to me, thought John.

John loved the pig field. It was right at the top, and he had always imagined he could smell the sea air. John was unlocking the gate.

"Oi."

John turned around.

"Yes, ma'am."

"You the farmer round here?"

"Well, I am one of 'em, ma'am. Are you Ok?" asked John

"I'm looking for my good-for-nothing husband. Not seen him in ages, not been near me, not even for a shag, but the bastard owes me money, so you got some twat called Rich working for ya? Cus this is where he said he was working."

"No, ma'am, all the season work is finished. One of the other farms has sprouts to pick, but we farmers do that and have a hot toddy and a game of cards afterwards."

"Lazy son of a bitch," she cried. "I'm broke, and I need a job or just some money. Do you have anything going on?"

"Sorry, ma'am, nothing,"

John felt sorry for the women. "You wanna give me a hand in this field? I have 20 quid on me."

"I'm in, sir, thank you. What do you want me to do? Oh, I'm Tanya, by the way?"

"Alright then, Tanya, let's get in the field, and I will show you what's needed," John started on the first pig pen. He scrapped out the mud and shit, checked the tin roof for holes, and then filled it with lots of fresh straw. He scrapped all the mud to one side so the pen was neat. "Just like that," said John. "I need all the pens done." Tanya looked around. She counted 30 pens. "What, all the pens for 20 quid?" John laughed. "If ya get em all done, maid, I'll double it!." Tanya started moving the bales of straw, first dragging them to each pen. "Hey maid, what you doing?" shouted John. "Clean em out first. I'll drop the bales near each one for you. No need to struggle too much, maid." Tanya was relieved; she was strong, but this was another level. But she was happy at last; she thought, here I am doing some work, helping the farmer and the little pigs. Tanya smiled to herself. Maybe the farmer would see she was a hard worker and give her some more work

. Farmer John came over. "You Ok, maid?" asked John. "Lovin' it," smiled Tanya. "Ok, I'm going to check the fences and fix the hose to the cottage to fill the troughs with some lovely fresh water. Then we can have a bit of lunch. I'm sure the wife made more than I can eat." "You have a cottage?" asked Tanya. "Yes, we have two. The farm hands stay in 'em in summer. They are empty now. I tidy 'em up in the winter but not got around to it yet." "Maybe I could help," asked Tanya. "Maybe maid, maybe," smiled John.

Tanya worked hard. One by one, she scrapped the mud and shit out, filled the pens with straw, and made each surrounding area as tidy as she could. She had 5 more to go.

Tanya shoved her big shovel into the pen, but something was blocking it. She shoved again and pulled out nothing. The pens were quite dark. Tanya leant in to see what was wrong. "Oh my God!" Tanya let out a scream. It looked like a person lying face down in the mud.! Tanya dropped the shovel and ran towards the cottages. Farmer John was making his way back. "You alright, maid?" "No, no, I'm not. I found a person, a body. Oh, I don't know what it is, but I've found something." John immediately wondered if he had left a pig to die and never noticed. How could he? An icy shiver went down his back. He was always so careful; he loved his animals. If this got out, he would be ashamed! Tanya led him to pen 25. John took a deep breath and, on his hands and knees, went in. He started feeling around; he felt a leg, a human leg, then another leg, then another leg! "What is it?" asked Tanya. "I think we have two," John replied as he crawled out of the pen. "Two what?" "Two bodies," replied John, who couldn't help but be relieved it was not a pig.

"You wait here," said John.

"No, I'm not waiting here. You wait here," replied Tanya.

"No, I'm not waiting."

"It's your field."

"You found em."

"Don't you have a phone?"

"Don't you?"

"Get on the tractor," sighed John. "Let's go; we need strong tea,"

Brandy, more like, said Tanya as she climbed onto the tractor

John explained the situation to his wife. Martha was not impressed that this woman had been helping her John in the field, but bless her, she was shaking and looked shocked. "Here, dear, have this." Martha handed Tanya a brandy with some sugar and hot water. "It's good for shock, dear. Sip it, mind." Martha wrapped Tanya in a blanket and sat her by the fire. "Poor dear," thought Martha. John was on the telephone talking to the police. "No sir, I dun know sir, I think so. Yes, two bodies. Yes, in the pig field, the top field. Ok, sir, I will wait here." When the police arrived, John was ready to escort them to the field. "I've fixed the trailer on the tractor. Ya, all need to get in. It's the quickest way now darkness is setting in." Serg was in no mood for this. He was just about to go home. Why the fuck did he answer the phone? "Come on, Serg, it's exciting," said Jessie as they climbed into the trailer. Serg climbed in the trailer along with the rest of the team, and John set off across the fields and towards the top field. John pointed to the pen, "Jessie, get in and see what it is," ordered Serg. Jessie was so excited he dived into the hut, the torch shining brightly. "Serg, it's two men! One is definitely dead, in my opinion," Jessie shouted as he made his way out of the pen. "Serg, what are we gonna do?" Serg sighed and scratched his head at all the fuckin'' places to find bodies in the middle of nowhere when it's getting dark! Why me? He thought, why me? "Ok, John, I am going to need your help. Would you be able to make a few trips up and down the fields for me, bring some people and equipment up here?" "Yes sir, no problem. I need the pen cleared as me pigs arrive soon," explained John. Serg was just about to respond with one of his cutting comments but thought better of it. The farmer was only doing his job after all, and maybe if he was nice, he would get some of that lovely homemade food that he had heard so much about! Serg made some phone calls. "Ok, John, if you could go back to the farm and wait for the next load of people and bring them up here, please. Then, I am going to need you to go down again as I need equipment up here. Is that alright?" "Yes, sir," replied John. "It's going to be a long night," sighed Serg!

Chapter Seven: November 8th
The Cottage

"Fuckin' fireworks! All that noise. Why don't they keep it to one night?!"

"I don't know."

"Did I ask you to speak? I told you to listen, bitch, and speak when I say. You've got some learning to do, but don't worry, babe, I'm an excellent teacher. I saved you, babe. I could have picked anyone, but I picked you. Yeah, I remember I had four, and I picked you for your long legs, big tits, small waist and nice round arse. I've always wanted someone like you, but that cold fish of a wife kept me away from a nice fanny, cold bitch. I swear I'll kill her one day! She's probably wondering where I am. I haven't been around to give her money or to shag her recently. Our money is running out, babe, only got what's left in the wallets; purses are empty! Got some cards. Do ya know any pin numbers, babe?"

Mandy was not sure if she should speak. She shook her head. Mandy's memory was coming back to her in small flashes, and he was filling in some blanks as he chatted away. But it was still a mystery where she was and who he was! "You're learning, babe. You know, you and me, babe, we make a great team. You are just so tasty, and I always wanted a woman like you. Now I have one, and babe, you're going nowhere without me." Mandy sat in silence. She had so many questions, but the thought of raising her hand to speak was too much for her, and she thought maybe gaining his trust was the best way. "I just look at you, babe, and I'm horny; come here." Demanded Rich.

Mandy dutifully got up from the chair. She was getting stronger by the day This stranger was giving her food and drink. He was washing her and had got some clothes for her. Every day, he would go out and return with food and clothes. Recently, he had returned with some makeup for her, but he was always demanding sex.

Rich was a sex addict, always had been. He could perform anywhere and with anyone, male or female. He loved nothing better than getting his enormous cock out and hearing the gasps! Everyone gasped when they saw it, and he loved it. Some women only wanted him for his dick, and some men only wanted him for his dick. He wasn't bothered as long as he was getting it out and shagging something. Yet all he wanted was to feel something for someone, something more than lust. He wanted something he had never had: LOVE. No one had loved him. They just used him mainly for his dick, but his don't-give-a-fuck attitude got him noticed, and for some reason, he was wanted by many people. He was not a bad man, just a misunderstood one!

"Come here bitch, come and stand over me and take your clothes off. You're still a bit skinny, babe," whispered Rich as he grabbed her. Mandy stood over him, legs open wide. "Wider girl, wider. He ordered, "That's it, stretch those lovely legs. That's better; now lower your sweet pussy on me." Rich's tongue went into action, darting in and out of her, licking and probing. Mandy moved to his rhythm, as much as she knew it was wrong, this stranger turned her on. She started pushing down on him, rocking back and forth. Her contractions were coming. Quicker "Oh my God, oh my… Fuck me. Fuck me," she screamed! "Na, you're a tart. You can fuckin' wait," shouted Rich as he threw her off him. "I say when you get fucked, now get dressed. It's fuckin' freezing."

Mandy was confused; this animal was abusing her, and yet she wanted him. Her pussy was throbbing,

"Hey, what ya thinking? Come here, babe." Rich held his arms out to her, "That's it. Come on, let me hold ya. Mandy relaxed into his arms. It was not long before she felt his hand between her thighs, gently stroking her, teasing her with his finger. "Fuck, you're wet, babe, really wet." His hand rubbed against her, and his fingers darting in and out of her. Mandy started moving to the rhythm of his fingers. He felt her fanny contracting, relaxing, contracting, relaxing. "Oh My, Oh My, Oh My," Mandy shouted. "That's it, babe, ride me fingers." Rich banged his fingers in and out of her, "Yeah, that's it, babe." Rich thought he would stop teaching her a lesson and make the bitch wait; after all, he was in charge, but his cock was throbbing, and she was moving and groaning. Her breathing was getting heavier and heavier. Fuck it, thought Rich. He withdrew his fingers and inserted his cock. "Now ride me bitch!" Mandy's pussy started contracting around his cock; he felt the pull. She was contracting hard, "Fuck babe," he shouted, "Fuck me." There was no stopping now. Mandy was riding him so hard she let out a scream. "Fuck it out of me," she screamed. His cock felt trapped, and it felt so good. Rich fucked her hard as she exploded, and he knew he was on his way. He exploded inside her, thrusting every last drop, which seemed to keep coming and coming. "Fuck me, babe, that was some fuck," smiled Rich as he cradled her in his arms, and for the first time, he felt as if he had just made love to a woman and not just fucked her! Is this love, he wondered. Am I in love now? Maybe? Rich had never been in love. He had been married a few times but never stuck around. Tanya, his current wife, was a witch; she never used to be, she was good in the sack, and he used to think she was hot, but she was lazy and only wanted him these days for money and his cock!

Rich would often think about Tanya. She was a real good fuck and game for anything. Rich smiled as he thought about the wild nights with Tanya; his fingers were tracing down Mandy's body, which was soft. Her skin was so pale. His fingers found their way between her legs. "Relax, babe, it's me and you now. I'm gonna take care of you." His fingers were inside her, and he started slowly finger fuckin' her. "I want you," he whispered. Rich started kissing her softly at first. He traced his lips to her breasts, sucking on her nipples, his tongue licking her belly as he made his way to her pussy. He started sucking her pussy, "Your'e tasty, babe," as he came up to kiss her. His tongue was soon back between her legs, darting in and out of her, sucking her lips. Mandy felt the urges rise inside her again. She started contracting her pussy, and her legs opened wider, inviting him in. She was pulsating now, pushing her pussy into his face. Rich turned around on her and placed his cock by her mouth, "Suck it, babe, suck it." Rich's cock was too big for her mouth; it was choking her as he pushed down, but she was lost in pleasure. Her pussy was on fire. She was gyrating now to his tongue; suddenly, she felt the heat rise within her. Her body started to shake her pussy was contracting so hard she wanted to scream, but his cock was fuckin' her mouth. Suddenly, Rich withdrew his cock from her mouth, flipped her over onto all fours and within seconds, he was inside her. "Babe, let me fuck it out of you. Go on, babe, cum all over me, let it all go," Rich shouted. Mandy was riding him so hard she screamed as she orgasmed, her body pulsing until she felt satisfied.

Rich smiled as he withdrew his cock and started stroking it, "It;s going in your mouth, babe," as he forced her head down on him. "Open wide, babe; you're a dirty fuckin' whore. Look, you dirty bitch, open your mouth fuckin' whore, open it, wider, wider, here it comes," Rich shouted as he pushed his cock deep into her mouth.

Mandy was struggling; she knew she had to swallow quickly, but she wanted to gag. She tried hard to think of how she could get rid of it. "Swallow, bitch." Rich grabbed her hair and pulled her head backwards, "Swallow," I said, "Remember I saved you, and this is good for you; now swallow." Mandy swallowed as she fought hard not to be sick. "There, not so bad; next time, just swallow, babe, don't make me mad. Now come and lie down with me." Mandy was exhausted; she laid down, closed her eyes and drifted off, feeling strangely safe in his arms. Rich lay thinking, was this love? Is this it?

Rich held Mandy tight. She needed him, depended on him; he was her saviour. She would have died! Rich's thoughts turned to the night he found her. His memory was sketchy. Rich remembered seeing his friend Hen and stealing a bag of powder on his way out! He must have been crazy on drugs and vodka that night! I'm not a bad man. He thought maybe selfish at times, but I'm misunderstood. I mean, I didn't kill anyone, did I? Everything I did was to protect her. That's why I did it, so they would never get to her, hurt her, tell her lies about me and spoil things for us, so it's all her fuckin' fault! Rich looked down at Mandy, sleeping in his arms. He wanted to be mad at her, but right now, he felt love for her. "What the fuck is that noise? Rich could hear voices. "No one ever comes up here. What on earth is going on?"

In the winter, the farmer would board up the cottage windows. Rich had managed to steal a key to the door in the summer. Rich knew the cottages well. He had a way of getting into the cottage next door without going outside, a hole in the wall hidden by a cupboard. Rich didn't want to get up from this beautiful, peaceful, loving feeling, but some noisy cunt was outside, and he needed to deal with them. Rich felt annoyed. He moved Mandy, wrapped her up in blankets and got himself dressed. It sounded like there were a lot of voices. What if they were after him?! Rich knew the woods well. He knew all the backways and shortcuts. He was like a wolf navigating his way through them. Rich looked at Mandy sleeping. Usually, he would tie her up when he left, but he trusted her now; he felt the love between them. She won't go anywhere, he thought. Rich made his way into the adjoining cottage and out through the back door into the lane. It was cold, dark and raining. He felt annoyed he had been disturbed. The voices were coming from the top field. He could not make out what was being said; he needed to get closer. He crawled around to find a gap in the hedge, but by the time he had found the gap, it was quiet. Whoever it was had gone, and the rain was getting heavier. Rich headed back to the cottage. He was furious, cold, and wet. When I get in, she's going to pay for making me do this. That fuckin' bitch will be sorry. I'll fuck her little pussy so hard that she'll beg me to stop, and then I'll fuck her some more! Rich's thoughts were running away with him. He was turning love into hate. He was cold and wet and feeling very disturbed.

Rich thought about the other women; maybe one of them would have been better. "Why? Why the fuck am I here? I don't deserve this. I got a wife, a house, and a handsome face. I'm no monster; they just make me fuckin' bitches!" Rich's head was full of dark thoughts about the women in the woods, the women in the van. Fuck, what had he done? And this one in the cottage, what was he gonna do with her?

Mandy was still sleeping when Rich returned. He looked at her; he blamed her for the mess he was in. He wanted to hate her, to hit her and make her pay for this mess. After all, it was her fault she needed to be looked after. He didn't want to be here. Rich's thoughts were dark and deep he felt angry and pent up. The only way to let it go was to fuck. He needed to fuck. He thought, looking at Mandy sleeping. I'll wake the bitch up!

Chapter Eight: November 12th
The Hospital

Cruz had been in the hospital for 7 days. He was doing well, getting visitors every day. His memory was coming back except for that day or night, which was still blank for him. Blood tests had detected a cocktail of drugs in his system! Cruz had never taken drugs, never associated with people who did, as it simply wasn't his thing. So, apart from having broken bones and being in traction, his mind was scrambled. The good news was he was healing, and his prognosis was good. The nurses were all lovely, some more than others, but he was making the best out of it.

"You alright Cruz? You're looking puzzled," asked Nurse Belinda, his named nurse for the day. "Yeah, nurse, I was just thinking, I don't climb trees, I hate heights, I don't like the woods, so how did I get there? Because I would not have gone willingly." Then a flash came to him: a van, an old van. "I had a van." "Do you have a van?" asked the nurse. "No, well, I don't think so. No, no, I have a car, but I drove. I drove a van." "Where to Cruz, where were you driving to?" asked the nurse. "I don't know!" "Ok, Cruz, stay calm. You know you can't drive right now, so let's just stay calm." "I know, I know, I'm just saying I drove. I know I did; I have a car. I need someone to check if my car is at home," begged Cruz. "Maybe when one of your friends comes in, they will do that, but please, for now, relax. Let's concentrate on getting yourself better. You were climbing trees, Cruz; you're a mad one," smiled the nurse as she touched his shoulder. Cruz smiled. He knew this was wrong. She was wrong; he would never be in a wood up a tree. Never!

Cindy, the daughter of Mr. and Mrs. Gilberts, had been taken off the ventilator, and she was making excellent progress. The Gilberts had been by Cindy's bedside since that first night, almost a week ago. They had made a makeshift bed, and every day, they would change over duties, praying for a miracle. Relatives, friends, and Terrance visited. The Gilberts always met the visitors in the cafe, and they would relive the nightmare every day. Today, the doctor joined them. The Gilberts had insisted the doctor needed a break, and they wanted to treat him to a coffee. "I guess, doctor, you have had no one so seriously Ill as our daughter," asked Susan. "I mean, she is so Ill, lucky to be alive, it's the Gilbert fight in her." The doctor looked up, "On the contrary, Mrs Gilbert, I have many patients here in this hospital who are extremely poorly, and Cindy is not one of them!" "Yes, but Doctor, to have a young person brought in under such circumstances, I mean, she must be the only one!" "Actually, no, she is not. We have three young people in the hospital, all in similar circumstances! Did you say your daughter was going out with friends?" "Yes, why?" "Were they male friends by any chance?" "No, they were not. How dare you suggest my daughter went out with men? She is to be married," huffed Susan. "She is?" "Yes, to Lord Arlington." "Oh, I beg your pardon. I have not seen him by her bedside. Is he not local?" "Well, I won't let him see her until she looks better! "But Mrs. Gilbert, you just said they are getting married; surely you need to let him see her," snapped the doctor. "No, No, I will not, now. Don't you have work to do, doctor?" Stuck up cow, thought the doctor as he made his way back to the wards. George shook his head. "Oh, you don't understand," shouted Susan. George looked up, "You're right, I don't understand. I don't understand how she can marry a man that has never visited our house. In fact, I think I have spoken to him a handful of times, and most of them were recent. He knows nothing about me, and more importantly, I know nothing about him. I mean, what does he do? When do they go out? Cus I don't know?" "Oh, George, shut up. He will be here anytime for a coffee, and for the record, I told Cindy not to invite him to our house. It's small and well, only 3 bedrooms with one bathroom!" George loved his home; it was smart, well-maintained, and in a good neighbourhood, nothing to be ashamed of. He looked at Susan, "You're turning into a right snob; nothing wrong with our home, and if Lord Snooty doesn't like it, well, quite frankly, he can go and jump." "George, shut up," shouted Susan; "Terrance will be here soon." "You know what, Susan, I'll leave you to deal with him. I'm going home; I am tired." "And quite frankly, Susan, I am disappointed in you," said George as he walked away, shaking his head.

Intensive Care

The unknown male had been in the hospital for 4 days and was responding better than expected. Every effort was being made by the Police to identify him and the deceased male they found.

Chapter Nine: Rich

Rich walked up the lane towards the cottage; he was feeling happy he had food and drink, and he had stolen some lovely perfume and makeup for her along with some clothes. "She is gonna be so grateful," thought Rich, his cock twitching at the thought of her on her knees, thanking him for being so good to her. Rich had not tied her up today. He had told her he was trusting her, but he had removed her clothes just in case. He left her instructions to wash and shave whilst he was gone. Rich knew the water was cold, but at least they had water she could wash herself bit by bit and wrap herself up in the duvet; she would be fine, he thought. "I mean, here I am out everyday hunting and gathering for her. All she has to do is take a wash in cold water!" Rich smiled to himself. He was turning into a proper provider. One day, he'll marry this one! Well, maybe! Rich was deep in thought, dreaming of the future as he continued up the lane. Suddenly, he stopped in his tracks. There were loads of people in the top field. "What the fuck!? Fuckin' hell, it's that fuckin' bitch of a wife. What the fuck is she doing here? No one comes up this way in winter." Rich knelt down to watch and listen. I bet it's that cow causing this fuss, he thought. Rich watched. Everyone had a stick. "Rich recognised the man in charge. It was old Serg, Rich had dodged him for years! Rich began to feel uncomfortable, he could feel his anger rising.

Serg started shouting, "Ok, Ok, gather folks. Thank you all for coming to help. I know time is precious, so thank you once again for giving up your time to help search this field. We are going left to right first; then we will go top to bottom, every inch. We are looking for anything, anything out of the ordinary, anything unusual. You beat your stick like this and you stay in your line all walk together. If you come across anything, shout and the constable will come and bag it. Oh, and if anyone shouts, you all stop and wait. Any questions? No? Ok, let's get started all over to the left." Serg pointed in Rich's direction. "Fuck, Fuck," thought Rich, as he headed back down the lane. He would have to go through the woods and around the back of the country hotel. It would take him hours; it's a long fuckin' walk. He had been gone since early morning. His woman would be missing him. She would be hungry for food and cock. Rich could feel his temper rising as he made his way down the lane. "Fuckin' idiots! Coming up here spoiling my fun. It's that cow; she's out to get me, fuckin' witch," Rich marched on down the lane, across the road and into the woods. It had started to rain. Rich was tired, stressed and now wet, his anger burning inside of him, but he kept going because he was in love with her, and she would be worried about him.

It was almost midnight when Rich arrived at the cottage. She was in bed, sleeping. Rich was in no mood for her; he was cold, wet and fucked off! Rich climbed into bed; it was warm and welcoming, but Rich felt disturbed. He lay awake thinking about his next move. He felt uneasy. He needed to know what was going on, what or who were they looking for? Rich decided tomorrow he would get hold of his friend Hen short for Tom Hennesy, the local drug dealer. Rich was fond of Hen. They had an interesting friendship!

Hen was a multi-millionaire. He had his own underground laboratory, where he imported ingredients from around the world and made top-class drugs. Hen employed a professional chemist to do the making and blending of the drugs that he sold around the world. Hen also loved to experiment.. not that he knew what he was doing but he liked to play. Sometimes, the blends worked sometimes. Well, let's just say they did not! In fact, a few times, it's been lethal.

Hen never got caught. He had too many people on his books, always someone willing to take the heat for him for money, and Hen paid extremely well!

The thought of Hen made Rich Smile. He was a small bloke, a very small bloke, actually, and he loved Rich. He would do anything for Rich. All he wanted was Rich's cock. He loved to watch Rich toss himself off; he would sometimes let Hen mouth him. Now that was fuckin' hot! Rich felt his cock spring into life just thinking about the times he and Hen had spent together. Rich started slowly stroking his cock, and his stroke got quicker as he imagined being next to Hen. Fuck, he was cumming. "Oh, fuck!" he sighed as he let it all go onto the sheets! Mandy was only pretending to be asleep; she had waited so long for Rich to return. She missed him. She didn't know his name, but he had something she liked. Mandy liked the way he looked at her, how he always wanted her. She knew it was strange, yet she knew it felt right. She felt him get into bed, and she was preparing herself to be rolled over and fucked. He never went to sleep without fuckin' her. But tonight, nothing! He felt cold and tense. When he warms up, he will want her. Her pussy was getting wet just thinking about him. It was then when she felt the bed rocking; he was tossing himself off! She lay still, thinking any minute now, he'd grab me; she was getting wetter. Her legs parted, ready for him. She expected him to jump her any minute. Her hands instinctively moved down to her pussy, realizing how wet she was. "Oh my God," she sighed. Then she felt it, his explosion all over the sheets! Immediately, Mandy felt rejected and unwanted as tears ran down her face. Why would he do this to her? Why? She imagined he had been with some other women.

Rich was deep in thought; he was trying to remember the beautiful times spent with Hen. The girl was making a noise, and Rich felt irritated. He prodded her in the back and angrily told her to shut the fuck up. She had broken his thoughts and all he had done for her, and this is what he gets. He couldn't even be left to think. Fuckin' bitch." The anger boiled within him. Without thinking, he whipped back the duvet; she was lying naked. He picked up his belt and whacked her on the arse. Mandy screamed out in shock and pain. "Shh bitch," as the belt came down on her again, "You stay like that. You deserve this," shouted Rich. The pain was intense. Mandy was screaming. She turned around to beg him to stop as the belt came down again, this time whipping her face. The force was so hard that it sent her flying onto the floor, banging her head as she landed. The lights went out!

Mandy woke up hours later, freezing cold with blood all over her face and hair. She was sore all over, and her heart felt broken. She slowly got back into bed, lying still so as not to disturb him; she felt full of anger. "How the hell am I here?" The problem was her memory was gone, almost like someone had rubbed away her past. She felt empty; all she knew was him and this cold, dark place with its boarded-up windows. It had 2 rooms; one room had a tin bath and a makeshift toilet. This room had a microwave, table, bed, and a chair. No carpets, they had electricity and running icy water, but where it was, she did not know. Why can't she remember?

Rich was dreaming he was running in the woods. He was angry; there were two women and he was chasing them. He didn't know which way to go. He felt panicked. The sweat was running out of him; then he tripped over one of them; she was lying in the leaves. He screamed, "No, no." She tripped, and I didn't do it. Run, gotta run! He saw the other woman slumped by a tree. He needed to get away! "Help me, I didn't do it; it was her fault." Rich's arms were lashing out, his legs moving all over the bed. Mandy laid still and listened.

She wanted to hold him and tell him it would be Ok, but she was scared. She wished this man would love her, hold her tight, and show her tenderness; that's all she wanted.

Chapter Ten: 16th November
Police station

Serg had called everyone in. He had requested help from the city. Serg had his map and stick ready, which reminded him of his London days! He had photos of the injured and dead, but what he didn't have was a suspect. Serg was going to work through what he knew, set a plan of action, and catch the bastard responsible. "What we got, Serg?" "Sit down. We need to wait for everyone. It's important we get this right. Grab a coffee or something."

"Morning, Serg,"

"Morning, Serg,"

The troops poured in. "Get some coffee, get ya self comfortable. We aint going nowhere until we have explored everything," shouted Serg. "I have some sharp minds in this room, so I'm expecting results," Serg thought these days were over. Well, behind him anyway when he left the city station, but now because of this shit, he was still working day and fuckin' night. Still, maybe one last job before he retires would do him good. Maybe he will be a hero at last! Serg cleared his throat, "Ok, troops, listen up. We are a sleepy little village. We are called Merryfield, for Christ's sake, but nothing's fuckin'' Merry about this! On November 5th, City Hospital reached out to us regarding a white male in his 20s who had been admitted with injuries suggesting a road traffic accident. He was found by the roadside along Castle Woods Arlington's side. The Guy was unconscious; he was still in the hospital, lucky to be alive, with no memory of what happened, in fact, no memory at all. Doctors can't explain why, other than Trauma! Did he see something? Did someone frighten him? Who fuckin'' knows! He's recovering slowly, I am pleased to report. Anyway, we know he's called Cruz, but that's it! Then, the following day, we got a couple of ramblers to report a body in the woods. Young Jessie here went with 'em and, sure enough, finds a body. I'm glad to say she was <u>alive (just), an</u>d thanks to TAZ, we now know who she is cus her parents cared enough to report their daughter missing. The girl is Cindy Marie Gilbert, and she was last seen leaving to meet her friends. She left in her car Reg CMG21 BMW Black 1. 8. Now, where is the car? She is also due to marry the prat that is Lord Arlington Junior—Terrance. He's been very quiet, not even sure he's been to see her in hospital. Why? I wanna know. I want him questioned! Then, if that's not enough, we were called to the Pig farm, and 2 males were found in a fuckin' pig hut! One dead, the other barely alive. He is now in the city hospital. He's critical, but I'm told he's responding to treatment. Again, N ID, no clues, no phones, nothing!" Serg sighed. "Four fuckin' young people found in my area, one of em dead and no fuckin' clues, that's why you're all here. I want every inch searched, and I want everyone interviewed. It makes no fuckin' sense." Drawing on the board, Serg pointed out, "So Castle Woods is here, and this is where Cindy Gilbert was found, not that far away from where Cruz was found, which is here. Do they know each other? Did they fight? Then, not too far away, two men were found. How did they get inside a fuckin' pig hut? Who are they?"

"Serg, Serg!"

"Yes, can't you see I'm busy?"

"Sorry, Serg, we have another body found in the grounds of Arlington Manor."

"What the fuck," sighed Serg.

Arlington Manor

Lord Arlington was pacing up and down the day room. Brandy in one hand and telephone in the other! The Lord had ventured out for a walk with his dog Trigger. He rarely went out alone these days. He liked people with him, but Terrance had commandeered all the staff to help him. Lord Arlington and the Trigger had set off in the grounds. Trigger had run on ahead as usual. They had been gone about ten minutes when Trigger started barking incessantly. The lord believed Trigger had discovered a dead bird or squirrel. What happened next took him by surprise!

"COME ON, BOY, COME ON, COME HERE! WHAT IS IT, GOOD BOY?" Trigger continued to bark. Lord Arlington approached the spot where Trigger was showing, "What is it, boy?" Lord Arlington looked down to see an arm sticking out of the leaves. "Oh, my goodness," he muttered. Lord Arlington knelt down and uncovered more leaves to see a female lying underneath them. "Oh my, oh my, what shall I do?" He had no phone with him and no helpers with him. He did not deal with anything these days; he didn't want to. The wife did everything, and he left her to it. She was younger than him and had much more energy than him, especially these days he was always tired. "Dam it, man, why did you agree to walk the dog?" he asked himself. "Come on, man," he thought, "Step up and take control." He could hear the wife saying, "Are you a man or a mouse!? Lord Arlington took a deep breath, stood upright, attached Trigger to the lead, and marched home. By the time he had reached the house, his mind was racing. "What on earth should I do? Quick, quick, help!" he shouted to the butler. "Quick, get me the phone and a brandy and get the family quick, Marley." Marley was the Lord's trusted Butler; he was as old as the Lord, and his pace was slow these days. "Here is the phone and your brandy; I will get the others, sir." "What on earth is going on?" shouts Terrance. "I am incredibly busy, and I…" His voice trailed off as he heard his father describing what he had found on the grounds. "Brandy, Marley, Brandy, quickly, I am in shock," shouted Terrance. Lady Arlington had just finished showering and rushed downstairs. "What on earth is going on?" she asked Terrance. Terrance always thought his mother smelt wonderful and looked wonderful. If only Cindy was like her. "Terrance, what is it?" "It's farther; he found a body in the grounds!" Lady Arlington sat down to listen. The Lord relayed the story to them, and Marley topped him up with Brandy. "Shall I run you a hot bath, my Lord, good for shock?" said Marley, fussing the Lord. "Marley, you spoil him. He can do that himself, anyway. The police will be here soon, oh and no more Brandy for him," said Lady Arlington. Lady Arlington got annoyed with her husband and his old butler. Her husband was old, lazy, and, quite frankly, boring. He would allow poor Marley to do everything for him. Still she had a good life; she must not complain. She is left alone to do what she wants with very few questions asked. She was deep in thought as the police arrived in van loads. Serg bounded in, "Ah, Lady Arlington, how the devil are you? I must say you're looking exceptionally beautiful." Why thank you, Serg, it is kind of you to say, but as I have only just showered, I must tidy myself. Please excuse me." "Of course, ma'am." Serg turned to Lord Arlington and Terrance, "Hello, Sirs. So, Sir, do you want to start at the beginning and tell me what happened?" Lord Arlington explained how he went out for a walk with his dog, where he went, how long he was out, and what he was wearing, eventually explaining how he came across the body and what he did next. "Did you touch the body, sir?" asked Serg. "No, no, I don't think so. I moved some leaves, but I don't think I touched the body." Serg turned to Terrance, "And where were you this morning?" "I was busy, sir." "Where were you busy?" asked Serg. "Well, I was around the house; I have a ball to organise, sir. It is taking such a lot of time."

"Taz, I'm gonna need fingerprints from these two," said Serg.

"Yes sir, and the lady?"

"No, no, no, just these two." Serg had sent a team out into the grounds, and it was not long before Jessie returned.

"Sir, we have found the body of a young female." Serg put his hands to his head. What was going on? What was he missing? After planning for the body to be removed and the grounds searched within an inch, Serg headed back to the station. "Come on, what are you missing?" He asked himself as he updated his board. Serg started again. "Found Cruz here, roadside about 5 miles from the country hotel! Fuck the Country Hotel. We need to go there. Cindy was discovered 1. 5 miles into the woods. Now, a body was found on the grounds of Arlington Manor. All on the same side of the road! But then we found the two men in the top field. The distances were not too far apart; it's possible someone strong could carry them or drag them, but from where?" Serg did not know what he was looking at, but now he had three young people in the hospital and two… well, it was too late for them.

Chapter Eleven: Helen's Story

Rich had taken the four women from the overturned car and put them into his van. They were all dazed and quiet, apart from one who was creating and shouting, banging the sides of the van. "Let me out, you stupid prick. Can't you see we need help? Let me out," she was getting on Rich's nerves. Rich didn't have a plan. He had no idea what to do or what he was doing! That stupid bastard Cruz had run into something on the road, and his precious van turned over and over and, by some miracle, landed upright, dented but nothing too serious. Everyone was unconscious except Rich. He got out of the van and started walking up the road. Then this car came round the corner at such speed, the headlights dazzled him, when suddenly the car skids off the road, crashing into a ditch and flipping over. Rich rushed over, but then he realized the car doors were stuck. Rich ran back to his van. Cruz had come round and was shouting at Rich. Rich always felt irritated by Cruz and now he felt angry towards him. It was this bastard that did this to his precious van. "Shut the fuck up," shouted Rich. "Did you go for help?" asked Cruz. "No, man, you're fine." "You're fuckin' useless," shouted Cruz. "What you doing?" asked Rich. "Calling for a fuckin' takeaway, what do ya think? "I'm calling for help." "We're fine, man; we don't need help, but some women in a car do, just up the road. Come on, man." "What about these two, your mates? They need help; they look in a bad way. I'm calling for help," shouted Cruz. "No, I said no, you can't." Cruz looked at Rich. "You're some fuckin' piece of shit, useless fuckin' layabout." Cruz did not see the blow coming. Rich had picked up a big branch and swung it at Cruz. It caught his head, knocking him off his feet. Cruz fell and rolled down into the ditch. Rich got in the van and started to manoeuvre it out of the ditch. Rich always made sure he was prepared to get himself out of trouble. He had flat planks of wood in the back of the van; always useful, he thought, when he nicked them from the farm! Rich smiled to himself, "He was such a good bloke!"

The noisy girl had gone quiet. Better check on em," he thought. Rich opened the van door as the girl jumped him; she was screaming at him, punching and kicking him. "Shut the fuck up!" "Don't tell me to shut up. Can't you see we need help? Take us to the hospital." Rich looked at the screaming women, not bad he thought! "I said shut up." Helen was raging. She looked around for something to hit this bloke with, but it was dark, and she had no idea where she was. "Take us to the hospital, man, please," begged Helen. Then Helen noticed the outline of a house, she began walking towards it. "Hey! Where you going?" "To get help." "Come back here; you're all fine." Helen ran. "Fuckin' bitch!" thought Rich as he ran after her. Rich was quick and fit, but so was Helen, except tonight she had been drinking, and she felt bruised all over, but the adrenaline had kicked in, and Helen was pumped.

Helen entered the gates to the house and ran up the driveway with Rich in hot pursuit. She had no idea where she was and figured if she jumped this gate, she might stand a chance of losing him. Helen found herself in some kind of woodland, she maneuvered herself around the trees, but she could sense he was near. She needed to pick up speed; it was her only chance! Suddenly, her foot caught in brambles, and she tripped, landing in a pile of leaves and mud. Helen lay still, thinking maybe he wouldn't see her. But Rich had eyes for the dark; he was like an animal. Rich stood over her. She was still trying to hold her breath. Rich placed his hand on her back. Suddenly, she kicked out at him, but Rich was quick and caught her leg. "Hey, that's no way to treat someone who saved ya!" laughed Rich. Helen kicked out again; this time, Rich was not quick enough, and her kick landed on him. The force and quickness surprised Rich long enough for Helen to get away. She started running straight into a low tree branch, which knocked her off her feet. It was not long before Rich had caught up! Helen was lying unconscious! Rich picked her up, and she had blood running from her head. "Ya must have hit ya head, missy," Rich whispered to her. "Never mind, ya safe now." Rich made his way back towards the van. He was tired and despite the girl being small, she weighed heavy in his arms. "Blimy girl, I'm struggling," whispered Rich as he tried to find a more comfortable position to carry her. As he moved his arms, his hand brushed her pussy. "Fuck, she's got no knickers on!" The thought of a pussy being near him was too much for Rich; he needed to look at least. He turned around and headed back to the woodland area. His mind was racing. She must be up for it, no knickers. I bet she did it on purpose. Rich lay her on the ground and opened her legs. Rich's dick was harder than concrete; his jeans were wet in anticipation! In a flash, his jeans were around his ankles; he couldn't control himself. I mean, she was asking for it, and he wanted to fuck this girl. She was teasing him, right? Rich slipped his fingers into her. She was smooth. He started exploring her as she moaned. She's enjoying it, thought Rich. "It was all an act to get me! I knew it! She's up for it." She was ready for him; Rich mounted her and began to ride her. Oh, it felt good getting his rocks off in the woods with a stranger. What a turn-on! Rich thrusted her hard.

Helen started to come around; she slowly opened her eyes to this stranger on top of her fuckin''g her so hard; it was painful. Helen was quick; she grabbed a stone from the ground and hit him on the head. "Get the fuck off me! Help! Help!" she shouted. Rich hated being disturbed mid-shag, and he didn't like being hit on the head. He felt betrayed by the bitch. Rich caught her arms and pinned them above her head while he tried to finish fuckin''g her. Helen was having none of it; She raised her legs and kicked and moved so much that Rich could not enjoy himself. "Bitch, you're making me angry," shouted Rich, pulling out of her. Helen slapped his face and kicked his balls. "That fuckin' hurt! I'm being nice to you, and this is how you repay me!?" Rich screamed. "You're a dirty piece of shit. I would never go near anyone like you. Look at you!" Helen screamed back. Women had put Rich down before when he was young, but no more. Nobody puts him down! This bitch is one big problem, thought Rich. But I like em feisty. Rich grabbed her, ripping her blouse, she had small tits, but right now, he would take anything. He wanted her, and she wasn't getting away. His dick was throbbing, and he needed to stroke it before it burst. He let go of the girl just long enough for Helen to take her chance. She sprang into action, kicking Rich's face and running for it. "For fuck's sake, this bitch is pissing me off." He needed to get her. Rich packed himself away and went after her. Rich knew the woodland well. He knew if she kept running, she would enter the big house's private grounds; that's not what he wanted. Rich moved like a tiger and waited for his prey. Helen thought she had outwitted him as she continued to run towards the house. Suddenly, something heavy hit her on the back of her neck. She collapsed to the ground.

"For fucks sake, Richard, what have ya done now! She's no good to ya now." Rich dragged her along the ground. "What the fuck am I doin'?" He stopped to catch his breath, nausea rising within him. "You're a stupid fucker; look what ya got ya self into!" Rich covered the girl up with leaves and made his way back to the van. "Fuck, what had he done! Who am I?"

Rich ran back to his van. He checked on the three women, and two blokes; not one of em looked good! Rich swigged his water; it made him feel better. His mind was racing. What was he doing? Rich turned the van around and headed back to the woods. He stopped the van, got one woman out, and carried her into the woods. He left her by a tree. "Sorry," he whispered. "Now what?" Rich moved the van and entered a lane; the van could only go so far up. One by one, Rich dragged the men out of the van, placing them in his wheelbarrow. Rich began to push the wheelbarrow up the hill. "Fuck me, this is hard." He thought they were heavy fuckers! He wanted to dump them in the woodland around the back of the country Manor. No one ever went around that way, but he was feeling too tired. Rich stopped at the top field. "This will do. No one comes up this way this time of year. " One by one, he dragged them across the field and placed them in a hut. Rich heard one of them groaning a bit. "Sorry," he whispered. Rich needed to rest; the cottage wasn't too far away. I'll leave the van here till morning. I can dump it then, he thought. Then he remembered he had two women in the back! One of them he fancied. She was his. The other, well, he would deal with her tomorrow!

Chapter Twelve: Jo's Story

Rich had taken his baby out of the van and into the cottage. He had put her to bed. Bless her, she was unconscious. Rich had taken her clothes off and had gasped at how beautiful her body was. Long legs, big tits, nice round arse, and a tiny waist, she was perfect. He'd made the right decision, and now she was his. Despite being tired, Rich had fucked her throughout the night, he could not believe his luck, but he had a problem., the other woman in the van. He needed to deal with her before it got light!

Rich made his way to the van; it was silent. Guess I should check on her. No, no, look what happened last time you did that, he thought. I'll just dump her somewhere. Rich headed towards the coast. It was still dark, and everything was good. Rich could hear banging sounds coming from the back of the van. "What the fuck? She's alive!" Jo was freezing cold. It was dark; she was disorientated but thought this box was moving. Jo felt around. "It's a van, it's moving." Jo screamed, "Hey mate, hello, hello. Oi, what the fuck is going on? Oi mate," Jo banged on the front of the van. "Hey, mate. Hey you, I say, mate, come on!" Rich could hear her, but it was noise he didn't want, so he took a swig of water. "Shut up!" he shouted. "Shut up!" Jo could not remember a thing; why was she in a van, and who was driving it? "OI, excuse me mate, I mean excuse me, sir," she shouted, "Can you hear me?" Rich pulled the van over. "Hey, I'm sorry, I rescued you from the roadside. I saved you, I'm taking you to the hospital, don't worry, I won't hurt you," shouted Rich. Jo thought he seemed caring. "So you saved me?" she shouted, "From what? I asked sir, from what? What did you save me from?" "Sir, can you let me out? Can I sit in the front with you?" Rich ignored her. "Let me out." Jo was banging on the van. "Let me out, you piece of shit, let me out. Sorry mate, I'm desperate for a wee." Rich had enough; he slammed on the brakes, and Jo went flying across the van. The back door opened. "no funny shit, don't make me angry. You wanna piss?" "Yes, please, Mr., what's your name?" "None of your fuckin' business." "Ok, Ok, just let me wee." Rich took her hand and dragged her through the woods. Jo thought he was handsome, not her type; she liked women these days. She had men in the past, but she found women to be gentle. They marched into the woods. "Hey, mate, can I just piss?" Rich stopped. "I'm not a monster; I won't hurt you. now, piss." Rich pointed to the ground. "Go by the bush; I won't look." Jo pulled her trousers and knickers down and squatted. Rich could hear her pissing. He looked around to see it running from her. Rich's mind turned to the golden showers he shared with Tanya, his wife. She could piss like no one else. She could stop on command mid-flow, make it trickle or gush out. His cock twitched. Jo let out a scream. "What the fuck?" snapped Rich. "I'm stuck, I'm stuck. Something got me. Can you help me?" Rich turned around and reached down by her side, "You're stuck in the bush, well, ya knickers are well and truly stuck. His arm brushed against her arse as he helped unravel her knickers from the bush. He liked a bit of arse action! Stop. Stop this, he thought. It's getting tight, and you need to get on. Rich freed her knickers. Stay still. I need a piss now." Jo watched him, amazed at the size of his cock. Rich was watching her. They all want this, he thought, smiling. "Do you want it?" he asked. Jo nodded as she got on all fours. "Come on, mate, it's been a long time since I was on all fours for a bloke." Rich felt anger towards this bitch. She was trying to control the situation, but what the hell? She was gagging for it, and a quick shag would settle him! Jo watched him as he approached her trousers around his ankles. She was ready to pounce, and as soon as he came near her, she would jump up and take him down!

Jo was quick; she sprung to her feet and charged for his legs, taking him down. They rolled around on the ground. Jo was usually strong but felt weak. "You stupid bitch, what ya think ya doing?" screamed Rich. "You're not fuckin''g me, mate, with your dirty dick," shouted Jo. Rich grabbed Jo's hair and punched the side of her head. Jo fell silent and slumped down to the ground. "That's better," whispered Rich as he dragged her back to the van, bundlerling her into the back, and set off for the coast.

"Hey Angus, where you off?" asked Rich. Angus was one of the local fishermen. He owned a big trawler and would often go off for weeks. "Boy, I aint sure; I go where the best fish is, somewhere warm, boy, somewhere warm! You wanna come? Cud cud do with a hand?" "No, no, I can't this time, but you fancy taking some rubbish out to sea for me?" "What is it?" asked Angus. "Oh, just something not needed anymore, ya know, no questions." "How much ya pay me?" asked Angus. "Look, mate, I got no money on me right now but Hen will see you right, "Oh, it's for Hen," questioned Angus. "Yea, yea." "In that case, back ya van up lad to one of em containers, put ya rubbish in, seal it, and I'll make sure it comes with me." Rich backed up his van, grabbed Jo, and shoved her into a square wooden container. He nailed the lid and left. "Sorry," he whispered.

Chapter Thirteen: The Cottage

Rich had not slept well; he had run out of special water. She had upset him, and he was having nightmares. He felt pissed off and scared! He looked down at his sleeping woman; her face was covered in blood. "What the fuck happened?" Rich recalled the events of last night. They were all mixed with his nightmare. "Did she try to run away? She must have done, then she tripped, and I carried her home?" He had no idea what happened. His memory was shot! Hen and his fuckin'' powder, it's all his fault. Whatever happened is his fault, thought Rich. He made a mental note to visit Hen soon. Rich smiled at the thought of Hen; he was slightly obsessed with him, and Hen was definitively obsessed with Rich. Rich was not gay but liked a bit of cock now and again.

The girl started to move and whimper, which brought Rich back to reality. Her face was black with bruises and deep cuts. Mandy looked at Rich, "Hey, what happened? Who did this to you?" Mandy remained silent. "Oh, I see, it was me; that's what that look means. Well, what did ya do to upset me, eh?" Mandy glared at him. "Come on, babe, it's ok. Just be a good girl, and we will be fine. I love you. See, I've said I'm in love with you! Now, let me show you how much I love you. Come here." Rich went to kiss her, and Mandy moved away. "Oh, you're playing hard to get!" "NO, I'M HURTING," Mandy shouted. Rich was shocked when she spoke. "I didn't ask you to speak; you know I prefer my women to be silent. Now come here," ordered Rich. "I'm sorry, I'm really sorry, babe, come on, you need some food." Mandy struggled to eat, but she knew she needed something inside her as she felt weak and cold. Rich watched her struggling to eat. "Hey, I'm gonna look after you; I'm gonna make this better." Rich picked her up and carried her to the bed; he boiled some water, gently bathed her wounds, washed her hair, and went back and forth with clean water. Mandy winced as he tendered her wounds. "Shh baby, it is ok." He wrapped her up in the duvet and gave her a hot drink. He told her how much he loved her and that they would be married. "I'm not a bad bloke. I'm misunderstood. I've always wanted a woman like you with a figure like yours, someone who listens to me and does not shout at me, someone I can look after, and someone who needs me, and that's you, babe. No one is going to spoil this for us." Mandy looked at him and wondered what planet he was on! Mandy knew not to speak, but she was taking it all in. Rich was relaxed as he spoke about the future. "We will have children, and I will get a proper job, an actual job, and we will live by the sea. Regarding the wedding, well I don't know who I should invite. Maybe we could have a quiet one, just you and me, babe!" Rich looked down at Mandy, and she was fast asleep. "She must have loved hearing about our future together," Rich sighed.

Rich felt unsettled. He wasn't sure whether to stay in, lie low, or go out and see what's happening! She was sleeping, not a chance of a shag. "Maybe I will go out and see what's going on." Rich got himself ready and made his way through the hole in the wall and into the next cottage. Mandy was not sleeping. She was aware of what he was doing. She had watched him dress and make his way out through the wall. Stupid idiot, she thought, as if I hadn't noticed the way out!!

Once he was gone, Mandy got up; she noticed he had not taken his rucksack. He goes nowhere without this, she thought. The temptation was too great. She rooted through it. "1, 2, 3, 4 purses! 1, 2, 3 wallets! What on earth!" Mandy opened one purse. It belonged to a Helen West. Mandy looked at the photo. "I'm sure I know her!

Helen West, Helen West!" Mandy was deep in thought when she heard him coming back. Quickly, Mandy threw the purses and wallets back into the bag and got back into bed. She then realised she had Helen's purse in her hand! "Shit!" She quickly threw it under the bed and prayed he wouldn't find it. Mandy lay thinking about the photo and the name Helen West, but she just could not remember. She knew she just looked so familiar!

Rich had been out watching the activities in the pig field. The coppers were searching it again. Rich heard one of em shout. "Serg found a piece of red velvet stuck on a bush!" Rich also noticed that the cow of a wife was helping the coppers again. Rich felt uncomfortable with the coppers being near. He needed to move on and take the little woman with him, but he had no plan and no money. Only one person could help him, and that was Hen, but he needed to get the lowdown from Tanya first, and she would tell him what was going on! Rich returned to the cottage. She was still sleeping. He lay beside her and planned his next move.

Rich had asked his friend Morris at the scrap yard to scrap the van, so Rich had no transport! Then he remembered the car he had hidden. It was battered, but he thought it was drivable! Rich planned to go out at dusk, find the car and head off. Rich would go to great lengths to cover his tracks, and hiding stuff was his speciality. He built fences, cut down trees, and moved bushes. It was complex, but it worked. I am such a clever bloke, he thought to himself.

Retrieving the car from hiding proved difficult because of its flat tyre, dents, and dirt, but Rich knew the BMW would have the kit in the back to at least temporarily fix the tyre.

It was hours later when Rich arrived at Tanya's. Tanya was outside smoking with her mates! "Oh, look who it is, look who it is, the fuckin'' king," shouted Tanya. All the women looked around, "Hey Tanya, he's back to give ya one," they all laughed. Rich hated this group of women. "Where ya been, ya fuckin' waste of space. I hope ya come with some money for ya wife, and I don't want ya dick." The women all laughed. Rich felt his blood boil, "Get in the fuckin'' house; you're making a show of yourself," shouted Rich. "Don't you tell me what ta do, and no, ya can't come in. I've got visitors," smirked Tanya. "Get out me way, you stupid bitch," Rich pushed past Tanya. "Where's your visitors? You're a fuckin'' liar." "Fuck off!" shouted Tanya. "I don't want you." Rich was angry, "I want a divorce," he blurted out. Tanya Laughed, "A divorce? Have it, I don't care; you're no good to me, your nothing but a ugly rough gipsy!" Rich swung around and grabbed her, "What am I? I'll show what I am bitch." Rich caught hold of her hair and dragged her along the floor. Tanya was screaming. "Shut up! Shut the fuck up, you dozy cow." Rich let go of her hair and dropped her to the floor. "Hey, I'm only messing; I thought you liked it rough?" Rich pushed his lips onto hers, his tongue darting in and out of her mouth. Tanya began to relax; she wanted him. She could feel his cock growing inside his jeans. Rich had his hand in her knickers, rubbing her pussy just how she liked it. "Fuck me, Rich, fuck me," she whispered. Rich looked at his wife, "Beg me bitch, beg me to make ya cum!" Rich's fingers were darting in and out of her, "Please, Rich, I beg you, please fuck me. I want you, Rich, please," Rich smiled. She played the game well; his cock was bulging and needed releasing. "Release the beast," he whispered. Tanya gasped as she released him, "Please, Rich, I want you. " Rich rode her hard, and Tanya took it. They fitted well together, and it felt so good. Rich pounded her until they were both satisfied and had no more to give. "Fuck, I've missed you," said Tanya as she looked at Rich, her handsome husband. "You're looking skinny, babe. You alright?" asked Tanya. Rich ignored her question. "Come here, hold your old man, and tell me what's been going on." Tanya fell into his arms and started telling him about the neighbours, how much she missed him and how she went looking for him on the farm. Then she told him about getting some work with the farmer for cash. Tanya told him she had come across two bodies of two men in one of the pig pens. Rich was all ears now. She thinks they are dead. "How awful is that?" "Yes, awful," replied Rich. "Poor bastards look like someone put 'em there." She did not know the names but thought they were locals. Tanya cried, "It's awful, Rich, two blokes the same age as you; it could have been you. " "Hey, hey, it wasn't, shhh…" Rich stroked her hair. Now he knew why the coppers were around. Rich was deep in thought; he needed to move, and he must get going. Tanya felt Rich tighten up, "What's wrong? You want me to relax you?" Tanya said, winking at him, "No, no, I'm just thinking." "What, you're refusing this?" Tanya stood up and started walking around him, "Look at me, Rich, I'm all women." Rich looked at his wife; she was all women. She was his type or at least the type he always went for. She is rough, with bright red hair, false this and that, tattoos, and quite a meaty girl. She was sexy and up for anything in the bedroom. Rich's cock twitched as he watched Tanya play with herself. "Fuck I ain't got time for this, I gotta go!"

Tanya had noticed her performance was working. She lay on the floor, "Come on, big boy." Rich was turned on; his dick was hard. "Fuckin' hell, Tanya, what ya doing to me!?" laughed Rich as he turned her over onto all fours. Rich entered her so hard she screamed. Rich slapped her arse, "Ride me bitch, ride me!" Tanya pushed back and forth on his cock as Rich slapped her arse as hard as he could.

Rich lost his load inside her and collapsed on the floor. "Well, finish me," sighed Tanya.

"Finish yourself."

"You selfish twat, finish me now; I'm horny, now finish me."

"Finish yourself, I'm going."

"Where's my money?"

"What money?"

"Well, I need money to live."

"Then get a fuckin' job. I aint got any money."

"So what, you just came back for a shag?" This woman was making Rich angry. She was questioning him, pushing him. Rich swung round and smacked her so hard she lost her balance. Tanya stumbled and fell backwards, hitting her head on the bedpost. Before she hit the floor,

Tanya lay still on the floor. "Serves you right, bitch," hissed Rich as he dressed. He needed to see Hen; now, he had spent far too much time here.

Chapter Fourteen: Hen

"Oi! White boy, what da ya think ya doin'? It's the middle of the fuckin'' night. " Rich looked up; it was one of Hen's Henchmen. "Fuck off, man, it's Rich, just fuckin' tell the big man I'm here, and I wanna see him." "No, it's fuckin' three in the morning, man. The boss is sleeping; now fuck off." Rich was in no mood, "Fuckin' wake him up, it's important, please. "Klep knew the boss liked this dude; what would be worse, the boss being woken up or the boss finding out his boyfriend had called and he had been sent away! "Wait here; I'll go see if the boss will see you." "He'd better," smirked Rich.

Hen was face down on a fur rug on top of his bed. He was naked, surrounded by naked men and women, all collapsed in a heap. The air was stagnated and heavy, and music was playing in the background. Broken glass and scattered sex aids filled the room. Klep wondered what the fuck had gone on. "Boss? Boss?" Klep didn't want to touch his boss; he had heard rumours of his boss sleeping with a gun. "Boss? Boss?" Klep looked around, picked up a cane, he started prodding Hen. "Boss? Boss?" "Fuck off!" "Boss? Boss, wake up; you've got a visitor." "Fuck off, or I'll fuckin' shoot ya!" Klep took a step back and retracted out of the den. He ran back upstairs to Rich, "He said to fuck off." "Did ya tell him it was me?" asked Rich. "Yeah, man, he's out of it, now fuck off! Come back later." "No. I'm here now. Now let me in. I'll wake the fucker." Pressing the emergency bell, Klep stood firm; he knew the others would be here in minutes. "Wanna take us all on, ya son?" Rich was surrounded. "Come on, son, let's see what ya got." Rich was in no mood for this. "I'm sure Hen will not be happy to hear how you treated me, his one love; I'll be sure to tell him. Maybe he will stop your--

"What's all the fuckin' fuss about?" the door swung open. Hen had a gun in one hand and a bottle in the other. "You fuckin' lot are meant to be protecting me, ya know, keeping me safe. Now, what's the fuckin' problem?" shouted Hen. "Ah, Rich, I might have known what ya want at this hour. Don't tell me you're in trouble, or maybe you come all this way for my dick?" laughed Hen, looking longingly at Rich. The group of guards looked to the floor, all feeling uncomfortable. Rich laughed, "Hey man, I came to see you cus maybe I want you." Hen looked at Rich; he would give anything for Rich to want him, but he knew Rich used him. The thing was, he couldn't say no to the fucker. "Come on, man, let me in, help me out, call your Dalmatians off." "Oh, so ya come to Hen when ya in trouble or maybe need some more shit? By the way, what did ya do with the bag of shit you nicked? How did ya get rid of it? Dangerous stuff, that batch." Rich was puzzled. "Get rid of it?" Ya, man, I left ya a message. Get rid of the shit. I got the measurements wrong. It was lethal, man. I mean, the highs lasted, but it fuckin' wipes the memory if it don't kill ya, so what did ya do with it?" "I used it." "What? All of it?" "Yeah, man, I put it in water bottles." "Where is it now?" "It's gone." "How you not dead?" questioned Hen as he looked at Rich. He was in love with him, always had been, and he cherished the times they spent together. "So, did ya have it all?" "No, man, I gave it to...?" Rich's memory was not good. "Gave it to who?" "I dun know man, I dun know names." "You're a fuckin' dozy fucker. If the pigs trace that shit back to me, I'll hunt ya down. Now fuck off out of here," shouted Hen. Rich looked at Hen, "Hey man, I'm sorry, man, I don't know what I'm doing. I know I need to get away. Will you help me, man? Please, I'm in trouble, man." Rich melted Hen's heart. "come with me," Hen reached for Rich's hand and led Rich to his private quarters. "Now tell me what ya want." "I need to get away; I need a van, some money and passports. I got this posh BMW. A bit battered, but it's Ok; you can have that."

"What do I want with a BMW? I got a fuckin' Bentley out there, but if ya asking me to get rid of it, I can do that for ya. Now let me see ya body, Big Boy!" Rich stripped off and lay naked in front of Hen! Hen's hands were all over Rich, "You're a beautiful man," exclaimed Hen, whose cock was hard.

Hen had a small penis, which is why Rich quite enjoyed it inside him. "Do ya want it?" gasped Hen. "Do ya want this beast inside ya, boy?" Rich nodded and got onto all fours. Hen entered him, his bollocks slapping against his arse as he fucked! Rich's cock was rock hard and dribbling. Hen was screaming, "Take that boy! And that! And that!" It was not long before Hen collapsed on top of Rich. Rich dragged Hen to the floor. "Now suck," he ordered. Hen was an expert. He pulled and sucked like no one ever before. Rich was so fired up that he exploded all over Hen, and Hen loved it. This is love, thought Hen; this must mean Rich loves him.

Rich lay down with Hen, holding him in his arms. Crazy fucker is mad for me, thought Rich. As he started to move, "Hey, spend time with Hen. " "No, man, I need to go, but I'll be back; ya can have some more of me," Rich smiled and winked. Hen melted, "Ok, Ok, I'll sort something out for ya, somewhere to go. Oh boy, leave the car keys; I'll deal with that problem for ya." "How the fuck can I get back?" "Walk," laughed Hen. "I'll get one of the lads to drop you. Anyway, where are you going?"

"Work."

"You work?" laughed Hen. Rich felt irritated. He was laughing at him. "Look, man, let me have one of ya vans, and I need some money." Hen looked at Rich, "Fuck ya! Ya come here, you want everything from Hen, but ya don't wanna spend time with Hen? No van, no money, no shit now. Fuck off!"

"Hey, hey, where did this come from? Ya know I'm mad about ya, ya know you're the only one I trust. Ya know I come to you, ya know I look up to ya. Come on, man, ya know I'm married, and she gives me a hard time."

"You always up to something, Richard, you're trouble."

"I ain't no trouble; it just follows me." Hen threw Rich some money, "Here, have that; no van. Get a lift from one of the lads." Rich knew when to give up.

"Ok, thanks. Look, I will be back soon. Oh, and a good shag. Thanks." Rich smiled and winked at Hen as he walked out.

Rich approached the lads, "Hey, lads, The boss asked if one of you could give me a lift, please." Rich hated saying please. Kramer was just leaving, "Yeah, I will; I can drop you at the crossroads." "Perfect! Thanks."

Rich sat in the back of the car and thought about his love. He had been gone a long time. Would she still be sleeping? They would leave soon and live happily ever after. Rich rested his head on the car door, but his mind wondered what he had given Angus. Rich was deep in thought as the car stopped. "Ya gotta get out now and walk, mate, unless ya live in that big house." Rich looked up, "No man, that's for those posh folk, ain't for me, mate. Thanks, man." Rich got out of the car and started walking towards the cottage.

November 25th CITY HOSPITAL

"Well, Cruz, you're doing just fine. A little more physio and you may be ready to walk!" Cruz had been having intensive physio and hydrotherapy. Cruz had worked hard to recover. He was a model patient and astounded the doctors on how quickly he was recovering. He had a few plates fitted in his knees, the spinal damage was improving, and even his memory was returning, although that day or night was utterly blank. Cruz remembers a van he was driving. He told the police, "I think I was with people!" The police visited most days just to check if anything else had come back to him. The police traced Cruz's relatives, and they visited when they could. His modelling agency had understood, and they agreed to wait and see what would happen; they did not want to lose him. Things were good. Cruz liked the ward. He liked the nurses, and some of them were fit. He had plenty of visitors, and now he was moving around and talking to other patients. Dr. Lopez stopped at the end of the bed. "Cruz, you ever taken drugs?" "No, Sir, never. I'm not about that. Why?" "No, no, I did not think so, yet we found a strange concoction of substances in your blood. We had never seen this before, so we sent some blood away for further investigation. We hope the results to be back soon. Ok, see you later." Cruz stared at the doctor, walking away, "Drugs me? Never. What on earth are they saying? Did someone drug me?" Cruz sat deep in thought; why can't he remember?!

"Cindy, my darling, you're looking amazing. Terrance will be here soon, spray some perfume, put some lipstick on." "Don't fuss, mummy." "Yes, but he is your husband-to-be; you need to impress him until you marry anyway." "Mother!" shouted Cindy. It was not long before Terrance arrived, "Hello, hello, how are you today? You're looking fine, Cinderella. I have a gift for you. "Oh, Terrance, you always spoil me," smiled Cindy. She was thinking diamonds or pearls would be fitting. Terrance pulled out a bag of oranges and a bag of sprouts. "Here, the oranges are for you, my dear, and Mrs. Gilbert, the sprouts, freshly picked this morning, are for you. They are rather nice; I have to say, grown on Arlington land, you know." Terrance stood holding the bags out, "Thank you so much, so kind of you. You're a very thoughtful husband-to-be. Any news on the date yet?" asked Mrs Gilbert. "Mum!" shouted Cindy, "maybe you will leave us alone." "Oh yes, of course you love birds." Terrance could think of nothing worse, but he had to go along with it. He had visited every day, paid for a private room, and had been a very good boyfriend. Mummy and Daddy had been tough on him, insisting he settle down, and this is the one. "Come here," said Cindy, patting the bed, "sit near me." Terrance dutifully sat down. "Why don't you kiss me, Terrance?" asked Cindy. "Er… Er, um, no kissing until we are married," replied Terrance. "When will that be, Terrance? Why don't we just get married tomorrow?" Terrance coughed, "No, no, we need a wedding fit for a lord and his lady." Cindy looked at Terrance, "Let me tell you something, I ain't waiting long. I want to be married by Christmas, so best you get planning. This accident could have killed me, and then what would you have done?" Terrance stared at her. Rejoice, he thought! Mrs. Gilbert walked back in, "You two love birds, alright?" "Yes, mummy, I was just telling Terrance I can't wait to be his wife, and I can tell how much he loves me, and guess what, mummy, Terrance has just told me the wedding will be before Christmas." "Oh my!" exclaimed Mrs. Gilbert. "This is wonderful news, Terrance; we really need to get a list." Terrance stood in silence; he felt sick. He needed his mummy!

A knock on the door disturbed the silence. "Hello, hello, only me again, your friendly policeman. Hello Cindy, Mrs. Gilbert, Sir, I wondered if I could have a word with Cindy." "No, not now. Can't you see we are busy?" snapped Mrs. Gilbert. "It's Ok, I was just leaving," said Terrance. Cindy held out her arms towards Terrance; everyone looked at Terrance who was standing by the door feeling very uncomfortable. He had no clue what to do. "Must go, busy," he shouted as he darted out of the door! "Ah, he is shy," explained Mrs. Gilbert. "Cindy, remember anything today? Maybe a car or a van?" "No, sorry, I don't remember. Why? "Well, we are getting pieces of information and just trying to fit them together. Well, if anything comes back to you, however small, write it down, Ok?"

"Yes sir, I will," smiled Cindy as Dr. López entered the room.

"Hello, Cindy, how are you today?"

"I am doing well, doctor, thank you."

"Cindy, I need to talk to you about something." Mrs. Gilbert immediately stood up.

"I told you, doctor, we will hear no more, and I told you I had to discuss this with the patient. Now, do you want me to get you removed?"

"What on earth is it!" asked Cindy.

"Look, Cindy, your recovery is going well, and you can go home soon;'a lucky girl. I am just going to ask you straight, Cindy, do you take drugs?"

No, never, Doctor."

"Ok, we found some strange substances in your blood, and, to be honest, I wondered what on earth you were taking. We have never seen such a mix. We sent samples of your blood off for further investigation, and we are waiting on the results, which will be any day."

"I have never taken drugs, Doctor, honestly." Cindy looked at her mother.

"Mummy, I never, honestly. I never. I don't. I would not take drugs."

"I know, sweetheart," said Mrs. Gilbert, comforting the now-wailing Cindy.

"See what you have done, Doctor; I told you to leave it. You can leave now," said Mrs. Gilbert, making Doctor Lopez feel like he had been dismissed. "Stuck up bag, not even a thank you for saving my daughter's life. Have some chocolate, doctor, some people!" Doctor López walked away, thinking of all the things he would like to say to her. Terrance had invited him to his Christmas ball; maybe he would go and accidentally let it all out then!! He smiled to himself; revenge made him feel happier as he made his way to the ICU. It was time to take the ventilation away from bed two. The police had established that this was Darren McGowan, originally from Scotland, who came down to London for a teaching job and the gay scene. He moved locations a few years ago when he got a promotion. He was a popular bloke, with cards, gifts, and donations for the unit arriving most days. His parents have been at his bedside day and night. People speculated that he might have been involved in illicit activities and that something went wrong based on the way he was discovered.

"Hello, Mr. and Mrs. McGowan; I am Doctor Lopez. I will look after your son today. May I ask you to leave the room and get a coffee or something? My team and I need to wake up your son and stabilize him. I am confident it will be fine; the signs are good, but I must warn you, sometimes things don't go as planned, but he is in safe hands, so don't worry. Mrs. McGowan cried. "Hey, try not to worry. I know it's difficult. I don't see a problem. We have been reducing the help to your son for the last few days, and he's managed; his heart is good, and there are no real injuries. Yes, he will be traumatised, but with help, that will improve." The McGowans walked out of the room and headed for the coffee shop. Mrs. McGowan prayed. Mr. McGowan just wanted to get back to Scotland and leave this nonsense behind. He had no time for hospitals, the English, or gays, yet here he was, being forced to deal with all three!

Chapter Fifteen: November 30th
The Police Station

Serg had called another meeting; only slight progress had been made, and Serg felt frustrated by all of it. He waited for the troops to settle. "Ok, Ok, we have crimes to solve. Call yourselves detectives?" Serg shouted, "What we know is the Country Hotel has confirmed that four guests booked under the name of Mike Mann never arrived!

We now know that Mike Mann was the man found dead in the pig pen. The man found with him is Darren McGowan, a teacher. He is still in the hospital and doing well, and we think he will make a full recovery. Thank God. The male found by the roadside is Cruz de Angelo. We think he was one of the four? Which means we are missing one. Obviously, this is speculation because Cruz can't remember a fuckin' thing! Now the girls Cindy Gilbert found in the woods, doing well, again can't remember a thing! We now know that the other girl found dead is Helen West, a personal trainer. She suffered a blow to the head, but the autopsy stated she had trauma in keeping with a car accident, just like Cindy! So where is the fuckin'' car? What were these girls doing? Mrs. Gilbert, Cindy's mother, stated her daughter was going to meet friends, but she did not know who they were. The dozy lord Arlington told us Cindy was meeting friends and going to the Country Hotel. Did we check this?" "Yes sir, I called them, no one by those names!" "Jessie, I want you to go to the hotel and check if they have CCTV, check who was there. I want a list of all the guests that day." "Sir, what else do we know?" "We are waiting on lab results. A strange substance has been detected in the blood of Cruz, Cindy, and Helen, so does this link them? Is Cruz the one who hurt the girls? It might be worth sniffing around the local drug dealer, our friend Mr. Hen, see if the dodgy shit is from him." "Serg, it's hard to get to Hen." "Yeah, I know, but start asking questions. Word gets back to him, and usually, he throws someone under the bus! That's my experience of the fuckin' rat. He likes the heat off him! Anyway, Cindy's car; where is it? The boys must have been in something to get them to the hotel. Where is it? Cruz keeps going on about a van. How did the bodies get to the wood, the pig pen, and the posh house cus they did not fuckin'' walk! This is a mess, and my name is on it. I want this mess cleared up. Do what you have to do to get answers. Jessie, go to the hotel and don't leave until you have answers. Taz, I want you to ask questions. Wake these sleepy bastards up, especially Hen. Why do I think he's involved?" "Will do, sir." "The rest of you keep searching, asking questions; whoever did this can't be that fuckin' clever! Now, all of you go and do the work," Serg commanded, sitting back in his chair, scratching his head and thinking.

His thoughts shifted to Lady Arlington, who intrigued him. Suddenly, he remembered she had invited him to the Christmas ball, and he needed a mask. He made a note to get one, something stunning, he thought, to impress her!

Chapter Sixteen: December 1st

"SHUT UP, stupid bitch! Shut up, I'm thinking. Bitch, why can't you be quiet? Slag! I'm not a bad bloke; misunderstood, that's all. Why can't you understand?" Rich's fist tightened up, tears rolling down his face. *"The key, where's the fuckin' key?!"* The sweat was pouring from Rich now. *"Fuckin' slag you made me, you were asking for it; you had no knickers on! Bitch, I didn't mean it; I'm a good bloke!"* Rich's arms and legs were moving around. The smell of blood was so strong Rich started to *urge. "Gotta get out, gotta run, no, no, don't, I don't want you! It's not you, I can't, I want a divorce, I don't want you. You won't make me stop. Stop. Ahhhhhh!"* Rich woke up startled, shaking and drenched in sweat. Mandy had been watching him. "Hey, you Ok?" she asked tenderly. Rich looked at her; she was perfect, apart from the scar on her face. Rich touched it gently, "Sorry, I am really sorry." Rich pulled her tightly to him, tears rolling down his face! Mandy lay still. She was unsure what she had just heard or what it meant, but this guy was troubled. Her memory was coming back to her in stages. She remembers a car and being in the back of a van. It was dark, and she was in pain as she rolled around, but that was it, and as hard as she tried, nothing else came back to her. That was all she could remember as Rich's mind was confused.

"What did I do? Did I kill her? Did I fuck her? I went to the shipyard. What did I do?" Rich looked down at Mandy. "Why is she here? I saved her, so what the fuck did I do with the others?" Rich felt annoyed with life; it was not meant to be like this. That fuckin' piece of shit, Hen, is taking too long. We need to get out of here. I have to sort the fucker out, go round and squeeze his balls, thought Rich. The thought of Hen stirred something up in Rich. His cock started twitching. Hen could do things to Rich that no woman ever could. Rich started stroking his cock as he thought of Hen and the times they spent together. Rich's breathing was getting heavier and heavier.

Mandy was woken up by him moving. She lay still as she listened to Rich toss himself off. Mandy wanted him; she wanted him to grab her and make love to her, she couldn't help it. This man aroused her like no other man had ever done; just being near him did something to her. But lately, he was rough and had hurt her. Despite loving this stranger, Mandy had decided she was going to leave him, so she lay still, closed her eyes, and prayed to be saved.

Mandy was getting stronger. He provided food, told her he loved her every day, and promised her a dream of getting away from here somewhere warm, he said. Mandy knew he was doing his best to look after her, but she was getting bored with him and was planning her escape she knew the way out. She had tried it several times when he had left her, and now that she had clothes, it was much better. She still had no shoes, but what the hell, she thought, that won't stop me when I'm ready I will go! She still had the purse, and every day, she would stare at the name and photo of Helen West. I am sure I know her, but where and how is a mystery.

POLICE STATION December 1st

"SERG SERG, I got something. I went to the hotel like you said. I was there for hours, but bingo, I got something. Four girls were at a spa day; one of them was Cindy, and one of them was Helen." "Who?" asked Serg. "The deceased girl." "Oh yes, carry on. I thought the hotel said no one under the names we gave was there?" "Well, that's it, Serg. The girls gave different names, B Bardotty, E Taylorford, M Monroeman, and R. HayMcwood." "Serg smiled. That's quite funny, he thought. "Ok, Ok, we got photos?" "Tomorrow, Serg, tomorrow. I had to sign a form to get the CCTC." "Did you recognise the others?" "No, sir, but we may be getting somewhere."

"Serg, Serg," Taz stormed in. "Just came in a BMW, number plate missing, looks battered and spotted coming out of guess where?" "Where?" "Our old friend Hen, Tomo's place, AKA local drug dealer Tom Hennesy." "Thanks, Taz; we need a plan. Put a watch on him." "But sir, you just gotta go in; he's impossible to watch." "Taz, I know what I'm doing. I need a car to drive up and down past his house. We need to unsettle the bastard." Serg sat back in his chair. Thoughts of ending his career on a high by bringing in Tom Hennesy and solving the murders, he would be due a medal! Serg's thoughts turned to his acceptance speech. I want to thank you all for coming; it's with great pride that I accept this medal for my services and the bravery I showed during my last year. It was difficult, but I did it. Thank you for my huge payoff. I will use the money to buy a place in the Sun, and you're all welcome. No scrap that bit, he thought. Serg smiled at the thought.

Chapter Seventeen: December 5th

The Hospital — update

Cruz was doing well. He was walking a little, and now he knows that someone drugged him with a cocktail of cocaine, dried mushrooms, Diazepam, and cannabis resin. The cocktail was lethal, causing organ failure and memory loss. Cruz's memory was returning, but in stages, he still had no memory of that fateful day or night or why he was by a roadside. However, he had recognised Darren, his mate Dazer, who was improving physically, but mentally, he had shut down. Cruz would visit Dazer every day. Dazer just stared ahead. He did not speak. Dazer's family had made a fuss of Cruz. They told him about Mike. Cruz could not remember Mike but thought the situation was dreadful. Poor Dazer!

Cindy was leaving the hospital today; she was moving into Arlington Manor, in her own wing, until she and Terrance were married. Cindy was so excited. She had only met the Lord and Lady twice, but she was sure they would love her. After all, once Cindy tied the knot, she would be secure. She would eventually own the big house. Cindy planned to have children quickly. She believed children would ensure they never got rid of her.

5th December

Arlington Manor

Terrance did not want Cindy in his home, but Mummy had insisted. "She is your girlfriend; poor girl has been through hell. Now she needs looking after, keeping safe, so step up Terrance." He had argued with his mother, but she had already instructed the staff to get wing 2B ready for her. "And no hankie pankie before marriage. I want you to have a pure soul on your wedding night," said his Mother. "Mother, don't talk of such things," said Terrance, who was feeling extremely uncomfortable. Lady Arlington laughed. Her son had a lot to learn; she knew he wasn't ready for marriage, and she also knew he never would be, so pushing him was the best way to ensure they got a grandchild. What he did afterwards, well, she didn't care.

Lady Arlington ruled the Manor house. Whatever she said happened, not that she told anyone she was clever and allowed her husband, the Lord, to think he oversaw everything. The truth was, he was not interested in anything unless it involved talking to his old butler friend, fishing, shooting and the occasional walk and watching TV in bed. Arlington Manor was huge, and Lady Arlington had it decorated exactly how she wanted. Upstairs, it comprised of wings, and each wing was a large flat. They each had separate wings. Lady Arlington refused to share her husband's bedroom because of his snoring, and although the Lord was unhappy about it, he couldn't be bothered to argue with her because she was exhausting. They had three guest wings, and on the ground floor level, a beautiful grand entrance hall that opened up into a large reception area that led into several lounges, one for TV, one for reading, one for music and a reception lounge for receiving guests. They had a ballroom, two dining rooms, many bathrooms and offices and an annexe, which was a self-contained apartment. The lower floor contained the kitchens, laundry and staff apartments. The day-to-day running of the home was quite time-consuming, but something Lady Arlington did with ease. Lady Arlington adored the manor house and the grounds. Love was the only thing missing in her life. She had never committed her love one hundred per cent. She always held something back. Her husband and past lovers called her selfish, not that she cared. She would just smile and move on!

5th December

Hens place

"That fuckin' piece of shit! You wait till I catch him, bringing the pigs near me. I knew the fuckin''fuckin' car was hot. He's a no-good liar, he can fuck off!" Hen was so angry; his scouts had informed him the coppers were constantly patrolling up and down the road. This was impacting Hen as he had to halt his supplies coming in. The cops had stopped the truck which was to carry the BMW to the scrap yard. They were fishing around, wanting to know why an empty car transported was needed. Fortunately, the guys were well-prepared. "They told the police that the boss always does his bit for the community and any abandoned vehicles he gets picked up to help the people out. The police were not buying it but had let them go. "We are watching you!" snarled Taz.

Hen was not a bad man. He was 49, had been in business since he was a kid, and watched his father run London with his gangs. His father was a monster, and Tom had learnt all the tricks, but unlike his father, he looked after people, he paid well, and he had hundreds of people in his books! The books were not exactly legal books, but they were books! People would do anything for Hen. They would take the heat for him, get locked up for him and all because he paid very well. He looked after children, and he would never hurt a child and if anyone did, well, it was game over! Hen had real money, more money than anyone imagined. He had a business in every town, every city and in several countries. He was a top dog; he had runners, scouts and guards everywhere. But right now, he was angry. The cops were watching everything. That fuckin' BMW would be linked to him. "Get rid of that fuckin' car. Drive it off a cliff or burn it; I don't care. Get it gone tonight when the pigs give up and piss off for the night!" "Yes, boss." "Find that bag of shit, Rich, and watch him. I wanna know everything: who he is with, what he is up to and--" "Hen! Hen! Sir! Mr. Hen!" Hen could hear the commotion; he pressed the safety buttons to secure the underground and looked at the CCTV. It was the fuckin' coppers! Hen put on his special shoes; one side was higher than the other, which gave him a limp. He got his stick and went out to greet them. He was greeted by Serg and six coppers. "Oh, you come to see Hen again? You can't stay away. Hen thinks you love him," Hen laughs. Serg had tried for years to get this man. Pin something on him, but nothing would stick. Slimy rat! Hen continued, "Sir, you follow Hen; you come to the seaside for Hen! I don't know why you follow Hen; I'm just a little old bloke minding me own business. I don't do any harm to anyone." "Look, you piece of shit," shouted Serg. "I know you; you're always up to something, you always have been, just like your father, and I'm on to you." "Sit down, Sir, you're angry; let's have tea." Hen snapped his fingers, "Get tea and coffee for the guests and some lovely biscuits." "Don't bother, thanks," snapped Serg. "I'm not here for fun." Serg held up a photo, "Do ya know this girl?" Hen looked, "No, never seen her." "This girl?" "No." "This man?" "No." "This man?" "No." "How about this one?" "No, what is this? Why are you showing Hen photos? Hen don't know em." Well, they all have one thing in common." Hen looked at Serg. "A strange drug combination in their systems, and I know you're the man with the drugs." "Here you go, again accusing Hen of dealing drugs." "I didn't say that," snapped Serg, "I said I know you have drugs, I know you import stuff. I just can't fuckin' catch you, but I will. I have people watching you. I will put you away before I retire. "Serg got up to leave and added, "Oh, and by the way, I retire in four months." Hen went cold. For the first time he believed the copper. He felt the heat had been turned up. He thought about the conversation and the photos. Were they all dead? And what strange substance? The last time he made a strange batch was about a month ago, and Rich stole it! "That fuckin' Rich again." "Find that fucker and bring him here!" ordered Hen.

Hen had accommodation underground. He had a drug receiving room, a laboratory where he employed experts to mix his cocaine with magic. That's why everyone wanted Hen's shit. It was the best. Hen would sometimes go into the lab and experiment with substances. Hen was doing just that a month ago; he had all kinds of shit mixed together. It wasn't until Charlie, the chemist, turned up and gave Hen hell for mixing such a lethal combination. "You will kill someone, man," he had shouted at Hen. "Get out of here; leave this work to me." Hen had left with the bag of powder. Charlie was the only person who could shout at Hen. He liked Charlie, he needed Charlie, and he paid Charlie extremely well. Hen thought about the bag of powder. It was by his bed. Rich had come around for money and a shag, and he was meeting some mates going away to a fuckin' spa. Rich took the bag of powder! Fuck, Fuck, Fuck, thought Hen. "That stupid boy would be the death of me. What if they were his friends and they were all dead!? The lying bastard told me he was going out with all blokes? The cops will trace the shit to me; I know it.

"Bring him here; find that no-good dog," Hen shouted. "Boss, we've been looking, but we haven't found him. Where does he live?" Hen did not know. In fact, Hen didn't know much about him. He knew he loved him; he loved his handsome face, beautiful Ice-blue eyes, his full soft lips, his strong shoulders, his perfect, amazing body and his cock, such a beautiful thing! But most of all, Hen loved the person. He knew he was a bad lad, but he liked that Rich didn't give a fuck about anything. But right now, as much as he was mad with the fucker he needed to protect him, they could run away together, thought Hen. We could live together happily forever! Hen was in dreamland, and it felt good.

Chapter Eighteen: RICH

Rich was clever; he knew how to hide, he had charm, and he could generally get away with whatever he wanted from anyone. Rich knew the police were out and about. He had been extra careful, only going out at night. Rich needed to get to Hen, get the passports and get out of there. The little woman was getting curious; maybe he should allow her to talk, get to know what she was thinking! "Babe, come here." Mandy looked up and hoped it was not for more sex. She was tired of him, sore everywhere and just wanted out. Rich patted his lap, "Come on, babe, I want you to talk to me. What's your name?" "Amanda," she said, "That's a beautiful name. How old are you?" "26" "Well, I'm er… er… The man that saved you." "What's your name? What do you do?" she asked. "Hey, I ask the fuckin' questions. Just call me darling," snapped Rich. "Sorry." "That's better. Speak when I say, babe, now tell me about yourself." Mandy told him she was born in New Zealand and came to the UK 8 years ago on her own to be a Nurse. She lives in the nursing quarters at the hospital; she has lots of friends and enjoys a good party. Rich watched her as she relived her life. She was more beautiful as she spoke; her voice was gentle and sweet. Rich smiled, "Yeah, I have seen you out; I always wanted you, but I was married." Mandy looked at him, "Was?" "Yeah, was. I think I killed her, babe." Mandy went cold and held onto the chair, the colour draining from her face. Rich was excellent at reading body language. He felt the change in her. Rich held her tight, "Hey, I was only messing, now kiss me." Mandy pulled away; she was in no mood for this. "No, I won't fuckin'kiss you; you're a dirty slob, now move away from me. Leave me alone." Mandy stood up. Rich was taken aback by the outburst; he sat still and watched her. "You lock me up in this dump like an animal; you tell me you love me, you force yourself on me all the time. You go out and leave me without shoes. You make me eat food I don't like. I AM SORE ALL OVER. I am tired, I don't know where I am or how I got here, and YOU expect me to be Ok? Quite frankly, I would rather you killed me than have to sleep with you again." Rich had heard enough. "Ungrateful bitch!" He got up and went to grab her, but she was quick; she picked up his rucksack and swung it at him. All the purses and wallets came tumbling out with a gun and a knife. They both stopped and looked at the floor. "That's my purse," Mandy shouted. Rich quickly gathered the items up. He was caught off guard.

Mandy knew he would be mad, but she was past caring. "Look, I am sorry," said Rich, "I know this is tough, but I am fixing it. I'm getting us out of here. I promise I'm taking you somewhere sunny, somewhere far away, where we can live and be happy forever. I'm not a bad guy; I love you. No one is going to take you away from me; no one! You're mine! Now be a good girl and make your man happy." Rich smiled at her as he dropped his trousers. "Come on, make me happy." Mandy took his cock in her hands and started pulling it. "Talk to me bitch, talk dirty to me," Mandy whispered about how she was going to take another woman, tie her up, spread her legs, lick her pussy like this. Mandy licked his ear; she whispered, "My fingers will fuck like this." Her fingers darting in and out of his mouth, "Suck them," she commanded. Rich sucked her fingers, the heat rising in him. "Oh my God, babe, sit on me, sit on me." Mandy did not want to sit on him, "No, over my tits," she commanded him. Rich exploded over her, consumed by emotion. Mandy felt powerful, asserting her voice and witnessing this idiot's weakness when his dick was out!

Rich wondered what had just happened. That was the first time a woman had taken control of him! Rich sensed she felt smug. He needed her to trust him, so he went along with her. "Babe, come here." Rich patted his lap, "You're such a beautiful woman; I love you." Staying silent, Mandy looked at Rich, "Ya know, that was some feeling I had, but babe, ya missed out. Let me bring ya on heat and take ya to paradise." "No, no, not now." "YES, now. You know ya want to," Rich held her tight and spread her legs, his fingers inside her. "Relax, babe, relax, it's gonna happen, relax." Rich knew the spot, and sure enough, Mandy was responding, "That's it, babe, let it go, trust me," Mandy screamed, begging him to be inside her. Rich smiled. Stupid bitch, he thought, "Who's in charge now?" as he mounted her!

Chapter Nineteen: 15th December
Arlington Manor

Cindy had settled well in the Manor house. It was a big house, very opulent. While she couldn't explore every part of the house, Cindy loved what she had seen. She had her own wing. Within her wing, she had a sitting room, a bathroom and two bedrooms. It was all decorated to a very high standard, maybe not Cindy's choice; she would have had bright pinks and purples, but for now, she went along with the creams, white and gold. Cindy assumed she had one of the smallest wings, as she hadn't received an invitation to the other wings; she did not know for sure, but looking at the building, she imagined the others were a lot bigger. One day, this will be mine, and I will have whichever wing I want, she thought. Cindy had her own maid and all her meals were cooked for her, which were served to her wing. "Why don't we all eat together downstairs?" she questioned Terrance one day. "You're not family, Cinderella," he responded. "You are a guest, and Daddy will not have guests at his table unless he has invited them. He feels awkward!" "Then let me meet him and get to know him. I am lonely here, Terrance!" Mandy cried, but all Terrance said was, "Go back home, Cinderella, go home." "I am home," she argued.

Lady Arlington was great fun. She would often come and chat with Cindy. Yesterday, she had arranged for tailors to visit to make clothes for Cindy, followed by beauty therapists in the afternoon, where they both had a pampering session that lasted hours. Cindy liked Lady Arlington. She wasn't stuck up like her son and seemed to be more normal, more in touch with people. Cindy got the impression it was her who steered the ship, and what she said happened. Cindy needed to impress her, keep her on her side, be a wonderful addition to the family, and go along with everything the Lady wanted for now! Today was going to be the best today, and Cindy had been looking forward to it. Lady Arlington had arranged for a vast selection of ball gowns and shoes to be delivered to the Manor for them both to try on to prepare for the Christmas ball, which was in nine days time. The ball was the talk of the house. In fact, it was the talk of the village and town! It was an open invitation, so the Arlington's never knew how many people would turn up, but it was usually in the hundreds. It was the annual celebration that everyone looked forward to, where farmers, doctors, shopkeepers and vets all got to mingle with the lords and ladies of the country, along with all their relatives and <u>dignitaries.</u>

This year, the Arlington's assigned Terrance the role of chief organizer. They had never trusted Terrance with such a role before. The Lord had insisted his son be more involved and that his wife step back in order to give him more attention! Lady Arlington hated the idea. She knew her son was incompetent, just like his father, but for keeping the peace and not rocking the ship she had agreed, at least to the Lord's face. "Of course, darling, what a grand idea," she said. However, in the background everything went through her. Terrance did not know, and it was a good job she had done this as Terrance was useless at organising and had no vision. He had ordered seventy Christmas trees for decoration for both inside and outside the manor, Lady Arlington had changed the order to three hundred. Terrance had forgotten to organise decorators and wreath makers, so the list got longer on what Terrance had forgotten. Meanwhile, Terrance was oblivious to the changes. He was too busy prancing around barking orders, mainly to himself, as no one really listened to him.

Cindy sat at the top of the stairs, watching the Christmas trees being delivered, followed by a team of decorators. It was a real buzz.

Terrance was in a state he had lost count of, the trees being brought inside, but it seemed over seventy. Maybe I ordered more, he thought as he tried to direct the team. Lady Arlington had given specific instructions to the team, clarifying that Terrance had no authority to decide where the trees should go and what decorations should be placed on each tree. Cindy watched on, slightly amused and embarrassed, as no one listened to Terrance. When we are married, I will make sure everyone listens to me, she thought. "Oh, there you are. Come on, we have dresses to try." Cindy looked up to see Lady Arlington smiling down at her. "It's a real buzz, but come, I am sure Terrance has it all planned; let's leave him to it," said Lady Arlington, reaching for Cindy's hand, "Come on, we have dresses to try."

Cindy entered the Guest wing, which had been turned into a shop full of ball gowns with matching shoes in various colours and styles. "Oh my," Cindy exclaimed, "This is the best day ever!" Cindy and Lady Arlington started trying on the gowns. Green, blue, black with feathers, without feathers, with lace, no lace, long, short, mid-length, red, burgundy, grey, white! "Oh my!" Cindy stopped in her tracks as she looked at herself in the white dress; it was amazing. She looked like a princess!

Lady Arlington walked in wearing a beautiful blue dress, "What do you think?" "Wow Cindy, you look beautiful; white really suits you. Maybe this is the one for your wedding, whenever that will be!" Cindy turned to Lady Arlington, "I love the dress, Steph. Can I keep it? Oh, and you look fabulous in the blue." Lady Arlington looked at Cindy, "No, not now, Cindy, choose a ball gown. We can ask for this one again once you have set a date." Cindy was not happy with the response, "But Steph, I have been thinking, why don't I get married? I mean, why don't Terrance and I get married on the same day as the

Christmas ball? The ball could be our reception." Lady Arlington looked at Cindy; she would make a beautiful bride in that dress, and what she said made sense; it would save some money, so the Lord would probably agree. However, it was not that long away, and Terrance would never agree. "I am not sure Terrance will agree," sighed Steph. "I will speak to the Lord, so for now, Cindy, put the dress to one side and choose another." Lady Arlington went off to try on more dresses. Cindy was not letting the dress escape her and instructed the dresser to put the dress in its bag and take it to her quarters. Cindy then picked a red dress, daring and sexy, it was low cut, split up one side. They would hate it, she thought, but she loved it; pure slut drop dress.

Lady Arlington had chosen the beautiful blue dress, two classic black dresses, one of them a lacy number, a grey fitted dress with deep pink trim, a fun flowery dress for summer, an emerald green dress, a beautiful dusky pink dress and a racy red dress! She did not know when she would wear them all, but she was happy, especially as she had chosen shoes to match all of them! The lord would have a fit if he knew how much she had spent. Best keep him in sweet, she thought. Although not too sweet, she had no intention of letting him anywhere near her. Not that he expected it these days except at Christmas and his birthday. With Christmas getting near, she planned to up his medication slightly to keep him sleepy!

Lady Arlington was speaking to Terrance, "Come on darling, sit down with mummy. I have been thinking, you have been working so hard; I think, sweetie, you need some fun, so let's not postpone the wedding any longer. Cindy's a nice girl, and you really need to be getting on with it, you know, produce some children, keep the name going." "Mummy, shh, not so loud." "Well, Terrance, you need to get on with it, I was thinking you could marry the girl before the ball! We will use the little chapel for the service in the morning, a few special guests for the day, and then the ball! It's perfect. Just think, by the new year, she could be carrying the next Arlington." Terrance stood up. He was not ready; he still needed his mummy to hold him, not some other woman. "I will hear no more," said Terrance. "Daddy will never agree. It is indignant; I feel like an object. It is unjust," Terrance stormed off to find his father.

The Christmas trees were all placed, and the decorations were coming on. It was looking magical. The lord was wandering around, trying to count the trees and losing his count at fifty. "Ah, Terrance, my boy, how many damn trees do we have this year?" "Seventy, Father." "Ah, good, much less than last year. That's it, boy, save us some money. Your mother spends the fortune like water." "Daddy, I need to speak with you in private," Terance explained to his father how mummy had proposed he marry the girl on Christmas Eve. "But that's the ball," exclaimed The Lord. "Exactly," said Terrance. "Mummy said it would save us money as we could use the ball as our reception, but I said it was a..." "A great idea!" shouted the Lord. "Yes, a great idea; we have everything organised, so why not? Just think, son, you could be getting your leg over at Christmas just like me," The Lord winked at Terrance, who felt physically sick as he ran off to hide.

Lady Arlington was in the garden talking to the decorators when Terrance came running out of the house. She followed him to his usual hiding place: the little summer house. "What's wrong now, Terrance?" she asked. "Father agreed it was a grand idea for me to marry, but I am not ready." "Look, Terrance, you will never be ready, my boy, so let's just get on with it. Produce some children, then you can leave her and play with boys or whatever it is you want! I know, Terrance, you don't want this, but it's happening, so get used to the idea; you will be married in nine days to the beautiful Cindy."

Terrance walked away, tears running down his face; he hated all of them, especially Cinderella. Terrance stood in the garden, looking at the lights on the trees twinkling, "It's beautiful." Terrance turned around to see Cindy looking at him. "Yes, it is and all for you, apparently," snarled Terrance. Cindy smiled, "Thank you, my dear Terrance," she said, touching his face. "It will be a wonderful day for us. We will never forget it; just think we will be married soon, and Terrance (she whispered), all of this will be yours," Cindy pointed to her body. Terrance blushed as he looked at her, "Now that I am to be married, I will help with the organising. Can't let you do everything; you may think I am lazy," smiled Cindy, walking away towards the grand hall. She had an idea for the table layout.

Terrance stood frozen to the spot; he hated this woman; she was vulgar and cheap, and now she was interfering with the organisation. Terrance thought about all the ways he could get rid of her!

"No, no, no!" Cindy shouted as she clapped her hands. "Listen up folks, I will need a top table now that I am to be married, and I want it here. Make it for nine people, and then I want the tables, each one to accommodate six guests around the edge. I want the centre left free! Do you all understand? Chop! Chop! It is getting late!" laughed Cindy. The team of staff looked at each other; they were never spoken to like this by the Lord or the Lady. Sometimes, Terrance would be a prick, but even he had learnt manners are everything. The team all agreed to do no more until they had spoken to an Arlington.

"Terrance, my dear, I have rearranged the grand hall; the little people are working on it now," explained Cindy. Terrance was still dreaming of ways to get rid of the vile women. "What have you done? I do hope you have not upset the workers Cindy. You must remember these people are not rich like me. They do not have a grand house; they have more simple homes like yours," snapped Terrance. "Excuse me, but I live here now, Terrance. I know it's hard for you cus you wanna get your hands on me, but Terrance, we need to wait until we are married," smiled Cindy. "But I wouldn't tell anyone if you fancied a quickie, ya know? A bit of finger action I could toss ya off, fancy it?" asked Cindy, looking into Terrance's eyes. Terrance was mortified, his face red with embarrassment. "I… I… er… I have to go," said Terrance as he rushed away to the bathroom. The thought of this woman touching him was making him want to vomit.

Lady Arlington was talking to her husband, "So darling Terrance and the young woman Cindy are to be married just before the ball! I have arranged the vicar, we will use the little chapel. I have arranged for the decorators to go in tomorrow and spruce it up! The ball will be their reception. It will be a wonderful day; now let's see if you need new suits to wear." Lord Arlington did not care, "Whatever darling, whatever you say." Whatever his wife wanted, she had. He wanted a quiet life; he was too old for drama, and he wanted to be left alone to do his own thing, to have good food and to make love to his wife at Christmas and on his birthday. "So, is it settled then?" he asked. "Yes, have you not been listening? Terrance is not too happy about it, but he will get used to the idea." The lord laughed, "Stupid boy, he will have a bit at last; it will be a happy Christmas for him, just like ours." Lady Arlington looked at her husband, "We have had our time dear, now don't fret; leave everything to me. Here, have your brandy, specially made how you like it."

16th December

Terrance sat quietly. He had done an excellent job of planning the ball. It was all coming together; the decorations looked stunning! But now he was to be married and expected to perform a sex act on that vile woman who was to be his wife! Terrance had never really fancied women; he didn't really fancy anyone but himself! His mother was his rock. She used to hold him tight and tell him it would be Ok. Her skin was always soft, and she always smelt divine. He felt safe with her and never planned to leave her. But now she was pushing him into the arms of another woman, a ghastly common woman! "Hello, hello, I say hello." Terrance looked up. Oh no, it was the dreadful Gilberts, Cinderella's parents. "Oh, my dears, Mr. and Mrs. Gilbert, how wonderful to see you," Terrance held out his hand. "Call me Susan," as she threw her arms around Terrance, "We are so pleased. We have heard the news that you have set a date; mind you, Terrance, you have not given me much time to get myself looking beautiful for the big day! Just think, my dear, we will soon be related, and I can come here to this magnificent house whenever I please. I mean, you won't be able to stop me! Now, where's my girl?" "Come along, darling." The Gilberts headed off to find Cindy. Terrance felt numb. Ignorant people, he thought. Did not ask how I was, say how beautiful the house was looking or offer to do anything! I cannot be married to her or her family. I need help; I need someone to get rid of them for me! Terrance then thought of Hen. He would do it for money! Terrance had hidden things for Hen in the past; they had an understanding. Hen frightened Terrance, but Terrance knew Hen liked money and cock, and he had both!

HENS PLACE

"Posh boy, why ya come see Hen?" Terrance was shaking; Hen's guards surrounded him. "So posh boy, what ya want? Some spice? Some magic? Or da ya want Hen?" Hen grabbed his crotch and laughed. "No, no, no, Sir, I come in peace; I mean, I'm peaceful, I mean, I'm careful." "Shut the fuck up!" shouted Hen. "What da ya want?" "I... I... I wondered if you wanted to come to the Christmas ball. It's... It's a masked Ball on the 24th from 7 pm," stuttered Terrance. Hen looked at Terrance, who was looking pale, "Sit down," ordered Hen. "Get him some tea. Now tell me what ya really want, cus I don't think ya come all this way, risking ya life to invite me to your fuckin' Ball, but thank ya anyway," said Hen. "I want you to get rid of someone for me," blurted Terrance. Hen looked at Terrance, "Ya come here to my home and ask me to get rid of someone for ya? What do ya think I am?" "I have money, lots of money," said Terrance, shaking. "How much money?" "A million. I'll give you a million." "Tell me all about it," said Hen. Terrance told Hen all about Cindy and her awful parents, how his parents were forcing him into marriage and how he did not want to share anything with Cindy, especially his inheritance, which stood in the Billions. Hen heard the prat's story, and while he felt slight sympathy towards him, he also found the situation amusing. The idiot did not know how lucky he was. Maybe time to have a bit of fun, thought Hen. "Leave it to me, and boy, leave ya invites on the table as ya go; I'll be in touch." "How?" questioned Terrance. "That's for me to know, and guess what, you'll find out," laughed Hen. "Yes, but how will I know what to do, where to stand?" questioned Terrance. "It's not fuckin' cluedo, now fuck off, posh boy!" snapped Hen. Terrance was shaking; he got up and made his way outside. Taking a deep breath. Thank goodness,

I'm safe, he thought. He did not know what would happen next, but he felt brave as he got in his car to drive home.

"Sir, the cops are still watching us; what do we do?" "Nothing, they will get bored, and now they have Lord Snooty on their list!" Hen laughed. "I'm no killer. He's an idiot, but for that money, I know someone who might be! Find me, Rich," Hen ordered. "Bring him to me; he can't hide forever. I have a job for him."

Rich

Rich was on edge. He needed to get to Hen. He needed out of here. Rich knew the cops were out and about; he also knew the lazy bastards went home at 10 pm. The woman was getting restless and on his nerves. He loved her, but since she could speak, she was talking too much, ordering him to do things, not that he was really complaining; the sex was amazing. She treated him like a little boy; she would smack him, tell him off, then fuck him. She would make him pretend it was his first time. Sometimes, she allowed him to take the lead. She had become obsessed with him and although Rich was satisfied all the time, he had lost the longing for her. He knew he needed out of this cottage and on to new pastures. Maybe he would feel better about her then! Rich decided tonight was the night, "We're leaving tonight," he announced to Mandy. "Why? Where are we going?" "Look, we can't stay here; we need to move on. A mate of mine is getting us the passports and money. It will be a long walk tonight so rest up now." "No, I will stay here." "No, you will come with me." "No, I don't want to. I will stay and wait for you." Rich could not be bothered; she would be alright. He trusted her, and she loved him. She would go nowhere. "Ok, Ok, stay, but I may be gone for a couple of days. Will you be Ok without me?" "It's Ok," she said, "I will keep my little pussy warm for you and guess what? When you come home, I will tie you up and have my wicked way with you." Mandy licked her lips, staring at Rich! Rich packed his bag, "Come here." Mandy came over to him and sat on his lap. Rich held her tight, sucking and biting her neck, "There's something to keep ya going, remind you ya taken." Mandy planned to sleep now and then, first thing in the morning, get out of this shit hole.

Rich walked down the lane. It was a bitter frosty night, and he had a long walk ahead of him. Rich reached the road and began to jog. Soon, warm up, he thought! It seemed hours before Rich even reached the crossroads. Maybe he could get a lift from a passerby? Except, the roads were empty!

It was 4 am when Rich reached Hen's place. He walked up the long drive away and into the reception office. He was tired, cold, hungry and in no mood for shit. "Oh, look who it is! Pretty boy!" said one guard. "Where you've been? We've been lookin for ya." "The boss is mad at you," smirked another guard. "Tell him I'm here; wake the fucker up," shouted Rich. Rich did not impress Joey, the senior guard; he lacks respect, the boss pays well, and no one disrespects the boss. "You're a fuckin' twat, mate, now get out of here," Joey points to the door. "Fuck off, man, I'm not going anywhere. Now, wake him up; he will not want to miss me. Now do as you're told," shouted Rich. Joey was mad; he pressed the emergency button. "You come here thinking you can say what you want, come with attitude, well it don't work with us. You're a fuckin' stupid twat who needs a lesson in manners." Rich was so intent on Joey that he missed the others coming in behind him. Rich suddenly realised he was surrounded by eight burleys; one kicked the back of his legs, and he went down. He was being dragged outside, and along the drive, the kicks and blows rained heavily down on him into his ribs, his legs, and his neck. It was the kick to his head that caused Rich to lose consciousness. "Stop," said Joey, "He's done for now. Dump him at the end of the drive." "Piece of shit!" one of them spat on him, "That will teach ya, cocky bastard."

Hen thought he had heard noises; he looked on the CCTV, but nothing, in fact, no guards. What the fuck am I paying for, he thought. Hen dressed and went upstairs just as the guards were coming back in. "Where ya been?" "Nowhere, boss." "I said where ya been? Why ya bleedin and why ya so dirty?" "Dunno, boss." "Dunno, boss." "Dunno, boss." "Well, you better start knowing, now talk." The guards looked at each other, and Joey stepped forward, "Well, boss, we had an intruder, so we had to deal with him." "Intruder? Who was it?" asked Hen. "Don't know, boss," said Joey. "Was it a cop? If it was a fuckin' cop, I'll kill the lot of you for bringing trouble to me door. Any sign of trouble, and you're all done." Hen pointed his finger at all of them, "Now tell me who it was." "Dunno, boss, never seen him before." "So what did you do?" "Just gave him a kick, told him not to come back." "So he got up and walked away, did he?" "Yeah, something like that." Hen felt they were hiding something from him. Joey was thinking of how to get rid of the body. He thought he would pretend to be sick and ask to leave, picking up the body and then dumping him somewhere! "So you fuckers, let me see this CCTV." Hen clicked on the machine. It was not that clear, but he saw Rich entering the office at 4 am. He watched them argue, then the guards piling in on him and dragging him away. "My Rich, what have they done?" Hen ran outside and down the drive, followed by Joey, who was expecting Rich to be by the gate. "So where is he?" asked Hen.

"Dunknow boss. He must have run off," said Joey, knowing it was not possible!

Lord and Lady Arlington had been out for a drive. The Lord could not sleep, so they went for a midnight picnic by the sea. They had fallen asleep in the Rolls and were now making their way home. It was almost 5 am when they came across Rich slumped by the roadside. "Stop!" shouted Steph, "That man looks in a bad way." The lord stopped the car. "Leave him, Steph." He sighed, "No, I will not hear of it; he needs help. Now help me get him in the car." They carefully moved him to the car; the Rolls had very comfortable leather seats, and they had several blankets to keep him warm. "Now what?" asked the Lord. "We take him home and look after him, of course." Rich was barely conscious, but he knew he had been moved. Blood filled his eyes, so his vision was impaired, but these didn't look like angry blokes. "Please, some water, just some water and somewhere safe," whispered Rich. "Stop the car," Lady Arlington climbed in the back. "Here, sweetie, have a sip of water; you're safe now, don't worry. Drive on, dear. Hurry." Rich dropped in and out of consciousness.

When the Arlingtons arrived home, Terrance was pacing, "Mummy, where have you been? I have been frantic with worry. Oh, and what's that?" pointing to Rich in the back of the car. "Terrance, get help; poor man needs care and rest. I will need help to get him out of the car and into the annexe. "Mummy, is this your project? Collecting tramps?" Terrance exclaimed, "Shh, the poor man has been beaten! Now, please, open up the annexe for me." They eventually got Rich onto a bed. Lady Arlington put Rich on his side, placed pillows around him for support, covered him with blankets and sat in the chair watching over him. She studied his face; bet he's handsome without the cuts and bruising, she thought, although he looked like no one had cared for him in a long time!

8th December

Rich had been out of it for sixteen hours. As he moved, he felt a softness on his head. He opened his eyes to see a beautiful ceiling and beautiful lights. Where the hell am I? he thought. He went to move, but the pain was too bad. He groaned. Immediately, Lady Arlington was at his side, "Hey, take it easy," she rested her hand on his shoulder. Rich looked at her. Who the fuck is this? he thought. "I'm Lady Arlington," she said, approaching his side. "You're in Arlington Manor, the Manor house. Lord Arlington and I found you by the roadside. You had been badly beaten up." Rich listened to her, "Here, sip this, sweetie; you need water and some chicken broth to make you strong, mend those bones." "Bones?" questioned Rich. "Yes, sweetie, we think you have cracked ribs. You really need to be checked. Will you allow me to get our private doctor to see you, sweetie?" Rich was in so much pain; he needed help, and he felt safe with her. "Thank you, ma'am, yes, thank you," said Rich. "Ok, sweetie, don't speak; try to sip this," Lady Arlington held his head into her bust and fed him water. Rich was in too much pain to even care what was happening. "Please, I need something for the pain." "I will get the doctor; now rest, sweetie." Lady Arlington had mixed a sedative in the water. She knew the doctor would not come until tomorrow, so she hoped this would help him sleep. It did the trick with her husband.

Rich opened his eyes. He looked up to see Lady Arlington smiling over him, "Hello, sweetie, the doctor will be here soon, so I think we need to get you washed and into something more comfortable and cleaner! We also need to change the bedding, it's very bloody! I have some silk loungewear for you." What on earth is silk loungewear, thought Rich. Is this bird actually gonna wash him? Yes, she was. She had the hot water ready and nice, warm, soft towels. What the hell, he thought, I need to be taken care of! Rich slowly sat up. "Can you swing your legs round, sweetie?" "I will try," Rich moved slowly. Everything hurt him, but he did it. Lady Arlington peeled away his jumper and T-shirt placed the clothes in a bag, and started washing him, his face, and his neck. She went down his arms, under his arms, down his back. "My… you're bruised, sweetie, you're black and blue; what happened?" "Dunno," said Rich. Rich knew exactly what had happened; that so-called friend of his Hen, little fucker had ordered his men to kill him. Rich tensed up at the thought of the betrayal. He better watch his back cus when I'm better, I'll get him. Lady Arlington was watching him, "Hey sweetie, you look tense. Come on, whatever it is, it will be alright," she sprayed his underarms and put a silk top on him. "Now, sweetie, we need to get your jeans off." Rich could not stand, "Don't worry, sweetie, I will remove them; lie down." Lady Arlington placed a towel for modesty over his mid-section; she undid his zip and gently removed his jeans and socks. She washed his feet and legs with gentle pressure.

This feels amazing, thought Rich. "Poor sweetie, you are so badly bruised; you must be in so much pain." Rich nodded, "Ma'am, I need a piss; I mean toilet." Lady Arlington smiled, "Of course," she handed him a bottle. Rich looked in horror, but needs must, he was desperate. He successfully pissed in the bottle and handed it back to Lady Arlington, who made nothing of it. She was used to this with her husband, bloody bottles everywhere. Thankfully, his butler picked most of them up. "Now your bits; we need to wash your bits." "My bits?" "Yes, sweetie, your man bits. Shall I get the flannel ready for you, or do you want me to do it?" Rich nodded. "Yeah, please." Lady Arlington removed the towel and gasped. She had never seen such a large penis before, she had seen her husband's tiny thing and two of the gardener's dicks, oh, and a builder some time ago, but this one was enormous. Lady Arlington soaped up her hands and washed him. She was gentle as she washed his penis, balls and his bottom. She could not take her eyes off his penis. She felt herself getting wet between her legs. It had been a long time since she had felt that! Rich was watching her. "Hey babe, I can't shag you; I'm in pain, but maybe when I'm better, hey?" "EXCUSE ME, HOW DARE YOU? I am a married woman who brought you into our home to look after you. I could have left you to die by the roadside, and you think it is Ok to disrespect me by being common and vulgar towards me!?"

"I'm sorry, ma'am, I'm sorry. I thought… Look, I'm sorry. I meant nothing; I'm an idiot." "Best you dry yourself," as she threw the towel at him. She helped him into the silk trousers in silence. "I need to change the bed; please roll to one side." Rich did as he was asked. "Good, that's all done, nice and clean. The doctor will be here shortly." Lady Arlington picked up the dirty laundry and headed out of the apartment. Rich lay in silence. Idiot, why'd you say that to her, he thought.

Lady Arlington returned with homemade soup and freshly baked bread, some butter, water, fruit and chocolates. "Here you go, something to eat." Rich felt she was frosty with him. He grabbed her arm. "Look, lady, I am sorry, I meant nothing. I am grateful. I guess I need to move on?" "No, no, I won't hear of it. You're not well; you must stay. I will look after you," she said tenderly. "What's your name?" Rich asked. "Lady Arlington," she replied. Rich smiled, "Lady A," nice, he thought.

The doctor arrived later in the afternoon. He examined Rich and concluded he had a few cracked ribs and lots of bruising, but in his opinion, nothing more. He gave Rich breathing exercises and painkillers. "You need TLC, lad," he said as he left the room. Rich did not know what TLC was, "What's TLC?" Rich asked. "Tender Loving Care, sweetie, tender loving care," replied Lady A as she held his gaze longer than normal. Now, Rich was not good at politics or business, but women he knew inside out. He was the best, and he knew she was giving him the signs! She may think she is not, thought Rich, but he knew women, and this bird was defiantly giving the signs!

"Come on, sweetie, you need a shave," Lady A was standing over him with a razor, Hot flannel and a small bowl of hot water. "Oh, and you're qualified to do this, are you?" asked Rich. "Of course, sweetie, now come on, you are in need of a shave." "Look, Lady A," Rich said, "I am grateful and all that, but I wanna shave myself; no woman is coming near me with a razor." Lady A looked at Rich. "Ok, do it yourself, but do it; you're looking a mess and need a shave! Oh, and I have ordered you a new wardrobe of clothes; when you're feeling up to it, you can try them on. I know they will look good on you! You can stay in this apartment until you are better. My family, that's my husband, son and his soon-to-be wife, live in the main house. They won't come down here but just in case the connecting door is locked and I have the only key! You can, of course, get out at any time you go out of the--" "Shhh, Lady, I'm not going anywhere," Rich smiled at her. Lady A felt her face blush as she tried to hide her delight when he said he was not going anywhere. Rich lay in bed; he liked the feel of the silk and the softness of the bed. He liked the fact he had a lady looking after him. He fell asleep thinking about his Lady A!

MANDY

Mandy woke up bright and early. It was dark inside the cottage, but then it always was. She was sure she had slept all night, and he would not be back until tonight, so it was her time to escape. She finished the bread and ate the last apple, drank some water, dressed and set about her exit. "Bye, cottage," she said out loud, "It's been a pleasure, but I must go!" She moved the furniture and made her way through the wall into the adjoining cottage. She had thought about this moment for ages, freedom at last! The cottage was barren and cold. She took a deep breath and opened the door to freedom. It was pitch black! Suddenly, Mandy felt scared. She did not know the time or where she was. Maybe she had not slept all night, or maybe she had slept for too long, and he would be back anytime. Mandy sat on the floor. "Calm down," she whispers to herself. "Calm down, it will be Ok; just wait, and it will be light soon." She pulled her knees into her chest and waited. It seemed like hours before it got light. Mandy was cold but determined to escape! Mandy opened the door and wished he was with her. He should be holding my hand, she thought. She missed him; she felt scared; she loved him! Mandy decided to go back and wait for him after all; he was trying to get them out of this mess, and he was going to take her somewhere sunny and marry her. It all sounded perfect. He was still a stranger in many ways but he excited her; he ignited something inside her she had never felt before! She knew she should escape, but the thought of being without him and never feeling his arms around her made her sad. Mandy decided to stay and wait for him.

Day turned to night; night turned to day. Mandy was hungry. He will be back soon, she thought, with fresh bread and fruit. The only thing she had was water, which she boiled for a hot drink.

As the days went on, Mandy began to feel weak and cold; her head was hurting, and her body was aching. She began to cry and pray.

Please, Lord, hear me. Please forgive me for my sins, but Lord, I need help. Please, please, help me. I have been selfish. I am sorry!

Mandy closed her eyes and drifted off.

Chapter Twenty: SERG

Serg was puzzled; how could he not solve this? Something was missing; the hotel footage had identified four girls, two he knew of but the other two, no idea. The lads had circulated the photos and were still following leads, so what is it, he thought. Serg decided to go for a drive; before he knew it, he had parked his car at the farm. He walked across the fields and into the pig field, which was full of pigs now, not his favourite animal. He stopped to catch his breath as he surveyed the land. The trees had been cut down and were bare. As Serg looked around, something caught his eye, "What the fuck!?" Serg climbed over the bushes to find a lane. It looked well used, he thought. He followed the lane, which turned into a path. The path led him to cottages.

"Well, well, well, dozy buggers didn't search here!" One cottage was boarded up, but the other looked open. Serg immediately called for backup. He walked back down the lane, following it to the road. How the hell did we miss this, he thought! The team arrived quickly. "Ok, let's go in," ordered Serg. "Nothing, Serg." "Empty, sir, it's bare." "Ok, ok, on to the next." Then Serg noticed something behind the table: a hole in the wall! Serg bent down to see a small tunnel; he crawled through it to find himself in the next cottage. "Cover the door, Jessie," Serg shouted. The cottage had a strange smell; it had rubbish on the floor, two cups and some clothes scattered around. Serg picked up the clothes. Male and female, he thought. Serg walked into the second room, "Oh my God, a young girl in bed, unconscious. Fuck! Fuck! Another one!" he shouted to the team, "Quick, get something. Get something; we need to get this girl out of here. Call the ambulance; get them to meet us at the roadside." Serg felt a faint pulse. He wrapped the girl up in the duvet, and between the six of them, they carried her out of the cottage to the awaiting ambulance. Serg ordered his team to fingerprint the cottage and bag everything. "Bag every scrap of evidence; don't leave a fuckin' thing!" he ordered. "Serg, Serg, a purse." "Bag it." "But Serg, it belongs to Helen West." Serg froze. Was this girl the murderer?

Chapter Twenty-One: Updates

HEN

Hen was on the edge of his nerves. He needed to find Rich. He had searched the lanes every night, he also had his team of scouts out to the hospital the village in fact every bloody where, but nothing; nobody had seen him. "Where is my Rich?" he shouted to himself Hen was emotional. "I love him; I need him." Hen banged the door with his fist in pure frustration. "Where is he?" Hen never got his hands dirty but fuck it. Taking out his gun, he downed his brandy and pills. He would kill anyone who stood in his way, he was gonna find him! Hen thought about the conversation they had: He had a wife but he had left her, he worked at the farm but not in the winter, that was all he knew how could he only know that about the man he loved? I bet he thought I was not interested in him. Hen began to cry. He had all this money he wanted for nothing, yet the person he wanted more than anything was gone!

HOSPITAL UPDATE

Cruz was ready for discharge, he was doing well; he had stayed in the hospital longer than necessary because he lived alone and he played on that. The nurses were all keen on him and one of them had invited him to the Arlington ball. Of course he had accepted especially as the nurses were organising his suit and mask.

Dazer was responding. Although he was frightened of everything, the doctor thought he was still in deep shock. He was to be transferred to a convalescent home but Dazer did not want to go, he felt safe with Cruz, he refused to speak to anyone other than Cruz so it was agreed he would stay with Cruz with some additional help each day.

Mandy responded well to fluids and food. The hospital confirmed she was a nurse at the hospital but they assumed she had gone home to New Zealand and had sacked her for not informing them. The staff looked after her and made sure she had everything she needed. The police came to see her every day, but she said she could not remember anything. "We know you had a male with you. Who was it?" asked Jessie. Mandy looked blank and replied, "I don't know, Sir." Mandy knew the police were not convinced, but it was true she didn't know him. She did not know how she got into the cottage or where it was, she did not know dates or time! What she did know was that she missed him. She wanted him to hold her, to tell her how beautiful she was; she needed him. She wanted to make love to him, to please him.

Jessie called in on her every day, trying to build a relationship with her. "Hi Mandy, how are you today?" "I'm good, thank you, sir. Now what?" "Hey, call me Jessie. I thought I would take you for tea or coffee. Fancy a walk?" "No, no, I only have a nightie on." "Ok, how about I get us a drink and a fancy cake and bring it back; fancy that?" "Go on then," smiled Mandy. Jessie caught her eyes as she smiled; he instantly felt something in his heart. When Jessie returned with the cake and coffee, he noticed she had brushed her hair and applied lip gloss. They chatted about cake for a while, and then Jessie said, "Look, Mandy, do you remember anything today about what happened to you? Like who bit your neck; that's some bite!" Mandy raised her hand to her neck as if to cover it. Jessie observed she went straight to the side. "So, who did it? he asked. Mandy looked at Jessie as tears started to fall from her eyes. "I don't know. I don't know; he never told me his name, I was not allowed to speak, I was locked away, I never went out, but he loved me, and I love him." The tears were streaming down her face. Jessie hugged her, "Hey, come on, you're safe now." "I was safe with him; he loved me," Jessie stroked

her hair. "Come on, it's going to be Ok; we can find him for you."
"You can?" Mandy looked at Jessie. "Yes, sure. Can you describe
him?" Mandy smiled, "Yes, he is tall, dark and handsome. Strong
jawline, lovely teeth with a strong muscular body and moody
looking." Jessie hated him already. "Did he hurt you?" questioned
Jessie. "Only when I did not do as he asked, so it was my fault."
"What did he do to you?" asked Jessie. "He punched me or hit me.
He belted me one time, and sometimes he would…" her voice trailed
off. "Yes, he would what?" asked Jessie. "Nothing, it doesn't matter."
"It does matter, Mandy. Did he force himself on you?" Did he rape
you, Mandy?" "No, no, he loved me, so it was his." Jessie was taken
aback by this poor girl; she was brainwashed, he thought. Jessie put
his arms around her, "Everything will be Ok. I will come back
tomorrow. We can talk some more." Jessie gave her one of his biggest
smiles and a wink as he left. She smiled back at him. Bless him, she
thought.

Jessie would return twice a day to see Mandy, and he would bring
in chocolates and magazines. He had even found some nice clothes
for her. They walked around the hospital chatting. Mandy liked him.
She was looking forward to Jessie visiting today, and she wondered
what mad stuff they would talk about today. They seemed to have a
lot in common. Jessie arrived with more chocolates. "Hey, looks like
they are letting you go home." Mandy looked up at Jessie, "I don't
have a home. I lived in the digs here, but they have Re-let my room.
What am I going to do? I don't have anywhere to go." Mandy started
to cry. "Come home with me; I have space," said Jessie. "You can
have your own room. I will take care of you until you're back on your
feet. I mean, it's nearly Christmas, and no one wants to be alone at
Christmas; you would be doing me a favour. I need someone to escort
me to a Christmas ball, what you say?" Mandy looked at Jessie; he

was serious. "This is so kind of you, Jessie. I don't know what to say." "Then say yes," he smiled. "Are you sure?" "Yes, I have room. I live alone. The company would be great. And the Ball; is that a yes?" "No, I have nothing to wear," replied Mandy pulling a face. "I will take you shopping. Come on, just say yes, it will be fun." Mandy smiled. She felt safe with Jessie. He was someone who would take care of her and be kind to her, she thought. "Yes, yes, Jessie, thank you. I will come home with you." "And the Ball?" "Yes, and the Ball," replied Mandy. "Great, we can eat, drink, watch TV, play games, walk, talk, anything you want," said Jessie with enthusiasm. "Sounds wonderful," Mandy smiled at Jessie; if only you were him, she thought.

RICH

Rich was healing slowly; his ribs were still sore, but he could breathe slightly easier. The bruising had come out all over his body, but he was feeling good. He had been slowly walking around the apartment in between, resting. Lady A was in and out of the apartment, bringing him food, drink, clothes, and aftershaves, and today, she turned up 'the several suits. "What's all that!?" questioned Rich. "Well, it's suits, sweetie and masks, which are all handmade and quite expensive," replied Lady A. "And what do I need these for?" asked Rich. "Well, sweetie, I wondered if you would like to come to the Arlington Christmas Ball, obviously, if you feel up to it. It is a masked ball so no one will know who you are, and it's here in the house and grounds, so not too far to go, and you may enjoy it, but no pressure, sweetie," smiled Lady A. Rich looked puzzled, "Why wouldn't I want people to know who I am?" Lady A. turned to Rich, placing her hand on his shoulder, "Look, sweetie, I know you're hiding something or hiding from someone or maybe many people. I know you're in trouble; you have done bad things. I have listened to your nightmares." Rich looked at her hand on his shoulder; it was small. He lifted her hand and kissed it, looking deep into her eyes, "For you, I will try to be there." She let him hold on to her hand as she looked at him; the electricity between them was sizzling, or was it just her feeling it? Lady A. pulled her hand away, "I must go," she murmured. Rich watched her as she retreated to the big house. What was that? He thought. He had felt nothing like that before. It was like electricity running through him.

Lady A. returned in the evening with a roast chicken dinner, a bottle of wine, a dessert and some cheese and biscuits, all served on a silver trolly. "Hello, here you go, something to build your strength up, a lovely chicken dinner fit for a king she said," smiling at Rich, "Would you like anything else?" she asked. Rich looked up at her, "You. I would like you!" Lady A. could feel herself blushing. She quickly pushed the Trolley to Rich and headed off out of the door. Rich smiled as she left the apartment.

Lady A. made her way to her apartment to collect her thoughts! She thought about his eyes, those lips and the urge inside her to kiss him. Pull yourself together, she thought, as she made her way down to dinner with the family, who were all waiting for her. "Come on, Mother, we are waiting for you," said Terrance. "It is rude to be late, and Father is hungry." She just wanted to be left alone with her thoughts and not listen to mindless prattle from Terrance or her husband, and now Cindy had joined the table he conversation was even more ridiculous. It was like listening to a bunch of imbeciles. The Lord insisted on sitting at the big table for dinner, which could seat twelve or more people. He insisted he sat at the head of the table with Terrance to his left, and any guests were down at the other end of the table. Problem was, the Lord was going deaf, so anything Cindy had to say had to be conveyed to him via his butler or Terrance. Neither were renowned for their listening skills. "Listening to you lot is like listening to a group of clowns in a bloody nursing home," shouted Lady Arlington, throwing down her knife and fork, "Now, if you will excuse me, I have a headache and will be returning to my quarters for peace." Terrance looked at his mother. He had never seen her like this before. "Ignore her; she is going through the change," shouted the Lord, laughing. "She has always been selfish, your mother, he continued. "SELFISH. Selfish woman! Always wants her own way, ignore her son." Terrance felt uncomfortable, but his father was right: Mummy wanted it all her own way. He looked down the table at Cindy, who was watching and listening to everything, "Cinderella dear, why don't you retire and leave the men to talk?" announced Terrance. "Yeah, think I will, some good telly on I'm missing, gonna take me dinner with me." Terrance shook his head. Vile women, he thought.

Lady Arlington returned to her quarters, ran herself a bath, and thought about the handsome stranger downstairs. She thought about the way he made her feel and the electricity she felt when they touched.

The following morning, Lady Arlington was up bright and early; the others were not awake, and she would be surprised to hear from the Lord until at least lunchtime. She may have made his nightcap slightly stronger last night. She had heard his comments about her as she left the table, so when making his favourite nightcap, she may accidentally slipped in more **medication.**

She carried the breakfast tray down to his apartment, opening the door. She expected him to be in bed, she planned to wake him up with a smile Maybe he would grab her hand again! She walked into the bedroom. "Morning, sweetie." She shouted, He was not in bed, her heart felt heavy, he's gone, she thought. Then she heard running water; she looked up; the bathroom door was ajar, and she could see him in the shower. She let out a sigh of relief, she knew she should leave him to it, but she couldn't move from the spot! Rich had noticed her but pretended he had not. He started soaping up his cock. The knowledge that she was watching him really turned him **on.** Lady Arlington couldn't take her eyes off him, completely captivated by his beautiful body and impressive cock. Rich was getting carried away, his cock was throbbing, and he was pulling it harder and quicker. He wanted to stop, but he couldn't. Looking across at the Lady "Come on in, help me out," he shouted. Lady Arlington felt mortified that he had seen her, she ran out of the apartment and back to the main house. Rich smiled as he thought about her, one day, lady, one day, but for now, a hand job!

Lady Arlington ran upstairs back to her quarters. She was flustered, but felt so excited and wet between her legs. She lay down with her favourite vibrator; thinking of him brought her satisfaction. She had several vibrators. They were a necessity these days. The only pleasure she got!

Lady Arlington could not get him out of her mind. I will speak with him, I will explain I did not mean to spy on him, but I was looking out for him in case he fell or something! She knew that was lame. Why didn't she just tell the truth? You're a gorgeous man, and frankly, I could not take my eyes off you!

Lunch time

Lady Arlington made her way down to the annexe, His lunch tray was made up with sandwiches and cakes. She had rehearsed what she might say to him. "Hello, sweetie, lunch for you," she called as she entered. "You Ok?" she asked. "Hey, yeah, just resting," Rich patted the bed, "Come and sit down. Come on, sit here with me. You never sit with me, always rushing off." Lady Arlington was unsure. "Come on, sit down. I wanted to say thank you for last night." "Last night?" she asked, slightly confused. "Yes, the dinner was superb." "Oh right, yes, of course." Rich looked at her, "Oh and if you're wondering, my wank was Ok." Lady Arlington stood up, "No, no, of course not. I mean, I--" Rich grabbed her arm and pulled her towards him. He began to kiss her gently at first, but his passion soon boiled up inside his tongue, darting into her mouth. She was returning the tongue action as if they were speaking to each other. She suddenly realised what she was doing and pulled away. "Hey, I'm sorry, I didn't mean to…" She put a finger to Rich's lips, "Shhh sweetie, it's forbidden, I am forbidden." She turned to walk away, looking back at him, "For now," she said.

Lady Arlington looked forward to meal times when she got to see him. She always dressed up for dinner, but tonight, she made an extra special effort! She carried in the tray, which contained homemade game pie and vegetables, followed by homemade dessert and sheep cheese with homemade crackers. "Hello, sweetie, how are you?" Rich looked up; he was still in bed, resting and watching TV. He smiled at her, "Hey, sit down; tell me about ya day." She sat down and started to chat with him. Rich felt the heat rising inside him. He wanted this woman. Rich grabbed her arm and pulled her into him, kissing her as he started to undress her, he unbuttoned her blouse and undid her skirt.

She had silk underwear on, the material felt amazing between his fingers. He had never felt real silk underwear before. He wanted to rub her panties over his face but was afraid to let her go. "Let me make love to you," he whispered, his hand rubbing over her silk panties. She was soaking, "Make me cum," she whispered,"Use your fingers." Rich slipped his fingers inside her, she started groaning, "That's it, keep them inside me, that's it, keep them still, now I'm ready. Bring me off," she screamed, "Now, now, do it now," she ordered. She started screaming as her body shivered and her pussy contracted around his fingers! Wow! Rich looked at her, smiling, "You gonna finish me?" "No, sweetie, I have to go, but feel free to have a go yourself or maybe save it!" "Save it? What the fuck for?" "Me, sweetie, me, when I'm ready, I will tell you." She kissed him passionately, dressed and left. What the fuck just happened, thought Rich, but he could not wait for her to come back!

The following morning, Lady Arlington returned with more food, "Morning, sweetie, how are you? Shall I put the tray on the table?" "No, bring it here, please." Rich was watching TV, "Where shall I put the tray? "Just here," Rich pointed to his lap. Lady Arlington put down the tray, "There you go, sweetie, I must go." Rich grabbed her arm, "Talk to me; why are you always rushing away? Come on, we need to talk about last night; you can't pretend." "Look, sweetie, you finger fucked me; I enjoyed it, and I want more, but it needs to be a secret between us, and it needs to be on my terms." Rich looked at her, "Ok, ma'ama, whatever you say." "MA'AMA? MA'AMA?" Lady Arlington exploded, "Don't ever call me that again because if you do, you will be gone." Rich was taken aback, "Hey, Ok babe, I was only messin', I am sorry. What's your name anyway? asked Rich, "Lady Arlington, I had told you once," she snapped. "No, no, none of that Lady crap; what's your name?" "Stephanie," she replied. "I'm

Richard," Moving the tray to the floor he grabbed her hand and kissed it, then placed it on his cock. See Stephanie, what ya do to me." His cock was bulging out of his trousers; she gently released him and began stroking him. She could not get over how big and beautiful it was. He was enjoying her gentle touch; it was like a velvet glove holding him. Rich closed his eyes; the feelings he was having were a mixture of pure pleasure, passion and lust. She was massaging his cock, and it was the most amazing experience. Oh, Steph, I'm gonna..." "No, no, not now, hold it back, HOLD IT." She let go of his cock, "Sweetie, keep it inside you; when I'm ready, I will take it." Rich looked at her, his mind racing, his cock pulsing. He just wanted to grab her and fuck her, but he held off. She had something, and he was scared to lose it. Steph smiled as she removed her knickers. She straddled him, teasing him, just letting the tip of his cock meet her pussy. She teased him until he was about to burst. "Please, please, let me in," Rich whispered to her, "Please, Stephanie, I need you." She was wet; she wanted him, but she would make him wait. She stood up, "No more sweetie." "I can't wait. I want you now," whispered Rich. "I know you do; I can see you dripping," she smiled. "Come on, babe, don't do this to me; my balls are hurting. I'm hurting," pleaded Rich. "Then finish yourself off. You will wait for me; when I am ready, you will have me!" Rich reached out for her, pulling her into him and kissing her passionately. "Ok, we do it your way; I will wait," he whispered. Steph looked at him; she stroked his hair and his chin; she traced her fingers around his mouth and gently kissed him. Rich had never experienced such gentleness. He looked into her eyes; they were dancing with mischief yet were soft but sexy. They made him feel calm like no one else had ever done! She intrigued him so much. Rich held her as he kissed her, his hands caressing her body; soon, his fingers were inside her. He slowly eased her down onto the chair and slid his mouth over her pussy, letting his tongue do the work. She had never experienced this before and was lost in the emotion of what was happening to her, the pure passion and pleasure of this man sucking her pussy. "Oh my God," she screamed as she pushed his head into her. Her body started to shake. He felt her tighten up and then explode. It was a beautiful moment for him. She lay silent in his arms; his cock was throbbing, "Please finish me," begged Rich, "It's so fuckin' painful." "I said, sweetie, you're waiting. Now I really must go." "No, no," Rich pulled her back, "Taste me." Steph looked at Rich, "I have never done that before," she whispered. Rich's surprise quickly turned into happiness when he realized he would be her first. "Come on then, let me guide you," he urged. She took his cock in her mouth and started sucking on it gently, following Rich's lead as he showed her the hand action he liked. He relaxed and let everything unfold. Her lips and mouth were soft and her touch even softer. "I can't hold it, babe," he shouted, "Don't stop, babe. Take it, fuck me, sit on it, oh my Oh, oh, babe!" Rich shouted as he exploded into her mouth.

She looked beautiful, Rich thought, flushed with his juices running out of her mouth. "Come here," Rich pulled her on top of him and kissed her, probing his tongue in her mouth, "You taste amazing, babe," he whispered." "I want you." She could feel his cock hard again against her leg, and as much as she wanted to move, she wanted to stay. No, don't do it, she thought get up and walk away, but her pussy was throbbing; her longing to be fucked was past caring about the consequences. She placed herself on top of him, gently at first. Rich pushed gently as he entered her. "Just take me, babe. I'm yours. Use me for your pleasure. That's it, babe. Ride me," he said. Stephanie found herself lost in emotion. She was riding a real enormous cock, not another vibrator! Rich watched her as she rode him fast, then slow, and then he felt the heat rising inside her. She was happy using him for her pleasure. Rich tried to remove her, but she had contracted so hard around his cock that she was going nowhere. "Fuck! Fuck!" he shouted. He had no choice; he grabbed her, rolled her over and made love to her. The passion was intense. Rich was lost in oblivion and emotion. He had never felt emotion like this as he collapsed on top of her. They lay quietly together. What have I done She thought. What have I done? I've crossed the line, he thought.

Steph started to move, "I have things to do," she said. "Like what?" questioned Rich. "Well, if you must know, I have to pick my outfit for the wedding." "What wedding is this?" "My son Terrance is getting married on Christmas Eve." "But that's the Ball!" "Yes, they are to be married in the morning." Rich stroked her hair, "Don't rush off, your outfit can wait, talk to me." Steph looked at him. "Did I cross the line?" asked Rich. "Line?" questioned Steph. "Yeah, ya know, just I… well, I cum inside ya; I'm sorry, but…" Stephanie raised her finger to his mouth, "Shh, there are no lines, sweetie; we did what we did because I allowed it; I wanted it." Rich was relieved; he liked it here, and he liked this woman. "So, am I invited to the wedding?" "No, sweetie, you're not; you will raise too many questions. The Ball will be fine; you can wear a mask, and I was thinking you could be Lord Smithye from the north. He cannot attend, and no one has met him yet, so this fits perfectly." "Oh, that's it; I can only come if I am hidden like your dirty secret," said Rich. Stephanie stood up and dressed, "It is not like that, and you know it, but like it or not, I am married, and you ARE my dirty secret, one that is hiding in my house being looked after, having all your needs met and now bloody moaning about not getting an invite to a wedding where you know no one, why don't you just go? The door is that way; take everything with you and go back to whatever you were doing." Shouted Stephanie angerly, "So the decision is yours; you are a free man. But if you stay, it's on my terms, and frankly, I don't care which way it goes." Stephanie left the apartment, banging the door behind her. Rich felt shaken by her outburst. Fuck it, Fuck her 'Ill leave, thought Rich Then he looked around. He had never experienced such luxury before. He had silk sheets, silk pyjamas, branded clothing, and leather shoes. He had food fit for a king, a warm, comfortable apartment, his laundry taken care of, and now, best of all, he was getting a shag. Maybe he would stay and play nice for now! Rich headed to bed. He was exhausted! The soft bed and silk sheets engulfed him. "I'm staying," he whispered, "Im staying right here!"

Stephanie joined the others in the lounge area, "Where have you been?" questioned Terrance, "You look well; you look a bit er… Not like yourself, mummy." Lord Arlington looked up from his paper, "Yes, my dear, you look rough," he said, laughing. "I am not well. I have been in bed; sorry I missed everything." "But mummy, I came looking for you; you were not in bed." "Terrance!" shouted Stephanie. "No more! I don't answer to you. I was in bed sleeping. I have just woken up, and guess what? I am going back to bed," Stephanie stormed off, leaving them all wondering what on earth was happening to her.

Stephanie lay on her bed collecting her thoughts; her mind was in turmoil. What if he leaves? She thought. Well, it's best now rather than later when you're more invested! Oh well, I will know when I go down tonight. She thought.

Stephanie opened the door walking into his apartment; she smiled as she saw him sitting in the chair watching TV. He was dressed in his silk pyjamas, he smelled wonderful, he had shaved, and he looked so handsome. Rich looked up at her and smiled, "I'm staying," he announced as he patted his lap, "Come here." Steph placed the tray down and sat on his lap. "Put ya arms around me," said Rich. She placed her arms around him. His aftershave was so nice that she felt wet just by smelling him. His eyes were smiling at her, and they held each other's gaze, smiling at each other, "I'm sorry," said Rich, "I'm sorry. I am grateful to you, Stephanie. I want to stay, and like you say, you're the boss," Rich winked at her. Stephanie felt butterflies in her stomach, her mind racing, "Make love to me, Rich," she whispered. Rich had not expected that, making love meant gentle; it meant more than a shag. Instantly, Rich thought about the girl he had left, in the cottage, he had made love to her because he loved her or at least he thought he loved her but now he was here in the arms of another woman, a real woman. Could he make love to her? Steph looked at him, "Rich, please, what's wrong?" Rich said nothing; he picked her up, "Put me down," she teased. "Woman, you're all mine." He slowly undid her dress, it fell to the floor, revealing stockings and suspenders. "OH MY! Woman" Rich gasped, He had never felt so turned on. Just looking at her made the heat in him rise. "Woman, you drive me crazy. Look what ya doing to me." His cock was erect, as he stared into her eyes, "Woman, look at me, I'm a wreck. I'm just putty in your hands, "LOOK AT ME!" he demanded. "I can't wait to make love to you, babe. I can't fuckin' wait; finger yourself, babe." She placed her hand over her pussy and inserted her finger, and within seconds, Rich exploded all over her! "Now I can make love to you," he whispered. Rich was gentle, loving and tender and took her to places she had never been. The ecstasy he felt was overwhelming. Rich had never felt such a connection with someone, and it was more than sex. It felt like the thing he had been searching for all his life. They both lay together in silence. They both knew they had crossed a line, and there was no going back. Stephanie turned to Rich, "You make me happy." "And you me," responded Rich. "I was thinking maybe you could come to the wedding as Lord Smithye. No one has actually met him as he only recently inherited the land from his father, so they won't know any difference," explained Steph. "I dun know, babe. I'm happy to come to the ball, but I don't think I'm ready for the day gig anyway. If someone got near you, I'd be on 'em. Can I watch from somewhere?" Steph felt a slight disappointment, but maybe knowing he was watching would be a turn-on. Steph smiled at him, "Ok, I will see what I can organise; now I really must go." "Did you choose your outfit, by the way?" Rich asked "You remembered?" She smiled, "Yes, I did." "Colour?" asked Rich. "Day is a beautiful Blue, and the night, well, let's keep that a secret, shall we? You must find me!" "Oh, don't worry, babe, I'll find ya, I'll know ya, I'll smell ya; you smell like no other woman has ever smelt. I'll know when you're near me; it will start twitching," Rich smiled at her. She kissed him and left. Rich lay in bed thinking he was in love. This was it. He had found what he was looking for at last. He had everything. I'm looking after myself for once, he thought. I know it's selfish, but I've struggled enough.

Chapter Twenty-Two
Christmas Eve

Everyone in the village, from the hospital staff to the police station, talked about the Arlington Ball and the upcoming marriage. Terrance had been inviting everyone. He did not know the numbers, so the caterers were on high alert. He had defiantly overspent the budget. Still, the place had a winter wonderland appearance. The trees looked amazing inside and outside, all decorated in matching themes depending on where they were. Fireplaces adorned with fresh garland; doors adorned with holly wreaths. The place smelt amazing. They also decorated the high ceilings with fir and holly and strategically placed mistletoe bushes throughout the house. It was perfect. The wedding invitations had gone out even though Terrance had tried to stop them.

"We invite you to witness the marriage of Terrance Arther George Arlington and Cindy Marie Gilbert. They are to be married in Arlington Chapel at Midday on 24th December 1989.

The reception will follow, and we will hold it in the Marquee in the west Garden from 2 pm until 6 pm. You're welcome to stay for the Arlington Christmas ball, starting at 7 pm. The Ball has a strict dress code. Gentlemen are to wear a tuxedo and bow tie all gentlemen are to be masked when entering the house. Ladies are required to wear an evening dress for the Arlington Christmas ball, and, of course, they must wear a mask when entering the house."

Terrance had laughed at the invitations. "It is very long, mother," he said. "Terrance, my dear, it is clear, so no one gets it wrong. Be clear, Terrance, be clear." Terrance wanted to be clear: he wanted to cancel the wedding; he was looking forward to the evening but dreading the day. He wanted mummy to be proud of him for everything he had done, organising the ball, but he did not want to marry the woman with any luck Hen will arrive and kill her. Suddenly, Terrance realised what he had done. It might be messy and its today; this will be her last day. How about he gets me? Terrance began to sweat; he had no time to cancel it! "You Ok, dear?" Terrance turned around; it was his beloved mother, "Yes, mother, yes, I was just making last-minute adjustments." "Ok, dear, but the dressers are waiting for you." Terrance looked at his mother, she had a beautiful inner glow to her, "Mummy, you look absolutely beautiful in that blue dress; I wish I was marrying you, Mummy." Steph smiled at him, "Well, thank you kindly, sir, now off you go."

Steph wanted to see Rich before the proceedings started. She had provided him with lots of food to keep him going. He now had a set of keys to his apartment and the CCTV room. Steph explained how he could get to the room without anyone seeing him. The camera guards were given the day off, and everything was going according to plan. Steph entered his apartment. Rich was in bed, "Wow, you look amazing, come here." "No, no, I'm ready. I can't." "Come here, woman, let me look at you." "Rich held out his arms. She edged closer to him like lightning; he grabbed her and pulled her on top of him. "My… you smell good," he said. "Richard, Richard, no, not now. I will be…" Rich's fingers were inside her, "You'll be what?" he asked. "Late," she whimpered, "Rich, my dress, let me take it off." "No, leave it on, then I know what ya done in it when I watch ya." Rich entered her and made love to her. Both grinding and gyrating together, her contractions started, he knew, "That's it, baby, come to me." They both climaxed with fireworks going off in their head. "Fuck me, Stephanie, you're doing things to me," sighed Rich. Steph gave him one of her smiles, "I must go, sweetie; look at my dress!" she exclaimed; "it's ruined." The dress was very creased and wet, her hair was a mess, and her perfect makeup was ruined. "Oh my goodness, look at me." Rich laughed, "You look lovely, a little flushed but lovely. You're too posh, lady." Steph smiled, 'Don't forget to watch everything. I will touch my hair when I think about you." She blew him a kiss and left the apartment. Rich lay in bed; he was slowly getting his feet under the table. He loved her fiercely, and no one would steal that from him. Now, with keys, he'd spy on the posh bunch for fun.

Terrance was pacing up and down the waiting lounge. What if HE turns up and kills her? What if he shoots me? Oh my, what if he kills someone else? What have I done? I can't let it happen. I have to stop him, thought Terrance. "Sit down, man, you're making me on edge, and where's your mother?" demanded Lord Arlington. "Making herself beautiful, I think, or maybe she's gone to see the tramp you brought home." "What!? He is still here?" exclaimed the lord. "Where is he?" "I don't know Daddy, in the outhouse, I think." They both laughed, "Pour me a brandy, son; your mother always loves to care for the poor bastards who have nothing. Your mothers very kind, really, just not to me." "What do you mean, Daddy?" asked Terrance. "Oh, nothing, son. I struggle to get it up these days, and she never wants to help me. She is selfish in that department and always has been." "Farther! Farther! Please, this is my day. I do not wish to have such words in my ears!" sighed Terrance. Lord Arlington drank his brandy. Maybe tonight, he thought, it was Christmas afterall.

Cindy was barking orders at anyone who listened. She had three dresses to choose from: they were on and off, her hair was up, then down, she flat shoes on then heel shoes. She had no idea! The wedding planner was in tears; the maids had left and refused to go back; Cindy's mother was fussing! "For God's sake, Mother, help me. I need someone to help me; you're useless, Mother," screamed Cindy. Stephanie quickly changed into a purple outfit; she tidied her hair and makeup. A touch more perfume, and she was ready. She looked in the mirror; her eyes were sparkling, dancing with mischief, and she felt amazing! Stephanie headed off to the bride's apartment. "Cindy, the guests are arriving; what is wrong?" "Oh, Steph, thank God! I can't decide which dress or veil or shoes or anything!" said Cindy, on the edge of tears. "Ok, pull yourself together," said Steph sternly, "It is this dress with those shoes and this veil." "But how do you know?" questioned Cindy. "Because I bloody paid for them! Now hurry!" Cindy stood in silence. She had just learnt who the boss was around here!

Rich was having fun studying the CCTV cameras. He didn't recognise anyone; they were all posh knobs arriving in Rolls and Bentleys, and most of them had their own drivers! They all looked wealthy, thought Rich. The women looked alright, not a patch on his women. Where is she? She had not arrived yet in the chapel. Oh, here they come, thought Rich as he watched Terrance and his father enter the chapel. So that twat is her son. Well, well, well. Rich recognised him. He was someone Hen used now and again. Rich laughed, and that's my competition. "Well, guess what, old man, I'm coming for ya!" Rich was loving this. Oh, at last, the bride. Cindy walked down the aisle. Rich thought she looked like a floating cake with a big veil covering her face. "She looks stupid," laughed Rich.

The little chapel was full of relatives, the lord, and the ladies of the country. Rich watched the proceedings with interest. He was not really into stuff like this, but he was interested to learn how the other half went about things. The priest dressed in a gown and spouted all kinds of stuff. Come on, man, hurry up, Rich thought impatiently. Restlessness consumed him as he wondered about the whereabouts of his woman. Rich scanned the chapel; no one was in bright blue. Maybe she had left him; maybe it was a setup. Rich started to panic, and then suddenly, it all seemed to be done. The man in the gown had shut up, and Lord Snot was going to lift her veil and kiss her. Terrance raised her veil and kissed Cindy on her cheeks. "Fuck me, man, kis'er on the lips," shouted Rich at the screen. The new Mr. and Mrs. turned to walk down the aisle. Rich looked at the screen; the bride looked familiar. If only he could take a closer look, it might come back to him. Rich didn't think she was an ex, but maybe someone he'd shagged at one of the wild parties! Rich shrugged his shoulders, "Who cares? That's all behind me now." Rich sat back in the chair and thought about his life. Rich had three older brothers. A mother who was no good and a father somewhere. His mother had taught him to steal, and his brothers taught him to survive. His mother went off with men all the time, leaving his brothers to look after him, but as he grew up one by one, his brothers would get into serious trouble, and one by one, they got locked away or ran away. His mother moved to Scotland with a truck driver, so at sixteen, he was left alone with no home or family. Thank God for his auntie; she looked after him and let him stay with her; she fed him and taught him every night about women. He was a quick learner, and soon, she was inviting her friends around for a bit of him. They loved him, and he soon learnt his handsome face and enormous cock would get him anywhere. Rich smiled as he thought about those times. He was young and eager, and he soon began charging the women, and he made a fortune. By the time he was twenty-one, he had enough money to move to London. He got a flat and tried to find work, but he had no qualifications. Eventually, he got a driving job. It was Ok, but he got in with the wrong crowd. He got married, got divorced, got into trouble and ran away. He met and married Tanya, and she saved him. They moved to a village. He got a job and tried to settle, but he always wanted more. It was then that Hen came back into his life. They had always got on, and Rich had always cared for Hen, but not now, he thought; double-crossing bastard. Rich was convinced it was Hen who had given the orders to get rid of him to prevent him from running away! Rich had drifted off in his thoughts. When he looked at the cameras the chapel, it was empty. Shit, I missed her, he thought. He quickly scanned the cameras; they were now having something to eat. Rich noticed his woman and felt relieved. She looked lovely, but she was in purple. Rich wondered if she had been with another man and if she had to change! He felt himself tense up at the thought of it. This is a fuckin' bore; I'm off. I will speak to her. I will know if she is lying! Rich locked up and headed back to his apartment. Rich was making his way down the corridor when he stopped; he could hear raised voices. "Kiss me on the lips, you'ree my fuckin' husband, now kiss me." "My dear, all in good time." "No, NOW I said, we are married." Rich listened; he assumed he must have kissed her as it went quiet. Daft Prat thought Rich, he'd be inside her by now! Rich smiled to himself. He knew women inside and out!

Once back in his apartment, Rich undressed and got back into bed. He was still recovering, after all, and he loved the feel of the silk sheets; he loved the comfortable bed and how fresh it all smelled. He was at home at last, and no one was taking this away from him. No one! He thought of Steph, his lady. He called her Lady A, which drove her mad, but he loved it; she was his. His Lady A was some woman: kind, warm, yet feisty. She was sexy without knowing it, and her eyes danced to him when they spoke; he liked her a lot, a real lot. In fact, who was he kidding? He was in love with her, and the thought of someone else touching her drove him crazy with rage! Not even the husband was allowed to touch her as far as Rich was concerned. She will get you into trouble, walk away said the voice inside him. Fuck off, I'm going nowhere. Rich fell asleep thinking about her and how happy he was.

Chapter Twenty-Three

The wedding reception was underway, the food and drinks were plentiful, and the speeches were long. Lord Arlington Senior had fallen asleep. He was several brandies in and found the table a comfortable resting place for his head! Cindy was having another meltdown; Cindy's mother was fussing. Terrance was on the edge of his nerves. A few of the guests were staying for the Ball, but most were going home. They were well-fed, had plenty to drink, and enjoyed some music, but it was Cindy who entertained them with her temper tantrums. "Terrance, take me to your quarters, I mean our quarters," ordered Cindy. "You have your own" Replied Terrance "That was before we were married; now take me to ours," demanded Cindy. "But I am in the main house," Terrance got up from the table. "Mother, mother. Mummy." Steph looked up, "Yes?" "I need to speak with you in private." Steph excused herself from the table, "What is it, Terrance?" "Mummy, this dreadful girl wants to move into my apartment." "Terrance," sighed Steph, "You need to have sex with her, we need an heir, so you have to do it, and the quicker you get on with it and make a son, the quicker you can play with whatever your little dickie wants." "Mother!" exclaimed Terrance. "Shhhh Terrance, get on with it. You never know; you may enjoy it! Now help me get your father to bed; look at him, fast asleep at the table. It is embarrassing. Then you can take her upstairs and make love to her!

Terrance helped his mother to get his father to bed. Lady Arlington had already prepared the lord's nightcap (sleeping tablets crushed into sugar, brandy and fresh orange) just how he liked it. Only today, she had made it stronger. After all, it was Christmas! They laid the Lord onto the bed, "Run along now, son; I will make him comfortable," said Lady Arlington. "No jumping on him, Mummy," laughed Terrance. Stephanie thought there was no chance of that happening! Sex had never been great with her husband, and these days, it was twice a year, his birthday and Christmas; even then, he needed help. He had special tablets in his drawer, which helped the erection, but they also gave him heart palpitations, so he would only use them occasionally. Lady Arlington had already removed the tablets and replaced them with something she found on the internet for depression! She had also ordered the latest batch of sedatives from the internet as the Doctor had raised concerns about the amount of sleeping tablets the Lord was going through! They looked the same, so she was not concerned. Lady Arlington wrote the lord a note for when he woke up; *"A little of your favourite tipple just for you, my dear, put you in the mood for later.S x"* Lady Arlington left the Lord sleeping. It was 6 pm, and the guests would arrive soon for the Christmas ball. She needed to shower and get ready for the evening.

Terrance made his way to his apartment, Cindy was waiting for him. "My husband, at last, come and sit with me; I must say your apartment is lovely it is very big. I will enjoy living here; we have plenty of space to grow as a family!" Cindy patted the seat, "Come on, darling, come and sit with your wife." Terrance felt mortified that this woman had already found her way into his private space. "Not now, dear; we need to get ready for the evening celebrations." Cindy knew he was not interested in her, but she was married now. Her plan was to get pregnant as soon as possible; that way, they could not get rid of her. She was going to be Lady Arlington if it killed her. "Come on darling, don't be shy, take my dress off." Terrance fumbled with the Zip, his hands shaking. "Hurry," Cindy snapped. "I am not used to this, can't you get a maid to help?" "No, I can't; now try harder, Terrance." It was no good; Terrance was a wreck, and his fingers were cold, and he was shaking. "Just rip it off me then," insisted Cindy. "I cannot do that; it is the best Silk made in India with bare hands," said Terrance. "I don't fuckin' care. I just want my husband, let's just get on with it, take me now, Terrance, in my dress." Terrance was confused. Where does she want to go now, he thought. He felt afraid to ask her. "I Cannot go anywhere with you; we have our reception, the Christmas ball to attend! Cindy looked at her husband, stupid brat, "Terrance, I want you to ravish me, you know, shag me, fuck me or whatever you posh folks call it" Terrance was horrified, "I cannot perform such things just like that; we must have a conversation first," exclaimed Terrance. Cindy looked up at her husband; I will never get up the duff at this rate, she thought. She grabbed Terrance and pulled him on top of her, holding his head and kissed him, probing her tongue in his mouth,. She pushed herself against him, rocking her body underneath him. Terrance began to feel sick; this woman was terrifying him. His body went tense, and he wished she would stop. Despite her hopes, Cindy felt nothing in his trousers. She let go of him. "Maybe tonight, darling, you will be more relaxed for your wife," she whispered to him. Terrance was flustered; his cheeks were hot, and his lips felt sore where she had pushed herself on him. Terrance smoothed down his suit as he thought about what to say to her. "Get me a maid; get me out of this dress," Cindy barked at him. "Yes, my love," as he hurried off.

Rich put on his clothes and prepared himself. He had four different masks and planned to wear all four. Rich headed towards the CCTV room. He wanted to know who was coming to this ball, and he missed his woman. Rich observed Terrance flapping around, the musicians arriving, and the bars being stocked. A new team of caterers had arrived. The decorations looked amazing, especially now that it was dark. This must have cost a bomb, thought Rich. The guests began to arrive. Rich watched them get out of their cars. No, he did not know anyone! Then he saw Hen arrive, the man had a mask on, but Rich knew it was him, a small compact man, well dressed slight limp! "For fuck's sake, what's he doing here!" Rich made a mental note of his suit and mask, one to avoid, he thought. "Oh, fuck, it gets better! Fuckin' coppers have been invited. Rich watched as car after car arrived, and people just kept coming. Then he saw her walk hand in hand with another man. It was his girl; she was not dead, thank God. Rich smiled as he watched her, she looked well and happy. Rich had thought about her a lot. He loved her, but his love was with someone else now. "Sorry!" Rich said to the screen as he reached out to touch her screen, "I didn't mean to leave you, but hey, look, it works out for the best." Rich had not seen his woman for hours. He missed her, he felt safe with her, he needed her. Rich had decided to tell her everything so they had no secrets. He really was falling for her and wanted her to know how much she meant to him. Rich headed back to his apartment; he lay on the bed, "Fuck it, I'll stay here. Let em get on with it!" But the thought of hiding behind a mask and pretending to be someone else turned him on. He needed his woman, and with any luck, he could persuade her to come back with him for a session! Rich picked the red mask. It was a full-face one, and it changed the shape of his face like a monster, he thought!

People were chatting and laughing. Rich made his way through the crowds; he picked up a drink and wandered around, observing everyone. Terrance had spotted the red mask stranger; that was a fine mask, expensive, he thought. "Good evening, Sir. I am Lord Arlington, Terrance, and this is my wife, Lady Arlington, Cinderella." Cindy bowed her head, "Me lord," she whispered, "So sir, where do you hale?" Rich looked at Terrance; he had no fuckin' clue what this twat was talking about. "I must say, you both look beautiful tonight, but I must go," Rich moved on quickly. He had forgotten who he was meant to be! Lord and Lady Maclothy were heading his way. "Good evening, sir. I am Lord Maclothy, and the beautiful woman by my side is Lady Maclothy. We are from Scotland, and you, sir? Rich felt an arm go around him. He immediately smelt her. "I see you met Lord Smithye. He is from the North counties and owns lots of land, looking for more land to purchase down this way, is that correct, darling?" "Yes, My Lady, I am indeed looking!" Lord and Lady Maclothy bowed and moved on. Lady Arlington went to move on, but Rich grabbed her arm, "Not so quick, I've missed you." "You are not meant to know who I am." Rich smiled, "Like I said, Lady, I know who you are. I can smell you, and I can see your body through ya dress. Let's go somewhere, I'm starving for ya!" "No, one must learn to wait," she removed his hand and moved away to mingle. Rich smiled; Game on, Lady.

Rich chatted as he moved through the crowds, his confidence growing every time he told his story. He was enjoying being a Lord! "Yes, I have lots of land up north Counties, My castle sits on some of my land and I have a river flowing through it, great for fishing!" Rich had just finished telling his story to a group of people. He turned around to find Hen right behind him. "Sir, I have been watching you. I am Thomas, and you?" "Lord Smithye," Rich shook his hand. Hen studied his hand, this man made him feel weak, just like Rich used to. "And what do your friends call you?" asked Hen. "Dickie; they call me Dickie." "May I call you Dickie?" asked Hen. "I have only just met you, Sir, so for now, call me Lord; far more appropriate." "Well, Lord, I would like to get to know you; you remind me of someone. I bet you are handsome under that mask?" Hen was trying to press up against Rich, "Excuse me, Sir, I must leave. I have business to attend." Rich made his way through the crowds and back to his apartment. Shit, the little fucker is like a dog on heat, sniffing me out! Thought Rich as he paced up and down the apartment. Maybe it is best I stay here; then Rich thought about his Lady A, He needed to see her, touch her, talk to her. Fuck it. Rich changed into a different suit and a different mask. He went for a grey/blue mask, which looked amazing on him as his bright eyes twinkled through the mask. Rich smiled at his reflection, "Yeah, man, you're hot; she will not be able to resist ya!"

The ball was in full swing; the guests were getting louder as the drink flowed. Rich didn't touch much alcohol; it did things to him, and he was not that guy anymore. Rich needed his wits about him, especially now that Hen was sniffing around. Why the fuck he's here is a mystery, thought Rich. "Come dance with me," Rich looked down; the person hugging his arm was Cindy, the bride. She was drunk and now dragging him onto the dance floor. Fuck, he had no option; this was his worst nightmare: dancing! but this was not dancing as he knew it. It was some old posh stuff; the men were in an outer circle, and the women in an inner circle. "Just follow everyone else," Cindy shouted to him. Rich followed the man to his right as he pranced around, twirling and bowing and going around in circles. "Then you get to hold the women and waltz around the room. Take yer mask off," shouted Cindy. "No, ma'am, I prefer the mystery." Cindy smiled, "Me too. You're very sexy, and you smell lovely." "Why thank you, ma'am." Rich looked at the bride; she looked sad, and she looked familiar. Had he met her before? Suddenly, he went cold; he had a flashback of the woods, the van, it couldn't be she was gone from this world! Rich's heart was racing. This isn't happening. It can't be; his mind was all over the place. "Hey, sir, you Ok?" Rich looked down, and another woman was before him. Cindy had moved on to another partner. "Yeah, I mean YES, ma'am." "Shall we dance,

Sir?" "Oh yes, of course, ma'am." Rich turned and swivelled, and on to the next woman and the next, a real collection of women passed through his arms, all charming, most of them were drunk and happy. Then it happened, his girl was in front of him, she was in his arms! Rich pulled her in tight, "You look beautiful," he whispered. "Thank you, sir." Rich held her waist; it was so small as he remembered he smelled her hair as Mandy pulled away to twirl. "You're going nowhere," came out of Rich's mouth. "I beg your pardon," she said, looking at Rich. Rich suddenly remembered where he was. "Oh, I'm sorry. I said I was unsure what to do, so don't go anywhere. How embarrassing, I have forgotten the steps." Mandy stared into the mask. Those eyes, that voice! As they danced the waltz together, Mandy felt a connection with this stranger, She looked at him, it was difficult with the mask on, but he had a strong jawline, In fact, the jaw was familiar. "Where are you from, sir" she asked. "Oh, a long way from here," Rich replied. "But where?" demanded Mandy "So many questions." "I am sorry; you remind me of someone." "I do? Someone nice, I hope!" "I thought he was nice. I loved him, but he didn't love me, so maybe not so nice." Rich pulled her into him, "I loved you; I'm sorry." "GET OUT of me way, love. My turn, move on." Rich looked to his left; it was a farmer's wife ready to dance with him. Mandy had moved on to her next partner. She felt puzzled; she was sure he said I loved you, but why would he say that? At every opportunity, Mandy glanced at the beautiful masked stranger, so tall and well-proportioned in build and jawline! Rich knew he had just held his baby. The question was, what would he do now? Should he let her know it's him and give all of this up to run away together? Rich continued to dance with the farmer's wife, then the shopkeeper, then a copper, then another farmer's wife, and so they kept coming. Eventually, he had his lady in his arms. "Having fun?" she asked. "I am now," he said. "You look beautiful; I have missed you so much," whispered Rich as he pulled her into him. She was the only one that stirred something up inside him besides his cock. She stirred raw emotion within him. Rich knew at that moment he wanted her, and he wanted this! "Run away with me tonight," Rich blurted out. "Excuse me?" "Run away with me tonight, or now, let's just go, just you and me. We don't need anything or anyone as long as we have each other." "NO I will not give this up for you or anyone else. I will not go on the run like some hippie, and I certainly will not live in anything but luxury." Such a blunt response caught Rich off guard; he did not expect it. "Please!" "No. Now shhh, sweetie, No More." Rich felt hurt; no one says no to him. Rich continued to dance with her; she was a wonderful dancer, and she captivated him. His emotions were hard to handle. He wanted to run away, but only with her, but for now, he held her tight as tears fell underneath his mask! The music and the everlasting dance eventually ended. "Time to eat," came the announcement. Rich grabbed a plate of food and headed back to his apartment.

The tall masked stranger had stirred up a few people. Mandy was sure she knew him, Hen was sure he knew him, and Dazer had been watching everything; he also thought he knew him. Cruz had come along with Dazer, who was in a wheelchair. Dazer was enjoying being out and observing everyone. He still refused to talk to anyone other than Cruz, but his senses were on full alert, and Dazer felt he knew the tall, masked stranger. He reminded him of Rich, and Dazer knew what Rich had done! Rich was dicing with danger. He knew he should stay away, quit whilst ahead, and go to bed. But fuck it; he was Richard Long, and he don't do easy. Fuck it; I'm goanna have some fun! He changed his suit and mask again, this time to all black!

Rich waited until he thought the food would be done, and the lights dimmed again for part two a bit more modern, he hoped! He needed to find her, his lady.

There was a time when I was everything and nothing all in one

When you found me, I was feeling like a cloud across the sun.

I need to tell you how you light up every second of the day,

But the moonlight, You shine like a beacon on the bay.

And I can't explain, but it's something about the way you look tonight,

It's a feeling I get about you deep inside.

Good old Elton; love this, thought Rich. The words are for my lady, who I need right now. Rich searched for her; she was nowhere to be seen. He started to panic. Where is she? Has she left me? He started to move quicker, pushing people out of the way as he searched through the rooms.

"OI YOU," called one drunk woman, "COME and dance with me." "No, no, later," replied Rich. "NO NOW!" The woman hung onto Rich and started swaying. Rich could see people laughing, and he hated it. I'll teach her to grab me. Rich picked up a bit of speed and began to travel around the room going round and round using the dance to look for his lady. "STOP! STOP!" shouted the woman, "I don't feel well." Rich sat the woman down. He turned to leave when he saw her in the background; she looked flustered and annoyed and who was the man with her? Rich edged himself nearer, hiding behind one of the many trees. Rich could see it was her old man, who was shouting at his lady. He felt his fists clench. Rich edged closer, only to find Terrance and Cindy behind another tree. "No, I will not return to my apartment until all the guests have departed from my house. I must ensure the house is safe!" "It's our fuckin' wedding night; come to bed with me, your wife," cried Cindy. Terrance got up and marched off towards the bar. Rich looked down at Cindy, who was crying. Rich went to say something to her but stopped himself as his lady was now screaming at her old man. Rich watched as the man raised his arm as if he was going to hit her. Before he had time to think, Rich was there, knocking the Lord's arm down, "Excuse me, sir, I did not see you." The Lord turned around, "Well, open your bloody eyes, man, now, if you will excuse us, this is private," said the Lord. "Well, actually, Sir, I came to ask the lady if she would care to dance with me" "No, she would not now piss off. Is it not enough you eat and drink for free? Don't think I don't know who you are," shouted the Lord. Rich was not sure what to do; he wanted to grab her and hit him. He looked at her, who was shaking her head, "My Lord, I will leave you," "For now," murmured Rich as he walked away and headed back to Cindy, who was still crying! "Hey, a bride should not be crying. What's wrong?" asked Rich. Cindy looked up and opened her mouth to respond when they heard screaming; his girl was running across the room towards them. Shit, thought Rich, who froze to the spot. "What the fuck am I goanna do? She knows it's me!" Mandy ran straight into Cindy's arms. The girls held each other tight. "Oh my God, I know you, but I don't know you, but I know you," shouted Mandy. "I mean, we know each other, but… Well, I can't remember your name." "I know what you mean," said Cindy, hanging on to Mandy's neck. "What happened to us?" Cindy shook her head. "We were friends, right?" Rich stood back, behind a tree relieved that this fuss was not for him but curious how his girl knew the bride. Rich could hear most of what was being said.

"So what happened to you?" asked Mandy "I got found in the woods, drugged, and left for dead. I barely survived. How about you?" Mandy recounted, "Dun-know, but I was found in a cottage and nearly died." "OH MY GOD, do you think the same person did this to us?" Cindy exclaimed. "Yes, the police informed me that there were four of us. They discovered poor Helen's body, but we are missing one person. I have been helping the police, and every day, bits of my memory come back. How about yours?" Asked Mandy. "Same, really. I can't remember, but to be honest, I dont care. I have all of this. now I am married," said Cindy. "So where is he, your new husband?" "Oh, busy, He is a very busy man, but he has promised me a night to remember," winked Cindy. Mandy smiled, "Well, it's been lovely catching up," she said as she hugged Cindy.

Rich had heard everything, "What the fuck!?" "Will you dance with me, Sir?" Rich looked down, it was his girl, "Sure." Rich took her arm and led her to the dance floor. Rich spun her round and moved to the beat of the music. Mandy suddenly felt alive, dancing with this masked stranger. The music slowed down, and she held him tight as they slowly danced. Mandy looked up at the stranger, "There is something about a man in a mask," she said, laughing, "Earlier on, I danced with someone who I thought I knew; he was tall like you. He had a blue, grey mask on and a blue-grey suit. Did you see him?" she asked. Rich shook his head. The music changed again; it was more upbeat, and Rich started twirling her around and around. Mandy had been drinking and was now beginning to feel quite giddy and slipped. Rich grabbed her to stop her from falling.. She felt the electricity run through her. It was him, she was sure it was him. "Why did you leave me to die?" she blurted out. Rich felt the panic rise in him; she knows, he thought. He raised his hand to check his mask was still on, "Phew, it was kay, don't panic." "Why?" she questioned. Rich remained silent as he led her to a table and sat her down just as Jessie came running over, "There you are. I have been looking everywhere for you. You alright? You look pale, darling; come on, let's get you home." Mandy stood up, tears rolling down her face. Rich felt his heartbreaking, "Sorry," he whispered. Jessie led Mandy through the crowds She turned to take one more look at the masked stranger; she knew it was him. He was watching her, and She felt their eyes connected. "Bye, my love, sorry, but I am a different person now," thought Rich.

Chapter Twenty-Four

Rich, who had been distracted from watching his lady found her still in some kind of disagreement with her husband, "Sir, excuse me, now may I have this dance with the lady?" "NO you may not, and she is no Lady. Now Piss off!" Rich stood back, "Excuse me, sir, I don't mean to interfere, but this is a celebration, and I see little celebration going on here, and you're the parents of the groom; you should be happy!" Lord Arlington swung around and squared up to Rich, "I told you to piss off, enjoy the celebration, be happy, eat and drink, do what you like, leave me to do what I like in my home with my whore of a wife! Don't think I haven't been watching you. I know who you are, nothing more than a dirty tramp. I want to know where you got your posh clothes from because someone like you could never afford such fine wear?" Rich felt his fists tighten and the heat rise inside him. Well, this night just gets better, thought Rich. Rich stared at the old man, no one was taking this away from him. His lady looked extremely upset, which hurt Rich deeply. "Sir, I will leave you, but you are quite mistaken. I am no tramp, I own land and a castle which has a beautiful river running through its land, wonderful for fishing! Maybe one day you will visit?" Lord Arlington looked up at Rich. "Like I said, piss off!" he shouted as he attempted to drag Lady Arlington away. Rich noticed he was pinching her arm. "Don't do that, sir, to a lady." "You still here?" replied the Lord. "Let go of her arm," hissed Rich. The Lord dropped his grip. "I'm watching you," he shouted. "And I you," Rich retaliated. His lady was rubbing her arm. "Thank you." Hey, no problem. Will you come with me now?" "I will, but I have to do something first. You need to wait for me," whispered Lady A. "I will wait as long as it takes, babe," whispered Rich.

Rich felt the best thing to do was to go back to his apartment and wait for her. He was happy she had said yes! Now, with the crowds diminishing, those that remained were drunk, high, or both! The band was packing up, so soft music was being played in the background. The bride was on another bloke's lap, nibbling his ear. Terrance was flapping around like a drunk penguin. The few remaining coppers, including the one called Serg, were still drinking excessively. Rich smiled to himself. That uptight bastard Serg had clearly let his hair down. Bet his head will hurt tomorrow! Then Rich saw two men who he recognised; one was in a wheelchair. I'm sure I know them. It's… It's… Shit, I can't remember their names. Wonder what happened to him. Rich was thinking about going over and what he would say when he noticed his girl marching back into the house, followed by the bloke she left with. Rich had a feeling this was not a good sign and hid behind the trees. He secretly thanked Terrance for the hideous number of trees which had come in very useful.

"ARE YOU SURE IT'S HIM, MANDS? You can't go accusing someone if you're not sure," shouted Jessie.

"I NEED TO SEE HIM UNMASKED. I know it's him; help me find him," screamed Mandy.

"Shit," Rich had heard enough. He needed to get back to his apartment, he was not ready to give this up. Mandy was pulling all the men's masks off as she made her way around the room. "STOP! Stop this, Mands," said Jessie, "Come on, it's over; he's not here. I should never have brought you out; you're not ready; this is all my fault. Come on." Jessie held Mandy's hand, "Come on, let's go."

Rich was back in his apartment, his mind racing: What if she convinces everyone? What if she talks to the Lord and Lady? What if his lady believes her? Fuck Fuck! Rich was stuck. Think Richard, think. He paced the apartment, thinking about what his next move would be. Rich changed into jeans, a jumper, a beautiful leather coat and a hat and scarf. He made his way outside via the back door. His lady had told him the door would take him into the grounds, but he had no clue where exactly in the grounds. He fought his way through the brambles in the hope of sneaking through the grounds to peer into the house to see what was going on inside. Rich wished he had practiced the way out before now as he felt quite disorientated. He walked around the building. He could see the driveway and hear laughter and music. Rich stopped in his tracks; it was her, hand in hand with her bloke, and she was shouting, "Why don't you believe me? It was him; he was here, please believe me." "Come on, darling, we can talk about this tomorrow. I can get a search out." "No, you don't understand. I love him, and he was here!" She shouted. "He's brainwashed you, the bastard. Come on, Mands, you're not well; let's go home. I will take care of you; he won't hurt you again." Rich watched and listened as Jessie wrapped her up in his coat and gently ushered away from the house and into a car, tears rolling down his face. She loved me, but I can't go back. I ain't that bloke anymore, thought Rich.

"So pretty boy, you hiding away like a rat,?" Rich turned around to see Hen, "What the fuck!?" "Shh, pretty boy, I've been watching ya! Ya worried Hen; Ya left me!" "LEFT YOU!?" shouted Rich. "Fuckin' piece of shit, you left me for dead, had me beaten up and left in the gutter; I should knock you out and do the fuckin' same," exploded Rich. "No, No, I knew nothing about it. I promise ya, why would I order that? I love ya and always have. I've been out me mind with worry when no one could find ya. I got rid of the guards who hurt ya. I'm a broken man, believe me," pleaded Hen. Rich looked at

Hen, "I love ya, pretty boy, tell me what mess ya in; Hen help ya." Rich took Hen's hand, "Come with me."

"Wow, look at this ya land on ya feet, like a cat with nine," laughed Hen. "Sit down, have a drink," snapped Rich, pouring a brandy for both of them. Rich told Hen how he was found by the roadside by the Lord and Lady, how the Lady had nursed him back to health, providing him with food clothes, and everything in this apartment. "You shag her?" asked Hen. Rich nodded, "Yeah." "I knew it; you shag anything." "No,No, it's not like that, she's different, older, classy, naughty she brings something out in me I never had before," smiles Rich. "Oh fuck, ya love her," teased Hen. "No, man, it's just fanny," said Rich. "But it's not, is it, man? She has given you all of this; you looked the most handsome tonight in your suits, all the highest quality. I mean, look what you're wearing now, the quality is better than mine! You smell amazing, very expensive, and all because of her, so pretty boy, what's next?" asked Hen.

H always knew he would have to share Rich with some women, so maybe a posh one was a better option. "Oh yeah, I forgot to say," said Hen, "Your wife's dead." Rich froze, "What ya mean?" "Ya know the woman you married; found dead. Had a fall, they say, banged her head. No one told you?" asked Hen. "No! No!" Rich slumped forward, "She didn't deserve that," he whispered. Rich thought about the last time he had seen her. They argued, but then they always did. He fucked her, but then he always did. He was desperate to get away, and he pushed her! "Oh No! Shit! It wasn't me. I didn't do it!" he said out loud. Hen had been watching him. "It probably was ya, man; ya a crazy fucker, ya know when ya get going, so pretty boy, what ya thinking?" "I'm thinking I'm not married anymore, I'm free!" smiled Rich. "You're a heartless fucker," hissed

Hen as he downed his second brandy. "Another?" asked Hen. "Yeah, why not? I'm celebrating," said Rich, who knew he should stay clear of alcohol, but what the hell! "So what is the local drug dealer doing at the posh Christmas ball?" asked Rich. Hen laughed, "All down to Lord Snooty, he invited me, well he asked me to kill his bride, he offered me a million," Hen laughed, "Stupid prick is scared shitless, he won't spend any time with his bride just in case, he's prancing around like a fairy on speed." so when ya doing it?" asked Rich. "I'm not, I'm no murderer," replied Hen. "So what ya doing here then?" "Come to wind him up, told him money upfront." "One million, ya say?" asked Rich. "Yeah, ya wanna do it?" asked Hen. "I want the million. I want to get as far away as possible. Did ya get those passports?" asked Rich. "Yeah, one for you and one is mine." Rich looked at Hen; daft fucker thinks I wanna run away with him. "Get the million first," ordered Rich. "What? Ya goanna kill her?" "No, man, knock her out with one of ya special cocktails. Got any?" "Always, man," smirked Hen. "Anyway, pretty boy, ya got something for Hen?" Rich looked at Hen, puzzled, "Ya know, what.s in ya trousers." Hens missed it. Rich felt irritated by Hen, he was an idiot, and Rich was not that person anymore. "Fuck off, man. Go and get the money from Lord Snooty."

The Ball was almost over; a few people were still chatting. Hen looked around for Lord Arlington; he was sitting down. He looked exhausted. Terrance jumped up as soon as he saw Hen, "Not here! I can't be seen with you," exclaimed Terrance. "Why ya invited me?" laughed Hen. "Yes, to get rid of my wife, have you done it? I can't go to prison. I would never survive," said Terrance, hanging on to Hen's jacket. "Relax. Relax and take ya hand off me fuckin' jacket; nothing happened yet. I told ya money first. No money, No deal." "I changed my mind," blurted Terrance. "Please, Mr. Hen, forgive me, but I can't let you do it. I will give you something for the trouble." "How much?" asked Hen. "One thousand." "Make it five thousand," smiled Hen. "Five!?" "Yes, call it hush money." "Ok, Ok, I will bring it tomorrow; now go," said Terrance as he clicked his fingers for a car. "Take my friend home," ordered Terrance. Hen was too tired to argue as he was escorted out to the waiting car. Hen fell into the car and then suddenly remembered Rich! He did not know how to get to him, and he was knackered anyway. Rich wasn't up for a shag Hen shrugged his shoulders; oh well, he'll come to me when he's ready, he thought.

Rich was pacing up and down, "Where is he? Stupid fuck!" Rich needed to know he had the money. He waited for what seemed like ages No sign of Hen, fuckin'' 'prick done a runner, thought Rich. I swear I will hunt him down. Rich had taken Hen's gun and stripped his jacket pockets, taking money and powder when Hen went to the bathroom. Hen had ruined Rich's plan, which was to take the money, get his lady and run. Now Rich needed a new plan. It was late; he was tired and not thinking straight. Maybe he should rest and deal with it in the morning. Rich looked at his Rolex watch. Fuck, it was the middle of the night. The good guy in Rich said sleep, man, you will feel better, your head will be clearer, and you can plan with her your future. The bad guy in Rich said, go and fuckin' get her. What if she is in bed with him? I'll kill him. Just take her man and run!

Rich made his way into the house; the party was over and everyone had gone. He walked around the mess was immense.. He took a swig of Brandy and headed upstairs. Rich had no idea where he was going; he had never been upstairs. He listened against each door.

"Quiet. Quiet. Quiet."

"Oh, sounds like a bit of sex going on!" He would love to watch, but no time!

On to the next door, he could hear talking, sounds like Lord Snooty; maybe he is talking to Hen, thought Rich as he opened the door. Rich looked around, "Wow, this is nice, all high ceilings and gold everywhere. Rich followed the voice, peering through the crack in the door. It was Terrance talking to himself, pacing up and down. "No, sir, I do not know. No, no, Sir, of course I have a guest list! But you do not have one, sir. My mother arranged it all, so I do not have the guest list. I do not know who murdered my wife." Rich was unclear about what he was rehearsing. Had Hen taken Cindy out and ran? Bastard thought Rich, the police will be all over the place, and they will pin it on me! Rich panicked. He needed to go, but he needed his lady! Rich headed out of the apartment, silence. Just as he was about to walk away, he heard her screaming; it was his lady. Rich rushed towards the screaming, opening the door and running into the apartment, "GET OFF ME, you dirty old man." "Shut up! You're a slut!" Rich heard the slap and her scream, "I am your husband; remember the one that picked you up off the streets and married you? Remember how I found you? You have never been grateful; you're a selfish bitch, always have been. Always wanted it your way, but guess what? I'm having it my way now. Open those legs for me!" Rich felt his fists tighten up. "Get off, I said. Do not come anywhere near me; you're nothing more than a lazy, dirty old man. Get off me! Get off me!" she screamed. Rich thought he heard the thud but wasn't sure; it had all gone silent. Rich waited, unsure of what had happened. He then made his way through the apartment, opening all the doors until he found her. She was standing over the Lord, who was on the floor. "What happened?" Steph turned around and ran into Rich's arms. "Hold me." Rich held her tight; Steph was sobbing, "I didn't do it, he just dropped," she sobbed. "Hey, it's Ok," Rich stroked her hair. "He was trying to force himself on me," Steph sobbed. "Did he?" questioned Rich. "No, no, I pushed him off, but he kept coming back on me. He pinned me down, so I kicked him as hard as I could; he just dropped." "Ok, Ok, we better do something," said Rich. Like what?" "I don't know, check him out, get help?"

"Leave him," said Steph coldly. Rich looked at her. "Leave him?" "Yes, the maid can find him in the morning." Rich looked at her, "You don't mean it; you're just angry. We need to get help." Steph removed herself from his arms, "I said leave him; I mean it, I am not angry; I am relieved. Please don't leave me. Can I come with you?" asked Steph. Rich smiled, "Lady, you're mine; come with me."

They made their way to Rich's apartment. Rich poured her a brandy and rubbed her shoulders as they sat in silence. Rich broke the silence. "Now what?" Steph downed the brandy, "It's time to party. Go put your mask on and one of your suits. Let me pretend I don't know you." Rich smiled. Fuck me, this is a strange night. "I will freshen up Me Lady."

Rich put on his suit and mask, sprayed her favourite aftershave and made his way back to the lounge. Music was playing in the background, and she was straddling a chair in a mask, stockings and suspenders. "Wow," Rich shook his head. Nothing should surprise him anymore, but this woman, well, she was full of surprises; she was immense.

"Oh, Sir, I did not see you there. I was practicing,"

"Don't let me stop you." Rich sat down and watched her. She squatted onto the chair, legs wide, pulsing up and down, then wrapped her legs around the chair and leant backwards, releasing one leg above her head, then the other leg, and then spreading them. Rich was speechless! She then eased herself to the floor on all fours with her arse in the air. She turned to look at Rich, as she slowly got up, and walked over to him, "Sir, excuse me, but you are so handsome. Will you dance with me?" "It would be my pleasure, My Lady," whispered Rich. They held each other close as they moved to the music, both lost in the moment, swaying in time together. Rich had never felt such a connection, his hands slowly sliding down her body, feeling her soft skin and silk stockings, "Kiss me," Rich begged. She looked at him, "No, wait." "Kiss me. I can't wait," Rich pulled off his mask, cupping her face and kissing her. The electricity between them was sizzling. "Why, sir, that is most inappropriate," whispered Steph. Rich smiled, "I know, and I want more," Rich picked up her hand, slowly kissing it, tracing his kisses up her arm to her neck. He bit her gently at first around her neck, nibbling her ears. Her breathing was getting heavier, and the passion inside her was rising. He released her bra, cupping her breasts; biting into her neck, unable to control himself he picked her up and carried her to his bed. She moved quickly and straddled him, tracing her fingers over his chest, down his abdomen, her nails scratching him. She slowly traced her fingers down his legs and back up to his cock, which was rock hard and trying to escape out of his pants. She removed his pants with her teeth and took his cock in her hands, stroking it slowly. Rich groaned, "Come here," whispered Rich. Steph turned around and sat on his face. Rich was lost in emotion, his tongue darting in and out of her, she was throbbing and rocking. Rich stopped to watch her. He felt an intensity he had never felt before. Rich turned her around and slipped his cock inside her. She contracted around it immediately and started to ride him. Rich quickly flipped her underneath him and took control. "More! More!" she screamed, "Fuck me! Fuck it out of me!" Steph screamed. Rich fucked her so hard that they both exploded together. They lay still, entwined together She began contracting her pussy, as she felt him growing inside her, and it felt so good. "That's it," she whispered, "You stay right there. I need you again." Rich stayed inside her whilst she squeezed and moved. He felt her rhythm change and her heat rise. "Oh, Rich!" she shouted as she worked herself off on him. "Wow, you're some sexy lady, but look what ya done to me." Steph smiled, "How do you want me?" she asked. "I would like to tie you up, smack you, bite you." "You won't hurt me?" asked Steph. "No, no, I could never hurt you; it's just a fantasy." Steph smiled, "Well, who am I to stop you?" Rich grinned. They put on their masks, and Rich tied her up with silk ties, spreading her legs wide. Rich had leather gloves and some feathers. He smacked her and teased her with the feathers, he bit her and kissed her. She was screaming for him to fuck her. He made her wait until she could not take it anymore. Rich mounted her and rode her, his emotions coming out of him like never before. He had never felt such feelings, and he loved it. They lay together, drifting off to sleep in each other's arms.

Rich woke up first. It was light; Rich stroked her body with his fingers. She murmured, "Hey." Rich "Hello, sweetie," she whispered. "Steph, what's next? What we gonna do?" Rich asked, "We?" Steph looked at him, "Yes. We." "Well," said Steph, "You are to remain here for now; you're my secret pleasure. I will ask for a divorce and then we will live happily together." "One problem with that, Lady," said Rich. "There is?" "I ain't up for staying and certainly not down here, being a dirty secret." Steph looked hurt, "Sweetie, it's safer this way; it won't be for too long. You need to trust me. You have everything you need, and one day, you can share all of this with me." Rich was agitated; this was not what he expected or wanted, but he didn't really have a plan. Yesterday, he was up for running away with

Hen and a million pounds; then, he wanted to run away with his lady and now this! Maybe she is right; he should stay hidden and just wait. Rich stood up, "Ok, we do it your way, but I want to keep the keys to the CCTV room. I want to watch everything. You need to get rid of your security guards." Steph looked at Rich, "I can't do that, sweetie; the Lord would never agree." "But you killed him, remember?" said Rich, staring at Steph. "I TOLD YOU, he fell! Anyway, he is probably sitting up in bed now having breakfast." "Best you go then, lady. Oh, and don'

t forget sack the guards !If you want me to stay, best you sort it." Steph was deep in thought; what if she had killed him? Rich broke her thoughts, "You Ok?" "Yes, sweetie, just thinking. Oh, Happy Christmas, sweetie," said Steph. "Oh, yeah, Happy bloody Christmas! Stuck here in this bleedin place." Steph swung around. "Well, it could be worse," she snapped, "You could be outside in the freezing cold with nowhere to go and with nothing. Why are you never grateful?" "You never say Thank you; in fact, you are quite rude. Now, if you excuse me, I will go, and your Christmas presents are under the bed, not that you probably want them and feel free to leave at any time." Steph marched to the door, but Rich was quicker. "Hey, not so quick, lady," said Rich as he blocked her exit, "What's brought this on?" "Excuse me, please, I wish to leave." "Not until you tell me what this is all about?" Steph looked up at Rich, her heart melting, She fancied him so much; in fact, she was in love with him, but he was younger than her, and who was she kidding? He didn't want her, maybe for money or the house, maybe even for her body, but not long term. Steph pushed him away, "I said get out of my way!" shouted Steph. "No, no, I don't think you did," smiled Rich, "You said I was rude and ungrateful." "Well, you are." Rich held her, "I'm sorry, I don't mean to be. I just want to be with you out there, not in here locked away. I want us to be together, Steph I love you." Steph touched his face and gently kissed him, "Ok, sweetie, I will be back later." Rich moved away, "Later, babe, later." She smiled at him and left. Christmas was never something Rich embraced, considering it to be for children, and Tanya frequently reminded him he was too selfish to have kids. He had never bought a Christmas present for anyone. Tanya used to buy her own. Rich smiled. He knew where he was with Tanya. She was rough, but she told it as it was. Rich felt a rise of guilt as he thought about Tanya; she didn't deserve to die. Rich had always had the devil on one shoulder and an angel on the other! But you killed her. No, I didn't, nothing to do with me; I'm no killer. But you are. No, I am not. I'm a decent bloke; just misunderstood. No, you're a murderer. Rich shook his head; the voices were getting louder. No, No, I am not. I didn't kill anyone, she fell. Yes, but you walked away just like you always do; you're a coward and a Murderer. No, No, I'm not. Fuck off. I didn't do it. Rich grabbed the headphones and put on some music to drown out the voices.

Step returned to her apartment, showered and changed. The maid would be here soon, then Steph remembered she gave all the staff time off over Christmas! Oh well, she sighed, I will cook. She made her way downstairs; the mess was unbearable. "Christ, Stephanie, why did you give all the help the day off?" She mumbled to herself. She made herself some tea, prepared the turkey and put it in the oven on a slow roast. She made a tray of tea for the newlyweds.

"Knock! Knock!" she shouted, "Happy Christmas, you love birds. Can I come in?" Steph continued into the apartment; she could hear groaning. She smiled to herself; maybe I should just leave the tray here, but her curiosity got the better of her. She slowly opened the bedroom door to see Cindy riding another man. "What on earth is this!?" she screamed, dropping the tray. Cindy turned around, "Not now, Grandma, I'm busy." Steph froze, emotions running through her; she picked up a vase full of flowers, marching over to the bed, she threw the flowers to the floor, and the water all over Cindy, "Where's my son, you dirty whore," Steph screamed, "Where is Terrance and who are you? Have you no morals, man? She only got married yesterday." "Hey, you mad witch," shouted Cindy, "I needed a shag, I needed a real man. Your son's weird; he wouldn't come near me, and this gentleman was happy to help me out, so do one Grandma." Steph dragged Cindy out of bed by her hair, "Put some clothes on and get rid of him," she shouted. "Look, it was only a shag. It meant nothing. Don't even know his name," exclaimed Cindy. "You're making this worse; I suggest you shut up. Being in bed with another man on your wedding night is bad enough, but not even knowing his name is another level and in my house!" shouted Steph. "Come on, Mother, don't tell me you're not shagging around. We can work this out; I'm sorry," cried Cindy. "I mean, I'm not ugly, am I? I wanted my husband to want me. I needed to be satisfied." "So where is Terrance?" asked Steph, who was slightly taken aback by Cindy's comment, does she know about Rich, or was it just Cindy being vulgar?

"We need to find Terrance, oh, and get yourself washed, you smell," snapped Steph.

"I don't mind helping ya find him, but I ain't washing mother. I like smelling like this; it's called 'sexy' laughed Cindy She enraged Steph so much that Steph caught hold of her hair, "If you know what's good for you, do as I say. Now get a fuckin' wash and get rid of him. I will wait for you downstairs in the Kitchen." Steph was unsure what

she would find, so her plan was to send Cindy in with Tea for the Lord. She could wake Terrance up later.

Cindy had showered and made her way downstairs. "What's up?" asked Cindy. "Nothing. I thought it might be nice for you to make up a tray of tea and biscuits for the Lord as it's Christmas and take it into his room," explained Steph. "I'm no maid," replied Cindy. Steph looked at Cindy, "Right now, you're nothing, so if you don't want this little mistake to ruin everything, the best thing you can do is do exactly as I say." "Ok, Ok, ma'ama," smiled Cindy. Steph could feel her temper rising with this girl, but for now, she may be useful. Steph helped Cindy put a tray together with beautiful China Cups and Saucers and the best Gold cutlery, a jug of milk, perfectly brewed tea, sugar cubes and the finest homemade biscuits. Cindy decorated the tray with a single flower. "What do ya think?" she asked Steph. "Perfect! Well done. He will love it; now you go and surprise him."

Chapter Twenty-Five

Steph watched as Cindy excitedly entered the Lord's Apartment. She was skipping with joy at being trusted to do this job. "Happy Christmas, me Lord, Happy Christmas to ya!" she sang. Steph heard the tray drop and Cindy screaming. Steph ran in, "What is it?" Cindy was howling and gesturing. There, on the floor, lay the Lord, face down, with Terrance slumped across the bed, both of them looking blue.

"No, no, this can't be happening, NOOOOOOOO, not my son!" Steph screamed. "We gotta do something, Steph," wailed Cindy, "Go get help, Cindy," Steph was checking Terrance for a pulse when she noticed the glass on the bed. It was the same glass she had left for the Lord's nightcap, the one she had made extra strong with extra drugs in it. "No, no, no, you stupid boy." Steph cried out loud. Steph picked up the glass and threw the glass out of the window just as Cindy returned. "Why are you opening the window?" she asked. "I need air," replied Steph. "I feel like I'm going to faint I need to sit down." Steph fell to the floor sobbing. "I called the ambulance," said Cindy, trying to comfort Steph.

What happened next was a complete blur to Steph; everything was happening around her: the ambulance, police, people in and out, every one of them shocked that such a tragedy should happen on Christmas Day. After being removed from the apartment, Steph and Cindy were being looked after by some support officers. Jessie was the duty Police officer.

"Do you want to tell me what happened?" asked Jessie. Steph looked up at Jessie, feeling slight irritation towards him because of

his abrasive manner. She let it go for now and recalled this morning's events, how they wanted to surprise the lord with a lovely tray of tea. "And Terrance?" asked Jessie. "Well, we did not know he would be there," snapped Steph. Cindy looked at the floor. Guilty, thought Jessie. "I'm sorry I am not getting this," sighed Jessie. "You both wanted to surprise the lord with tea, yet it was your wedding day and night only a few hours ago, as in yesterday, and yet you did not know where your husband was, and you Lady Arlington had not seen your husband," said Jessie, looking at Steph. "Look, officer, we all have our own apartments; the Lord and I have had our own apartment for years, and No, we do not sleep together, so the last time I saw him was yesterday evening when he returned to bed." "And Terrance?" asked Jessie. "Look, Terrance had just got married, and he was busy making sure the ball was a success, which I think you came to and enjoyed? So I didn't really see too much of him as I said, he had just got married, as you know. I am sure he had other things on his mind," snapped Steph. "Sorry, Lady Arlington, I know this is upsetting for you," explained Jessie, turning his attention to Cindy. "Cindy, why was your husband not with you?" "Well, he was missing." "Missing from where?" asked Jessie. "from our apartment." "Why was he missing?" "Because we had a row." "On your wedding night? Didn't you go after him?" "No." "Why?" "Dun know I was drunk." "Were you angry with him?" questioned Jessie. "Yes, I was." "How angry?" "Very," said Cindy. "Angry enough to kill him?" asked Jessie. "What? No, I would never." So why didn't you go after him?" asked Jessie, sensing she was not telling the truth. "Because she had another man in her bed, that's why," shouted Steph, "She was shagging another man and my Terrance must have known!" Cindy looked at Steph in disbelief. "I thought we were not goanna say any more about

it." Steph turned on Cindy. "My son is dead, probably of a broken heart because his cheap tart of a wife was bouncing on some other man on their wedding night after everything we have given you." Steph raised her hand to slap Cindy. "Hey hey," shouted Jessie as he caught Steph's arm, "That won't help, come on." "So where is the man now?" asked Jessie. "Gone," replied Cindy. "Name? What is his name?" "Dun know, just someone I met last night at the ball." Jessie sighed, turning his attention to Steph. "And who were you with last night?" "I beg your pardon?" asked Steph. "Who did you sleep with?" asked Jessie. "Like I have told you, we have separate apartments. I slept alone," replied Steph. Jessie had noticed the big love bite on the Lady's neck. Well, someone is sleeping with her, he thought.

"So, who else is here?" asked Jessie. "No one. I gave all the help the day off for Christmas." "And when did they leave?" "About 5, I think." "Do you usually do that?" "Yes, it's my gift to them." "And the mess, who does that?" asked Jessie. "Well, the plan was for all of us to clear it and to cook dinner as a family." Jessie nodded, "I will need a guest list"

"I don't have that, Terrance organised everything." "Ok, CCTV, then I can go through that," said Jessie. Steph nodded. Jessie got up, "I am sorry for your loss, Lady Arlington. "Cindy, the apartment is out of bounds, the bodies will be picked up shortly. We will be back, but for now, we will leave you in peace," said Jessie. "And oh, before I go, who was the tall, well-dressed man with a mask on all night?" "I don't' know, we had many tall men in masks," replied Steph. "Yes, but this one stood out." "I don't know, officer." "Strange because you were talking to him quite a lot," questioned Jessie. "Oh, maybe it was Lord Smithye, quite a charmer." "And where can I find Lord Smithye?" asked Jessie. "I don't know, he lives North. He was a friend of Terrance." "So where is he staying? Because to go North after such a party would be reckless," said Jessie. "I don't know, I think some of the guests stayed at the country Hotel, but I don't know if he was one of them." "So, is he a farmer?" asked Jessie. "I don't know." "You don't know much, do you?" questioned Jessie. "Look, I think I remember him saying he inherited land and he was looking to buy more, so maybe he is a farmer," snapped Steph. "So this tall, handsome stranger comes into your home, You speak and dance with him a lot, but you don't know him?" "Yes, that is correct, officer, it was a masquerade ball that's part of the fun. I did not know half the people here last night, including you, my dear son organised it, he invited the guests, and now he is dead, and if I am not mistaken, this is the reason you are here, not to ask details of some fuckin'' farmer," Steph exploded. "Well, that's just it, Lady Arlington, I did not get an invitation, it was Serg who was invited and told to bring along whoever. "And your point is?" asked Steph. "Well, my point is how about this handsome stranger was not invited, and he just turned up, gate-crashed, shall we say?" stated Jessie. "You know, Sir, I am tired. My husband and son are lying dead, and all you are asking about is some man at the ball who may or may not have gate crashed what is the point of the conversation or you ?" snapped Steph. "The point of me, ma'am, is that I have had several young people hospitalised, of which your daughter-in-law was one. Three people were killed, and one thing they all had in common, well, no, two things: drugs in their system and DNA belonging to a… Oh, look at me, getting carried away. Can we search the house?" "No, no, you cannot! It is Christmas Day. I would like some respect to grieve my son and husband. Now if you don't mind, please, go," Steph burst out crying. Jessie nodded, "Ok, I will leave you in peace for now, I am sorry once again for your loss, oh, and by the way, we have a witness who recognised the tall handsome stranger, so I am not making this up, it is important we find him ; we think he is dangerous, so if you remember anything," Jessie stared at Lady Arlington who stared back at him not giving anything away. Jessie thought he was good at reading body language. He knew when someone was lying, but Lady Arlington was not giving him anything!

Chapter Twenty-Six

Steph watched as the bodies were removed, the apartment was locked, and the police got back in their cars and left, Steph slid down the wall, crying, "My son. My son, my darling son, my only son." Cindy came over to comfort her, "Hey, come on, it's just you and me now; we will get through this," whispered Cindy. Steph looked at Cindy. "No, you must go, call your parents, go stay with them." "No, I like it here, I live here," Cindy replied. "I SAID GO ! I want you gone!" shouted Steph. "This is all your fault, NOW GO, my son is dead because of you," shouted Steph. "Hey, Lady, this is my home. I am married, and you never know I might be pregnant, so guess what? I'm staying." Steph got to her feet. "Don't push me. I said go, take one of the cars and get out of here NOW," said Steph in a calm but frightening manner" "Ok, Ok, I will go for now."

Steph wandered around the house; the turkey was burnt, and the mess was just too much. Steph made her way to Rich's apartment; he would be wondering why she was so late. Rich was fast asleep in bed, still with headphones on! Steph walked over to the bed and shook him. Rich stirred slowly, opening one eye and then the other. "Hey," he whispered, "I slept like a log, must have been the excitement or the brandy," he joked. Steph sat on the bed, tears falling down her cheeks. "Hey, me Queen, what is it?" said Rich, trying to recall the events of last night. Steph fell into his arms and broke her heart. Rich held her tight, "That's it, babe, let it all out; you're safe now, I've got ya," said Rich as he stroked her hair. Eventually, the sobs subsided. "Now tell me what's wrong," whispered Rich.

Steph told him how she had found Cindy with another man, how she felt unsure going into the Lord, so she made Cindy go in first and how they found him still on the floor, but worse than that, Terrance was in his father's bed and had drank his father's cocktail and was dead. "Cocktail?" questioned Rich. "Yes, I was drugging the Lord to keep him sleepy, keep him away from me. Only the doctor was getting suspicious of the amount of drugs I was ordering, so I got some from somewhere else. They looked the same!" explained Steph. Rich smiled. He loved this woman; he knew they were the same! Steph told Rich about the police and how they were interested in him or Lord Smithye, something about a witness who had identified him as someone else and something about three or four other people being found and all linked to him Steph looked at Rich. "What did you do?" Rich looked at her. "Honestly, I dun know I was drugged myself, but I don't think it was good." "You going to give yourself in?" asked Steph. Rich looked at her, "You gotta be fuckin' joking, No way, I'm gonna have to leave, just don't believe 'em. I'm not a bad man, come with me?" pleaded Rich. "Where? Where will you go? Please don't leave me; I need you," begged Steph. "I need you too, but I can't stay here; they will lock me up, and that ain't happening, I have a friend who can get me a passport, once I have that, I will make my way somewhere," said Rich, tears rolling down his face. "Please believe me, you're my Lady A I love you, and I don't want to leave you, but I need to protect myself I don't want anyone else I want you, Lady, your lips, your body, your mind. I'm crazy for ya, One day, I will tell you everything," cried Rich. Steph looked at him, she loved him so much. "Hey, sweetie, I cannot come with you right now, but I can help you, we have a secret Villa in the canaries, I will give you lots of instructions for the villa and lots of money, take Terrance's passport. I will join you when I can." Rich did not know where the canaries were; he had never heard of them, he had never been out of the country, never been on a plane, and frankly did not fancy it. "Look, sweetie, trust me, you will want for nothing. I will give you the codes for the villa, for the safe where you will find plenty of money, we have land out there and a thriving business producing wine and Banana rum! You can take one of the cars, get yourself to an airport and stay safe, my darling." "You promise me you will join me?" asked Rich. "I promise," said Steph, "Try to stop me," she smiled, kissing him, her hands all over his body. "Come with me," she led him back into bed, kissing every inch of him. They were unaware of the cars speeding up the drive; suddenly, the banging on the door burst their bubble. "We know you're in there. Open the door!" shouted Jessie. "Fuck!" Rich ran to look at the cameras. "Fuck, it's the coppers!" "Open the door; I have a warrant. I know you're in there, Lady Arlington." Steph had ran upstairs to get something "Here," she threw Rich some keys. "Take a car here a passport with all the info you need; I will get them upstairs, then you go be safe, my darling." Rich had only had two choices: stay and face the music or take a chance.

Steph answered the door, "What is this?" she asked. "I am grieving my son and husband." "I'm sorry, ma'am, but we have reason to believe you have a guest here who we are keen to speak to," said Jessie, looking around. "Come in, officer, bring your troops." Steph ran upstairs and into one of the back-facing apartments, followed by Jessie and the team of police. "What was that?" asked Jessie. "I need the bathroom," replied Steph. "Oh, oh, sorry. Ok, Ok, we start here; we have a warrant. I want this place searched," ordered Jessie. The team dispersed in different directions, "What are you looking for, officer?" asked Steph. "Signs me lady, signs."

"Of what?" asked Steph. "I will let you know when I find it," replied Jessie. The case where all the villa documents had been stored was still out. "Going somewhere?" asked Jessie when he noticed the case. "Yes. To a friend, although I feel like driving away," sighed Steph. "DRIVE AWAY!? shouted Jessie. "The fuckin' cars!" Jessie ran to the front window just to see the taillights of a car at the end of the driveway. "DAMN! DAMN!" Jessie slammed his hand down, "How many cars do you have?" questioned Jess. "One," replied Steph. "Ok. How many cars are usually parked here?" Steph knew they had seven cars, one for each day of the week. "Four, officer." "Four?" "Yes." Jessie ran downstairs; he counted five cars! "Ok, stop the crap; you have five cars parked. "snapped Jessie "Maybe someone left a car overnight? Officer,. Still, I don't know anything about the cars," said Steph. "Maybe Lord Smithye left a car," said Jessie. "Maybe," she replied, "Unless--" "Yes?" questioned Jessie. "Unless it was him in bed with Cindy, I did not see too much of him. Still, he looked tall with dark hair. She had rejected my son on their wedding night; he must have been devastated," cried Steph, "Where is she now?" asked Jessie. "I don't know, she ran off, just left," said Steph. Jessie looked at Steph, she looked pale, her eyes swollen through crying. He was about to ask her more questions as the search teams returned.

"Nothing, Sir"

"Nothing?"

"Nothing here."

"Ok. Downstairs!" ordered Jessie.

Steph put on her best performance. She threw herself to the floor and began to cry and cry, her mind turning to Rich, and the thought of not seeing him for a while made her sob. Jessie tried to comfort her but she was getting worse. She started to hyperventilate, and the officers were getting uncomfortable "Jess, I think we leave her in peace; she just lost her husband and son, and it's Christmas," said one of the officers. "When Serg finds out you're in for it, it's not respectful, Jess. "Ok, Ok," said Jessie in frustration, we come back tomorrow." "You goanna be Ok? Do you want me to stay with you? asked Jessie. "No, no," sobbed Steph, "I want to be alone to pray." "I can arrange for someone to come over and be with you. You should not be alone at a time like this," said Jessie. "The maids will be back tomorrow. I will call a friend, don't worry," whispered Steph.

Jessie got up from the floor, still unsure if he should leave her, but it was Christmas after all, and he had Mandy at home waiting for him. He was annoyed he was working; it was not his turn, but Serg was sick, so it fell to him to cover. "Ok then, if you are sure, we will go," said Jessie. As Jessie left the house, he was still looking around for clues or anything unusual. He spotted the CCTV cameras, making a mental note to come back first thing and seize the footage.

Steph had been watching them from the top of the stairs; as soon as they had all gone, she went into action; running into the CCTV room, she wiped all the history and cut a few wires until all the cameras went black. Next was Rich's apartment. It smelt of him, but she had no time to cry; she stripped the bed, bagging everything but one sheet. She bagged all the towels and any remaining clothes, not that he had left much. She smiled; he must have really liked her choices.

They had an old incinerator, which they used for getting rid of stuff; time to test it out, she thought as she loaded the bags into it. The machine was noisy, but it seemed to mash and tear whatever was put in it. Steph smiled; so far, so good! Running back into the apartment, she cleaned every inch of it, mainly with bleach. She hoovered and polished and rearranged the furniture, made up the bed with clean laundry, and removed every piece of China glass and cutlery. The apartment looked bare as if no one ever stayed in it. Steph ran upstairs with the sheet and into Cindy's apartment. She exchanged the sheets putting the one from Rich bed onto Cindy's. Cindy's apartment was a mess, her bridal gown, which cost Steph thousands strewn all over the floor, her underwear all over the floor, makeup everywhere, food everywhere. Steph looked around; ungrateful bitch she thought she would pay for this!

Chapter Twenty-Seven

RICH

Rich needed to get to HEN. His plan involved setting a few things straight, acquiring the passport, and potentially enlisting HEN's aid in reaching the villa. He trusted HEN. He was the only person who had helped Rich in the past, and yes, they had a questionable relationship, but Rich quite liked it.

"Happy Christmas, man," said Asif, the duty guard. "I'm here to see HEN," Rich responded. "He out, but he left instructions if you turn up, let you in," said Asif. "What da ya mean he's out? It's fuckin' Christmas, man, the twat never goes out, now stop messin," snapped Rich. "Like I said, man, the boss not here; he's gone see family; someone died now you going in or what?" "Well, how long will he be a few hours?" asked Rich. "No, man, he said a few days; now you going in?" "No, I can't wait," snapped Rich.

Back in the car, Rich slammed the steering wheel in frustration! Now what? He did not have a plan. The only thing he was sure of was he knew he would not fly. Rich did not understand how something so big could fly like a bird, and, with his luck, the bloody thing would come down in some remote place, and he would be left to survive on fuckin' berries! No, he did not fancy it. Traveling had never crossed Rich's mind until now. His lady said the villa was in Grand Cannie or something like that, in Spain, so best he heads for Spain. Rich remembered the time his first wife took him on a ferry to get booze and cheese from a big supermarket. Maybe that was Spain, he thought. He remembered it took a day to get there, and they spent most of the time shagging and sleeping. They nearly missed the ferry back home. Rich smiled; he rarely thought of her, She was nice like all of em to start with, but she wanted to know where he was and what he was doing all the fuckin' time, She became obsessed with him, clinging on to him, and then she gave his mate a blowjob in exchange for fixing some shelves in the kitchen. Rich only found out cus the boys were talking about her in the pub. He didn't know she had never learnt to swim when he chucked her in the pool at one of the fancy parties she liked to go to in front of all of her posh friends The look on their faces, Rich could see them now all gasping and flapping as he just walked away! Rich had been driving on autopilot, his head full of memories. Before he knew it, he was heading to the port. Now, all he needed to do was to secure his place on the ferry.

Finally, Rich spotted the boarding signs. It won't be long now, he thought. Rich had never done this before and was slightly nervous as he joined the queue. He lost himself in dreams of the Villa and how life would be with her, just the two of them. They did not need anyone else, just him and his lady! He would be the man about the house and she would cook and clean and perform in the bedroom. Life is gonna be so good, thought Rich.

"Hello, Sir, have you booked?"

Rich was startled, "Booked?"

"Yeah. Have you booked, you know, to get on,"

"No, I'm a first timer, a virgin," said Rich, smiling and winking at the girl. Who blushed?

"Oh, I'm sorry, sir, but without a booking, we won't allow you on," said the girl.

"Oh no, I will miss my sister's wedding. I'm a fool. I should have booked. What do I do?" Rich asked, gazing into her eyes.

"Well, Sir, but I mean meet me, no I mean go to the booking office and book the next ferry and then join the queue," said the girl gasping. Rich knew he had this girl in the palm of his hand.

"But the queue is miles long. How about I leave the car and walk onto the ferry? Can I get on?"

"Yes, of course, but you cannot leave your car here."

"You have it, baby, you have it," said Rich, smiling at her.

The girl shook her head, "I can't do that, Sir; you're desperate to get to this wedding, ain't you?" she asked.

"Yes, yes I am; my sister has a disease, and we don't know how much longer. Oh, I cannot talk about it, sorry it's important to her but never mind, I'm a fool for not booking," This stranger's vulnerability touched the girl; he was not only the most handsome man she had seen in a while, but he seemed like a genuinely caring soul.

"Look, you only have a small car. I'll get you on; leave it to me. Pull in over here." Rich waited whilst the cars behind him were all given the go-ahead to board.

"You're in luck you're on," the girl announced as she returned. "One lorry, not turned up, must be your lucky day." Rich looked at the girl, "Thank you, it was my lucky day when I met you; maybe when I get back we can meet up?" smiled Rich as he handed over the passport and money. The girl was flustered; she glanced at the passport. "You look better in real life." Rich looked up, "I do?" "Yes, sorry, not being rude; I mean, passport photos don't really do anything for anyone, do they? I see some real Munters," laughed the girl. Rich held her hand and kissed it, "I look better in the nude; maybe you will find out one day," whispered Rich. The girl was now bright red and almost wetting herself, "Sir, you must go now, follow that car. Safe travels and see you when you get back. Bye for now."

"Goodbye, what's your name, so I can ask for you when I get back?" asked Rich, keeping up the act. "It's Honey; everyone calls me Honey Bee as I'm always buzzing," she laughed. "Bye then, Honey bee, laters," smiled Rich as he drove off into the ferry. Rich thought about Honey. Poor cow, bet she's on heat now, I bet she would have been an easy lay for me, but I'm not that man anymore. My Lady is the only one for me. She is the only one that can put me in my place, the only one that makes me feel I'm on fire. Rich parked the car and headed up to find a seat on deck with no idea what would happen next.

Chapter Twenty-Eight

JESSIE

Jessie was telling Mandy all about his day, "It sounds bad; come and relax with me," said Mandy, patting the seat next to her. Jessie snuggled up to her, "I will find him, Mands; I promise you I will lock him up for what he did to you," Mandy smiled. "I know, but I want to forget it. I was thinking of getting away, a fresh start." "When?" asked Jessie, feeling quite hurt that she wanted to get away from him. "I don't know Jess, just something I need to think about, maybe go travelling, or maybe I will go home to New Zealand." Jessie sat up, "I know, Mands, how about a holiday together, just you and me, what you say? "Well, we could go travelling, Spain, France, Italy. We could travel for a few months," said Mandy, excited by the prospect. "I don't know, Mands, if I can get that much time off work, but I could get a week or two off, and we could go somewhere hot, just you and me," said Jessie as he smuggled into her, he was falling for her, and the thought of her by his side in the hot sun with very little on was very appealing to him. Mandy and Jessie had been getting to know each other.

Jessie was a kind and caring bloke. He had made Mandy more than welcome in his home. She had her own bedroom, but they shared a bathroom. Jessie would often catch sight of her in her underwear, but he was too much of a gentleman to try anything besides he wanted her to trust him. Mandy got the sense Jessie fancied her. He would bring home gifts most days, which were usually flowers or perfume, but she was desperate for a shag. She wanted him to be demanding, to rip her clothes off and take her. Just like **he** did, she missed **him** so much. She would spend hours just looking out of the window, dreaming **he** would find her and scoop her up and save her from this normal, unexciting life she suddenly had. What's wrong with you, Mandy Cane, She would ask herself**. He** was an animal, but I loved **him. He** was a real man, and when **he** made love to me, well, nothing else mattered. But **he** locked you up. No, I could have left; **he** left you without food. No, **he** went out every day to get food, **he** took care of me, **he** left you to die, something happened to him, I know it, **he** loved me, and so the conversations would go around and around in Mandy's head.

Chapter Twenty-Nine

ANGUS

Angus had been at sea for weeks. He was sailing alone, as no one turned up to help him. Bloody lazy buggers, no bugger wants to work these days, Angus moaned to himself as he set sail. Angus did not have a family, so taking off for months was nothing to him. In fact, he enjoyed it. He loved the sea and the challenges it threw up. Angus liked to daydream as he sailed. He found it relaxing, but the boat was rocking a bit more than usual. The sea was getting rougher by the minute. Best I hanker down me thinks I'm in for a rough one.

"HELP! HELP! Please HELP!" shouted Jo, not knowing where she was or what was happening. She was cold and wet and being tossed around from one side to another. "HELP," she shouted as the crate she was in got tossed upside down.

Angus shook his head, "Your hearing things now, silly bugger!"

The crate banged into the side of the boat, then into the other side. Bang. Bang. Bang. The crate was being tossed around like it was a feather. Each time the crate hit the side of the boat, it began to break up. Soon, Jo could push her way through the side. Where on earth was she? It was dark, cold and stank of fish. Jo crawled out on her hands and knees. She was in a bloody boat, and the sea was rough. The sides of the crate were being thrown around. She found a space in between the ropes and boxes. She needed to wait this out and pray! Stay with it, Jo, she thought, stay with it. You have come this far. Don't give up now.

The sea eventually calmed down. Hours had gone by, and Jo had drifted off to sleep. Startled, Jo opened her eyes to find a big, burly fisherman standing over her.

"Hello, my dear, what are you doing down here?" asked Angus

"Hey, I mean, Hello, I'm Jo. I'm not a stowaway. Don't get mad at me, please. I was in that crate," said Jo, pointing to the broken crate. "Some bloke knocked me out and put me in it. Don't hurt me; I mean no harm," said Jo.

Angus sat down on the floor. "Don't worry, maid. I won't hurt you," said Angus as he held out his hand. "Come on, let's have a cuppa, and you can tell me all about it. I'm Angus, by the way."

It was the best cup of tea Jo had ever had. She devoured a packet of biscuits as she told Angus what she could remember, Angus filled in the Blanks; he knew Rich. "Dirty rotten bastard, when I get home, I will have him. Animal!" said Angus. "Well, love, I can't let you off yet. I'm heading, well… I don't know where I'm heading; the navigation broke in the storm, and I'm following the sun. I could do with a hand if you fancy earning, ya keep?" smiled Angus.

"Thought you would never ask." Jo smiled. Angus showed Jo the bunk bed, shower and toilet, and most importantly the Galli. "Help ya self to what ya want; we can get more when we eventually stop." "Thank you, Angus-. Thank you," said Jo.

Each day that past Jo got stronger and more confident with the boat. She enjoyed the ever-changing seas. One day rough and wild, the next calm. She found it astonishing how rapidly the weather at sea shifted, going from brilliant sunshine to torrential rain. Food was running low although they had plenty of fish, she like fish but not every day! Angus was entertaining, and they got on like a house on fire. "So, do you know where we are heading?" asked Jo. "Well, if I'm not mistaken, we will be in Madeira tomorrow or next. We will stop for a few days and get some supply of fish," joked Angus. "So, when do you actually fish?" asked Jo. "When I get where I want to be," replied Angus. "No rush, maid, plenty of fish for everyone," Jo smiled. He truly was a lovely man.

Angus had never bothered with women, too much trouble, and to have one on a boat. Well, he never would. No good will come of it, as his father would say. But this maid was different, and he didn't really get a choice. Angus looked over at Jo, she was strong like a bloke, quick to learn which meant he could rest whilst she stayed at the helm. She was an absolute delight to be around, captivating and hilarious. He liked her. His blood boiled over when he thought about Rich and what he had done to her, poor maid. It made him shudder to think he was going to tip the crate into sea, had the seas not been so rough. He vowed to himself he would kill Rich when he got back home, but who was he kidding? He was no killer, "Hey, you coming to do any work, or ya gonna sit on ya arse all day dreamin," shouted Jo. Angus looked up, "Sorry maid, I was miles away, but yea, I think I will sit here all day and let you do all the work," laughed Angus. "Well, you might want to join me. I can see land, and I ain't got a clue what to do," shouts Jo. Angus immediately got up.

"Maid, that's Madeira, a wonderful island. It has a big fish market," laughed Angus. "You and your bloody fish! For a fisherman, you don't actually catch any," said Jo, smiling. "Hey, maid, plenty of time to do that when the time is right. Anyway, why trouble myself when some poor bugger has already been out and done it for me!?

Now watch and learn maid watch and learn how to enter a port and dock," said Angus has he took control of the boat.

It took hours to sort out the paperwork before the boat could moor. The authorities gave them a beautiful spot and allowed them to stay as long as they pleased. Jo saw money exchange hands, but she asked no questions. She had made a list of supplies they needed and hoped Angus had some money left, as she had none. "Angus, this is embarrassing, but I don't have any money on me and we need stuff. I need stuff, like women's stuff." Angus looked at Jo, "Maid, I have money; that's one thing I do have. Ya never have to worry about that; I knows the position ya were in, and look, if ya don't wanna be seen with me, I understand. I will give ya money, and ya can do what ya want," said Angus.

"What do you mean?" asked Jo, puzzled. "Well, you might want to stay on this island, get ya life back together or get ya-self home," said Angus. Jo looked at Angus, "I am not staying on this island unless you are. I am coming with you; I'm a fisherwoman now," she laughed. "All I need is supplies, and we will go together, although I could do with a change of clothes." It made Angus happy to hear she was not leaving him. "Maid, you can have whatever ya want; I'm not short of money," he said, smiling at her.

Chapter Thirty

19th of January

It was halfway through January, the longest month. It had been a particularly cold and wet month so far. The funeral for both Lord Arlington and Terrance Arlington was today. According to the autopsy results, the cause of her husband's death was a heart attack, and her son passed away because of an allergic reaction to medication, resulting in anaphylactic shock. The entire village and nearby town were talking about it. *"Terrance took the overdose because he found Cindy with another man. Oh yes, the other man was lord Smithye; I thought he was too good to be true,"* said the farmer's wife.

The police search of the big house had come up with nothing; despite Mandy's statement, the information from Dazer and the DNA all pointing to Richard Luck, the police search was fruitless. Cindy was useless. She did not know who she had slept with but thought he was tall, dark and handsome! Jessie suspected Richard Luck was hiding away like a rat. He won't go far, he is too comfortable, and he thinks we are a load of idiots, he told Serg.

A sense of curiosity gripped the locals, drawing them to the funeral to glimpse Cindy and the Lady. Many of the locals proclaimed they would know who was telling the truth just by being present at the funeral! Lady Arlington was no fool. She knew the local folks liked scandals and a gossip, as well as the free food and drink provided. She smiled to herself as she got herself ready. If only they knew half of it! Steph chooses a well-coordinated black and grey outfit. She had a grey rose attached to her hat. Cindy had moved back into the house because her mum and dad were ashamed of her and were giving her a hard time. Cindy also dressed herself in black and grey. She had tried to copy Lady Arlington, but her choices looked tacky when they stood side by side.

The relationship between the two women was strained. Steph tried to keep her distance. She knew Cindy had men most nights she heard her scream and giggle. Steph felt jealous of Cindy having fun having sex. She had that glow about her, the one you get from getting your needs met. She desired that glow more than anything. "I heard you last night," Steph blurted out, "You have wasted no time. I thought you would have at least given it a rest last night, as it's your husband's funeral." "Look, lady," snapped Cindy, "I'm a woman who needs sex. I need to know men desire me; nothing wrong with that. Try it sometime. Anyway, I am trying to get up the duff and give you an heir, and then when you go, all this will be mine. I'll be properly sorted." Steph looked at Cindy, not quite believing what she had just heard. "You're nothing but a tramp!" screamed Steph, "And if you get pregnant, it won't be an Arlington!" "Calm down, grandma, it will be an Arlington; remember I married your son? I'm an Arlington," smirked Cindy. Steph looked at Cindy, "Look, lady, don't take me on if you know what's good for you," turning on her heels, Steph walked away. Call me selfish, she thought, but she is having none of this. If she wants to play games, then so do I!

The funeral was a heartbreaking, sombre affair. Lots of people wanted to say a few words. Lady Arlington sat alone at the front and all she could think about was Rich. Everyone attended the wake afterwards, some out of courtesy, but for others, it was a chance to see Cindy. She was the talk of the event! The nerve of her, she killed him, ya know, drugged him she did, left him to die. She killed the lord prancing naked in front of him on her wedding day. Look at her, not a tear, the Hussey, look at her. They say she was in bed with that bloke they want for murder. And so, the gossip continued. Steph walked around listening, making pleasant conversation. Everyone felt sorry for her. She looked lost; no one could understand why Cindy could come back to the big house. Well, I bet she's blackmailing her. Poor lady, all this and no one to share it with. See, even the rich folk don't get it all they laughed.

Lady Arlington found Jessie. "Can I speak with you, please?" "Yes, of course; how are you?" asked Jessie. Within seconds, Serg was making his way over. "Anything wrong, Stephanie?" Serg asked, pushing Jessie out of the way. "Oh, Serg darling, nothing wrong. I just wanted to speak to Jessie. I think I have remembered something." "I will take it from here. Thank you, Jessie," said Serg. Jessie had received a right bollocking from Serg when he found out what Jessie did on Christmas day. Jessie was sure Serg fancied Stephanie any opportunity he was going to see Lady Arlington! Jessie moved away; I need to get away from here; he thought maybe travelling with Mandy was not such a bad idea!

"So," said Serg, putting his arm around Lady Arlington, "You must be exhausted. It has been a troublesome time for you, and today, well, very hard. Come sit down, my dear and tell me what's on your mind." Lady Arlington began, "I keep having flashbacks of the man in Cindy's bed the night they poisoned my son. He was tall and dark. I think it may have been the man you are looking for, and I am frightened she is still seeing him. She goes off, and then I hear a man here at night. I am too scared to come out of my apartment. I think, if I may be so bold, you should watch her," said Lady Arlington, putting on her best acting. "I will do more than just watch her. I cannot have you frightened in your own home. Oh, no, you leave this with me," Serg placed his hands on her shoulders and gave them a squeeze. "Don't worry, my dear, I will take it from here. Oh, and Steph, maybe one day when you are feeling up to it, you will let me take you out for tea or a drive or both?" Serg waited for her response. She smiled at him. "You are so kind Serg."

Serg walked away. Was that a yes or a no? He needed to impress her. She needs to like him. He quite fancied living in a big house like this, he thought.

Why does everyone want my fuckin' house, thought Steph as Serg walked away. He really is very obvious!

Cindy was drunk and making a beeline for Jessie, "Hey, you're a lovely boy, handsome, clever; you taken?" asked Cindy. "No, well, yes, well, not really, we are in between things," said Jessie. All Mandy heard was No. "Well, why don't you come with me upstairs for a bit of alone time?" Jessie was mortified but also curious to get her alone; maybe she would talk. "Lead the way," said Jessie. Cindy took his hand and made her way to her apartment. She had been put on the ground floor; it suited her. She could nip in and out whenever she wanted. Cindy dragged Jessie onto the bed, "Hey, not so fast," exclaimed Jessie, "Talk to me." "Fuck talking, kiss me," demanded Cindy as she forced her lips onto Jessie's. "Get off me!" Jessie shouted as he pushed Cindy away. "What the hell you doing? Have you no shame ?" Jessie shouted as he stormed out of the apartment. "Serg! Serg! I need to tell you something. Serg" shouted Jessie He was just about to tell Serg what had happened when Cindy came running into the room; her dress ripped at the neck, her hair a mess, and mascara running down her face. "Help! Help! I have been attacked." Everyone fell silent; Steph ran over to her, "What did you say? What do you mean?" "He tried to rape me," cried Cindy pointing to Jessie and bursting into tears. Steph looked at Cindy, then at Jessie, who was talking to Serg. Jessie went to say something. "Leave it, Jess, I've got this," said Serg, walking over to Cindy, "I will need you to come down the station so I can take a statement," said Serg. "What, now? No, I'm not coming!" shouted Cindy. "Oh, I think you are. I need to investigate your claim against one of my officers," said Serg, who was getting quite agitated by this woman. "Oh, don't you worry, love, I don't want to take it any further; he probably didn't mean it," laughed Cindy. "But I do," said Serg, "You will come with me, and you will come now. Don't make any more of a scene. Cindy, come willingly, or I can cuff you?" Cindy looked at Lady Arlington. "Do something then!" she shouted, "This happened in your house, it's all your fault!" shouted Cindy. "Walk away. Walk away, ladies," ordered Serg as he marched Cindy out to the waiting car.

19th of January ————Maderia

The weather had not been kind to them. The wind was always in the wrong direction according to. Angus, not that Jo was complaining, the island was lovely, people were friendly, a bit of sun in between the winds, and the food was superb. Jo and Angus laughed and chatted most of the day. They played cards, did a spot of fishing, went for walks, and explored the island. Jo had got lots of new clothes. She saw Angus as a father figure, and Angus saw Jo as the daughter he had never had. "I think we'll be moving on soon, maid," said Angus. "The winds are turning in our favour." Jo felt a slight disappointment; she liked it here, and part of her wanted to stay, but the thought of Angus doing the next crossing alone hurt her. "Ok, Ok, if we must, I will stock up today and get the boat ready," smiled Jo. Angus knew Jo was enjoying it here on the Island. "We can always come back here one day, maid; it will be a nice straight sail down to La Palma in the Canaries, lovely and warm. Do a bit of fishing and then head back."

Jo looked at Angus; she was with him until he said to head back. No way was she heading back; she would work on Angus to stay!

19th January Huelva Spain

Rich had been travelling for twenty-something days. Once he got off the ferry in Santander, he purchased a map and set off on an adventure across Spain. He spent his days sleeping sometimes in the sun but usually in some low-budget hotel. He would swim in the sea when he could, and he even got involved in the local food and picked up bits of the language. Rich liked to travel at night, taking the odd day and night off, but most nights, he would be on the road; he liked it this way. It gave him time to think, although he only had two things on his mind: Stephanie, (his Lady A) and the villa. He thought about her all the time, and he felt selfish for leaving her, but he justified it to himself. She wanted me to be safe, he thought. He really hoped she was ok and once they were together, that would be it. Nothing or nobody was coming between them.

Rich felt pleased with himself; he had never been outside of the UK before, and yet here he was, driving on the wrong side of the road, eating Spanish food; although that cold soup was a step too far for him, he liked paella and an omelette made from potatoes with ham. Rich smiled to himself. All you need to do now is get yourself on this ferry, and in two days you will be in Las Palma, then find the villa that's when your new life will start.

19th January Evening Arlington Manor

All the guests had gone, Steph sat alone, Cindy was not back from the police station, and the maids had gone home. Just you then, girl, she said to herself. Just you. Now what? Steph wandered around the house, she found herself in what used to be Rich's apartment. She was staring at the bed, remembering all the wonderful times she had spent with Rich. She longed to hold him, to kiss him. She needed to be with him as soon as possible her heart ached for him. Steph sighed as she continued to walk around the house. She did not love it anymore. It felt wrong now, every room felt cold. She wanted something different, something more exciting. That's it, she said to herself. Sell it and get out; go be with your man, and don't come back! She smiled. The decision felt right. Tomorrow, I will start the ball rolling!

19th January evening at Jessies

Jessie arrived home to a lovely meal made by Mandy. "Hey, what's this?" asked Jessie. "It's a farewell dinner, Jess. I'm off. My parents sent me a ticket. I'm going back to New Zealand," explained Mandy. "When?" "Tomorrow, Jess, tomorrow night." "How long for?" "I dun know Jess, maybe forever." Jessie looked at Mandy, "I thought you wanted to go travelling." "Yea, I do, but I need to see my folks, Jess; I need to go home." She could tell Jessie was disappointed; he had been good to her, and they had grown close. They had been sleeping together, and it was nice, but Mandy could not get **him** out of her head. It was **him** she wanted, not that she would ever tell Jessie, so it was best she left. "Let me come with you, Mands; I'm fed up with my job. I will just quit." "No, Jessie, you can't do that. I don't want you to come with me," blurted Mandy, who was still thinking about **him.** "Oh, I see," said Jessie, pushing his plate of food away. "Sorry Jess, I will come back, then we can go travelling, but I need to see my folks," said Mandy. "Yea, of course you will," replied Jessie, getting up from the table. He had developed feelings for this woman, especially since she had made her way into his bed. He made love to her most nights and thought they had something, but the bitch was happy to just walk away. Jessie felt sorry for himself; he felt his career was stagnant with a boss he hated because he was doing all the hard work and Serg was taking all the credit. It was Jessie who had linked everything to Richard Luck, but once Lady Arlington was implicated, Serg took over the case, Jessie was sure Serg had destroyed evidence that tied her to Richard Luck! "I don't know why I bother"; he said out loud to himself. Mandy came into the bedroom. "Jessie, I am sorry, that was mean of me. I just need time with my family, so why don't you come out in a week or two?" Jessie looked up, "What? To New Zealand?" he said excitedly. "Yes, why not?" Jessie's face lit up. "It's a deal. I'll be with you before you know it Mands," he said. Jessie pulled Mandy into his arms. "Make love to me," he whispered. Mandy knew what to do; they went through the same routine every night. She slowly undressed and teased him, sliding up and down his body with hers. "Oh baby, please, no more, please baby, please," moaned Jessie. "Have you been a good boy?" she asked. "Yes, yes, I have; please let me, please," moaned Jessie. "No, I don't think you have been good. I think you have been a naughty, naughty boy," whispered Mandy, getting out the cane. Jessie loved the cane. "Bend over," Mandy commanded. Mandy whipped his arse, each whip getting harder. "Take that, you naughty boy!" Jessie's arse was red, and his cock was rock hard. Mandy bent over, sticking her arse in the air. "Now you can have me," she whispered. Jessie had no sooner entered her than he emptied himself inside her. "Oh, Mands, that was wonderful," sighed Jessie. Mandy lay beside him. She felt nothing. The only reason she had agreed to sleep with Jessie was because she felt guilty and saw sleeping with him as some kind of payment for her keep. She hoped she would feel that electric feeling she had felt with **him,** but she never did. Jessie liked to be smacked hard and to be told he was naughty, so Mandy just went through the motions to please him. "Oh yes, babe, you're wonderful," sighed Mandy. She never asked Jessie to pleasure her; she only wanted **him** to do that. She could not imagine opening up for anyone else ever again, and something inside her knew she would find **him** again.

Chapter Thirty-One: January 30th

STEPHANIE ARLINGTON

Steph had been busy packing up. The entire estate was to be sold at auction tomorrow. The estate had generated prime interest from América and experts predicted it to be one of the biggest sales ever.

Steph wanted to be at the auction to ensure she got the correct price. She had given instructions that the lowest she would go was one hundred and fifteen million pounds.

Serg had been a regular visitor, and he felt annoyed Stephanie was selling up. He quite fancied being the Lord of the manor. "Well, my dear, you will be able to buy whatever your heart desires. What will you do, my lovely?" Serg asked her. "I don't know, Serg, we will see," replied Steph. Serg was growing frustrated with her. She never gave him a straight answer. Despite inviting her for tea, he only got to kiss her hand. Whenever he suggested a holiday together, she would dismiss him, yet she fascinated him. The more she pushed him away, the more he wanted her. "Stephanie, my dear, why don't you share your plans with me? I'm a decent bloke; I am looking for love, and frankly, I will do anything for you," blurted Serg. Steph looked at Serg; it was true he would do anything for her. He had got rid of evidence that may have incriminated her. He had upset Cindy so much she had run back to her parents; he had helped her pack up and had taken her out for dinner and tea, but he wasn't who she wanted. He had tried to kiss her. Luckily, she moved quickly out of his grasp. The thought of kissing him made her nauseated. She only had one man on her mind. "It is too soon, Serg. I am not ready for any relationship," explained Steph. "Now, please be respectful of my feelings and if you cannot, then please leave." Serg was going nowhere; this woman had everything he wanted, "Of course, my dear, I understand we have all the time in the world," said Serg. Stephanie wished he would get a big case and be so busy he had no time or get moved somewhere else. She had made her mind up to leave as soon as the sale went through. Steph had sold the cars and most of the furniture. It was just the land left to sell. "Do you own any more homes?" asked Serg. "No, why?" asked Steph. "Oh, just curious. I wondered why you had plans for a villa on the wall; I mean, it looks stunning," smiled Serg. "I don't know what you are referring to," responded Steph. Serg held out his hand, "Come, my dear, let me show you; maybe it is something you have forgotten about," Steph declined his hand. "Just show me," she snapped. On the study wall were plans of the villa. Damn it, she thought, how many times have I walked past those and not noticed them. "Oh, that old thing, well, those were plans my Terrance drew up; he wanted to buy land one day in France and build a villa, so he had plans drawn up. He hoped once he was married, it would happen," Steph cried. "Now look what you have done; I am all upset again; please leave, please leave me alone." Serg felt hurt, "Look, my dear, I think we should take the plans and maybe build the villa in the south of France in memory of your Terrance; what do you think?" asked Serg. Steph was getting really bored of this man, "Do you know, Serg, you have given me an idea; I think I will get a villa built in France just like you say in memory of my son. Maybe when it is finished, you will come out and stay," said Steph, "Well, my dear I would be delighted, imagine us in a villa in the sun, you will have a pool and maybe a jacuzzi, oh my days I can retire in the sun," said Serg dreaming. Serg looked at Steph, "You know, my dear, I thought you would never ask me, but now I know we will be together. Maybe you would consider marrying me?" asked Serg. Steph went cold at the thought of this man touching her. "Run along now, Serg; I really need some alone time to pray," responded Steph. "Oh yes, of course, my dear, you have a big day tomorrow ; you need all the beauty sleep you can get," smiled Serg. Steph decided it was not worth her energy responding to him, She had to think of a way to get rid of him.

31st of January- Stephanie

It was the big day, the moment of truth. How much was the house and land worth? The town's people and farmers were worried a big company would buy the land and build houses. The auction room was full. Stephanie had dressed up for the occasion, she had chosen a black suit with lemon detail. She had, of course, shoes, a handbag and diamonds all to match.

Despite Jessie leaving today, Serg had decided it was more important to be by Stephanie's side. He was really irritating Steph. He was noisy, wanting to know all the details of her business. Steph had invented a sister who lives in America. She informed Serg once the sale was over; she was heading out to America to see her sister for a month. Serg had looked at all the intel he had on Steph, and he could not find any sister, but if he asked her too much more, she would get suspicious of him, and he did not want that, as he was so obsessed with her. Steph was no fool; she knew Serg wanted her, so she had to always be one step ahead of him, "May I say, my dear, you are such a smart, beautiful woman," whispered Serg as he gazed at Steph, "I have a gift for you," Serg handed Steph a small box. "Thank you. What is it?" she replied abruptly. "I was thinking, Steph," Serg continued, "I can never get hold of you, so you need a mobile phone. I hope you like it. I was thinking we could go somewhere for lunch once this is done and celebrate, we could talk about our plans, I mean your plans, you could tell me all about your sister," said Serg. Steph sighed, "I have no intention of carrying this around with me. I do not have a phone by choice, and I certainly won't be having this one. The fact you cannot get hold of me is exactly how I want it, and no, I will not have time today, maybe another day," said Steph sternly, handing back the box. "Oh, and what, may I ask, are you doing today?" questioned Serg. "No, you may not ask; in fact, stop asking me bloody questions," said Steph, sitting back in her seat. Serg sat down in silence, crossing his arms like a child who had just been told off. Play it cool. You're obviously coming on strong. Play hard to get like you're not interested. She will soon come round. I mean, what woman could resist a hardworking, respectable police officer? She will be lucky to have me, thought Serg

The auctioneer was ready. BANG BANG went his hammer, the auctioneer's voice booming over everyone. PLEASE, PLEASE, LADIES AND GENTLEMEN. IF I MAY HAVE SILENCE, I SEE SUCH A WONDERFUL COLLECTION OF FINE PEOPLE HERE TODAY, ALL EAGER TO HEAR ABOUT THE WONDERFUL ARLINGTON MANOR ESTATE. The auctioneer continued, "We are so pleased to have the lovely Lady Arlington here today, and Lady Arlington, please may I extend my sincere condolences to you for the loss of your husband, a dear friend of mine and your son in such tragic circumstances. I am sure the whole of this hall will join me in wishing you well, and if I may be so bold to applaud you for being so brave." The hall erupted in applause, Stephanie stood up, "Thank you so much, John; thank you, everyone, for coming today and showing an interest. It is very kind of you all."

"HEY, LADY, why ya sellin' our land?" shouted a farmer, "Ya putting me out of business and home." "The Lord would never have done that," shouted another farmer. "HERE! HERE!" shouted another, "Yes, Lady, you don't have to do this; it's our land, our homes are here; we love it; we don't want no cheap houses on our land." "We don't want this." "HERE! HERE!" "Pound signs, that's all this is, you don't care." "Well said," the heckling continued, the shouting getting more intense. Steph had not realised or thought about the impact this sale would have on the farmers; all she thought about was getting out of this place and into bed with Rich; she was so selfish.

Steph whispered into Mr McCormack's ear, "Stop the bloody proceedings." McCormack was the family solicitor; he had supported them for years. He was not very keen on Stephanie; he thought she treated his friend The late Lord Arlington disgracefully. But needs must, he needed the money "What? I beg your pardon. I mean, excuse me," he exclaimed. "Stop the bloody proceedings I need to think," snapped Steph.

"Well, ladies and gentlemen," shouted the Auctioneer as his hammer banged on the desk, "Quiet! Quiet! Please, we need to get on. Today, we have the wonderful Arlington Manor and land, 5000 acres, no less. Currently, 2000 acres are farming land. The manor house and grounds are a mere 1000 acres, with the remaining land being woodland. We have considered our assessment of the land in the following ways: The environmental impact, location, economic impact, appearance, and planning permission. Now, I will go through each point. We have, of course, a valuation in mind, but the bidding is open. Oh, just one minute, someone just asked me to halt the proceedings. Well, this is highly irregular! Please. ORDER! ORDER!" shouts the auctioneer.

The noise in the hall was immense, with everyone talking and speculating. "ORDER! ORDER! Ladies and gentlemen, if I could ask you to step outside for a break whilst I talk."

The hall emptied as everyone went off to get some refreshments. Serg was unhappy, "What on earth are you thinking?" he snapped at Stephanie, "This delay will cost us, I mean, you. Why did you stop the proceedings?" Steph looked at Serg, "Because I did. Now if you don't mind, you have been asked to leave the hall," said Steph sternly. "But I am with you; I am at the front with you if you haven't noticed," replied Serg. "No, No, you're not. Now, please go." Snapped Stephanie. Serg walked away, bitch he thought, she can't speak to me like that. I love her, and I had plans for that money! Steph sighed. He really is a nuisance, she thought. He needs to go!

Lady Arlington said to John, the auctioneer, "This is most inappropriate stopping the proceedings. It will cost you." "Shh, John, I know, but I have changed my mind. I want to sell the manor house and its grounds only. I will keep the rest. The grounds are big enough for a developer to build on. The house alone is worth five million, so John, I am looking for eighteen million lowest. Now, do you want to sell and earn some commission or not?" said Steph. "Yes, yes, of course, but the delay will cost you," Steph laughed. "Then I want nineteen million, John, so shall we get on with it? Remember, if you don't get me what I want, you earn nothing; that was the deal." John stared at Steph; she can be a real hard bitch; he thought to himself. He had heard from the Lord when they used to go shooting together that she was bossy and so selfish, and it was her way or nothing.

"Well, John, are we starting or not?" demanded Steph. "Yes, of course, anything you want, my dear," said John with a hint of sarcasm.

The hall was soon full, with everyone eager to hear the latest developments. BANG! BANG! Went the hammer. "Ladies and gentlemen, without further ado, we have a slight change to the sale today; we are only putting forward the beautiful manor house and its land, one thousand Acres of land, Ladies and Gentlemen, with planning permission to build more homes so whoever the new lucky owner is can take forward if they so wish. So, will someone start me off?"

"FIVE MILLION," shouts someone at the back. "Sir, five million is nothing; this is prestige land, an easy commute to the major city."

"EIGHT MILLION," shouts someone else. "Sir, eight million is nothing; the land alone is priceless."

"SEVENTEEN AND A HALF MILLION." Everyone turns around to see a well-dressed man with staff fussing over him. "Sir, that is more like it; you truly see the value."

"EIGHTEEN MILLION!" shouts another.

"NINETEEN MILLION!"

"TWENTY MILLION!"

"TWENTY AND A HALF MILLION!"

"TWENTY-ONE MILLION!"

"TWENTY-TWO MILLION!"

"IM OUT."

"TWENTY-TWO MILLION POUNDS, I say twenty-two million pounds going once, twenty-two million pounds going twice; anybody else wants to offer me more?" After what seemed like a long silence, the hammer went down, "SOLD to this fine gentleman and your name, sir?" asked John. "Lord Smithye, my name is Lord Smithye." A silence and gasp went around the hall. Steph looked in horror; it was her husband's cousin, the actual Lord Smithye. Serg was quick to his feet. "Lord Smithye?" he questioned. Steph decided the best thing was to ignore him and play dumb. "Yes, and who may you be, Sir, sitting with my auntie?" Serg smiled; he liked this bloke; he had recognised me, and the Lady were together. "Oh, I have heard such a lot about you and wanted to meet you. I must say you are looking nothing like the description I was given, but then I am guessing you were not at the Christmas ball or in Cindy's Bed," Serg blurted out. Lord Smithye took a step back just as he opened his mouth to protest at such degrading talk. The hall doors were pushed open, "Where is she, lying cow? Where is she? I'm gonna kill her." Everyone turned around to see Cindy with a gun in her hand and clearly drunk. "Put the gun down, Cindy," ordered Serg as everyone moved out of the way. "Oh, there she is, cuddling up to you now, is she? At least you're better than that tramp she took in. Did she tell you how she likes to look after down and outs?" Serg looked at Stephanie, who was staring wide-eyed at Cindy, wishing the ground would swallow her up. Cindy continued, "I didn't kill my husband; she did, and she killed her own husband, and I'm gonna kill her." Cindy aimed the gun at Stephanie, who froze on the spot, "Anything you want to say, Lady?" shouted Cindy. "No? Nothing? Not even sorry!" shouted Cindy, still aiming the gun at Stephanie. Suddenly, the farmers charged at Cindy from behind, knocking her to the floor. Cindy pulled the trigger as she fell; the bullet flew through the air, hitting the metal gong and rebounding into Serg's chest. Serg fell to the floor, and Stephanie started screaming, "Do something! Get an ambulance, get the police." "Don't worry, Lady, she ain't going nowhere," said farmer John, who was sitting on top of Cindy. Had ya sold our land, we would have let her shoot ya," laughed John. Steph held her head in her hands; it was total mayhem. The paramedics were making Serg stable before moving him. The police were dragging Cindy away, who was screaming obscenities. The auctioneer was banging his hammer, shouting ORDER, ORDER, but no one was listening; the crowds were all talking and laughing. "So when do I get the keys, my dear? It is, after all, mine now." Steph looked up to see Lord Smithye smiling down at her. "Hey, not so fast. I am Lady Arlington's solicitor; we have papers to sign, and if I am not mistaken, you need to transfer the remaining money, so shall we say tomorrow at noon?" Lord Smithye clicked his fingers and whispered something to his staff, "I have the money now, and I want the keys now. I can sign now." Stephanie looked at McCormack, who was shaking his head, "I am sorry, Lord, the papers need to be drawn up; tomorrow at noon is the best I can do." "Very well, tomorrow at noon it is, and I do not expect any further delays. I want you out," snapped Lord Smithye as he bowed his head and left the hall. "So, what was that about?" asked McCormack. "I don't know, I guess he is keen to get in the house," replied Steph. "No, not him, that woman; what was that about?" asked McCormack. "She was drunk. Anyway, best I get going and finish packing." Steph walked out, leaving McCormack wondering what she was hiding now. Unknown to Steph, he knew a lot about her and he intended to

use it to get some money out of her.

Steph made her way back to the house; most of it was packed up, just a few personal things. She called the hotel and asked them to prepare their suite as she would stay there for a while. She called the hospital, but Serg was still in the theatre. She called the removal company, "Yes, we can do it tomorrow, but it will have to be at 6 am and is it still going into storage?" asked Mike. Stephanie paused, "No, Mike, dump the lot or sell it. I don't care," sighed Steph. She wanted a new start with fresh stuff around her, and even though her furniture was expensive, she had no plans to buy another bloody manor house in England. Steph felt like a weight had been lifted bit by bit. She felt she was getting closer to her man.

RICH

Rich got off the ferry. He was tired of travelling for almost six weeks now, nonstop. The sun was beating down; the air smelt fresh, and for the first time since he left the manor house, he felt safe and at home. Rich had spent a lot of his time thinking about the future. He was turning over a new leaf. No more trouble; no one knew him. He would settle into being Stephanie's partner. Rich looked down at the information Steph had given him about the Villa. It was the last time he saw her; he missed her so much he wanted to share his adventures with her, but most of all he wanted to make love to her! Rich had never gone so long without a shag, but he was saving it all for her!

The villa was in Monte Leon, about an hour's drive away. Come on, son, you're nearly home, Rich whispered to himself. The island was barren in parts but beautiful in others, thought Rich as he drove through the towns. Rich was enjoying the drive; he was taking it all in; after all, this was home now! As Rich approached the Villa, the air seemed to change; it was fragrant and clear. "WOW!" Rich gasped. The villa was behind an access-controlled gate, but he could see how grand it looked. He was expecting something small, but this, well, this looked like a mansion. Rich fumbled through the paperwork, looking for gate instructions. "Gates, gates, nothing about bloody gates, what do I do now?!" he got out of the car and pressed all the buttons. "Senor, Senor." Rich looked up to see a man running down the driveway. "Senor, senor, I so sad. Welcome. Please, please. How you say, come in." The man gestured for Rich to drive in as the gates opened. Rich drove up the drive, almost to the Villa door. Rich did not have time to get out of the car before the man was by his side. "Senor, senor, welcome, how you say congratulations." The man held out his hand; Rich shook his hand. "Welcome, senor, welcome please, senor I Migel." "Hello Migel, I am Rich." "Yes, senor, please I," said Migel, pointing to the cases. "Oh no, it's Ok. Thank you." "Senor, this is my job." Rich shrugged his shoulders and nodded as he looked around in amazement. What a beautiful place, and to think this is my home now, thought Rich.

Rich entered the villa. The entrance reminded him of Arlington Manor. It was spacious and elegant, but this one was full of natural light with natural materials of wood and Ratten. The kitchen was a large industrial one with a lovely dining area. The lounge area had plush furniture. Walking through the villa, Rich came across a beautiful internal square garden. He looked up. The roof was different coloured glass which the sun danced through, creating patterns on the walls; it was truly spectacular. The bedrooms, of which there were eight, all went off from this garden. Each bedroom had its own bathroom. Wow, thought Rich as he walked back and down the other side of the Vilia and there it was, the master bedroom. Yes, this was built for love, he thought, an enormous bed, lights that dimmed and changed colour, mirrors everywhere, including the ceiling, but all of them had a shutter so at the touch of a button you could have mirrors wherever you wanted. The bathtub was big enough for four, thought Rich.

The main garden had a lawn and palm trees, which led to a barbecue area, the other side was the swimming pool, an enormous swimming pool. As Rich continued exploring the grounds, he came across a small house and two cottages; he smiled to himself; my days of living in a small cottage were well over. He then thought about the girl she was nice; and a good fuck, but he never wanted to live like that again. He felt trapped and responsible for her. Then she started getting demanding. Rich felt a shiver go down his spine. He shook his head and body. Oh well, that's behind me. I have moved on, thought Rich as he continued exploring his new home. He came across the tennis court, a jetty, a sauna and a cave stocked with wine! Wow, whistled Rich.

Rich made his way back to the house. Migel had brought in the cases and was unpacking his stuff; he was just about to protest then realised that this is what the little man does and that he needs to act like a wealthy person, "Senor! Eh senor!" shouts Migel, "Senor er, how do you say er, maid no, no, er, half no, other half yes," Rich looked at Migel, who was waiting for a response. Rich shrugged his shoulders and gestured with his arms as if to say I don't know what the hell you are talking about.

Rich ran a bath, putting some beautiful smelling stuff into the running water; the bubbles were insane; it's been a long time since you have done this, he thought as he lay soaking. He tried to remember the last time he had a bubble bath; a wave of sadness came over him as he realised this was the first time. When he was a kid, his mother would put all the boys in one bath and scrub them one by one. Being the youngest, he was sometimes first but usually last; he hated bath times as a kid, then as he grew up, he showered wherever he was, often quickly as he was always trying to escape some women. Then there were the strip washes when he had no bath or shower, blimey he thought, look at me now! Rich was enjoying the dreaming of what was and what will be. He had been soaking for some time and feeling a bit wrinkly! Just as he made a move to get out of the bath, Migel came running into Rich's annoyance. "Senor, senor, I have my Hermana, yes," shouted Migel. "Don't you know to wait?" snapped Rich, getting back into the bathtub. "Senor, please." Then a girl appeared, "Who the fuck are you?" snapped Rich. "Sorry sir, Migel, my brother asked me to come here. His English is not good and mine is perfect," she smiled. "I am Lozena." "Well, thank you, Lozena, but I am in the bath and want to be left alone," replied Rich. "Sir, yes, of course, but my brother Migel is puzzled. Sir, where is your wife?" "My wife is dead," replied Rich, "Now, if you would please both leave and do not disturb me again." "Of course, Sir," said Lorena as she translated back to Migel. Migel gasped as he heard the news, kissing his necklace.

Rich got out of the bath, feeling relaxed but tired. He was ready for bed. Drying himself off, he noticed someone watching him through the crack in the door. Rich smiled; dirty little bitch. He knew she was giving him the eye; Rich walked around the bathroom, his body bronzed except for his boxer lines. The thought of someone watching him took him right back to the apartment when his lady was watching him; he missed that woman, the smell of her and her soft skin next to his. He wanted her! His cock was responding in agreement. Damn it, I wanted to wait, but need's must, thought Rich as he started stroking his cock. It did not take long before he had satisfied himself. Whoever had been watching had fled. Dirty bastard watching me! Bet her old man gets it tonight, thought Rich, smiling to himself as he made his way to bed.

Chapter Thirty-Two: February 10th

JO

It had taken them 20 days to sail from Maderia to the Canneries. Jo was unsure why it had taken so long, other than Angus had no clue, but they were here at last, and it felt good. Angus had secured a place to moor for two weeks, "Then we go, maid, make us way back home," said Angus. Jo ignored him. We will see, she thought. Angus's spot was next to the fishing trawlers, which were all working boats in and out of the harbour most days, bringing back lovely fresh fish. Angus's boat, although also a fishing boat, stood out like a sore thumb because of its luxurious appearance and clean interior. Not a fish in sight! Most of the fishermen were welcoming, but the crew on the adjacent boat were rough, thought Jo, and one of them gave her the creeps. Her senses had kicked in this man gave off a dangerous aura! "Shall we go exploring tomorrow?" asked Jo. "Get out for the day; what do you think?" "Yes, maid, that would be good Are you sure you want me with ya?" asked Angus. "Of course, I am not going anywhere without you." Angus smiled; he was really fond of this girl.

The following day, they left the boat early, hired a taxi and went off for the day to explore the island. Jo fell in love with a place called Playa de Ingles; it was the Gay capital; although not a capital, it was a small town with beautiful beaches, high-rise buildings and cute shops selling wooden willies, willies on a rope, rock willies in fact they were everywhere. Jo loved it. She got a sense of freedom and expression. She felt comfortable and knew she had found home! Angus on the other hand was shocked to his core with men holding hands, men kissing openly and naked men on the beaches. "Whatever is the world coming to?" he said to Jo as they had a coffee whilst people watching. Jo held his hand. "Come on, old man, this is the new way to be, you can be who you wanna be with no judgement," laughed Jo. "I'm too old maid to change, it ain't right maid, I mean look at that girl, she hardly got any clothes on, and she be eating, it's just not right," explained Angus. Jo smiled. "Well, get used to it, old man, cus this is the way of the world now." Angus nodded; he knew the world was changing He just didn't know how he would change with it, but now he had Jo, she would keep him up to date. "Ya know, maid, I be the luckiest man when that bastard put ya on me boat cus look at me now, I found a daughter." Tears welled in Jo's eyes. This man was adorable. "No, I was the lucky one, although I have to say It didn't feel lucky at the time," she Laughed.

They continued their tour of the island. It was dark when they arrived back at the boat. "I am sure I locked up and turned the lights off," said Angus as they approached the boat. "You did; why?" asked Jo. "Well, the lights are on, and it looks like someone is inside," said Angus, tensing up. Shit thought Jo picking up a stick, "What ya gonna do with that?" asked Angus. "Dun know, but I need something."whispered Jo.

As they approached the boat, the strange fisherman that Jo had taken a disliking to was just climbing off the boat. He did not appear to have anything with him. "Hey!" shouted Jo raising her stick above her head, "What the fuck ya doing, man, on our boat?" The fisherman turned and smiled at them showing his almost toothless mouth and his cold black eyes. "He is gone now, maid, put ya stick down," said Angus. "Yea, but the cheeky bastard was on our boat; he broke into our boat, Angus," shouted Jo. "Maybe I didn't lock it, maid; boats are everybodies in a harbour. It's an unsaid rule if the boat ain't locked," said Angus, Jo knew he was lying what she didn't know was why he was lying. Jo could smell the fisherman. His aura was heavy, as if he had just brought a big black cloud and dumped it on the boat. Jo searched around the boat. Nothing was missing or out of place. "Cheeky bastard," continued Jo. "Drop it, maid, no harm done," said Angus.

The following morning, Jo was up early on deck with her cup of tea, watching the comings and goings of the harbour. The fishing boats were coming in loaded with fresh fish. The fishermen were loud and jolly, not that she could understand everything but she got the impression it had been a good fishing trip. The fishing boat Ecardo, which moored opposite, had not gone out. Someone was definitely on it, thought Jo. She was sure she could see movement. Something about that boat gave Jo the creeps. "Hey, maid, you up early?" shouts Angus. "Yep, thought we could have a day just lazing around and get to know the neighbours," laughed Jo. Angus looked at Jo, then looked across at the Ecardo, "Come on, maid, come on in, don't stare at that boat, It's bad news, maid, bad news," said Angus as he made his way back below deck. Jo felt puzzled. What was he talking about? She followed Angus below deck. "You gonna tell me what's goin on? Why you so freaky?" "Ah, nothing, maid, just daft old sailors' superstitions," said Angus. "Tell me, Angus, what's wrong?" "Look, maid, they no fishermen in the Escardo, they pirates, maid, pirates. They evil men, and they don't like women on boats, we need to go," explained Angus. Jo was unsure about what she was hearing. Yes, she got a bad vibe from the boat and the strange man, but pirates! Surely, they don't exist anymore, and now Angus wants to leave. "Tell you what," says Jo. "Let's have another day out. Let's find somewhere that does a nice English Breakfast." "Now ya talking maid, then we make plans to leave," smiled Angus. Jo was thinking of plans to move on slightly, not leave. She loved the island. "We can discuss now, let's get ready, chop chop," laughed Jo.

Jo and Angus headed out for the day. They had a full English Breakfast in Jo's new favourite place, Playa de Ingles. "Come on, Angus, let's get a bus and explore the rest of the Island, Maybe find an English Roast dinner somewhere," said Jo, holding her hand out to pull Angus up from the chair. "I'm full, maid, can't move put me in a taxi and send me back to the boat. You carry on, enjoy yourself," said Angus. "I just want to sleep, maid." Jo was having none of it, "No, we stay together. I will come back if that's what you want," Angus looked at Jo, He really liked this girl. He needed to protect her from the pirates. They hated women on boats; rumour had it they burnt boats with women on them; maybe staying out was best. He had heard they were going tonight, not that he knew much Spanish, but from what he had seen, the boat was definitively getting ready to go out. "Ok, Ok, you win. We explore, but by taxi, so I can snooze," Angus smiled.

They eventually arrived back at the boat at 10 pm, both of them shattered but happy they had laughed, eaten loads of food, sunbathed and managed some shopping. "thank you for a wonderful day, Angus," said Jo. "My pleasure, maid, goodnight, maid." "Night, Angus."

That was the last time Jo saw Angus. When she awoke the following morning, Angus had gone. At first, she thought he was sleeping in; she had made her tea and sat out on deck enjoying the morning sun. The Escardo boat had gone, much to her relief. It was late morning when Jo began to worry. Strange, Angus is not up yet, she thought. Jo made him a drink and ventured down to his cabin.

"Hey, sleepyhead," Jo called out. She stopped in her tracks when she saw that his bed had not been slept in and he was nowhere to be seen!

Chapter Thirty-Three

STEPHANIE

Stephanie had been at the country hotel for a week. She felt relaxed and ready to move on. The financial settlements had all come through. She had paid the solicitor, the auctioneer and everybody else that needed it. Stephanie drew up arrangements for the land, giving the farmers far more choice in what to grow or use the land for, but now they pay rent to her. The new arrangements pleased the farmers, especially as Stephanie had invested money in new machinery for them and a new milking station.

The new Lord had already submitted plans for his land. He wanted to build a small town with shops and restaurants and a leisure centre. It was to be called Smithye Town. Stephanie shook her head as she read about his plans. She felt a touch of sadness, but it was fleeting as her mind moved to Rich. She thought about him a lot, dreaming of the times they had spent together and imagining how life would be once she got to the villa. Steph was certain Rich would be at the Vilia causing havoc, but she had no way of knowing. What she was certain of was the connection they had, and her feelings and her senses both told her he was safe and waiting for her.

Serg was doing well. The force had retired him early and, thankfully, sent him to Cornwall for recovery. He would be back soon, and she really needed to be gone, she thought.

After being released on bail, Cindy waited for her day in court. Stephanie received information that she would be a witness in court, not that Stephanie had any intention of turning up for it. Stephanie felt sorry for Cindy. After all, the girl had married her son, and maybe things would have been different if Terrance had just shagged her on their wedding day, thought Steph. Rumours were flying around that Cindy was pregnant. Maybe she will send her some money, McCormack was visiting later. She would speak to him.

"My dear Stephanie,"exclaimed McCormack, kissing Stephanie's hand, "Would you like tea?" asked Steph. "Oh yes, and some of the finest cake and maybe some ice cream and double cream on the side," he said to the waitress. The waitress looked at Stephanie. "Yes, put it on my bill, but just tea for me, please." "Hey, why you not joining me in some sweet afternoon delight," asked McCormack, smiling at Stephanie.

Stephanie ignored him, wanting to get rid of him as soon as she had signed everything. "Let's get on, shall we?" said Stephanie. They spent the next few hours going through papers and signing deals. "One more thing before you go," said Stephanie. "I do not want to proceed with prosecuting Cindy, so please plan to get the charges dropped." "No, can do, not your choice," said McCormack, leaning back in his chair, displaying his enormous belly and tight crotch." "Then make it my choice!" demanded Stephanie. "No. Can't Police don't need your permission; they have enough evidence; besides, she shot one of their own, so that's it; nothing I can do," said McCormack, speaking with his mouth full of more cake. He was really starting to annoy Stephanie. "Well, I want to give her some money. She was married to my son, after all, so can you arrange that?" asked Stephanie. "I don't advise that," said McCormack, who was now eating the remaining cream. "It will look dodgy." "DODGY?" shouted Stephanie. "What do you mean? She was my Daughter-in-law." "Who you shafted," said McCormack. "Now leave it, Stephanie, we don't want more complications, do we?" said

McCormack, finishing the ice cream. "What do you mean more complications?" asked Steph. "Look my dear Stephanie, your husband was a great friend of mine; he trusted me. I am guessing, my dear, you will head off to your luxury villa. You know, the one no one knows about apart from the trusted family solicitor? You see, your husband, my friend, trusted me with everything. It may be in your best interest to do the same. Obviously, my rate will be slightly higher now. The lord was a friend, so he had mate's rates," McCormack laughed. "But you, well, you're a cold-hearted bitch, selfish to the core. I can keep your secrets, Stephanie, for a price, let's call it professional fees!" smiled McCormack. Stephanie remained calm, her eyes turning to Ice as she stared at McCormack, disliking him more by the minute. "Why don't you have more cake and cream, Ian, because if you are blackmailing me, it had better be worth it, so tell me, what do you know, then I will decide what happens next," said Stephanie "You're one brave bitch I give you that, but you see, your dear husband told me about your affairs," laughed McCormack. "Well, this should be interesting as I didn't have any" snapped Steph. "Not only a cold bitch but one that tells lies; I have evidence. Oh, I forgot to say I have photos, my dear. It is certainly you up against the wall with your frilly knickers down, having a bit with the gardener. It's also you carry on with a young builder in the summer house; you like a bit of afternoon delight, not to mention the tramp," said McCormack, who was now pissed off he had to tell her what he had. Steph went cold when he mentioned the Tramp. "What are you talking about, a tramp?" snapped Steph. "Yes, you and the lord found a tramp. According to the Lord, you were looking after him well, in and out of his place like a dog on heat. The lord could smell him on you; shall I go on?" asked McCormack. "You disgust me!" shouted Stephanie, "now get out!" "Your fee has just gone up; I will be in touch with the details," said McCormack, struggling to get up from the low chair. Stephanie sat in silence. Bastard, she thought, now what!

Stephanie had been sitting and thinking for hours. What was she worried about? She had money and nothing to stay here for. She could sell the villa and move. McCormack would never find her. Is it really that easy, she thought? Yes, it is you can do anything you want. Her internal conversation spurred her on to book a hotel in London, a spot of shopping, then a one-way ticket to her beloved villa and, with any luck, her handsome lover would be waiting all fired up and ready for her. She smiled as she thought of Rich and knew this was the right thing to do. Nothing, and no one would take this away from her.

RICH

Rich had slept for days, just getting out of bed to drink water, eat and wee! He really needed the rest and to recharge. He awoke today feeling just that. Rich showered and dressed all before Migel appeared. "Senor? Senor, you out of bed?" shouts Migel. Rich nodded, "Senor, senor, you go out, plan? Ah, how you say stay in villa in sun?" Rich could not help but feel irritated by this dude; he was in and out like he owned the place. Rich did not respond to Migel, noisy prick, thought Rich. Migel was looking at Rich for a response, but Rich just walked away. Migel felt disappointed. The young lord was always so pleasant now. He's an arrogant snob, thought Migel although far more handsome than he remembered!

Rich pulled up a sunbed and lay in the morning sun, but he felt restless, and before long, he was on his feet exploring the villa. First, he visited all the bedrooms, trying all the beds for a bounce; the rooms were beautifully clean with everything in its place. He made his way outside towards the house and cottages. Just as he turned the corner, he saw Migel and Lozena coming out of the small house. They were arguing, both animated and loud. Rich hid behind one of the trees, assuming they would leave soon. To his surprise, he witnessed Migel grabbing Lozena, pulling her towards him and kissing her passionately. "Fuck me," Rich thought, "That's his sister." Rich wanted to move on, but he was stuck. If he moved now, they might see him and think he was some dirty pervert! Rich looked on as the pair ripped each other's clothes off. You got a nice body, babe, but fuck me, you need to shave, thought Rich as he continued to watch them. Migel was a small-built man, but his cock was impressive. Wow, good on ya, man, nearly as good as mine. No wonder she wants it laughed Rich to himself. Lozena went on all fours, allowing Migel to mount her like a dog in heat. Rich continued to watch as Migel banged away. Hurry, dude, do the deed and fuck off, thought Rich. I don't know how much longer I can stay in this position. My fuckin' foot is cramping. Rich was rubbing his foot. He could hear Migel slapped up against her arse. She started to scream. Then it all went quiet. Rich looked up to see the pair getting dressed. "Damn, I missed the best part, but at least those dirty bastards will be gone." thought Rich.

Rich made his way through the garden and towards the cottages, "Senor, good morning." Rich turned around; it was Lozena. How the fuck did she get behind him? "Senor, what are you doing here?" asked Lozena. "Why can't I come here?" "Oh yes, of course, sir, but this is for servants; it is servants' quarters." "Who lives here then?" asked Rich. "Migel and I share the house, and in the summer, the cottages are let to people working the land." "What land?" asked Rich. "Er, your land, sir, your farmland. We grow tomatoes, bananas, strawberries and lemons," Lozena replied, looking puzzled. "And what is your job?" asked Rich. "I help Migel, sir." "That's your brother, right?" questioned Rich. "Yes, sir, my brother, He very busy and needs help. He get very angry, no er stress, and he need to be relieved. He does everything: the swimming pool, the grounds, inside the house, shopping, laundry, cleaning everything, sir, whatever you want, he will do!" said Lozena, smiling at Rich. "Anytime you want to go out, Senor, I take you, I come with you, help you be your guide. Rich looked at Lozena; her face was flushed. She was a pretty girl, but he got a strange vibe from her, one that told him to stay clear of her. "Well, that's nice of ya. I will let you know, bin nice talkin to ya.!" Rich walked away; thank fuck for that strange bird, he thought. He made his way down to the jetty. It was overgrown with reeds. Rich made a mental note to get Migel out here to cut them down. He stood at the water's edge. So why a jetty and no boat, he thought. "Boat in the boat shed," Rich was startled, Lozena was standing behind him; she had changed into a see-through lace dress, Rich could see she had no underwear on. "Shall I show you, senor?" "No. No thanks," said Rich, pushing past her, his elbow accidentally brushing her nipple. "Excuse me. I am sorry," said Rich, "It was an accident." "Don't be

silly; I won't tell if you won't. Anyway, it was nice; maybe you would like to feel more," said Lozena, looking at Rich. "No, I ain't interested," snapped Rich as he made his way back to the house.

Rich poured himself a drink and sat in the sun. It was not long before Migel was fussing around him. For fuck's sake, what is it with these two.? thought Rich. "Senor! Senor, you have some food? Migel make the best tapas you want?" "Yes, yes," said Rich, just wanting him to go. "Senor, please come" Migel had produced a lunch fit for a king. The selection of tapas was beyond anything Rich had ever had before. "wow, thank you. Is this all for me? I won't be able to eat all of this. "Si, Senor." Rich sat down to enjoy the food when Lozena walked in. "My brother says you asked us to join you. How kind of you," said Lozena, smiling at Rich. As Migel and Lozena chatted in Spanish and devoured most of the food, Rich sat quietly, taking it all in. Rich felt his temper rising, fuckin'' ignorant pair! Rich got up from the table, angrily pushing away his plate. He picked up some bread and a banana, shoved them together and bit into the sandwich, staring at both of them. "My brother thinks you don't like the food," said Lozena, who had tomato juice all around her mouth. "I don't," Rich responded, "It's shit. I want you both to go once ya eaten all the fuckin' food and cleared all the mess up and don't come back. I don't need any help," snapped Rich as he walked away heading outside to cool down.

Rich made his way to the cave; it was cold and damp, and it had beautiful lights expertly structured into the walls. Wow, Rich let out a whistle. This is some place. Bottles of wine adorned the walls, all secured in racks. Rich picked a bottle. He did not know what the label stated, but someone had written a year on it. He picked up more bottles. All had a year recorded on them. "That's when they were made and bottled here on the estate." Rich turned around to see Lozena, "You again! You following me?" snapped Rich. "Yes, I am. Problem with that?" asked Lozena. "Yea, I do, I don't want ya following, now piss off!" said Rich. Lozena laughed, "You play hard to get. I see in your eyes you want this." She lifted her dress, exposing her pussy. "You a man, you need a bit of this; it will be our secret. Look, It's wet for you," smiled Lozena. "Just fuck off!" shouted Rich, "I ain't interested." "Not so quick, senor; why you not understanding me. I am here giving you free pussy, no commitment, just slip it in me, relive yourself; we say no more." Rich began to panic. "Will you get out of my fuckin' way? I ain't interested in ya," Shouted Rich as he pushed past her. Lozena lost her balance, slipping on the wet floor. She fell backwards, banging her head on the cave floor. Rich heard the crack as she hit the ground. "What the fuck!?" Rich ran out of the cave and into the daylight. "Fuck! What the Fuck just happened!?" With sweat pouring from him, Rich ran back to the house jumping straight into the pool, swimming the lengths of the pool as if his life depended on it. He swam until he exhausted himself, eventually relaxing in the spa jets. *What on earth just happened? Why does this shit follow me around? Why did I walk away?* Rich's mind was full of thoughts. What the fuck do I do? He lay on the sunbed, thinking. "Senor! Senor! You like *alimento?"* shouts Migel. Rich had fallen asleep. "What?" he questioned with his eyes half open. Migel was pretending to pick up something and put it in his mouth whilst rubbing his stomach. "Oh, food," said Rich, nodding. "Yeah, why not?" Migel prepared a salad with fish and steak with four different dressings. Rich smiled. "Perfecto, Migel, perfecto!" Migel bowed his head and left. Rich enjoyed the food, eating most of the steak and fish, getting bread and dipping in the dressing. Migel had left him alone,which was the best bit thought Rich as he stretched out his arms. He was relaxed, full of food and ready for bed, then the image of Lozena lying on the cold floor came flooding back to him, fuck, what am I gonna do!

Chapter Thirty-Four

JO 6 AM

Jo had spent the last four days looking for Angus. She had asked everyone, but no one had seen him. Jo believed the Escardo crew had something to do with it. It seemed strange that the boat went out to sea, and that was the last time she saw Angus. Jo hoped the silly fool had agreed to go proper fishing with them and he would come back soon. Jo was awake but lying, thinking about Angus and what to do next, when she heard a commotion on deck. What the fuck is going on? Jo threw on some clothes and headed to the deck. The crew greeted her from the Escardo, who must have sailed back in last night. They were picking stuff up, dropping it or throwing it into the harbour. "Hey, what do ya think ya doing," shouted Jo. The man Jo had described as odd, the one that gave her the creeps, pushed his way through the men and approached Jo. *"Este es Nuestros BarcoBébé Tu Viejo lo aposto,"* he shouted as they all laughed. *"Se escapo llorando como lina bebe. "* The men were laughing. Jo stood her ground, staring at the strange man whose eyes were blacker than black. She could smell the anger and hatred within him, almost like it oozed out of him. *"Asi que senora empaque sus cosas y vayase porque estoes mio y no megustan las mujeres enmi barco ahora is, "* he shouted. Jo continued to stare at him. She did not know what he was saying but felt it was not good, "Ma'am." Jo looked up to see a young lad standing on the wall. "Yes?" said Jo. "Ma'am, the man says you must leave the boat. It is his boat; he won it in a competition." "He is lying. Ask him what competition." The young lad exchanged Spanish. "No, ma'am, it was a bet; your husband was gambling, and he lost. He gambled the boat, so you must leave," said the boy. "Ask him about Angus; where is

Angus, the man from this boat, please," said Jo. Again, the lad exchanged Spanish. A few of the men laughed, but others looked away. "He is gone, ma'am, he er… walked into the sea." Jo dropped to the floor. "No, no, not Angus," Jo screamed, "He would never do that,." The men surrounded Jo, "Ma'am, you must go; they do not want you on this boat. They think it is bad luck, ma'am. A woman is bad luck on a boat." The men picked up Jo. "Get your fuckin' hands off me," Jo shouted as she fought them off. They all backed off, apart from the odd one. He shouted something at the boy, "Ma'am, he said if you don't go, he will… well, he said he will er… he said he will force you," said the boy, who was visibly shaken. Jo sensed things had turned. After collecting her few belongings, she was escorted off the boat. Jo stood by the young boy, who actually looked older now that she was near him. "Thank you," Jo said as she handed him ten euros. "No problem. What you do now?" he asked. "I don't know; head for Playa and see what happens. I will go to the police and report this," said Jo. "If you know what's best, you will leave it, ma'am; they are not nice men; they will hunt you down and hurt you." Jo looked at him, "What did he really say he would do if I did not leave the boat?" The boy blushed, "he said he would cut your tits off and throw them to the sharks." Jo felt suddenly sick and shaken. "You Ok, ma'am?" asked the boy. "Yes. Thank you. I better go." Jo walked away, tears rolling down her face.

The taxi dropped Jo off in Playa De Ingles. She would find somewhere to stay and then figure the rest out. Jo had money. She had collected all the cash Angus had hidden on the boat and Angus had insisted on her having access to his bank. Jo's eyes welled up as she thought about Angus and that she may not see him again. She walked around looking for somewhere open, eventually, she found a cafe open, "English; do you speak English?" asked Jo. "Yes. Sure, ma'am." "Oh That's a relief," said Jo as she sat down. "Is it always this quiet?" asked Jo. "It's early. No bugger up yet, all out partying last night." Jo smiled, "Sounds fun." "Yeah, it is fun here at night but not so good when you have to get up like me; anyway, what you want?" "A large coffee and some toast and somewhere to stay," replied Jo. "Oh, how long you staying?" "Forever," Jo replied. The guy looked at Jo, "Running away from something?" "You could say that." The guy nodded. "Yeah, most people are, especially here we are all running from something." "You can't be running; you look sorted," said Jo. "I'm living the dream I work in a cafe during the day and a drag bar at night, no time off to enjoy the sun and still can't pay my rent. It's not all; it's cracked up to be. This town is full of people running away, hiding away from life, but it's hard, ma'am." Jo looked at the guy; she could see the pain in his eyes, "Go back then," she said, "Go back." "No, no, no way, I can't go back." "Then get a better job." "It's not that easy out here if you're not Spanish. Sure, I speak the language, but I ain't Spanish, so all the good jobs have gone. I could sell drugs, but I am not into that shit. I stay clear of that, but it's difficult trying to make an honest living." Jo could see the tiredness in the guy, "Well, at least you have a place to stay; I am going out to get a room, so wish me luck." Jo smiled at the cafe owner, "See you later?, " "Yep, I will be here as usual," he sighed.

While it was still quiet, Jo walked around for a while, getting a feel of the area. The street cleaners were busy, and the smells from the bakery shops wafted through the air. She booked into a hotel for a week. That would give her enough time to find Angus, she thought. The hotel provided a clean and comfortable environment. The room offered a view of the beach. It had everything she needed for now. She showered, then headed out for something to eat. She wanted to explore the town and talk more to the man in the cafe. She was sure he would know who to speak to about missing persons. The cafe was bustling with people, and the poor man struggled to keep up with the work. Jo watched him for a while, "Hey mate, let me help you," as she picked up some dirty dishes. For the next two hours, Jo washed dishes, served the food and cleared tables while the man took the orders and cooked the food. Eventually, the cafe was quiet, and Jo could sit down. "Here is a coffee; you deserve it; thank you for your help. You were great!" Jo looked up as the man came and sat with her. "I enjoyed it. Is it always that busy?" asked Jo. "Yes, I always get a rush when everyone is heading out. The next one will be lunch, it's loads of sandwiches and takeaways, then it can go quiet. Anyway, what's your name?" "Jo. And yours?" "Robin, and I am pleased to meet you, Jo. I can't pay you for your help, but I can offer you a nice Breakfast," smiled Robin. "Hey, it's Ok. I don't want you to pay. You needed help, and I really enjoyed it. I would love breakfast. Thank you. Will you join me?" asked Jo. "No, I have to get on with the preparation for lunch and bake the cakes. A woman's work is never done," laughed Robin. "Did you find somewhere to stay, by the way?" "Yes," said Jo as she explained briefly her plans to stay in the hotel for a week, then get somewhere more permanent. Robin had heard it all before: so many people running away from something, so why not run away to the sun, get a little job, spend days in the sun, and party at night? All sounds wonderful, but the reality was it was a fuckin' hard life if you wanted to make an honest living.

Jo walked around the town. It was getting busier. The shops were all open, displaying their items trying to entice people in with special offers. Jo stopped to buy the latest fake designer gear. She tried on the latest perfume and purchased some beach shoes. She walked along the beach and then headed back to the hotel.

Jo lay on the bed thinking of Angus and how much she missed him. The thought of not seeing him again made her really sad. Despite that, she felt contented. She felt like she fitted in and that everything would work out!

It was 9 pm when Jo woke. Fuck, I have been asleep for hours. It's fuckin'' dark; Jo smiled to herself. Sea air always knocks me out, but I'm starving. She showered and headed out. "Madam, you are not going out alone, are you?" Jo looked up to see a mature man at reception. "Yep. Why?" "Well, madam, it is rough out there; a woman should not be alone. It is how you say, a man's world; it is not for the ladies." "Look, anyone tries it on with me, well, let's just say I hope they like hospital food because believe me, what I have been through over the last few months, I ain't scared of no one," replied Jo. The reception man threw his arms up, shrugged his shoulders and walked away. That told him, thought Jo. I'm no little pussy woman! Jo made her way into the centre of town, which was already full of drunken men. Jo smiled to herself. This would mortify Angus to see men holding hands wearing very little, some in drag, some in suits. Jo had even passed some drug dealing going on and a few having sex! Jo was unsure why most of the people were men. It's lively, thought Jo, who was desperately looking for a place to eat.

Jo found herself in one of the many drag bars. She ordered a drink and a burger. The drag act was Ok, the burger was Ok, but the beer was nice and cold. Various men joined her throughout the night, all drunk and wanting to tell her their problems. Jo sat and listened as, one by one, they dumped their shit and left her with her beer! At least the music banged, she thought. "Hi, I'm Karen." Jo looked up to see an attractive woman in her 40s wearing very little, bending over her. "Hi, I'm Jo." "I've been watching you; you're new around here," said

Karen. "Yes, came in today." "Ah! Holiday,?" "No, no, I'm staying. I want to stay forever." Karen laughed, "Oh honey, that's what they all say, but best of luck to you. I will see you around then, Jo, maybe we could hang out. Do you do lines?" asked Karen. "Lines?" questioned Jo. Karen took Jo's hand and kissed it. "Don't worry darling, to make this place work, you might need it. Maybe one day I show you what it can do," said Karen, winking at Jo as she left. Wow, thought Jo, she was some hot mama. I'm gonna like it here!

Stephanie

Stephanie arrived at the villa at 2.30 am. She had been travelling for twelve hours. The flight delay of four hours caused Stephanie's transport to not wait for her as it was past midnight, leaving her with 15 cases and the need to find someone to help her.

She made her way into the master bedroom. Her heart skipped a beat. There he was, sleeping, a thin sheet covering his body. He looked tanned and beautiful. Tears welled up inside her as she felt relief that he was here and the anticipation of the future. She was tired from travelling so took one of the other bedrooms to rest.

The Villa 10 am

Rich could not believe how long he had been sleeping. The sun and doing nothing made him tired! Rich showered and dressed, expecting Migel to come in at any moment. Then he remembered the cave and Lozena. He went cold Fuck I never went back, what's wrong with you, man? Fuck, what am I gonna do now? thought Rich, slamming his hands against the wall. You're a fuckin'' idiot; that's what you are, he said to his reflection in the mirror. Rich made his way to the kitchen for breakfast. Strange Migel was nowhere to be seen. Then he saw the suitcases rushing over to them to check the labels. One case was unlocked. Rich opened it, and it was full of silk underwear. Rich touched the fabric, rubbing the material on his face and smelling her scent on the garments. Rich could hardly breathe. She had made it! Tears ran down his face. I need to tell her everything; she needs to know I am not bad. Rich headed for the bedroom to find his lady.

Rich stopped in his tracks; he could hear her talking to a man who sounded like he had a cockney accent. She had brought someone with her; his heart sank. "Get out of here, Migel, do some bloody work. I have 15 cases that need unpacking," she laughed. Rich felt stupid. The prick could speak English. He felt his fists tighten up. He hated being made to look a fool. Rich burst through the door. "Morning, beautiful lady." Steph looked up to see her Rich. She held her arms open. "My darling," she sighed as Rich fell into them. They kissed and cuddled for hours, taking in the emotions. It wasn't about sex; it was more than that. It was a connection, a connection that had broken and was now repairing.

Hours had passed, and Rich and Steph were still in bed holding each other, kissing, being silent together, lost in the emotions they were feeling. Stephanie had never felt such a strong connection with someone; she wanted him so much. Rich had never felt such powerful emotions towards anyone as he felt for this woman. It hurt him to think of anyone else looking at her, let alone talking to her. Rich knew this could be dangerous; he knew feelings like this ignited not only passion but extreme jealousy within him, and it was something he was going to have to work hard on! Steph broke the silence, "My darling, shall we get up and eat and enjoy the last bit of sun?" "As long as I'm with you, I don't care what we do," replied Rich. "Come on then, sweetie." Steph got out of bed and began to dress. Rich watched her.

He really adored this woman, but why hadn't he ripped her clothes off and fucked her? His dick wasn't hard. "You look puzzled, darling; what is it?" asked Steph. "Nothing," replied Rich. "For this to work, we need to be honest. Now, what's wrong?" Rich looked at her, "I love you; I have wanted nothing more than to be with you, but me dick's not hard, and well, I didn't think about fuckin'g you." Steph smiled, "It's Ok; we needed to reconnect on a deeper level than just sex, I think we have connected, and do you know what? My pussy is wet for you, so I think if you were to slip a finger in, I would probably cum all over you," Steph smiled. Rich grabbed her, inserting his finger, "Fuckin'g hell, babe, you were not lying." Rich had only been in her for a minute when he felt her riding his fingers. "There, go for it, babe, that's it, just let it go," whispered Rich. Steph screamed as she let go of all the tension. His cock was throbbing; Steph sat on him and rode him like she was riding a stallion. "That's it, babe, Harder, babe! Oh, my God babe, I'm--" Rich screamed like he had never screamed before, lost inside his woman as he gave everything he hadto give.!

They lay silent for a while. "Come on then, time to eat. Do you feel better now?" asked Steph. "Much better," smiled Rich. "I think I could go again." Steph smiled, "Not before we eat. I'm starving," she turned to Rich, "Things will be good, sweetie, but we need to be honest with each other about everything; no surprises." "About everything?" questioned Rich. "Yes, everything, for this to work, no secrets, but let's get some food. I imagine Migel has been busy," said Steph, holding her hand out to Rich.

Migel had not been around. In fact, nothing had been done. Her cases were still in the hall, the pool checks were not done, no food was prepared, no laundry was done. "This is strange," said Steph,

"Migel has not been around. I saw him early this morning, but nothing has been done." Steph prepared the food for them. "What's the deal with him?" asked Rich. Steph laughed, "Don't tell me he told you he did not speak English and acted dumb around you." "Yeah, he did." "He is a cockney lad. Spanish parents as gay as you like, that's why he was acting strange around you," laughed Steph. "Lying little bastard," said Rich. "Hang on, he's not gay," said Rich. "Yes, yes, sweetie, he is." "No, no, I saw him; he was fuckin'g a woman outside his house" Steph looked puzzled, "Why would he be fuckin'g anyone outside his house? Unless he knew you were watching, dirty pervert," laughed Steph. "No, I was out walking, and they just started, so I hid until it was over," Rich explained. "You say a woman, are you sure, sweetie?" questioned Steph. "Yeah, I know the fuckin'' difference; he introduced her as his sister when I first arrived." "Oh, Lozena," said Steph. "Yes, that's her." "What!? And he was fuckin'g her, are you sure, sweetie?" questioned Steph ",YES! I was minding my own business; first, they were arguing, then he was fuckin'g her," explained Rich. "She is strange," said Steph, "I don't really like her here; to be honest, she gives me the creeps; maybe Migel isn't gay anymore," said Steph. "Steph, it's his fuckin'' sister! That's sick; you need to get rid of them," said Rich. Steph looked at Rich, "I know they are strange, but Migel is a hard worker. Did Lozena come on to you?" asked Steph. "NO," replied Rich. Steph looked at Rich. "And the truth is?" questioned Steph. "YES," said Rich. "When, where and what happened?" "Nothing fuckin'' happened. What do you take me for?" said Rich, raising his voice. Steph looked at Rich, "Like I said, we need to be honest; now tell me where" "By the jetty, she came on to me. I pushed past her and ran away " said Rich. "The girl is strange, Rich; you need to keep away from her. I will ask Migel to move her out, Now, sweetie, let's go for a walk. Take me to the jetty," said

Steph. "I can take you up the jetty if you wish, me lady," Rich replied, winking. "Stop it, young man or I will punish you." Rich looked at Steph, smiling as she held out her hand, "Come on."

They walked around the grounds, chatting about the villa, the gardens, and their plans. Migel was sitting outside his house. "Migel, Migel, anything wrong?" shouted Steph. Migel looked up and signalled for them to come down to him. "What is it, Migel?" asked Steph. "It's my sister; she missing. I don't know what to do; she is not well, she cannot be alone, she needs medication, she not well, she not let me know," said Migel franticly. "I am sure she will be back soon; maybe she has gone shopping," said Steph. "No, you not understand. She is not allowed out alone; she knows this. What am I going to do?" "We will help you look for her," said Steph, elbowing Rich. "Oh yeah, man, we will look," said Rich, who was getting bored with the conversation. "No" protested Migel, "She not here; I look everywhere, she gone. She not well, she not allowed on her own." "Migel, you take what time you need. If you need to search the Island, then do it. Maybe she has taken herself to the hospital or something," said Steph, not really knowing what to say. "We will manage things here; you check friends and family, favourite places, and I am sorry to say again, but maybe hospitals," said Steph, rubbing Migel's shoulder. Steph and Rich walked off, "Oh, I bet you have not seen our cave, have you? Come on, let me show you," said Steph excitedly. "You know, babe, I am not feeling good, think I may lie down," said Rich. "Ok, sweetie, the cave can wait," said Steph, gently rubbing his back as they made their way back to the house.

Rich lay down on the bed. Steph left him to rest as she unpacked her cases and prepared some food. "Hey, sweetie, how you doing?" she said gently. "I have made some food. Do you fancy a little something?" "Dun know, babe, I am tired, don't think I fancy anything," moaned Rich. "Ok, sweetie," said Steph walking away. Rich lay in bed thinking about the women on the cave floor. She must be dead by now. How the hell did I get into this fuckin'' trouble? It follows me. Why me? Why didn't I tell Steph? Why didn't I go back? I'm not a bad man.

Rich's mind was all over the place as he tried to sleep. He was thrashing about in bed. Steph watched him. He was clearly having some kind of nightmare. She decided not to disturb him and to sleep in another room.

Rich felt agitated, and she did not care she's left him. She thinks she's in charge. He needs her, and she is nowhere near him. He got out of bed, feeling annoyed as he walked around the house. She had clearly had food and left him nothing. He poured a drink. Bitch, who does she think she is? Nobody does this to me. Rich finished another brandy and went to look for her.

Steph was sleeping; Rich entered the bedroom and climbed into the bed, pushing her so that she would wake. "Hey, how you feeling" murmured Steph. "What do you fuckin'' care?" snapped Rich. "Excuse me?" "You heard me. You're a fuckin'' bitch leaving me alone. I needed you, and you left me; you don't care. In fact, I don't know why I'm here," shouted Rich. Steph felt disoriented, but she could feel the tension in Rich. "Ok, what on earth is this?" she asked. "Like I said, you're a fuckin'' bitch; you don't give a fuck about me, leaving me alone when I needed you," shouted Rich. Steph got out of bed, quickly slipped on a silk robe to cover her naked body and left the room without saying a word. Rich lay in bed, wondering what just happened.

Steph made her way to the master bedroom. She climbed into bed and tried to sleep. She heard Rich enter the room and climb into bed next to her. He went to cuddle her. "Take your fuckin'' hands off me!" said Steph. Rich ignored her, "I said take your hands off me," as she tried to remove them. Rich held her tightly, "No, you're not going anywhere." Rich pulled her into him; his cock was hard and slid between her legs. "Get off me!" protested Steph. "No, I don't think so."

"I said no!" "And I said YES, it's time you learnt who is in charge around here." Rich pulled her hair, her head went backwards as he sunk his teeth into her neck. "Stop! Stop!" she protested. The more she struggled, the more turned on Rich became. "Ya know, ya getting it, so just relax," whispered Rich. "Fuck off!" snapped Steph. "I said no" Rich had hold of her; she was going nowhere. He slipped his finger inside her. "So you don't want it? Hmm, I think you do; I think you're a fuckin'' liar," he whispered as his cock entered her from behind. "Rich, no, no!" she screamed. It was too late. He was riding her. The force of his fuckin'g was intense. He was only thinking of power and dominance, and it felt good. He knew her no'S were role-play. "You're a fuckin'' bitch do ya hear me? You take it when I say you're all mine, and I'll fuck you when I want," Rich whispered to her as he emptied himself into her. Collapsing on top of her, they both lay silent. Steph tried to move. "Hey, not so fast; I'm not finished with you. You're mine; no one else is ever gonna make love to you, no one else will ever touch you, and no one else will ever satisfy you," Rich whispered into her ear as his fingers worked her pussy." "Come on, babe, let it go. Come on babe, let me have it, let me taste you. Tell me, babe, tell me when." "NOW! NOW, RICH! NOW!" Rich smiled as he lay down, feeling totally satisfied. Steph lay down, feeling satisfied but concerned and confused. Steph knew shouting at him would just ignite him. She did not know how to play this, and she desperately wanted to shout at him. She sensed she had just experienced a dark side to him. "Babe," whispered Rich, "I'm sorry I got carried away. I don't know what came over me. Babe, say something. "Yes, you got carried away, Rich," said Steph. "Did I hurt you?" asked Rich. "Yes, a little; my insides are sore; you really went at me." "I know, I know, it's you. I just want you, and then I think about someone else having you, and I see red," said Rich. "What's this about Rich? What's going on? You don't have to be like this with me," Steph said, looking into his eyes. "I can't go to prison, Steph, and leave you for someone else." "What are you talking about, " asked Steph. Rich started to cry, "I'm sorry, Steph, I have let you down, but it wasn't my fault; I'm scared, Steph," said Rich Steph was puzzled, "Rich, what is it? Tell me?" "The girl. I think I killed her," Rich blurted out. "What, girl?" "You know the one missing? I think she is dead." Steph sat up, "You had better tell me everything." Rich explained what had happened. "I should have gone back." "Yes, you should; well, you should never have left her," shouted Steph, shaking her head. "Why the fuck didn't you get help?" "I don't know, I forgot. Don't ask me," shouted Rich.

"Ok, Ok, let's think about this: when it's light, we have to go to the cave and call for help," said Steph. "No, no, we can't do that," said Rich. "So what do we do?" "We pick up the body and put it in the lake," explained Rich. "What!? I can't do that." "Yes, we must, it's the only way." "I can't do that; it is not right." "It's the only way, Steph, trust me." "No, Rich, I won't do that." Rich looked at Steph; he thought she understood him, he thought she would support him, but no, she wanted to do things her way. "I trusted you," said Rich. "I opened my heart to you, and now look, you don't love me; you're just fuckin'' using me. If you loved me, you would help me," said Rich.

"I do love you, Rich, but this is not the way that poor man needs to know where his sister is; he will never get peace. Think about it, Rich, do the right thing," begged Steph. "Stay out of it, Steph; let me deal with the mess the way I want." Shouted Rich "NO, RICH, we do things together," Steph held his hand. "TOGETHER," she said.

Chapter Thirty-Five

BACK IN ENGLAND

"Mr Henerson, pleased to meet you, McCormack," as McCormack held out his hand to shake Hen's.

"Please sit down, tea, coffee?"

"Tea, milk and sugar, and some of the finest cakes, please."

"Well McCormack, word has it you're an excellent solicitor, discreet I hear, for a price."

McCormack laughed. "Not sure I understand."

"Oh, I think you do, sir; not everything is legitimate. I am told you make it safe, and money buys your silence," said HEN, staring at McCormack.

"Well, Mr. Henderson, what can I do for you?"

"Information, McCormack, Information," Hen continued. "£1000, I give you right here and now to know where Lady Arlington is."

"Mr. Henderson, you insult me."

"£2,000."

"£3000."

"£4000."

"£5000. Exactly how much do ya fuckin'' want?" shouted Hen.

"That will do," said McCormack.

"Ok, so where is she?"

"Spain."

"Spain? Fuckin'' Spain? Where in Spain? It's a big fuckin'' place," shouts Hen.

"Well, that will cost you a lot of money."

"Ok, McCormack, stop playing games."

"Hey, Mr. Henderson, please remember you want something from me, not the other way round. Information is power, and right now, I have it. Also, I am a very loyal man. I get paid to be loyal, so I bid you a good day and thank you for the tea and delicious cake," McCormack got up to leave.

"Hey, finish your tea."

"No, thank you, sir; I really don't want to be seen with you. I know who you are,"

"One million," shouted HEN.

McCormack stopped in his tracks. "Excuse me, sir, what did you say?"

"You heard me; I said one million quid for the information."

"I will think about it, as I said. I am very loyal."

"But how loyal? Two million loyal?" asked Hen.

"Mr Henderson, I work with very wealthy clients, so one million two million three million does not really turn my head," said McCormack, walking away.

Hen was furious. Fuckin'' wanker; no one walks away from me. He was not sure what his next move would be. Hen called his trusted people, "follow McCormack. I wanna know everything, where he goes, who he works with, what his weaknesses are, I want to know fuckin'' everything about the wanker, everything do ya hear me!!" he shouted

McCormack got back into his car. He was relieved to be alive. Mr Henderson had quite a reputation, but I'm in control. He wants what I have, smiled McCormack to himself. Henderson's interest in the posh bitch's location intrigued McCormack. Speaking of her, the fuckin'g bitch never paid him. McCormack laughed to himself. The bitch has no idea what I know; I know where the Vilia is, and I know how to get to her through Migel. McCormack smiled when he thought of Migel and the times they had spent together. They met in a bar, and it was not long before Migel became McCormack's servant; one day, Migel over- heard the Lord talking about his plans for Spain and all the land he had. It wasn't long after that Migel was in Spain and became the general manager. McCormack never found out what he had to do to get the job. Anyway, best I contact the bitch. I think five million will keep me quiet for now!

BACK AT THE VILLA.

Rich woke early, "Hey princess, wake up; we have a body to get rid of," whispered Rich. Steph had been awake most of the night thinking about the situation. Steph rolled over. "Rich, I can't let you get involved with this; it's too risky. I'm scared, Rich, something will happen to you." "Hey, this is all my fault; it's my mess; now come on," said Rich, grabbing her hand. "No, listen, Rich, there is another way." "What would that be?" asked Rich. "We send Migel to the cave to get some special wine, we tell him we are celebrating, he finds the body, we all act surprised and upset, and he deals with it; the end. Rich looked at Steph, "Your plan is too simple, Steph; it won't work."

"Why?" asked Steph. Rich thought about it. "I don't know why, it just wont " "You need to trust me. It will work. In fact, you need to go out for the day and leave everything to me," said Steph. Rich was no coward, but maybe she was right; he needed to stay out of trouble, but he was the boss, he was the man; she was his woman, and man is always boss, thought Rich, staring at her. It was as if she knew what he was thinking. "Rich, I know you like to be in control, but sometimes, sweetie, brute force and testosterone need to be put to one side for calculation and control," Rich smiled. Maybe she is right on this occasion. They showered together, made love, and showered again. "No, not again, sweetie," laughed Steph. "Maybe later now, put it away." "Oh, come on, babe, it's standing erect for you; it wants your mouth around it, pleeeease," begged Rich. Steph could not resist; she knelt down in the shower, the water cascading down on her, Rich's cock in her mouth; she sucked and licked him until he was ready to burst. "Babe, now babe, I'm gonna… ahhhh," Steph's mouth held on to his cock as Rich emptied into it. "Fuck me babe, I'm weak;

my legs are jelly," Steph smiled. "That's how I like my men," she winked.

They ate breakfast and Rich set off for his day out "are you sure" he asked "yes now go and Rich stay out of trouble" said Steph smiling at him "I love you Steph and when I get back I'm goanna" "shhh don't tell me" laughed Steph "Now go" Rich looked at Steph I'm gonna ask you to marry me he thought.

Steph felt nervous, but it was the only way to protect him. With the rumours and Serg's account, she had enough reason to suspect that whatever he had done back home wasn't good. She had never asked him; she hoped one day he would tell her. Steph was no fool. She knew being with Rich came with risks, but her feelings for him were immense. She had never felt so much passion for someone, and she did not want to give that up at the moment. She experienced a sense of aliveness with him, feeling wanted and desired as a woman should. In her heart, she knew he was bad, but right now, he was what she needed. No ties, no fuss, no commitment.

Steph made her way down to Migel's house as he was making his way to the main house. "Morning, Migel; I was on my way to see you. How are you? Is there any news on your sister?" asked Steph. Migel held his arms out to greet Steph. "I am sorry I overslept. I just coming to do my jobs, I tired been at hospital all night," said Migel. "Hey it's Ok. I told you to take all the time you need, so are you ill?" asked Steph. "No, no, not me, my sister; she have operation on her brain last night," said Migel as he started to cry. Steph felt confused, "Come on, let's get some tea, and you can tell me all about it." Steph held onto Migel as they made their way back to the house, "Please take a seat. Do you want Tea, coffee, or brandy?" asked Steph. Migel looked shattered, "Coffee with brandy, please." Steph's mind was racing as she made the drinks. Must be some kind of mistake, she thought. "Here you go now, start fromat the beginning." Migel sat back in the chair, "My sister, she was found in the street, someone attacked her. Hit her over the head and left her to die, brutal the attack, brutal. Lucky someone found her, when they did, she had a clot on her brain and last night had surgery, it's touch and go, touch and go if she will ever be the same again," said Migel, crying. Steph listened, feeling really confused by what he was saying. "So where exactly was she found, and where was she attacked?" "They found her in the service lane to the fields," said Migel, crying. "So, who found her?" asked Steph. "I don't know, some kind man walking his dog. I don't know anymore. She has been unconscious." "So, how do you know she was attacked?" asked Steph. "It's the only explanation for such an injury. Whoever did it raped her and left her to die," Migel broke down crying. Steph froze, her mind racing with all kinds of thoughts; she poured large Brandy's for both of them. Migel downed his immediately and looked for another. "Yes, help yourself," said Steph. Migel got up from the chair; he was a little unsteady on his feet as he made his way to get more Brandy; a note dropped out from his sleeve. Steph noticed it but decided not to say anything; it would be a shopping list or something. "What hospital is she in?" asked Steph. "Why?" "I will visit her," said Steph. "No, no, she would not like that, she can get a bit er strange, she know you don't like her, and she don't like you," said Migel "Sorry ma'am, but she not well, she saying things." "What things?" asked Steph. "Ignore me ma'am, I tired it's probably nothing," said Migel. "What things is she saying?" asked Steph. "She saying your man attacked her." Steph looked at Migel, "So when did she say that Migel? Because you just said she was unconscious, so when did she say that?" demanded Steph. "Look, I don't want no trouble, but that's what I heard and-" Steph interrupted.

"And you are going to blackmail me? Well, I thought more of you, Migel, but they all come out of the woodwork eventually. You're lying, Migel, and we are done. I want you and your sister gone from my land; find yourself somewhere else to live. I am not unreasonable. I will buy you a house for your services, but if you ever come back for more, I will make sure everyone knows what you and your sister get up to; I think you will find out, it's illegal."

Migel was feeling brave; he had Brandy inside him, and he was fired up with anger the bitch had just sacked him. "You think you can just dismiss me like that? I know too much; you have a big shock coming to you," Migel laughed. "We will see who's laughing when McCormack gets hold of you." "McCormack?" questioned Steph. "Yes, yes, you did not know I know him, he after you, he asked me to leave you a note to scare you, frighten you out of your little silk panties," laughed Migel, who was very drunk and was now searching around his sleeves for something. Steph watched him closely, edging closer to the kitchen drawer. She may need something to protect herself, "Migel, I think it is time you left; we have nothing more to discuss. You need to pack and leave." "I not going anywhere, lady, you cannot dismiss me like some cheap labour. I have given years to this place to your family; this is my home, and I not leaving." "You are, Migel; YOU'RE LEAVING NOW!" Steph screamed. Migel looked at Steph, who was holding a long knife in her hand. "Don't think I won't use it, now fuck off out of my house and don't come back. Pack your things up and find yourself somewhere else to live; now go!" Migel was unsure if she had the nerve to do anything. Should he push her some more or leave her? "Feeling brave are you? I know the big fellow is not here; now he's a stud. I wouldn't mind a bit of him myself, not sure what he's doing with you, an old bird, guess it's your money, and you're an easy fuck, or so I have heard," laughed Migel.

Stephanie felt the anger rise inside her, "I said fuck off! I gave you the opportunity to leave, but oh no, you have to stay and push me." Steph was quick before Migel could move; she had the knife up against his throat. "One move, and I will cut it; the choice is yours," whispered Steph. "Now, what were you saying? How do you know McCormack?" she asked, prodding the knife to his throat; a small trickle of blood ran down his neck. Fear filled Migel's heart. "A long time ago, he became my friend. He introduced me to your husband, who gave me the job and the house here. We only a few times. Mostly for business but a. few times, I helped him in other ways. Honestly, it was nothing." Steph dropped to her knees, "You had sex with my husband?" "Yes, well, just a few times, but it was nothing," said Migel. "Look, it was a long time ago. Anyway, you were not interested in him. He told me you were frigid, but you looked good on his arm, and you would make a good nursemaid; that's why he let you stay," laughed Migel. Stephanie was still on the floor, trying to take it all in, looking up at Migel, who was laughing at her as he continued to spread dirty, disgusting things about her husband and her marriage. It was all too much for her; she felt intense anger and hate towards her husband and Migel. Her hand tightened around the knife as she plunged it towards his cock, "You fuckin'g bastard, how dare you talk about me like that? I put up with a husband who could not get it up for years, thinking it was me and all the time he was doing you?" Steph was shouting, and Migel was screaming, "Stop, you mad bitch, I'm bleeding. Your husband is dead now. STOP, STOP!" The Red mist that had come over Steph lifted as she looked around at the scene; she had a kitchen knife in her hand. Migel was in front of her with his trousers down, wrapping a tea towel around his cock, which was bleeding profusely. There was blood all over the floor. "What happened?" she said calmly. "WHAT HAPPENED !?" shouted Migel, "What happened? You tried to kill me by cutting off my cock, that's what happened! You're a mad bitch; I should have you arrested for this!" Stephanie looked at Migel, "Then do it."

"No, you're more useful to me, not locked away. Anyway, Mr. dickie will be Ok. Besides, the money you are gonna give me, I will afford a dick transplant and a house," Migel smiled. "Now, I think I have the power, so I fancy a house like this; in fact, this one would be just right. Maybe you and lover boy could move to the little house, and I stay here and pretend to be posh, but all the time, I am nothing more than a dirty cheap slapper, just like you," said Migel. Stephanie felt cold inside; she was in no mood for this idiot. She picked up the knife, using it to tear her dress; she then put it to her throat, causing blood to ooze from a wound. "What you doing?" said Migel, still nursing his bleeding cock. "You see, you tried to rape me, and this was self-defensive. You pushed your way into my house knowing my man was out, we had words, and you tried to rape me. I used the knife in self-defensive," Steph smiled. "Remember who has the money, and money influences outcomes; now let's get things straight. We say no more, I will pay you to fuck off and never return, and I will buy you a house which you and your sister can live in; that's the deal. Take it, or we can call the police right now." "What about my stuff? What about wages? What about money for the future?" asked Migel. "All about the money," laughed Steph. "Money really is power, and I have loads of it," she continued. "Tell you what, I am not unreasonable. Book yourself into a hotel near the hospital and look for a place; I will make sure you have enough money. Once you are settled, you can come and get your stuff. No, cancel that. I don't want you near this place again. I will get it delivered. As for ongoing money, I won't be paying you. You will get a lump sum, and that's it. Make it last or not, up to you," said Steph, with the composure of a lawyer. Migel looked at her; she was one cold Bitch; all the rumours he had heard were true. She was the one in charge; her poor husband just provided the title and the fortune. They all said she was a selfish bitch, and look at her now cold, calculated in a dress ripped to shreds covered in blood and still calling the shots like a pro, more like a prostitute, thought Migel. In fact, that's how she met the lord; she was a posh man's escort. "You're nothing but a prostitute. I know how you started, and you're still doing now," sneered Migel. "I know where I came from. I don't need you to remind me, but like I said, I have the money, and right now, you need me more than I need you. I'm getting bored of your company now, and as nice as it is to talk history, I'm done talking to you, so you need to go." Migel knew it was over; he had nothing left to throw at her, his cock had stopped bleeding, and he needed to visit his sister and now find a hotel. Without saying a word, Migel walked out of the house and back towards his accommodation for the last time. Stephanie slid to the floor, both in exhaustion and relief. What the fuck had she just done? She needed to collect her thoughts, put her game face on, clear up this mess and wait for her man to come back. Could she lie to him? Well, it's not lying, she thought. It's just not telling him everything! Steph reached out to stretch her arms when she touched the note that had dropped from Migel's jacket that said,

Hey bitch, bet you thought you got away from me; first mistake that will cost you an extra million. Second mistake, you never paid me, that will cost you another million. Had the local drug dealer sniffing around looking for you, why? Price of five million to keep quiet—Mac.

McCormack, that's all I fuckin'' need, and all this time, he has been using Migel. Steph shook her head. Fuckin'' lot of wankers. Let's see who's got the balls around here, thought Steph. You wanna play McCormack? Then let's play. Although Steph was slightly confused about the reference to the local drug dealer, unless that was someone else, her husband was shagging. Steph called Martin Newton of Newton and Newton.

"Martin, it's Stephanie Arlington."

"My dear, how are you? I heard about your tragedy. Bless you."

"Martin, I want to sell the villa. I want you to sell it and I don't want it publicly advertised, just a few selective clients. No questions, Martin. I just want out."

"And the land?"

"Negotiable, but not at this moment. I want to keep the businesses, but if it's a deal breaker, then maybe. Obviously, a handsome profit for you. Now, when can you come around to view?"

"How about tomorrow, my dear?"

"It's a deal. Oh, and Martin, I am looking for another villa, again, something exclusive and expensive. See you tomorrow at, say, noon?"

It was 9 pm when Rich returned to the villa; the villa was silent. Where was his woman? Rich dropped his keys. His mind immediately went into bitch has left me. It was all a plan to get me out for the day. She's gone. The bed was empty. Then he caught sight of her in the bathtub. She had dimmed the lights; soft music was playing, and a beautiful aroma was swilling in the air. Rich smiled. "Room for one more?" Steph was startled, "Hey, I was miles away." "Anywhere nice?" asked Rich. Steph smiled, "Come in." Rich dropped his clothes within seconds and was in the bathtub. He also made a mental note that she never responded to him when he asked her where she was in her mind. They chatted and laughed, washed each other, made love, in fact, anything but address the elephant in the room. "Shall we eat, darling?" asked Steph. They prepared food together, and Steph poured herself a brandy. Rich noticed she downed it quickly and was pouring a second. "TELL ME, Steph, tell me what happened. Was she dead?" asked Rich. Steph picked up Rich's hand, "No, she is not dead. Migel said she was found in the lane, someone had attacked her, and well, she is in the hospital, and she is not doing too good," explained Steph. "Where is Migel now?" asked Rich. "At the hospital, I think. We had an argument, and I told him to leave." "Ok, so when he comes back, I will talk to him and get more information," said Rich. "No, he won't be coming back; I sacked him and told him to leave, as in pack up and get out. I said I would buy him a house and—" "YOU DID WHAT!?" shouted Rich. "Why?" "Because I did not like his tone or what he was saying. Besides, I don't need him; you can look after everything," said Steph. "What the fuck do I know about pools or business? Anyway, I'm not your hired fuckin'' help, Stephanie, why do you do this sort of shit? You don't think. Why don't you leave things to me? I'm the man of this house," shouted Rich. Steph looked at Rich, "One more thing," she said. "Yes?" sighed Rich. "I'm putting the villa up for sale; I don't want to stay here." Rich banged on the table "WHY? WHY? WHY? Don't you think my opinion is worth anything, eh? Why can't you wait? Eh, WHY Stephanie!? WHY?" shouted Rich, his face up close to hers, his eyes full of anger. Steph calmly got up from the table and walked away, saying nothing.

Rich banged down his hand. Fuckin'' woman drives me crazy. Rich poured himself a large brandy. Her plan is to sell this place and leave me. She is gonna do a runner. He came around today, and they made this plan. That's why she was in the bath - she has someone else, she shagged him! Rich marched into the lounge, Steph was listening to music. "So, who is he? Tell me who was here, who, and where? Tell me where you shagged him?" shouted Rich. Steph looked at Rich, "What are you talking about?" asked Steph. "Bitch, you had a bloke here all day, that's why you sent me out, so your posh bloke could come around. Now tell me who it is, tell me who ya bin shagging, cus so help me Steph, I'll fuckin'' kill him. I told you NO one was gonna touch you. I told you, Stephanie, you're my woman. I need to know where, Stephanie. Where did you fuck?" shouted Rich.

"Calm down, Rich, you're scaring me. No one came around; I called the agents, and they are coming tomorrow. I have been alone all day, thinking and trying to do the right thing. Ok, I may have acted in haste, but I panicked. Migel said his sister was attacked, and I-" "Oh, I see. You thought it was me. You thought I attacked her? Well, fuck me, Steph, who do ya think I am? A monster?" "Right now? Yes, I do. You're shouting at me like it's my fault. all All I have been doing all fuckin'g day is trying to save your arse, and yes, I want to sell this villa, and if you would bother to ask why, I could tell you I am being fuckin'g blackmailed by the family's solicitor and Migel who by the way I took a knife too and cut his throat and his fuckin'' cock. So yes, I want out. I want to go where no one can find me. So thanks for asking; my day has been great!" screamed Steph.

Rich slid to the floor, hands covering his face, "I'm so sorry, I mess everything up. I am ashamed of myself. I thought things would be different with you, but I'm doing it again, treating you badly, and you don't deserve it. I'm scared, Steph, scared someone will take this away from me," said Rich, sobbing. "What? So, you push it away?" she asked. "Yes, maybe. I don't know, I've had nothing nice like this, or like you before. I don't know what to do cus I don't deserve it. Steph, I didn't care about anyone and ended up getting involved with the wrong crowd. I shagged women as timepass, but it all changed when I met you. I would do anything for you. Please forgive me, Steph." Steph got up from her chair, "I am going to bed; I don't want you in my bed tonight," she said coldly. "I think it's our bed," said Rich, "And you don't get to send me away, lady. We will sleep in the same bed tonight," said Rich. "as long as you stay on your side," she said as she walked away. Rich smiled, she's a feisty cow, I give her that.

The following morning, Rich woke early. He prepared breakfast and planned to take Steph out for the day to get her away from the villa for a day. "Here, my darling, breakfast in bed for my princess," shouted Rich as he walked into the bedroom with a full tray of food. Steph opened her eyes. Last night came flooding back to her. "Thank you, this is nice," she smiled. Steph sat up in bed, poured some tea, and sipped in silence. "I am sorry, Steph honestly, I am. I thought I would take you out for the day; what do you think?" "No, I cannot today," she said. "Besides, it's raining. Look." Rich looked out; it was raining heavily. "Fuckin'' typical; I wanted to take you out, show you how sorry I am," said Rich. "I know, sweetie, I know," Steph smiled at him. Rich noticed her eyes were not dancing.

"Let me bathe you," said Rich.

"No, I don't want that."

"How about a massage? I have excellent hands."

"No thanks."

"How about a cuddle then?"

"No, not right now. I must get ready. The agent is coming around."

"Well, I'm staying around."

"Yes, of course."

It was noon when the team of estate agents rocked up, led by her old friend Martin Newton. "My dear Stephanie, how are you? It has been such a long time. You look glowing, my dear, glowing the Spanish sun; suits you although not today; bloody rain has swept in trying to kill our joy." Steph laughed. Martin had always been over the top, but he was a very respected agent, and if anyone could sell this villa quickly, it would be him. "Martin, it is wonderful to see you and your team, thank you so much for coming around so quickly. Can I get you tea or coffee?" asked Steph. "No, no, my dear, we are going for a power lunch after this; we aim to have this sold quickly, my dear. It truly is a beautiful place and the land, my dear, can we see the land?" Rich had entered the house and was watching everything. "Is this your hired help, my dear? Maybe he could show us the land," asked Martin. "No, this is my partner," said Steph as she held out her hand to Rich. Rich grinned as he walked over to her. "Oh, I see," snapped Martin, "Pleased to meet you, sir. Now, we must get on, so can we see the land?"

"NO, not right now; I am not selling it. I may rent it out, I have a vinery, fields of Tempranillo grapes and Muscadine grapes, then I have acres of land that yields Bananas and land that grows undercover organic crops. But like I said, I am keeping those at the moment. I mean, we, that's right, darling?" asked Steph, looking at Rich. "Yeah, I mean, yes, at the moment, darling," said Rich, kissing her neck.

The team took photographs and made small videos. "What about the furniture?" asked Martin "I'm leaving it." "What? All of it?" "Yes, all of it." "I think you should go to Auction." "No auction. I told you I did not want this advertised. I only want it offered to a selected few, do you understand?" demanded Steph. "I understand, my dear, only a fraction of people could afford this. I am thinking in the region of eight million euros; that is my estimate. What are your thoughts?" asked Martin. "Yes, I am happy with that," said Steph as she looked at Rich, who nodded.

"I think I know someone who may be interested," said one of the team. "But I think you will get ten million." Steph turned to the young lad, "Then do it, and if you get me ten or over, I give you a million." "This is most irregular," snapped Martin. "Martin, this young lad is keen; let him do his job. Stop being so bloody old and boring; you will still get your cut," said Steph, winking at the young lad.

Once they had all disappeared, Rich patted the seat next to him, "Come sit down, babe." Steph sat down, smiling at her man, "So, fancy a bit of young lad, do ya? I saw you winking at him," said Rich, who had grabbed her arm. "Take your hand off me. I am not doing this, I was just encouraging and trying to get the best price, and frankly, Rich, it wouldn't hurt you to step up and do these kinds of things, so don't fuckin' start," snapped Steph. "Hey! Hey! I was only messin'. Come on; chill out, babe. Tell me all about McCormack and Migel," said Rich, backtracking, but his mind was racing, she fancied that young Spanish dude. I mean, she didn't want me, what if it was him here all day? He seemed to know his way around. Rich's fists tighten up. "Are you listening to me?" asked Steph. "Sorry, babe, what were you saying?" "Oh, don't fuckin' worry yourself, no doubt I will end up dealing with it, just because the family solicitor is trying to blackmail me and some drug dealer is after me and all this time Migel was involved with them, not to fuckin' mention the fact I got a knife to him cut his throat and his cock!" exploded Steph.

"Hey! Babe, I am sorry. I'm rubbish at this relationship stuff; I get so jealous. Now tell me again; start from the beginning," begged Rich.

Steph explained all about McCormack and Migel and about the note. "I know who that is; I don't think he is after you, babe; it's me he wants." Steph looked at Rich in horror, "No, not like that; he likes me. Well, he's obsessed with me, actually. He's helped me out a lot. I never dealt drugs; we were just good friends. I ain't proud of some things I've done, but needs must; when you want something, you sometimes have to do stuff," said Rich, who could feel Steph tensing up. "Look, babe, in my world or old world, you did what you had to do to survive. He was obsessed with me, and well, I used that to my advantage. It was when I said no, he had me beaten up; that's when you found me" said Rich. "Don't hate me, Steph, I'm different now, I promise," begged Rich. Steph put out her arms, "It's Ok, come here, come, let me hold you. But how does he know you're with me?" asked Steph as she stroked his head. "I dun know, baby," whispered Rich, as he moved his head down until he was being cradled like a child. Steph held him tightly, gently rocking him. "It's going to be alright," she whispered. Rich felt like a child; he felt uncomfortable yet comfortable. It felt wrong yet right. Rich relaxed into her; he felt safe. Steph started unbuttoning her blouse, "Here," she whispered. Rich opened his eyes to see her breast exposed and her nipple standing erect. "Suck it," she ordered. Rich sucked on her nipple for what seemed like ages as she cradled him. "Hey, greedy boy, try this one."

Rich switched sides and continued to suck on her nipple until he fell asleep. He felt so comfortable, he felt wanted, and he felt safe. He had never experienced anything like this before. It wasn't sexual; it was something else, something deeper, something so personal to them.

Steph eased herself away and left him to rest. Something did not add up; she felt Rich was lying to her, and one thing she had insisted on was the truth, however bad. Steph looked at Rich sleeping, he was handsome, sexy, and a lot of fun, but these moods of his and the lying were getting to her. She needed a man to be a man and take care of her, yet here she was again taking care of another fuckin'' man. For her, the crack in the relationship had started.

Rich lay thinking of why Hen was asking around after Steph. It could only be to get to him. Problem was, when Hen wanted something, he would get it. Rich was in love with Steph, and he only wanted to be with her; he felt such a deep connection with her. The days of messin' around with Hen were over. He needed to step up and take charge, and yes, moving out of here was the best thing, somewhere new, somewhere they both choose. He was going to ask her to marry him!

Chapter Thirty-Six

JO

Every day, Jo would do a shift at the cafe, catch the bus, return to the harbour, and stare at the boat, and every day the strange man would chase her off, shouting something in Spanish at her. Three weeks had passed since she got kicked off the boat, and there was still no sign of Angus. The police showed no interest, and no matter how much she asked around, nobody knew anything.

Jo was helping Robin out at the cafe, not for money but for something to do. They had become good friends, and Robin invited Jo to move into the flat with him and share the rent. The flat was clean but basic; she had her own bedroom and shared everything else. Robin was out most nights at the drag bar, where he turned into Rubella, the redhead. He had long red hair, very red lips, and beautiful fitted dresses. Some nights, Jo would watch the show and wait for Robin to finish. They would walk home together, grabbing chips or curry if the tips had been good. They would chat and laugh all the way back to the flat.

Jo was waiting at the bar for Robin to finish when a group of women came into the club, all singing and laughing. They hugged each other, danced, and sang along to the tunes with big smiles on their faces. Jo watched them. She missed having friends. One woman came over to Jo, "Hi, bet you don't remember me. I'm Karen. Couldn't help but notice you staring at me. Everything alright? Do you fancy me?" "Oh, no, I mean, sorry, I was just thinking how wonderful it must be to have good girlfriends," said Jo. "Yes, it is; you should get out more and make more friends. Everyone comes alive at night on the island; only the old come out during the day," she laughed. "So do you?" asked Karen. Jo blushed, "No, no, nothing like that," said Jo. "Ah, pity," smiled Karen. "Anyway, see ya around." Karen planted a kiss on Jo's cheek and headed back to the group. Damn it, thought Jo. Why did I say no? She is hot, but she said, see ya around, so ya never know, thought Jo.

Jo thought about what Karen had said. What if Angus was around at night, having a great time, and then sleeping during the day? Maybe she had been searching at the wrong time of day?

Robin had just finished his gig, "Well, girl, how was I?" he asked. "You were shining like a fuckin'' bright star; you get better every time I watch you," Jo replied. "Are you sure?" Questioned Robin, smiling. "Yes, of course, you are so much better than the blonde bombshell. She has nothing on you," Robin laughed. That's Terry. He's been doing this for years. Anyway, let's go home, girl," said Robin, holding his hand out. "Robin, I'm gonna go down the harbour; just wanna check a few things out." Robin looked puzzled, "The harbour? You're not a hooker, are you?" asked Robin, concerned. "Don't be fuckin' daft. Do I look like one? Of course not, I just want to find someone," responded Jo. "Oh, we all want that girl," laughed Robin. "No, not like that, it's a long story," said Jo. "I'm listening; I think I need a drink," said Robin. Jo told Robin how she was involved in a car accident, dragged from the wreckage, put in a van, and then moved to a crate on a boat to be dumped at sea. That's where she met Angus. She escaped from the crate because of the rough sea. Jo talked about Angus and how good he was to her. "He was like a father to me," she explained. Jo told Robin about the boat and their journey together, how she loved Maderia, and they were only staying one more night when Angus disappeared, and every day she had been back to the harbour to look for him. "But how about he comes out at night, and that's why I can't find him?" said Jo. "So why did you leave the boat?" asked Robin. Jo explained that the fishermen, who Angus had told her were pirates, came on board one morning and took it over, saying Angus had gambled it and lost it, but he loved that boat and would never do that. I know he wouldn't; something is wrong," Robin listened. "Fishermen are strange, Jo, really strange They don't like women on boats or gays like me. They are a tough breed, they only like other fishermen. Best leave it, Jo," said Robin. "No, no, I can't. I need to go tonight. I need to see for myself.,. "You got money?" asked Robin. "Yes. Why?" "Well, it's a long shot, but maybe a Rat Boy will be your best option. "Rat Boy?" asked Jo. "Yes, it's a group of young men who work in the harbour. Fishermen should not be gay, but some are, and let's just say they talk a lot and they like a Rat Boy. They trust them; they keep quiet, but for money, they will talk." "Can we go now?" asked Jo. "We can, but I can't promise we meet one."

Jo and Robin left the club every night and went to the harbour. They would walk around looking for a Rat Boy, looking in pubs and clubs but nothing.

Tonight, Jo noticed the Escardo boat had gone out. Angus's boat was moored. It looked lost and empty. "I'm getting on it," said Jo. "No, no, don't, it's bad luck, don't Jo," begged Robin. Jo jumped on board. "I'm only looking," shouted Jo. Robin felt very nervous, he lit a cigarette to calm his nerves. "Nothing to see; it's locked up," said Jo as she made her way back to Robin. "Hey, I didn't know you smoked." "I don't, just when I'm nervous," said Robin as he flicked his cigarette into the water. "Come on, let's go," said Robin. They were just about to get into the car when Robin grabbed Jo "A Rat Boy!

Come on." Jo looked up to see this small blonde boy. He was a pretty boy with bleached blonde hair and a strange walk. "Hey!" called Robin, "English?" "Yea, man, any fuckin'' language you want." Rat Boy made his way towards Robin just as Jo caught up. "Hey man, I ain't into no women unless she wants to watch at a price," laughed Rat Boy. "Can we talk, man?" asked Robin. "Cost ya." "How much?" asked Jo. "100€." "Come on, man, we just want to talk." "Still a 100€," said Rat Boy. "Ok, where can we go?" asked Jo. "We not going anywhere. I go nowhere with women; now, what ya want?" Jo handed him the money. "I am trying to find an old man called Angus. He owns the blue fishing boat in the harbour, but he's missing. I think the Escardo men may have something to do with it," said Jo. "Can't help you, and if ya know what's good for ya, you will drop it. Keep away from the boat," said Rat Boy as he threw the money back at Jo. "I don't want ya money, and I don't want anything to do with ya. The streets have ears and eyes now go," shouted Rat Boy as he ran away. Jo and Robin looked at each other, suddenly both feeling uncomfortable. "Come on, let's go. He knows something, and I don't feel safe anymore," said Robin.

They had just got back to the car when they heard an explosion. "What the fuck!?" shouted Jo. The harbour was lit up in flames. It looked like a boat was on fire. Strange, thought Jo. Angus's boat was the only one in the harbour! "Nooooooo… the boat!" shouted Jo, "Noooooo, the boat! My boat… Angus's boat!" Jo was screaming as she ran towards the burning boat. "Jo, we gotta get out of here; nothing we can do now. Jo, come on," shouted Robin, dragging her away and towards the car. "Come on, Jo, we can't save it." Robin got Jo in the car, who was hysterical; he was about to drive off when someone was frantically banging on the window. "Let me in, you cunts, let me in." Robin looked round to see Rat Boy; he opened the door, "Let me in, you fuck wits." Rat Boy climbed over robin and into the back seat, "Now drive. Fuckin'' drive. DRIVE!" he screamed. Robin and Jo looked at each other. What the fuck had just happened, and why did they both feel scared?

RICH AND STEPH

Rich had settled, he and Steph had laid everything out. She knew most of his back story, and he knew hers. They talked about the future and were both excited to find their own villa. They had viewed several exclusive villas. Rich liked all of them, but Steph found something wrong with each of them. Today, they were going to view a beautiful villa not too far away. This one had its own beach, but it was a hell of a lot of money. They had several people interested in their villa. Steph had left the agent to negotiate the best price. "Hey babe, when we finish looking at the new villa, well possibly our new villa if ya don't find anything wrong with it," laughed Rich, "I would like to take you out. Let's go somewhere, even if it's just a walk and a coffee; what do ya think?" asked Rich. "Lovely," said Steph. It would be good to get away from packing and away from this villa, she thought. Steph was on edge. Migel had been back several times, unknown to Rich, demanding money. Steph eventually paid him to disappear. Problem was, she didn't trust him. The last time he came around, Rich had gone out. "Bitch lady, I come for money; call it hush money. Oh, I see you're packing. Going anywhere nice?" "Not that it's any of your fuckin'' business, but we are going back home." Steph hoped she had planted the seed in his tiny brain, but he was a slippery character, and the sooner she was out of this villa, the better. "Hey, what ya thinking?" asked Rich, who had been watching her."You were miles away; what's wrong?" Steph looked at Rich, "Nothing, sweetie, just thinking this villa was so special to me once upon a time ; now I can't wait to get rid and start again with you, my handsome bit of rough." Steph reached out for Rich, "When I say rough, sweetie, I am referring to your chin," she said playfully, rubbing his chin, "It's rough for my delicate skin." "Oh yea, because you are such a delicate little fragile flower," Laughed Rich. "You're the toughest fuckin'' bird I have ever known, and I love ya; in fact, I have been meaning to ask you something," said Rich. "Ask me later, sweetie, we are going to be late for the viewing. Come on," said Steph, holding out her hand.

The villa was magnificent, beautiful uninterrupted sea views and nicely laid out gardens planned to be aesthetically pleasing throughout the seasons. It had its own beach and long driveway, which was more like a private road. Lemon trees, intermingled with magnolia trees and jasmine trees, lined the drive. The smell was Devine. It was just as beautiful inside the villa, with a large reception room, beautiful kitchen and dining area, two lounges, and its own gym. Sauna and swimming pools inside and outside. It had 17 rooms upstairs made up of 7 bedrooms, 7 bathrooms, an upstairs lounge area, a master bedroom, and a master bathroom. "Wow," Rich let out a gasp. He had never seen such a beautiful place. Steph watched him. He was like an excited child. It made her breasts ache watching him. She needed him to suck them, "I will take it," she said to the agent, who was nonchalantly drinking coffee, thinking this was another noisy couple wasting his time. He spat out his coffee in surprise, "Er… excuse me, excuse me, I am sorry. Er… my English may not be good, but you say you buy?" "Yes," said Steph, "I Buy." "But you not asked price." "No I haven't, but I give you 11 million today; call someone." The young agent was still in shock, "The cost is more like 13 million." Steph smiled, "Well, best of luck with that; it's an empty shell, just been built, probably will have a few teething problems. It still needs some work doing to it, so no, I have had second thoughts; 10 million is my offer, now call." The agent dutifully called the office. "Ma'am, my client say no, he say 12 million." Steph smiled, "Tell your client I give him 11 million; that's my final offer, and we will walk away." Rich observed everything; this woman really turned him on; she was cold and calculating yet soft and sexy. He just wanted to rip her clothes off. "What you thinking, sweetie?" she asked. "I was thinking how much I love you and how much I would love this to be our new home. A new start where no fucker knows where we are." Steph smiled, "Don't worry, sweetie, it will be ours." The agent returned, "My client agreed to 11 million if you sign today." Steph held out her hand, "Agreed. So where and when do we sign?" Rich smiled. He gets to sign something and own something, fuckin'' hell, who would have thought! The agent asked them to attend the office in town. "Give me a few hours to get everything ready," said the agent. "Come on, babe, let's go celebrate," said Rich. "I feel I might get lucky," winking at Steph.

It was a hot day for the time of year. They parked the car and walked along the beach hand in hand. Rich stopped, grabbing Steph and kissing her passionately, his tongue probing her mouth. "I love you. I want you. I need you," he whispered, "Let's go somewhere." Steph could feel the hardness in his shorts. "Come on then," she grabbed his hand and ran into the sea, laughing as much as Rich was complaining. They were waist-high in the sea. Rich picked up Steph and tried to maneuver her onto him, but the sea had other ideas. Rich did not see the wave coming. It took him off his feet, both of them falling under the water. Steph came eup first, laughing. Rich had banged his head on something and was bleeding and not impressed. "It's not fuckin'' funny, Steph. I was trying to be romantic, but you have to make fun of everything. Look at me, my best clothes fuckin'' ruined, not to mention me best shoes, and now I got a fuckin'' bang on me head." Rich was furious. "Hey, Ok, don't get like this; it was fun. Let's go home and get you changed." "No, I wanna book into one of these hotels and pretend we just met," said Rich. Steph was not keen, but she knew to keep the peace it was better to go along with it. They picked up a few new clothes, shower gel, and a towel and headed off to find a hotel room.

The Sunrise Hotel was the first hotel to have a room available. It was two stars, not what Steph wanted, but Rich insisted it had to be this one. "About time you roughed it, lady," he said. The room was clean but basic. The bed was the hardest bed Steph had ever lay on. Oh well, she thought, a bit of shagging should make him happy. Then we can go home.

"Come on then, sir, show me what you got picking me up like that," said Steph.

"You're a cheap tart standing around dressed like that. You're asking for it."

"I'm no tart. I'm a respectable married woman, so if you don't mind, sir, I will be off. I am not used to such poor quality."

"You want quality? I'll give you quality when I fuck you. Because you're going nowhere, lady. See this? It's going in you. I'm going to fuck you, and if your husband complains, I'll fuck him too." Steph looked at Rich, who was immersed in the role play, and as Rich always does, he was taking it too far.

"No, no sir, my husband will kill you; he gets so jealous. Best I go."

"I don't care." Rich grabbed her and bit into her neck, sucking it hard. "There! Now ya husband will know you've been up to no good. He will know a real man has had ya." Rich's fingers were inside her. "Now tell me ya don't want me, eh? Tell me, do ya want me?" Rich whispered, "Yes, yes, I want you!" screamed Steph. Rich bent her over and entered her from behind, his balls slapping against her arse as he fucked her. Emotion overcame Rich as he exploded inside her. Hisbrain felt it had electric running through it,he felt completely vulnerable, something he had never experiencedbefore.. It was like being on drugs, and he wanted more! "Wow, babe, that was some feeling, but I aint finished with ya." Rich slipped his fingers into her wet pussy, "Come on, babe, let me bring you off." "Suck my tits!" she demanded. Rich ripped her bra, exposing her breasts, and latched himself onto one of them. She was soon rocking and contracting. "That's it, more! Yes! Yes! More… Oh fuck me!" she begged. Rich's cock was hard again and ready as he slipped inside her; it was enough to make her body contract and shake as she hit new heights in pleasure, her secretions gushing out of her, "Fuck me, babe, you're some hot woman!" "Come here, let me hold you," said Steph as she cradled him in her arms. Her breasts were aching to be sucked. "Suck them!" she ordered. Rich moved his head to accommodate a nipple in his mouth, and he gently sucked on it as he fell asleep.

They awoke two hours later, both feeling chilly and starving. "Come on, let's shower and go out and eat. Come back for more, shall we, sexy stranger?" said Rich. Steph really wanted to go home, but he was having fun, and the sex was amazing, so maybe a few more hours in this dump she could do.

They walked a short distance, found a decent restaurant, and settled in for the evening with the drinks flowing. They laughed and chatted like long-lost friends; anyone watching them would see the chemistry between them, and anyone near them would feel the electricity between them. "Shall we watch a show?" asked Steph. "Why not? I've never been to a drag show before," laughed Rich. "They are very good or very bad," replied Steph. "A bit like me?" Steph looked at Rich, reaching out for his chin, "Exactly like you," as she leaned over the table to kiss him.

Rubella was first on. She was funny with a pleasant voice, thought Steph. "More drinks, babe," asked Rich, who was feeling uncomfortable. Drag was not really his thing, although the bird-on-bird action going on around him was a good watch. But he was not that person anymore. He was respectable and almost a married man, he just needed to find the right time to ask her. Rich stood at the bar waiting for his turn; eventually, he got a space using his weight and height to push in. "Oh, I am sorry," said Rich to the women sitting at the bar. "It's's Ok, M-..." Jo looked up at Rich she could not finish her sentence. It's him, it's that fuckin' animal that left me to die. Rich looked at Jo. She looks familiar. I know her from somewhere, he thought.

Jo stared at Rich. This isn't happening to me, she thought. Rich began to feel uneasy; his senses started kicking in. He paid for the drinks and headed back to Steph. "You Ok, sweetie? You look like you saw a ghost?" "I dun know, babe, some woman at the bar; she looks familiar. I got a bad feeling from her," said Rich. "I think I'm gonna be sick." Rich ran to the toilets.

Jo had been watching Rich. I know it's him, she thought. "You alright, bird?" Jo looked up to see Rat Boy. He was now living with them and working in the club. It was crowded at home, but he was hardly in. He was always out and about doing something or someone for money. He would come home with hundreds of euros most days. This meant the rent was always paid, which was a relief for Robin, who worked day and night for very little. "So you alright or what?" "Oh, sorry, I just saw someone who tried to kill me; long story," Rat Boy put his arm around Jo. He didn't like women, but she was Ok, "Hey, come on, you're with us now; no one will hurt you, especially now that you have me." Jo looked at Rat Boy and smiled; he was a cute little bloke but no match for most men in build or stature, yet he was quick and knew many people. "Point him out, point him out, I find out," Rat Boy said excitedly. Jo pointed to Steph, "Well, he was with her, he's…" Before Jo could finish her sentence, Rat Boy was at the table with Steph, "What's a beautiful woman doing sitting alone?" Steph looked up and smiled, "Madam, you are sat alone; this is a crime." Steph laughed, "It's Ok, my er… my… er friend has just gone to the bathroom." "Your friend, madam, is very handsome." Steph just realised this bloke was after Rich, and she had just called him her friend. "Well, when I said my friend, he is my…" Rat Boy placed his hand on Steph's shoulder, "Hey, you don't have to explain to me; I get it; he's your bit on the side." Steph was just about to protest when Rich marched back to the table, knocking Rat Boys' hand away from Steph, "Can't leave you 5 minutes darling without some dirty pest bothering you." Rich put his arm around Steph, staring at Rat Boy, "You can go. Piss off!" shouted Rich. Rat Boy smiled and started shouting, "*Eres unidiota asesino le observare y estare en todos los rincones. paga*ras a mi amiga por lo *que hiaiste maldito cerdo sucio maldito maldito bastardo.*" Rich had heard enough, "Come on, let's go." He took Steph's hand and marched out of the club. "What was that about?" asked Steph. "Fuckin'g dirty little bastard, come on, let's go to bed," said Rich kissing her passionately, in the hope she dropped the questions. They were oblivious to the Rat Boy following them.

JO was shaking. She wanted to leave the club, but she had promised Robin she would stay for both his performances. Rat Boy came running back into the club. "They cheap," he announced. "They stay in cheap hotel; it must be for sex. No one stays in that hotel for rest; bed's rock hard," he said excitedly to Jo. Rat Boy loved drama. "I know, owner, tomorrow I find out." He put his arm around Jo, "It will be Ok; you have us now, and no one will hurt you again. Now I must get back to work," he said, laughing. Jo had grown fond of this bloke that had barged into their life; he was full of fun, full of contradictions and very inappropriate, yet he had a beautiful side to him, and even though the living arrangements were not ideal, she would not have it any other way. He knew everyone, and for those he did not know, he made it his business to know. Jo was unsure what he actually did for work, yet he earned a lot of money. "Ask no questions, my dear, but if you do, I charge you for the answer," he would say to her. Jo assumed that's how he earned his money connecting people, with what she was not sure about and thought it best not to ask.

"Let's go home; I don't want to stay here. We have a beautiful bed at home," said Steph. "We can't risk it, babe; we've bin drinking. Come on, babe, I want you. I can't keep waiting. My cock is rock hard for ya," said Rich as he dragged her into the room. "Come on, babe, maybe I can suck your tits." Rich knew she could not resist him once he was sucking on her.

Steph cradled his head as he latched onto her nipple, "Talk to me, tell me your fantasy," whispered Rich. "I wanna be fucked at the same time as you sucking my tits. I want to hold you and be fucked by someone else." Rich stopped, "What did you say? You want someone else to fuck you? I've fuckin'' told you nothing or no one is going inside you, only me; you're not even having a vibrator. We discussed this; you're mine, you agreed, Steph. Call me selfish, but this is how it is, Steph. Don't make me mad," shouted Rich. "Hey, calm down; it was just a stupid thing to say. I'm sorry," said Steph, "Come on, come and relax. Come on, sweetie, come and suck." She cradled him in her arms as he sucked on her nipple. It was not long before he was sleeping.

Steph was uncomfortable. The bed was hard, and he was a heavy weight lying on her. She slowly rolled him to one side, needing some pleasure to help her sleep. She slid her fingers inside her wet pussy, trying not to make any noise or movement. He would be annoyed with her. Rich was not sleeping; he was uncomfortable, and he could not get the woman in the club out of his head. He knew her, but where from? He just could not think, and that stupid little twat, what was his problem? Rich's mind was racing. He felt the covers moving and realised what Steph was doing. "You dirty girl," he whispered as he rolled over "Let me." Rich's fingers took over, and soon, she was riding them. Rich mounted her, "Here babe, this a real man, ride this." They made love for hours; the sweat poured out of them soaking the sheets. Eventually, falling asleep from exhaustion.

Rich felt disoriented. Where the fuck was he? It was 5 am, and he could hear voices. It sounded like an argument in the corridor. He made his way to the door to listen.

"What kind of time is this!?"

"Fuck off, old man."

"Don't you tell me to fuck off. I've been waiting for you all night. Where have you been."

"Enjoying myself, old man, enjoying myself with some nice young cock, not an old shrivelled one."

"You're nothing but a dirty, drunken waste of time and money. Go and find someone else to take care of you and put up with you. Maybe you could use and abuse them."

"Don't you fuckin'' worry, finding some old bloke won't be hard, but keeping him hard is the fuckin' problem?"

Rich had heard enough. He felt annoyed by the blokes. He was just about to open the door to give them a mouthful when someone beat him to it.

"Oi, I'm trying to fuckin'' sleep. I need my sleep now; if you two don't shut the fuck up, I'll shut you up."

"Fuck off, man, mind your fuckin'' business."

Rich heard the click.

"I said I needed to sleep. I'll blow your fuckin'' balls off."

The gun went off several times; Rich jumped away from the door, realising what had just happened. He slid down the wall to the floor, holding his head in his hands. What the fuck? Trouble! It follows me. The coppers will be all over this. I can't get caught; they can't find me here! Rich's mind was racing: you need to get out, get away from here; you can't be found here. Rich looked over at Steph; bless her, she had slept through it. No time to wake her; she would be Ok; he could hear the sirens. I gotta go. Without thinking of anyone but himself, he dressed opening the door. There was blood and bodies everywhere. Some were groaning for help. Rich stepped over them without a thought, making his way to the fire exit. Once outside, he drew a deep breath. Now get home. He reached in his pocket for the car keys. For fuck's sake! He remembered she had snatched them because she wanted to go home. Now I've gotta fuckin'' wait for her.

Rich walked along the beach, thinking about what had just happened. Why did you run? You didn't do it, so why run? What are you scared of? you always run. That was who he was, but he'd changed, so why again, why not stay and help? And who is that woman in the club? Why did she unsettle him and the little man who the fuck was that, and what was he saying? Rich's mind was racing with questions. He sat on a wall, he could see the front of the hotel. The police were in and out and people had gathered. Rich watched as the police marched away with someone in handcuffs. People were wailing as they were being escorted out of the building, followed by bodies in bags. Where the fuck is she, he thought.

It was the banging on the door that woke Steph up. She had no idea where Rich had gone or what had happened. The policeman did not speak English, and although she understood some Spanish, she did not believe her translation: murder, shootings. No, she must have it wrong. The policeman instructed her to wait in the room. She was not sure why, unless Rich was involved. Oh my God, he's dead, he's been shot. Steph began to pace up and down; what will I do without him? I can't believe this has happened. Why now? Why me!? Eventually, an English-speaking police officer arrived, "Excuse me, madam, I am sorry for the wait; we just need to take details from everyone in the hotel.

"So you heard nothing or saw anything; you slept all the way through it?"

"Yes, that is correct," responded Steph. "And the person with you, madam?" asked the officer. "Person?" asked Steph. "Yes, ma'am, you have a partner?" His head nodding towards the clothes.

"Oh, him, I don't know, officer, it was just sex. Someone. I picked up. Is that a crime?"

"No, no, ma'am, it is just, well, you don't need to do that. Oh, I'm sorry. I mean, it's Ok, but we need a name."

" I don't know, I did not ask. Like I said, it was just sex. I needed sex."

"Description."

"Of what?"

"The man."

"Oh, short, stocky, bald brown eyes, pleasant smile,"

"Was he, er… Spanish?"

"Yes, yes, he was."

"Age?"

"Don't know."

"Ok, was he young or old?"

"About 50."

"So, the man you had sex with was in his 50s, short, fat and bald?"

"Yes, that's right."

"Ok, I will need an address in case we need to ask you more questions."

"Of course, officer, Arlington Manor House, Arlington estate, Merryfield, EX732TD."

"So, you're on vacation?"

"Yes, came for a hen party."

"Hen party?"

"Yes."

"Whose?"

"My friend's."

"Who is that?"

"Marai Jenkins."

"Where is she?"

"I don't know. I left them in one of the bars."

"So, where are you staying?"

"Staying?"

"Yes, which hotel?"

"I don't know, I think it's a villa. We came straight to the clubs. I got drunk and, well, here we are."

"So, how will you find them?"

"Who?"

"Your friends."

"We will meet on the beach. Don't worry, officer one of us always does this. We always meet up," smiled Steph.

The officer shook his head. Crazy women. He did not believe her, but if he raised his suspicions, he would be told to stay on duty, and he was looking forward to some time off. Fuck it, he will sign it off. "Ok, ma'am, thank you. Oh, one more thing, ma'am, you really don't need to pick up men; you're a beautiful woman. Maybe try to find someone who will give you what you need; this is, well, how you say tacky?" the officer smiled, "Anyway, when you are ready, I will escort you out. Shall I wait outside whilst you get changed?" Steph looked at the officer, "No need, I can use the bathroom. Just give me a minute or two."

Once outside, she thanked the officer and headed for the nearest coffee shop. Rich noticed Steph walking out of the hotel with the officer. She was chatting and laughing with him. The officer was far too close to his woman; then he touched her shoulder. Why is he touching her shoulder? Rich followed her to the coffee shop.

"Coffee, please," Steph sat down and felt like crying. She put her head in her hands in the hope it would all be a bad dream!

"Room for one more."

Steph looked up, "Where the fuck were you?" she snarled. Rich was taken aback; he thought she would throw her arms around him. "I panicked; I heard the shooting and left." "Oh, that's it; leave me with some mad fuckin'' gunman on the loose, run away as long as Richard is alright, then fuck everybody else," shouted Steph. "No, no, it wasn't like that; I was scared," said Rich. "Of what?" asked Steph.

"The coppers, I knew they would be all over the place, and I panicked and ran. Don't be angry with me, Steph," pleaded Rich, "I did it for you." "Don't be angry with you? I want to scream at you right now; you must have stepped over those poor people. Why didn't you help them? Who are you? And what do you mean you did it for me? How fuckin'' dare you," she shouted. "Keep your voice down," whispered Rich. "No, no, I won't keep my fuckin'' voice down!"

"Is everything Ok, ma'am?" asked the waiter.

"Yes, thank you."

"Coffee, sir?" the waiter asked Rich.

Rich looked at Steph, who nodded, "Yes, please."

"Steph, I waited for you. I wasn't gonna leave you. I'm sorry, Ok? I was scared," Rich confessed. Steph looked at Rich, "It's all about you, all the fuckin'' time. It's always about you; I'm scared, I'm sorry, I'm this or that. All I can say, Rich, this is getting to be a habit of walking away and leaving people to die." Rich went cold, as if someone just walked over his grave. "Hit a nerve, did I?" she asked. Rich remained quiet. Steph paid for the coffee and walked out of the café, followed by Rich.

"Where are you going?"

"Back to the car."

"Come on, babe, let's go for a walk along the beach." Rich grabbed her arm, "Come on, babe, you know I love you; you knew living with me would not be easy, but look at the fun we are having," laughed Rich as he gripped her hand tightly. Steph walked in silence with him along the beach. "Let's get some breakfast, babe; maybe you will feel better once you're fed. I know I do," Rich winked. Steph was hungry, and a full English sounded just right. Maybe he was right. She would feel better when she had eaten. "Ok," she said.

They found a lovely café and sat down to have breakfast. Rich ordered, "Two full English, please, with tea and plenty of toast, please."

"Wow," said Steph, "You actually ordered something and said Please?" Rich smiled, "Yeah, and I always say please." "No. No, you don't, Rich, but anyway, like you were saying, life is difficult with you," whispered Steph. "I didn't say that," snapped Rich just as breakfast arrived. They devoured the breakfast in silence.

"Talk to me, Steph."

"I don't want to."

"Come on, you can't ignore me forever," smiled Rich. She was about to answer him.

"Well, look who it is, the murdering English bastard." Rich and Steph looked up to see Rat Boy standing at the table. His eyes rolling around, and the smell from him, he was clearly stoned. "Fuck off!" shouted Rich. "Dirty fuckin'' tramp." "And you're nothing but a dirty English murdering bastard, and I'm coming for you," shouted Rat Boy. Rich stood up he towered over Rat Boy, "Look, boy," said Rich sternly, "I don't know what your fuckin'' problem is, but boy, one more word and I will put you outside. Now fuck off!" Rat Boy was feeling like he could take on the world, and this monster hurt his friend, "You don't scare me; you're nothing but a murdering English." Before he could say anymore, Rich had picked him up, and they were outside. "Now tell me what this is all about?" ordered Rich.

Rat Boy whistled, and just like rats, lots more Rat Boys appeared from nowhere. Rich looked around. They were closing in on him. Rich picked up Rat Boy and threw him over the wall and into the sea. Turning to the group, "Who's next? Come on then!" shouted Rich as they all ran in different directions.

Chapter Thirty-Seven

LUCUS

"HELP, HELP; I CAN'T SWIM. HELP! I'M HURT!" shouted Rat Boy. "HELP ME PLEASE!" Rich looked over the wall and walked away. Steph had watched it all, and once again, he walk's away; she thought, "HELP! HELP!" Rat Boy's cries were weak. Steph ran to the wall, ripped the Bouy from its home and threw it out to Rat Boy. "Here, get inside or just hold it. Can you do that?" shouted Steph. "Don't panic. Stay calm. Just hold on, and I will get you," she shouted. Before Steph got to the water the emergency services had arrived. "stand back lady" shouted one of them.

Getting Rat Boy out of the water, they wrapped him in foil and blankets, and the cafe supplied a hot drink. Steph sat next to him. "Thank you," said Rat Boy. "You saved my life." Steph looked at the young bloke. "Least I could do. I'm sorry," she said.

"Why are you sorry?"

"Doesn't matter; what's your name?"

"Rat Boy."

"No, your real name. What is it?"

"Lucus."

"Hello Lucus, I'm Steph. So what does Lucus do?"

"I'm a Rat Boy. I pleasure men for a living. I do drugs, beg, steal, borrow. You know, all the nice things. I'm a nightmare, lady."

Steph smiled, "Here." She gave him 300€, "Buy yourself some dry clothes." Lucus looked at her, "And for my silence? Or do you want me to tell them how I found myself in the sea? Attempted murder, I think."

"How much?"

"500. No 1000 euros."

"Deal. I don't have that on me. How do I find you?"

"You don't. I find you. I believe you will pay it."

Steph opened her purse. "Here, another hundred euros. I will get the rest. Meet you here tomorrow at about 12. Oh, and Lucus, no funny business. We have a deal.?"

"Sure thing, lady."

Steph made her way to the car, where Rich was waiting for her.

"Hey!"

"Don't you fuckin'g hey me! Get in and don't speak to me."

"Steph, please listen to me," begged Rich.

"I said don't speak to me," snapped Steph as they drove home in silence.

He knew he had some explaining to do, but how could he explain what came over him? It's an emotion that overtakes him when he is angry; he doesn't really understand it. All he knows is he's a good man but misunderstood. No one gives him a chance; people always pick on him, and trouble follows him. It's not fuckin' fair!

Steph was sunbathing. Rich watched her stretch out just in her knickers, moving her body to the music. He needed to let her know he was a good man; he was her soulmate, and he needed to show her he was worth sticking with.

Steph had showered and was making something to eat. "Is that for both of us?" asked Rich.

"YES."

"Steph, come on, we need to talk," begged Rich.

"No, we don't. I'm done talking to you. I want some space from you," snapped Steph. Rich felt hurt and rejected. He could feel those emotions rising inside him. "I said I'm sorry. I said I wanted to talk," shouted Rich.

"And I said I wanted some space," snapped Steph.

Rich grabbed her arm and pulled her away from the kitchen."Sit down," he ordered. Steph sat down then immediately stood up, "I said sit down." "I don't want to; what you going to do? Make me? Or maybe you are going to throw me over a wall or knock me out, leave me for dead. Is that it, Rich? Is that what you're going to do?" shouted Steph.

Rich took a step back, "No, no, I would never do that. Is that what you think of me? Is it?" Rich looked at her, waiting for a response. Steph said nothing. "Look, Steph, this is a difficult time; we will get through this. We love each other, and we need each other; we need to stick together. We are moving to a beautiful villa soon, our villa; a new start. Just you and me; we don't need anyone else."

Steph stood up, "Rich, it's over. I'm not the right woman for you, and you're not the right man for me. We have had fun, but it's over." Rich stared at Steph, not believing what he had just heard. She was dismissing him, not wanting him. This can't be happening. Everyone let him down, but not her. He would not let it happen. "Steph, you're angry. Please think about this: we are good together," said Rich. "No, no, we are not. You left me in a hotel with a gunman; you walked over bodies, not stopping to help anyone; you threw a vulnerable person who could not swim over a wall and into the sea; you could have killed him and you just walked away. Who are you? What are you capable of? I don't know you, I don't want to know you, I don't want any more of this," cried Steph. "Well, I didn't kill my husband or murder my own son, did I?" Rich retaliated. "GET OUT!" shouted Steph, "GET OUT of here! How dare you say such things to me? GET OUT!" "No, I aint't going anywhere. I will give you space, but I ain't leaving, lady. Best you think of a way through this," shouted Rich as he marched off.

Steph woke up early. She had cried herself to sleep and felt like shit, but she had things to do. She showered and got herself ready to leave the villa.

"Where are you going?"

"I'm going out."

"Where?"

"What's it to you?"

"I asked where."

"I have to go to the bank. Is that Ok? Unless you are going to pay for the Villa? No? Thought so!" snapped Steph.

" I will come with you."

"No, I don't want you to."

"Why, what you hiding?"

"Nothing. I need some space."

"Where else you going?"

"Nowhere else."

"Ok, I expect you back in an hour, maybe two."

"And if I'm not?"

"Then, lady, there will be consequences."

"Oh, that's right, here we go again. Threats! Threats! Threats!" snarled Steph. Picking up the car keys, she headed out. She needed to get to the bank and find Lucus.

"I didn't think you were coming, lady," said Lucus.

"Sorry, got held up."

"You got the money?"

"Yes, I got it."

"Here, put it in this bag," said Lucus, handing Steph a plastic bag.

"Not so fast," said Steph. "I want to know why you called my man a murdering bastard. What did he do?" Lucus looked down at the floor. "I dun know. I was high or something. I hear things, you know. Now, the money."

"No, what did you hear and from who?" questioned Steph.

"Just someone."

"Who? It's worth another thousand," said Steph.

"Look, lady, all I know is he captured my friend and put her in a crate, then asked the fisherman to dump her in the sea. He bad man; you saw what he did to me. Now, can I have the money?" Steph felt sorry for him; she could see he was badly bruised and scared, "Where do you live?" "Nowhere, Anywhere, Why you ask?" "I just wondered if you lived with this friend," asked Steph. "Yes, I do." "Another thousand for you if you take me to her. Lucus quickly calculated he would get three thousand euros, maybe four if he pushed her. He needed the money; he needed his own place. "Ok, I take you."

They walked for about half an hour. "Wait here," said Lucus. Steph looked around; she was outside a small block of apartments. The sun was shining and drying all the washing people had on their balconies; everyone seemed friendly, all going about their day. Music was blasting out from someone's apartment, which contributed to the feel-good vibe. "Hey lady, come." Steph looked up to see Lucus signalling her to come in, "Follow me, lady." Steph followed Lucus to the third floor. "Here, come in." The flat was small, and it was obvious several people lived in it. Steph noted it was clean but not tidy. "Here, lady, this is my friend Jo." "Hello Jo, I am Steph, pleased to meet you." Jo looked at Steph; she looked like a nice woman; she thought, "So you wanna know about the scumbag you were with?" asked Jo. "Well, yes," Steph replied. "Sit down," said Jo. Steph sat down and looked at Jo, "I'm from Merryfield, a little place in England; you won't have heard of it. I was a trucker, with plenty of friends, minding my own business; all I did was go out one day with some friends; it's patchy. I was drugged, but my memory keeps coming back in bits; I know it was him. I will never forget his face when he hit me or the look in his eyes when I asked to go to the toilet. You see, lady, I was in the back of a van, I think, with some others. It was cold, and I was freezing. I must have passed out. When I woke up. The van was being driven. I was banging on the van and shouting. I needed a wee; the man let me out; it was him, the eyes I will never forget them. I swear down it was him; he took me in the woods and ." Jo started to cry. Steph gasped, "Did he?" "No, no, nothing like that. We both had a wee, and I tried to get away but he caught me and knocked me out. I must have passed out again. When I woke up I was in a crate being tossed around. Ya see, lady, the bastard had put me in a crate, then on a boat and told the fisherman, my Angus, to dump the rubbish at sea. I could have been a goner, but the rough seas saved me and Angus of course. That's when I met Angus; he told me the bloke was called Rich. Angus knew him and said he was a bloody nightmare, always up to something." Jo was sobbing as she recalled her story. Steph held out a hand to her. Lucus, who had been listening, came running in with tissues. "So where is Angus?" asked Steph. "I dont know, he disappeared." Jo told Steph all about the boat, about the fishermen and how she would go looking for him every day. Then the boat went up in flames, and now she lives in fear of the fishermen finding her. Tears ran down Steph's face; she could feel the pain in this girl's heart. She looked at Lucus, who was also crying; bless him, he's also lost, she thought. "Who else lives here?" asked Steph. "Robin. It's his flat; we are just guests. He's been the best friend, letting me stay here and now, Lucus, although I think Robin may get something from Lucus." Jo smiled at Lucus, "A lady never tells," smiled Lucus. "Lady, you need to stay away from him. It was him, lady. I guess you never heard of our little town, but it was nice, people were nice, but he was a bad one. You gotta get rid, lady," said Jo, looking at Steph. Steph smiled, "Your town sounds nice here." She gave Lucus his money and Jo a thousand euros. "What's this?" asked Jo. "Look, love I have money, so I can help you. Take it, give some to Robin, help him out," said Steph. "Are you with him?" asked Jo. Steph hesitated, "Yes. Yes, I am for now."

"Does he know you're here?"

"No."

"Will you tell him?

"No."

"What you gonna do?"

"I don't know."

"Stay safe, lady. You seem like a lovely woman. Don't let him hurt you. Get rid."

"I don't know how to," answered Steph, "I dont know how to."

The villa was quiet, with no sign of Rich. She put down her keys; maybe a nice soak in the bath would soak away her troubles. She ran the bath, collected some clean clothes, poured a drink, put on some soft music and looked forward to a nice relaxing hour. "Why do ya need a bath?" Steph jumped; she had not noticed Rich. "I said, why do ya need a bath?" "I dont need a bath; I want one," replied Steph.

"You bin with someone else?"

"What!? What do you mean?"

"You bin shagging someone else? You bin gone long enough. I said 2 hours. Now, where you bin?"

"No, I haven't been shagging anyone. I don't want anyone. I want you. I'm fuckin'' mad for you, Rich, but you scare me. This scares me."

"So, where you bin? Answer the fuckin' question, bitch."

"If you really want to know, I paid off the young lad you threw in the sea to keep him quiet. Then I met his friend who claims to know you. She recognises you from Merryfield. She told me you tried to kill her, you put her on a boat and sent her out to sea to be dumped like rubbish. Ring any bells? No? Well, that's where I have been, paying off your mess again and look, I'm back. What does that say about me? I'm stupid or a fool, eh? What does it say, Rich?" Rich looked at her; she was half naked, trying to get into her bath to relax, justifying herself to him. A monster, cus that's how he felt. She had come back to him after everything. "Well ?, if you have nothing to say , excuse me, but I would like a bath," said Steph. "I'm sorry, babe. Here, let me wash you, scrub your back, massage your shoulders. Steph lay in the bath while Rich washed her. "Sit up, babe." Rich scrubbed her back and massaged her shoulders. "Come, babe, let me massage you on the bed."

Steph lay on the bed, and Rich expertly massaged her. His hands were powerful, and it felt wonderful. Once he had finished, he got her some water. "Here, you will need water," Rich said, smiling at her. "Steph, I'm not a bad person; I'm a good man, just misunderstood. I need you, Steph; I can't share you. I know I've been bad. but I don't know about a fisherman or a boat. Steph, I was off my head most of the time on drugs. I've got no idea, Steph; my memory is bad. Man, please, believe me, Steph. I won't keep going on. I'm going to give you space, and if you want me to leave, I will. I can't hurt you anymore. I love you. I know you have cleaned up my mess time and time again."

Steph listened to him. She could tell he was sorry. She also heard as he spoke her involvement in everything he had done by cleaning or covering it up. You're a stupid woman, a weak woman falling for this man. She did not know what to do. She loved him. "I am sorry, Steph, say something. I will go tomorrow if you want me to," said Rich. Steph wanted him to hold her, kiss her, grab her, take control of her; it turned her on, not this soft shit he was coming out with; she liked it rough. She wanted him to bite her, fuck her, but how could she tell him when he was trying to be gentle and kind? She kissed him on the forehead. "Let's talk tomorrow." She hoped he would grab her, take her, but he didn't. Rich knew what he was doing; he could see the lust in her eyes. He knew she wanted him; he knew she could not live without him.

Rich went to bed, happy he was in control. I'm a selfish bastard but so is she, he thought. We work well together, and I ain't giving this up or her, and if anyone tries to make me, I'll kill 'em. Rich smiled to himself. It's all working well.

Chapter Thirty-Eight

HEN

HEN was getting frustrated; he had been following McCormack for weeks. The fucker did very little. He had the occasional visitors to his home. "They look like hookers gov," said his scouts. HEN was missing Rich, and it was McCormack who knew where he was. He was pulling the strings well no more. It ends today. HEN had followed McCormack into his office.

"Well, this is nice," McCormack turned around.

"Oh, Mr. Henderson, what do you want?"

"Well, that's no way to speak to a customer."

"I'm busy. I have no availability, so if you don't mind, piss off."

"I do mind, and I've checked you have nothing today; in fact, you don't really do anything, so I was wondering where do you get your money from?" said Hen as he started walking around the office. "Ouphs," said Hen, laughing as he pushed a plant onto the floor. "Ouphs, I'm so clumsy today," as glasses smashed onto the floor.

"What is it you want!?" shouted McCormack."

"You know what I want. I want to know where Lady Arlington is."

"Why?"

"Cus, she got something of mine."

"I told you, Spain."

"Spain is a big fuckin'' place. Now, where in Spain?"

"It will cost you."

"No, no, it won't; you're testing my fuckin'' patience. Now tell me where?"

"I don't know."

"Liar, do you like this office?"

"Yes."

"Would you be sad if it went up in flames?" McCormack looked at Hen, "What a stupid thing to say to me because if it does, I will know who to…"

"Let me stop you, dumb wit; you will be in it, so you won't be talking to anyone. Or maybe that posh flat you live in, do you like it? I said do you like it?"

"Yes, of course I do."

"Well, I have someone in it right now just waiting for me to give the word." McCormack felt the colour draining from him. Is this shit really happening? "You're bluffing; now piss off!" shouted McCormack.

"Nooooo, I don't bluff, let's call him, even better, let's video call him," snarled Hen.

"Yes, boss." "McCormack don't believe you in his flat; show me the flat." Hen handed the phone to McCormack, who watched as Hen's henchman walked around his flat.

"Ok, I have seen enough; what do you want? Don't touch anything in my flat," McCormack handed back the phone to Hen. "Wait for instructions; don't do anything yet. Make ya self a tea or something," said Hen to his guard.

"So, McCormack, you ready to talk?"

"I do deals, I told you."

"And I told you deals are off the fuckin'' table; now talk!" shouted Hen as he slammed down his hand onto the desk. "Where is she?"

"Canaries!" shouted McCormack.

"Ok, still too fuckin'' big. Which one?"

"Gran Canaria!" shouted McCormack.

"Ok, still too fuckin'' big. WHERE?"

"Look, I don't know any address. I have never been; all I know is it's in Monte Leon district. Posh, I believe."

"so, when was the last time you spoke to her?"

"I don't, I mean, we don't speak, she always has her phone off, she just transfers money to me, although a payment was due a few days ago and still nothing. It's usually in my bank by now."

"Maybe she run out of money," laughed Hen.

"No, I doubt it. She got plenty, bitch better pay me," said McCormack. Hen looked at McCormack and started to laugh. "Exactly why is she paying you?" asked Hen. "To keep quiet, keep her secrets." Hen shook his head. This guy is a real dumb twat.

"Well, my friend, you're coming with me," said Hen.

"Where?"

"Gran Canaria."

"No, no, I'm not going; I don't like heat and I don't like flying," said McCormack, dabbing his forehead.

"Like I said, you're coming with me. Pack your fuckin'' case. I will let you know the details."

"I don't have a passport," shouted McCormack.

"Liar, you do, well, no, technically you don't. I have it! You don't think this was the first time in your gaff, do ya?" Hen laughed. "I know more about you than I want to, let's just say cock rings and prostitutes tut tut tut but all their own. Now pack ya case and wait to be told when ya being picked up, and oh, sorry about the mess," said Hen as he made his way out of the office.

"Will your man… Will he do anything!?" shouted McCormack.

"Not unless I tell him to."

McCormack sat in silence; he was shaking. He should have stood up to him, called the police, and shouted for help, but who was he kidding? He was shit scared of him; he didn't want to get hurt, he knew his reputation, and now he was some kind of work bitch for a drug lord.

I could be his sidekick, a bit like Sherlock and Watson, or more like Crockett and Tubbs. Maybe it won't be so bad, he thought. If we become friends, he will look after me, I could do some deals with him. Yes, maybe this is the break I need. McCormack's mind was racing, full of future thoughts of how life would be, as he made his way to his flat to pack his case and wait.

Chapter Thirty-Nine

THE VILLA

It was the day of the move. The new villa was ready at last. Steph had paid professional designers to redecorate exactly how they wanted it. Every piece of furniture was new, all chosen by herself and Rich. Steph had ordered flowers for every room and for the kitchen to be stocked with produce. All they had to do was move in. "So when they movin' in here," asked Rich. "In about an hour's time, so we have to go," said Steph. "One last look around. I liked it here," said Rich, like a child having something taken away from him. "No, come on, Rich, the cleaners are here. All we have to do now is move ourselves, now, come on." "So who's movin' in?" asked Rich. "I dont know, some bloke from América, a rock star or something," said Steph. "Who? Who is it?" asked Rich, who was quite excited now. "Who, Steph? Who is it?" "It's meant to be hush-hush." Rich laughed, "Hush-hush? What the fuck!? Who is it?" Steph knew he was not moving until he knew, he was quite childlike in some ways. "Morgan L Jackson. Now come on." "Wow, he's one hot rocker. I'd fancy him myself if I didn't have you." Rich laughed, "Who would have thought me, Richard Luck, living in a better and bigger Villa than Morgan L Jackson, the rock star? Phew! Come on, babe, let's go to our bigger and better villa. Rich was the happiest he had been in ages. He was about to move into a big beautiful villa, one they chose together; in fact, both of them chose everything in the villa. Rich had given Steph space. He slept in a separate room and was respectful and gentle with her, and boy, was it working. She could not get enough of him, but he would push her away. "No, babe, not until you are sure; I won't stay where I am not wanted. I don't want to bring more trouble to you. I love you, babe, and I want to marry you, but not like this; you have to be sure." Rich would play the game pretending to be sad and demur.

Steph loved the new villa. She had made sure no one knew where they had moved to. Steph bribed the agent to remain silent. She had cancelled McCormack's monthly fee. Paid off everyone who needed paying. She felt happy that no one should bother them now. Rich had been different since she had told him it was over. He had given her space and would not sleep with her. He was attentive, kind and respectful, not at all like the Rich she knew and fell in love with. This Rich was Ok, but it was getting boring now. He did as she asked. No arguing, he made polite conversations. Yes, they laughed and chatted and she got to know him better, but the passion, the sulkiness, the rough diamond spirit she loved had gone. He was reminding her of her late husband. "Yes, dear." "No, dear." "Anything you want, dear." Steph wanted passion; she wanted the old Rich back. Not this boring shit. What's wrong with you? She asked herself, he is doing what you asked, giving you space. What more can he do? "So, which room is mine?" asked Rich as they wandered around the villa. "This one, of course," said Steph, "This is the master bedroom. I thought you would have this?" said Rich. "It's for both of us, Rich; it's our bedroom," said Steph, patting the bed. "What you mean is you want me back in your bed?" asked Rich. "YES, YES, I do!" Oh, I don't know Steph, not long ago you wanted me to go, you wanted space you really hurt me Steph and now…" said Rich, looking at her sitting on the beautiful large bed that should be theirs.

"I know, I know, but it's different now; you're different. We have a new start, please, Rich," Steph pleaded. "No, not yet, Steph. I'll sleep somewhere else until you are sure, just in case you change your mind. I won't carry on like we were. You either want to marry me or you don't, Steph. I know I have money, but it feels like I'm your child, and I'm getting an allowance. I know you're not hiding money from me. I have seen your bank accounts, and I have seen the thousands that come in every month from your businesses, but I don't know what they are, Steph. I want to be involved; I want it to be ours, so until you're ready for that, I'm staying away from you, cus you're hurting me, Steph, breaking my heart, you are," said Rich as he walked away smiling to himself.

Steph sat on the bed and wondered what she had done. She had pushed away the only man that lit her up. Maybe it was for the best. Maybe she should just let him go and live a quiet life but the thought of letting him go made her stomach knot up. She needed him; she needed passion in her life.

Rich was in the kitchen preparing food, "Come sit down, darling; I have lunch to serve you," said Rich, who had prepared fresh strawberries, cream, bread and butter and asparagus "This is a mix," laughed Steph. "I know. I thought it would cleanse your palette," replied Rich. Steph looked at Rich and shook her head, "What's wrong?" asked Rich. "It's you. You're strange, and you're not the man I er… well, you're different." Steph stuttered, not sure what to say, "But darling, you wanted me to change to be more caring, remember? All I am doing is trying to please you; I am a good man," said Rich. "I know you are, Rich; I know you're misunderstood," sighed Steph, "But this is not you."

Rich smiled "All I am doing is giving you space to think. You asked for space, and that's what I'm giving you. I realise I have been too much for you," said Rich as he walked away, smiling to himself.

Steph made her way back to the bedroom. This was all too much.

Rich expected her to come running after him, begging him, so he waited and waited. Where the fuck is she.he thought as hewalked around the Vila. He felt a sense of pride walking around this beautiful big villia, it was   his villa. With his name on the deeds. So, where the fuck is she? Rich searched the pool area, the gym, and the sauna. She was nowhere to be seen. He began to feel a slight panic as he raced around the villa. Suddenly, he caught sight of her fast asleep in the big queen size bed. He wanted to slip into the bed; he wanted to slip inside her, but she needed to beg him; she needed to know who was in charge around here.

Chapter Forty

HEN AND MCCORMACK

The flight was uncomfortable; McCormack hated flying, and Hen wasn't keen on McCormack. "I will call you Mac, and you call me Tom," said Hen. Our story is we are a couple."

"But I'm not."

Shhh," said Hen, "you will be who I say. We need a back story. So, as I was saying, we are a couple, and we're looking to buy a villa, Ok?"

Yeah, Okay. Are we married?"

"No, no, no! We're not fuckin' married," snapped Hen.

"Ah, maybe we should get married. That could be our back story," said McCormick.

"Oh shut up, leave the talking to me," said Hen.

It was a hot day. Mac hated the heat. He was overweight, so any heat made him uncomfortable. The hotel was decent. It had everything they needed and was close to shops and bars. "So, the plan is we will visit the estate agents, find the expensive parts of the island, try to find out what people live in the area, find out if any are for sale, that kind of thing," said Hen. "Is that Ok?" "Yes. Shall I stay quiet?" asked Mac. "Yes, not like a mute, just like a quiet person," said Hen. "What does a quiet person do?" asked Mac. "Are you fuckin' joking me? Just stay quiet. I will say you are shy or something." Mac wiped his brow. "Ok, I think I got it. So, how long have we been together?"

"3 years."

"Where did we meet?"

"In a club."

"What do we do?"

"Well, I am a businessman."

"What business?"

"Does it matter?"

"It might"

"Ok, I own property."

"Where?"

"England."

"Well, what am I?" asked Mac.

"Well, you're a solicitor."

"I thought we were pretending."

"Ok, what do you want to be?"

"Hairdresser. Always wanted to be a hairdresser."

"A hairdresser? A fuckin' hairdresser? To be a hairdresser? I'm with a hairdresser. Ok. Ok. If that's what you want," said Hen.

Mac smiled; he might enjoy this game, "So tell me again, why are we going to the estate agents?

"To find her, we ask around, find the expensive villas and bingo, we will find her."

"So why don't we go straight to the villa?" asked Mac.

"Because we need the address, dumb wit," snapped Hen.

"Oh, I have the address at home."

"You do what?"

"I have the address, but it's at home in the safe," said Mac. Hen looked at Mac, "I don't fuckin' believe you, idiot! I get someone round to your gaff now." "No point, I don't know the code." "What do ya mean ya don't know the code? It's your fuckin' safe!" Exploded Hen. "Well, not exactly; the codes belong to the people paying me to keep quiet; in this case, it's her."

"What? And you don't know it? Why didn't you tell me? I know professional people who open safes; I COULD HAVE GOT IN IT!" shouted Hen .

"Well, you didn't ask. Anyway, you only get three chances, and it spurts ink at you," snapped McCormack.

"Brilliant. Fuckin' brilliant! Come on, you have wasted enough of my time and remember, we have a backstory," said Hen .

ESTATE AGENTS

"So, sir, we are here to buy property somewhere very nice, somewhere high-end, upmarket, somewhere expensive," said Hen to the agent.

"Senor, bunenos dias. Mi ingles no es buena, tengo que conseguir a mi amiga! ok."

"What's he say?" asked Hen.

"Something about good morning and English friend," said Mac. "I thought you knew Spanish?"

"A little."

"So, what do you know?"

"I know aeropuerto, **autobús**, hotel, desayuno, cerveza."

"Ok, ok, what does that mean?" asked Hen.

"Well, I'm asking for the airport, the bus, the hotel, breakfast and beer."

"Typical. Fuckin' typical. I'm with someone whose Spanish is worse than a child's."

"Well, you don't know any," replied Mac.

The agent came back with his friend.

"Hello, I'm Robin, the owner of the cafe next door. My friend doesn't speak English, so if you're ok with it, I can translate."

Yes, yes, tell him we want to buy something expensive, something big, a villa in the best area. You know, like a gated area," said Hen.

"Tesis idiotas están desperdiciando el tiempo. Quiero comprar una villa cara en la zona más exclusiva de la isla," said Robin to the agent. The agent shook his head, "No es posible porque, no son espanoles los ingleses solo pueden comrar tras!"

"Oh, he said no, not possible," said Robin.

"No, no, he said more than that," demanded Hen.

"Well, he said it's not possible to buy in the expensive gated community unless you are Spanish, and, well, you are not. So English buyers only get lower property," said Robin, shrugging his shoulders.

"Tell him I want higher property. Tell him I have money," snapped Hen.

"Look, sir, it is not possible. It can only be Spanish. Anyway, I must go now," said Robin as he headed out the door. Hen, Mac and the agent all stood in silence. "What now?" asked Mac.

"Look at the pictures. Find something expensive," ordered Hen.

Mac looked at the adverts scattered around. He quite liked all of them, 100,000€ for a tiny house. It looked nice, but he thought it was expensive for such a small property, it must be somewhere expensive. "Look, honey," shouted Mac, "how about this one?" Hen marched over, "Honey? No, you stupid fucker. That's a house. We are looking for a villa! Come on, let's go!" Hen marched out of the estate agents, followed by Mac, leaving the agent shaking his head. *"Idiotas,"* he whispered under his breath.

Robin rented the space, but the *Cafe le Bow* belonged to him as his little business. Jo and Lucas invested the money they received into the cafe and paid the rent in advance on the flat. Robin was not happy when they told him all about the English man and the Rich woman, but the money made life a little easier for them, so he accepted it and hoped it would not come back and bite them.

"You worry too much," laughed Lucus. "You need taking care of." And that's how it started. Robin and Lucus became a couple, no more RATBOY. Lucus committed to Robin. They both did drag at night as Rubella and Lic-no-cane, and they were the talk of the town. Jo still searched for Angus, but she was happy. She worked in the cafe and the club, saving her money to one day buy a big house or a boat for all of them.

Cafe le Bow was busy. "Hello again," said Robin. "Did you find somewhere?"

"No, not today, but we are looking." "I was wondering," said Hen, "if maybe you knew someone who spoke English who would show us around the Island?" "You need a travel guide for that, sir Now, do you want coffee?" "Yes, two, please." "and some of your lovely cake," added Mac.

Robin came over with their order, "I dont think I made myself clear; I will pay you 1000€ to show us around the Island," said Hen. Robin was surprised, "Sir, I don't think YOU understand. This is my business, and I cannot leave it to show you around the island, but I am sure you will find someone. You may need to up your offer, though, as four hours won't get you around the island. It will take a good twelve hours, if not two days, if you want to see it all." Hen looked at Robin, "Thank you, mate, but how about I give you 3000€ for a day's work? We don't want to see the whole island, just a few spots," smiled Hen. "It's tempting," said Robin, "but I can't close for a day. I bake everything myself — the bread, the cakes, and I am building up my business , I am just getting known , so, sorry."

"Now what?" asked Mac. "Just relax, just wait, watch and listen," said Hen. Mac was not sure what he was watching, but he sat in silence, watching and listening.

The cafe was getting busy and Robin was run off his feet. . "Where were you? I'm run off my feet," exclaimed Robin. As Jo and Lucus arrived at the café "Sorry baby, we went looking for a house, but we can't afford it yet," shouted Lucas. "Okay, tell me about it later, now put your pinny on, bitch," laughed Robin. Lucus came over to Hen's table, "Have you two gentlemen finished? Shall I clear the table?" "The coffee was so nice; we'll have more, and I think a selection of your finest sandwiches, one of every filling and a selection of your cakes," said Hen. "Wow, that's some order, sir. Thank you," said Lucus, skipping off to tell Robin about the order, which would be about 200€

"Sorry about the wait, sir," explained Lucus as he placed the variety of sandwiches down. "Shall I bring the cakes later, sir?" "Yes, thank you." Said Hen looking at the selection of sandwiches which looked amazing. The bread had been freshly baked, and the filling was very generous. No wonder he was busy, thought Hen. Mac, , loved food and had devoured his share so quickly that he was watching Hen. "Are you not going to eat that last sandwich?" "N--" Before HEN could get the word out, the sandwich was in his mouth. "Um, waste not want not," said Mac as he chomped on a ham and Stilton sandwich. Lucus came over with more coffee, "On the house and here is a little honey brandy; helps with digestion." "Do you work here?" asked Hen. "Yes, of course. That's my love; we work together," said Lucus, smiling. "And you two?" "Yes, he's my love," said Mac, grabbing Hen's arm. "Oh well, in that case, you may enjoy our show. We put on a show along with some other queens every night; it's great fun! You should come. I will get you a voucher — free entry," said Lucus as he skipped off. Hen removed Mac's hand, "Keep your hands to yourself," whispered Hen. Lucus returned with the voucher and the cakes. "Know what, we cannot eat anymore. Any chance you could wrap these fine cakes up for us, and can we have the bill, please?" asked Hen. "no problem, sir."

"Here you go, sir, cakes all neatly wrapped and your bill." Hen made his way to the counter, "Here, young man," he gave Lucus 300€. "Keep the change." "Thank you, sir." Lucus could hardly wait to tell the others how much tip they had been left. Robin told Lucus about the conversation he had earlier with the pair and how they offered money for a tour of the island. "I can do that, easy money," said Lucus excitedly as he ran out of the cafe, hoping to catch the pair, but they had disappeared.

Hen and Mac headed back to the hotel, both in need of sleep. "Shall we hold hands?" asked Mac. "No, fuck off," replied Hen. "But what if someone is watching us?" questioned Mac.

"Like who?"

"I don't know, but we have to stay in character, you said." Reluctantly, Hen held his hand out as Mac gripped it tightly.

"Don't swing my hand; we're not fuckin' kids," snapped Hen.

"Ok, ok, ok, calm down, dear," smiled Mac. Hen looked at Mac, "I will swing for you in a minute."

"You just said not to swing."

"What?"

"You just said not to swing your arms, then you said I'll swing for you in a minute."

Hen sighed and closed his eyes. Why oh why, he thought. Why me? Why did I end up with this idiot?

"Shall we go out tonight, dear," asked Mac. "Yes, we are going to that club; the more they see of us and the more money I throw at them, the more they will want to help me. Watch and learn, watch and learn," said Hen.

"So, did I do well today?" asked Mac.

"Yes, you did."

"So, do I have to stay silent tonight?" asked Mac.

"Look, I never said stay silent. I mean, speak, obviously, but stay in character. Remember our back story, ok?" said Hen.

"Ok, dear."

It was the only club around that got busy before nine PM, and it was buzzing with activity. The drinks were reasonable and not watered down. The place itself was clean, the food was decent, and the entertainment was excellent.

"Hello again." Hen looked up to see a tall, beautiful woman greeting him

"Hello," replied Hen, looking puzzled.

"We met earlier today in the café." Hen stared at the women. "Did we?" "Yes, you asked me to be your tour guide," laughed Rubella. "That's you!? I mean to say you're beautiful. I mean, you're a handsome man. I mean, — were a man— no, I mean I'm—" Hen stumbled over his words. Rubella laughed. "Please come in and sit down. Would you like a drink?" she asked. "Brandy, Make it a double," replied Hen, still staring at Rubella. "And you, sir." Rubella turned to Mac, who was staring at her with his mouth open. "Oh, same, same as him, please."

Hen could not get over how beautiful Rubella was, and he was a bloke. Hen looked at Mac. Maybe they could make him look like that, he thought. Hen was deep in thought when Lic-no-cane came over with the drinks. "Here you go, gentlemen. Do you want a tab or pay now?" "A tab, please, miss," replied Hen. "That's a bloke," whispered Mac. "No, it's not; shhh, she will hear you," snapped Hen. "Yeah, it is; he's with that other bloke, the one you can't stop looking at," laughed Mac. Hen looked up to see Rubella and Lic-no-cane kissing. "Well, I never," he sighed, looking at Mac, "Don't get any fuckin' ideas." Mac laughed. He liked this bloke. He was so miserable, he was funny.

Most people had left the club. The show had been fantastic, and the drinks had flowed. "I'm going to have to give you the bill now, gentlemen. We are closing," said Jo. "No problem, miss. Here, 500€ should settle it," said Hen. "Sure thing, sir. It was 290€. I'll just get your change." "No, keep the change. It was a great night," said Hen. "Thank you, sir! Glad you enjoyed it. You will probably enjoy the weekend. It is carnival time. It's a Spanish bank holiday, so we celebrate being alive. I am told everyone comes out to party, so hopefully I'll see you?" asked Jo. "Oh, yes, sounds right up our street. When you say everyone comes out, what do ya mean?" smiled Hen. Jo laughed, "Not like that. I mean the whole town and surrounding areas come and party. Everybody under 80 will be here; no one wants to miss this one time to dress up and party." "Perfect! Perfect! Sounds perfect," said Hen.

Chapter Forty-One

THE NEW VILLA MAGNOLIA

Rich and Steph had settled into their new villa. The hard work was done. All that was left to do was get him back in my bed, thought Steph. Rich was playing hard to get. He was attentive and kind, and whatever she wanted apart from him; she got. He would do anything for her. They chatted and laughed, even hugged each other, but he would pull away and tell her she needed to be sure. Steph was getting bored with this Rich. He was too nice. Whatever she wanted, she got. No argument, no moodiness, no passion. He would kiss her cheeks at night before heading off to bed. Steph ached for him to be in her bed. It was all she could think about. She needed to sort this out once and for all, and no time like the present. Rich was lying in the sun. He looked so good, thought Steph.

Steph got herself dressed: stockings, suspenders, best silk underwear and her beautiful red dress, a spray of perfume, some heels, and she was ready. She picked up her keys and sunglasses. "See you later, darling, I'm heading out," Steph shouted, smiling, hoping he would care enough to look up. Rich looked up. "Ok, hey, where?" Within seconds, he was off the sunbed and standing in front of her.

"Where you going?"

"Just out, darling."

"Where?"

"What do you care? You take no notice of me these days, so I'm going out."

"Of course I fuckin' care, so I'll ask again, where ya going?"

"Look, Rich, I'm frustrated. I need to get laid, and I was hoping some tall, handsome man would notice me," Steph said, smiling.

"What, so you're going out to find someone?"

"Maybe, if he plays his cards right,"

"No, you're fuckin' not, lady." Rich grabbed her and dragged her into the bedroom.

"Take that fuckin' dress off; you're going nowhere," Rich screamed at her.

Steph stood up, still playing the part, "I will not take it off, and I am going out. You don't want me, so I'm going to find someone that does," she shouted. Rich felt his blood boil like never before. The thought of someone looking at her, yet alone touching her, made him mad. Suddenly, Rich lashed his hand out, which landed across her face, knocking her off balance. "No one is coming near you, no one, do you hear me?" shouted Rich. Steph's face was stinging, "Oh, that's it, use violence!" shouted Steph. Rich ran over to her, grabbing her throat. "I'll show you fuckin' violence," he hissed at her, pushing her to the floor, one hand around her neck, the other tearing her dress from the neckline. Steph started to panic. She began hitting him as the pressure got too much around her neck. Rich was straddling her, his one hand around her throat, the other holding on to her ripped dress.

He suddenly realised what he was doing. He let go of her neck, tears streaming from his eyes. Her neck was bright red, and her lip was bleeding. Rich looked down at her, "You made me do this, you made me. Did you hear me?!" he shouted. Steph just looked at him. "I said, did you hear me?" he shouted. Steph nodded.

"Speak."

"Yes."

"Yes, what? Yes, you made me do it. Is that what you're saying, is it?" questioned Rich.

"Yes," whispered Steph.

"You're just like all the rest of 'em. Can't just have one man, can you? Think you could sneak out and get laid? What do ya think? I'm so fuckin' stupid I won't notice, is that it, eh? You think I'm stupid? Eh?"

"No, no, Rich, please, this is not you."

"But this is me; I'm a fuckin' animal. I told you, no one is going to touch you. I told you no one is gonna fuck you, only me. I told you, didn't I?" shouted Rich.

"Yes, yes, you told me," whispered Steph. Rich grabbed her silk bra and tore the cups, exposing her breasts. She had those stockings and silk knickers on that drove him crazy.

"You dirty fuckin' bitch, going out in this? This is for me only." Rich's hand came down across her face. Steph started to cry.

"Rich, stop. Stop, you're hurting me."

"Shame. I've just fuckin' started," as another blow hit her head.

"No, Rich. No, not like this. Please, Rich, No! No! No!" shouted Steph.

It was too late; Rich was inside her. No nice foreplay, no nice kissing; he was so angry, his thrusting was hard and aggressive. His rhythm was fast and furious. "Take it bitch, fuckin' hell, I'm cumming!" he shouted as he collapsed on top of her. Steph lay still for a while; every part of her was hurting, and she needed to move. "You're going nowhere, lady. Like I said, you're mine."

"Please, Rich, let me get up."

"No."

"Please, Rich, not like this."

"I said No." Steph's face and throat were throbbing, her back hurt, and her insides felt raw. She looked at her best dress in tatters and her best silk underwear in bits, everything ruined. This game had gone horribly wrong. How could she have got it so wrong? Maybe she doesn't know him after all? She was, however, strangely turned on by his dominance and passion. What's wrong with you, she thought. This is wrong. He has just raped you! But Steph was lit up inside; her flame ignited. She wanted more.

"Let me get up."

"No."

"I need to pee."

"No, pee here."

"No, don't be vile. Let me get up."

"Vile? Vile? Did you just call me vile?" Steph did not see the slap coming until it landed across her face.

"So you wanna pee, do ya? Well, guess what? You ain't goin' anywhere. You will just have to let it out here." Rich's cock was rock hard inside her. "You're nothing more than a dirty Hoare," he whispered to her. "You're my dirty Hoare. Mine to use and abuse, fuck when I want. Now tell me what you are?" he demanded. "TELL ME!" he shouted.

"I'm yours. I'm your Hoare, I'm yours to fuck when you want," cried Steph. Rich smiled, "That's better; now, on your knees bitch!" Rich pumped her until he was satisfied, collapsing in a heap on top of her.

Rich stired as he felt Steph crying underneath him. "Hey, come on, I know you're sorry," he whispered. "I need the bathroom, please." Rich rolled off her . Steph rushed to the bathroom, followed by Rich. "I just want to wee!" snapped Steph. "Well, I'm watching in case I see something I like," smiled Rich. "Leave me alone to wee," sighed Steph. "Come with me," said Rich holding his hand out, "Come on, let me suck your tits; you know how it relaxes me." Steph followed him to bed and cradled him whilst he sucked on her tits. Tears running down her face, she felt sorry for herself. All the money I have and look at me! Stuck again with another fuckin' useless man. What have I done?

Rich was awake bright and early. He had been getting up early, going to the gym, and having a swim all before breakfast, but this morning was different. He was back in the master bedroom and back in control. Their game got a bit out of hand last night, thought Rich, but she would never do that again, and he won't let her out of his sight, so this morning, he had made her breakfast and got back into bed. "Hey darling, wake up. I have a surprise for you." Steph began to stir; she could hardly open one of her eyes. she turned towards Rich, "OH My GOD, what happened to you!?" shouted Rich." "What happened, Steph?"

"It was you, Rich, you did this."

"No, no, don't say that you made me. You forced me; it was a game, right?"

"No, Rich, you were v--" Steph stopped her words. "You were angry; you hurt me, Rich."

No, it's all your fault. You made me do it. I wouldn't hurt you. I love you. Rich threw his arms around her, "Come here, baby, let me take care of you. I'll make it better." Rich gently stroked her face and neck.

"You could have killed me, Rich," Steph whispered.

"But I didn't. I love you. Maybe now you won't go out without me, and maybe now you realise I'm in control."

"Yes," whispered Steph, "I'm sorry. It was all my fault. Please forgive me,"

"Hey babe, I forgive you; I'm not a monster. At least you admit it's your fault, but don't fuckin' do it again, okay?"

"No, I won't."

"Good girl," Rich gently kissed her, "Poor baby, your lips are cut; let me kiss your other lips." Rich made his way down her body, gently kissing and sucking on her. With one finger inside her, he could feel the heat rising and her contracting. "That's it, baby, let it out, let it out. You're all mine," he whispered. "Please, please," she begged. "Please, what?" he teased. "Please fuck me," Rich smiled as he mounted her. "Here ya go, babe, work ya self-off on that." It was not long before she was screaming. Rich pounded her until he had no more to give!

It was late afternoon when they woke. Rich felt relaxed. "Hey babe," he whispered as he traced his finger over her body. "Hey," she whispered back to him. He looked at her. Her lips were swollen, her eyes bruised, and her neck was various colours ranging from red to black. Rich traced his fingers over her neck. Steph pulled away, "Hey, I'm sorry, is that painful?" asked Rich. "Yes, it's sore." "Look, I'm sorry; you won't make me do it again, will you?" Rich asked. "No, I won't," she replied. Good , now run a bath for us; we need to wash before we eat, and we wash together and eat together. In fact, we do everything together, ok?" Steph looked at Rich, "Ok," she said meekly, "I'm glad we understand each other, babe. I will look after you," smiled Rich.

They chatted and laughed in the bath. Steph made food for both of them, and they watched a movie and cuddled together. They made love softly and passionately. He told her he loved her like no other woman. "I'm obsessed with you. Call me SELFISH, but only my lips are meant for yours. Only my arm will be around you. It's me and you, babe. I love you." "I love you too," whispered Steph see did love him, but this was not how she wanted to live like a prisoner frightened to go out and speak to another man. No, this was not for her. She felt trapped. "What ya thinking?" asked Rich. "Oh, nothing special, darling." "Tell me what ya fuckin' thinking, woman. I felt you tense up, so what were ya thinking?" demanded Rich. "Well, if you must know, I was thinking about us. Look at us now, all loved up, but look what we had to go through. I mean, look at me, you hurt me" "Shhhhh." Rich put his finger to her mouth, "We agreed not to talk about it. You made a mistake. I have forgiven you; no need for a sorry again, babe." Steph looked at Rich; his eyes had hardened again, "Ok, ok, ignore me. Now kiss me, you handsome beast." Rich smiled, "With pleasure." Rich kissed her passionately, "No one is taking you away from me," he whispered to her, "do you hear me? No one!" Rich picked her up and carried her to bed, "This is the best place for you. MY bed. You're my whore, now dress up for me, just like a whore. Pretend I am that man you were meeting." Steph sighed, "I'm tired, Rich; I just want to sleep and cuddle you." "I said dress up for me, or do you only dress up for him?" "It's only you, Rich, only you." Steph began to cry as she dressed for him. Blue silk dress, silk underwear and stockings, a spray of her special perfume, some heels and she was ready to perform.

"Well, hello, sir. You called for a woman?" Rich sat up in bed smiling, "Sure did. My wife has gone out, and I need someone to ignite my fire." "Well, sir, allow me." Steph started to unbutton her dress slowly, "Come here, come here," urged Rich. "No. No sir, all in good time," said Steph as the dress fell to the floor. "Fuck! You're gorgeous," sighed Rich. Steph got on her hands and knees and made her way across the bed. She began to lick his ears and then his chest sucking on his nipples, her tongue tracing down his abdomen. She made her way down his legs, gently sucking his inner leg to his toes where she sucked on his toes as if it was his cock , which was rock hard and busting for her. "No more, I need you," Rich moaned. She took his hand and placed it on his cock. "Let me watch you, sir," she whispered. Rich smiled, "I call the shots slut, now let me watch you bring yourself off. Stand over there and do it. Spread your legs!" he ordered. Steph was happy to oblige; she needed gentleness. Her fingers worked her pussy like they were playing piano, and it was not long until she felt the heat rising in her and her pussy contracting. "Stop. Don't you dare without me, bitch, no more. I said can't you wait for me!?" shouted Rich. Steph could not stop herself. Rich moved like lightning, grabbing her and was inside her before she had time to protest. "Fuck, babe, that was hot," he panted as he fucked her. All Steph could do now was pretend, he had ruined her moment and was now enjoying himself inside her." Wow, babe, that was hot," he whispered as he collapsed by the side of her. "Now you can sleep, good girl." The tears ran down Steph's face as she fell asleep.

PREPARATIONS

"So, shall we go shopping?" asked Mac.

"Shopping"? questioned Hen.

"Yes, we need costumes for the celebration. Apparently, everyone dresses up."

"No, we won't be " said Hen.

"Come on, it will be fun. We will meet lots of people, apparently everyone or is anyone attends. It's a massive celebration. Everyone dresses up in masks and costumes. They say it's wild," said Mac, who was very excited. Hen gave it some thought; he thought about Rich; if he was here, this would be right up his street, and he would surely be here. "Ok, let's go shopping," said Hen. Mac clapped his hands and let out a scream in excitement. "Calm down, you're like a fuckin' child," said Hen. "Oh, I'm so excited. It's going to be fun; come on, we need the best costumes," Mac held out, his hand dragging Hen out of the hotel.

"Shall we go to the carnival night? It's a mask-up night. You know how much I like to mask up," said Rich. "Yes, it's usually a brilliant night; let's have some fun," laughed Steph. "Do we have masks?" "Yes, of course, I packed them. When I packed up the manor, they were in one of the many chests." "Come on then," said Rich, "let's go find."

"Robin, have you got everything ready for tonight?" asked Jo. "Yes, don't panic. Everything is in order. Trust me, it's all done. Loz is just putting up the decorations. Our costumes are here. We are ready, Jo. Don't panic; nothing will go wrong," said Robin, who was beyond excited. He wanted to make the club *the* place to be, so everything was bigger, brighter, and camper than usual.

"Have you heard the fishermen are going to Playa's celebration tonight?" "Mad Bot has rounded up a gang." "He still blames RATBOY for the boat fire, and he heard he's in Playa." "Don't think I'll go tonight. It'll get messy if *that* lot is going."

Hen and Mac had chosen costumes and masks. Hen had gone sophisticated—Bond, James Bond. And Mac was a **chicken.** "Why a fuckin' chicken?" asked Hen.

"Well, it fitted nice, and besides, it'll be fun. Never been a chicken before," replied Mac.

"Yes, but I am Bond. How can I be seen with a chicken?" snapped Hen.

"Well, they had another chicken outfit left. We could both be chickens. I mean, no one would know who we were," laughed Mac.

"You know, that's not a bad idea. Get the other outfit. I'm sure he will be here tonight," said Hen.

"Who will be here tonight?" asked Mac.

"What?"

"You said, 'I'm sure *he* will be here tonight.'"

"No, I didn't. I said *she* will be here tonight."

"No, no; you definitely said *he*."

"No, don't fuckin' argue. I said *she*. Now go and get the outfit."

Steph and Rich spent hours going through the chests. "Are you sure you packed 'em?" asked Rich.

"Yes, of course; about 20 of them and some costumes. Look, you take that chest, and I'll take this one. They must be in one of these."

Steph came across not only the masks but a bottle of pills. She was sure these were the new ones she had sent away to sedate her husband. She shoved the pills in her pocket.

"Found them!" she shouted. "Look, all different styles and colors. We can dress up now, darling. Would you like a drink, darling?" asked Steph.

"I can drive tonight."

"Well, if you're sure, you can spoil me," laughed Rich.

"Of course, darling. Let's start with a drink. You run a bath, and I'll bring in a special drink for my special man," smiled Steph.

Steph was not too sure about the tablets but figured one would not hurt him. It just might calm him down, and she could always pop another one in a drink later.

Robin was now Rubella, the policewoman; Lucus was Lic-no-cane, the nurse, and Jo had dressed as Cowboy Jo. The club was ready, and they had decorated it with not an inch to spare. As for the extra lights, well, Jo thought they had too many, but the boys wouldn't listen.

"Don't worry, it's safe. It's only one night," said Robin.

"Yes, but the sockets—look, they're overloaded," exclaimed Jo.

"You're a worryworm, Josephine," said Robin as he kissed her forehead. "But I love ya."

Jo smiled. She was so happy she had found these two. Robin was just adorable, and from the very first time they met, they hit it off. As for Loz, well, he sort of came into their life through bizarre circumstances, but it was meant to be. He and Robin were an item now and were talking about getting married.

Yes, she felt very content. She would like to meet someone—and you never know, maybe tonight would be her lucky night!

"Are you ready yet?" asked Steph.

"I'm feeling lightheaded," said Rich. "How much bloody brandy did you give me?"

"Brandy? No, darling, you had orange juice with a dash of vodka and a sugar rim. Just how you like it," replied Steph. "Maybe another one would help?"

Steph made another special drink with another tablet.

"Here, darling, more orange juice for you."

Rich smiled. "You're spoiling me. Wow, you look stunning, me lady. Think we should stay in, and you can spoil me all night," he said, grabbing her. "You look proper nice, I mean—wow," he whispered.

Steph had found a long gown with a corset middle that pulled her waist in so much it changed her figure. The dress was in red and pink; colors that shouldn't go together, but they worked well on this dress. She had fitted a big hairpiece, her makeup was foxy, and the mask she chose was red.

"You really are a stunning woman, babe. I mean, look at ya. Can't see ya black eye now—good girl. We don't want anyone thinking ya been in a fight, do we, babe?" said Rich. "Anyhow, what do ya think of my costume?"

Steph was shocked at his choice. He had dressed as a lord, but she thought he looked ridiculous. She wasn't brave enough to tell him.

"Well, I'm speechless… You're so, so, er… handsome. So much a lord."

Steph wasn't sure what to say. Rich had trousers that stopped at his knees, with long socks that came up to meet them. His suit was red velvet with gold buttons and cuffs, and to top it off, he wore a white frilly shirt with a black sparkling mask.

Rich smiled. "Why, thank you, me lady. It's all for you," he said as he swigged his drink.

"Well, how do I look?" asked Mac.

"Like a fuckin' chicken," replied Hen.

Mac was oblivious to Hen's sarcasm. "Oh, that's good. You look good, too," said Mac as he flapped about the room.

"So, what's the plan? Are we still trying to find Lady Arlington?" asked Mac.

"Shh, keep ya voice down. Yeah, we find the bitch. I have some photos—here, put one in ya pocket. Show the photo around and ask if they know her. Say we found some jewellery, and we need to give it back, ok?" said Hen.

"What jewellery?" asked Mac.

"What?"

"What jewellery?"

"We don't have any jewellery—we're pretending."

"Oh, ok. So what if they ask what we found?"

"Say a bracelet and a ring."

"Where?"

"Where?"

"Where did we find it?"

"I don't know. On the fuckin' street."

"So how do we know it's hers?"

"I don't know. No one will ask you those questions. Just say nothing. In fact, leave it to me."

"So, am I being quiet again?"

"Yes. I mean, no. You'll need to ask around, but don't get carried away. You don't have to go into detail. Now come on," snapped HEN.

"Oh, I don't like this game. I don't know the rules," said Mac.

The fishermen were drunk before they even arrived in Playa. They were all rough, hearty men who stood for no nonsense. Tonight, the pack comprising ten fishermen was on a mission to cause as much chaos as possible. They were anti-everyone who did not look like a fisherman or a woman.

"Estamos todos listos! Todos nos preparamos! Todos estamos listos para pelear! Vamos, vamos a darles!" (We're all ready, we're all tooled up, we're ready for a fight. Come on, let's give it to them!) they chanted loudly.

The celebrations were in full swing; the carnival floats made their way through the streets; they were loud, colourful and full of alcohol-fueled men and women, all singing and shouting. The atmosphere was incredible, with music coming from the clubs and bars mixed with laughter and shouting. People were everywhere, most of them in fancy dress and most of them drunk. Robins club (club de petirrogos) was full. In fact, Robin was sure they had allowed far too many in. Oh, it's only for tonight. It won't hurt just for one night, he thought.

Chapter Forty-Two

CLUB DE PETIRROGOS

The fishermen had pushed their way into Club de Petirrogos and they were out of control. They were helping themselves to drinks, insulting people as they pushed past them, grabbing women's arses, spitting everywhere. Minora, the leader, was standing on a table. He was looking around when he noticed RATBOY behind the stage curtain scratching his head, having just taken his wig off. Minora signaled to the rest, who all fell silent to listen. "Nosotras nos quedamos aquí. Lo he visto. RATBOY está aquí. Nos deshacemos de la RATA." (We stay here. I have seen him. RATBOY is here. We get rid of the RAT.)

Mac and Hen were having a great time. They had sung along to cheesy pop songs, joined in with street dancing, stood for hours having photographs taken with many people, and now they were making their way through the town. Hen was always on the lookout for Rich, but so far, there had been no sightings of him. Mac had been showing the photo of Lady Arlington to as many people as possible, but again, so far, nothing—no one recognized her.

"Hey, come on, seats! Quick, let's grab them," said Hen.

"Ah, that's better. My legs are killing me."

They sat in silence for a moment, taking in not only the wonderful feeling of resting their legs but also the atmosphere around them.

"It feels different up this side of town," said Mac.

"Yeah, I thought that. Still, the club sounds banging. Maybe we go in later," replied Hen.

A man pushing a woman in a wheelchair approached them.

"Excuse me, sir. English?"

"Yes," said Mac.

"Ah, thank goodness. Sir, this is my sister. I need to use the toilet and get a drink. Please, can I leave her with you? Please?"

Mac looked at Hen, who nodded.

"Yes, that's fine," said Mac.

"So, how are you?" Mac asked the woman.

She looked at him blankly.

"Well, I hope you're enjoying the madness. It's fun, isn't it? This is our first time. I don't mean like that—oh no, we've done it a lot. I mean, first time at the celebration. Is it yours?" asked Mac.

The woman stared at Mac. Hen had been listening and hit Mac on the arm.

"Shut the fuck up. She's not interested in your jib-jab."

"She might be. She might just be shy," said Mac, getting out the photo of Lady Arlington.

"You seen this woman?" Mac asked, showing her the photo.

The woman looked at the photo. Her expression changed, and she started twitching and kicking. Her breathing became irregular, and she was making strange noises.

"What the fuck have you done?" asked Hen.

Mac was standing over the woman, trying to keep her calm.

"Breathe—one, two, three."

"What is it? What is it?"

Mac turned around to see the man had returned.

"I don't know! She just started kicking, and then this! I was chatting to her, then I showed her a photo, and then this," explained Mac.

"What photo?"

Mac got out the photo.

"This one. We're looking for this woman, and I'm asking everyone if they know her."

Migel looked at the photo, "I know her, well, we know her. Used to work for her. Mad bitch. She got rid of me. She lives in a big villa not that far away with her—how do you say—fancy man. Evil bastard. Although, they suit each other. She tried to kill me, but she paid me well for my silence."

"How well?" asked Hen.

"Enough to keep us going."

"How about I pay you more to break your silence?" asked Hen.

Migel looked at the two men dressed as chickens, "Look, I don't know you, but not being funny—you don't look like someone who has the kind of money to match her. I'm talking millions, 'cause that's what it would take," said Migel.

"Like I said, I can pay you. I can match what you got from her and more for the right information," said Hen.

Migel was still unsure, but the thought of more money made him excited, and the thought of causing them some pain made him happy.

"Okay, look, I'll meet you here on Sunday at 12, and we'll discuss." Migel held out his hand to both men.

"Don't fuck me around, son," said Hen.

"Mate, I hate the bitch, and if you're gonna cause them pain, then I'm in. But the money needs to be on the table. Oh, and one more thing, the bloke she's with, if he's going spare, I wouldn't mind a bit of him," Migel laughed.

HEN immediately felt his blood boil. He's talking about my Rich. Cheeky Spanish bastard.

"Let's just keep it professional, shall we?" said Hen coldly.

Rich and Steph had been enjoying the carnival. They had stayed down the quieter end of town and were now heading to the main square, moving toward the music.

"I'm really tired," yawned Rich. "Can we go home?"

Steph looked at Rich. "How about a coffee, darling, then we go?" She squeezed his arm. "Come on, darling, I need a coffee to drive."

Rich smiled at her. He had been feeling strange all evening; it felt like the flu. He ached all over and could easily go straight to bed, but she was having so much fun, and he had never left early in his life, so he wasn't gonna start now!

Suddenly, he felt Steph tense up, and before he knew it, he was being dragged into the nearest coffee shop.

"Hey, babe, what's on?" asked Rich.

"Oh, sorry, I saw this one was open, and, well, we can still hear the music, so I dragged you in. Sorry, is it wrong?" she asked.

"No, no, of course not, babe."

"Tarde, señora y señor, ¿qué puedo conseguirte?"

"Dos cafés, por favor, con leche," said Steph.

"No hay problema, señora. Eh, ya se está poniendo un poco difícil. Los pescadores están causando grandes problemas. Mucho más seguro aquí, pero si empeora, cerraré."

"Gracias, señor," said Steph.

"What did he say? I didn't know you spoke Spanish," said Rich.

Steph laughed. "I don't, just a little. Anyway, it's always best to keep something hidden."

Rich looked at her. "So, what did he say?"

"He asked if we'd had enough of the noise. Then he said the fishermen were causing big trouble and we were safer here, but if it got worse, he would close."

Steph was staring across the road at two chickens.

"Fancy them, do ya?" asked Rich.

"What?"

"The chickens. Fancy a bit of their cock, do ya? You ain't stopped fuckin' staring at them since we got in here," snapped Rich.

"Don't be daft, Rich. I'm just watching the goings-on, it's fun."

"No, you're definitely looking at someone. Now fuckin' tell me, is it him?"

"Who?"

"Your other man."

"Don't start that again, Rich. I don't have another man. You're the only man I want."

"I don't believe you. Now tell me, Steph." Rich banged the table.

"Okay, if you must know, I saw McCormack, and he was talking to Migel."

"Who the fuck is that?"

"The solicitor who was blackmailing me, and he was talking to Migel, who was pushing his sister in a wheelchair."

"Are you sure?"

"Yes, of course I am! I saw him clearly; he had the top half of his chicken costume off. I know it was him. Let's just--" Before Steph could finish her sentence, Rich was up out of his seat, pushing his way across the street into the club.

Steph sat alone in the coffee shop. Now what? she wondered. He would be in the red mist, and someone would get hurt. She felt exhausted by his moods. I guess I sit here until he comes back, then I pick up the pieces of whatever he's done. We say no more about it and carry on just like we normally do!

"Cafés, por favor."

"Señora, café."

"Gracias, señor."

Lucus was feeling uneasy. The fishermen were getting louder by the second. Robin was due on stage soon, and the fishermen were an unforgiving lot—they did not understand anyone different from them.

Lucus stopped Jo. "Jo, we need to get Robin. I fear the worst. The fishermen are here, and it's getting out of control."

Jo peered through the curtains. It was wild. "Where is Robin?" she asked.

"I thought he was with you."

"No, I haven't seen him in ages."

The fishermen had made a beeline for the chickens, pretending to catch them. When they did, they tried to ride them, spinning them around and around. Mac and HEN were exhausted. Every time they tried to get away, they would be pulled back into the burly arms of another fisherman.

"Aquí, gallina, gallina, dale un vistazo a esto." (Here, hen, hen, have a peck at this.)

One of the fishermen grabbed HEN's head and forced it into his crotch.

"Aquí, gallina, gallina, cloc cloc, voy a sonar tu cuello." (Here, hen, hen, cluck cluck, I'm gonna wring your neck.)

Mac felt hands around his neck. He started to panic, his arms flapping and legs kicking. The fisherman let go, laughing as the others cheered.

Then, the music started to get dramatic. The lights dimmed, and out came Rubella to do her act. Everyone started singing along, clapping, and whistling at her, except the fishermen.

"¡Maldita sucio raro, poniendo de los nervios, cierre para arriba!" (Fucking dirty queer, getting on my nerves—shut it up!)

One of the fishermen threw his beer bottle at the stage to the cheers of the others. Then, another fisherman hurled his glass at Rubella, hitting her shoulder.

"Hey, hey! Stop that! No room for that in here," shouted Rubella.

"¡Mierda, queer sucia! ¡Nadie quiere escucharte!" (Fuck off, you dirty queer! No one wants to listen to you!)

With that, another glass was thrown, smashing into Rubella's forehead. The force of the blow knocked her backward, and she slipped on the wet floor, crashing down with a thud.

"¡Ahí, eso la calló!" (There, that shut her up!) one of the fishermen shouted to the amusement of the others.

One by one, they climbed onto the stage, yelling and inciting the crowd.

"¡Hola, españoles! Tenemos que mantenernos unidos contra los turistas y maricas." (Hey, Spanish people! We need to stick together against the enemy—tourists and queers.)

"HEY! HEY! STOP!"

A team of security guards had been called to deal with the fishermen. One by one, the guards tried to remove the men, but they were ready. Out came knives and spanners.

People started screaming as the scene turned violent.

Suddenly, a loud explosion stopped everyone in their tracks. The lights went out, and the club fell silent.

"I can smell smoke!" someone shouted.

Panic erupted. People ran for the doors, screaming—but the doors were locked.

"We can't get out!"

"HELP! HELP! HELP!"

Rich had been watching the fishermen's antics with the chickens. He wasn't too sure which one was McCormack, but he'd take both of 'em out and be done with it, he thought.

Rich was near the stage when the explosion went off. Crowds pushed past him to get out of the front, but he figured they would have a back door, so he made his way towards the back of the building. Sure enough, a queue had formed, all frantically trying to get out. Must be my lucky day, thought Rich as he watched the chickens get out of the back door. Rich pushed his way through and found himself outside in an alleyway.

Hen and Mac were standing against the wall, trying to catch their breath.

"Hey, you fuckin' piece of shit," Rich grabbed a chicken and dragged him along the alleyway. Rich started punching him, "You will never fuckin' demand any more money from me or her ever again, do ya hear me?"

Rich kicked at the chicken with such force his entire leg hurt. He rained blow after blow down onto him; then he realised the chicken was not moving.

"Fuck!"

Rich turned to walk away. It was then he saw him—HEN had been watching him. HEN had removed his top half and was just about to say something when the second explosion happened, knocking them both off their feet. The roof of the club seemed to lift up, then came flying down onto them in bits, followed by bricks and cables.

Steph had been in the restroom when the first explosion happened. She was lucky, as the explosion had caused the café windows to shatter. The café owner was shouting and crying. Steph stood in shock at the scene as she walked back into the seating area. It took her a moment to collect her thoughts and understand what had happened. It was then she realized her Rich had gone into the club across the street—the one that was in flames.

"Señora, debe irse a casa!" (You should go home!) shouted the café owner.

"Señora, no es seguro!" (It is not safe!)

"Mi amor, necesito encontrarlo!" cried Steph.

The café owner shrugged his shoulders as he shoved her out. "¡Ve, ve!" he shouted at her.

Steph joined the army of people, all wondering what to do. The fire crews were trying to pry the doors of the club open, but the heat was too intense for them despite the water cannons aimed at the flames. Steph stood rooted to the spot, looking at the burning club. She felt empty. Why did she say something? Why didn't she just go home with him?

"Why, why, why?" she screamed.

Then the second explosion happened. This time, it seemed to be at the back of the building. Steph stepped back as the roof appeared to blow up, and debris started to fall. She felt helpless, lost, almost invisible. Everyone else seemed to have someone. She sank to the pavement, head in her hands, wondering what to do.

"Looks like it's my turn to save you."

Steph looked up, it was Lucus. "Come on, you can't sit there. You're not safe."

Steph took his hand, and he led her to a makeshift base on the green. It was far enough away from the flying debris but close enough to see what was going on.

"Here, you'll be safe. Stay put," said Lucus.

"Hey, where are you going?"

"I'm trying to find Robin and Jo. My life is over without them. I love them. He is the love of my life. I need to find him," explained Lucus.

"And I need to find mine. I'm coming with you," said Steph.

"No, no, it's not for ladies. Stay here. If I find someone fit, I'll bring 'em back for ya." Lucus winked at Steph as he started to walk away.

Lucus had only gone 100 yards when the third explosion happened. This one caused a fireball to form, engulfing the club like it was made of paper. Lucus stood still, tears running down his face.

"That's it," he wailed. "No one survived that. I lost—I lost him. My love, my love!"

Steph held him in her arms.

"I can't go on. They were my family. I love them," wailed Lucus.

Tears were rolling down Steph's face. My Rich, my darling Rich, where are you? Please, somebody, tell me you're safe. Lucus and Steph held each other, trying to comfort one another.

"OH THANK GOD!"

Lucus and Steph looked up to see Jo and Robin holding each other up, covered in blood. Lucus screamed and jumped into their arms. "I thought my life was over without you! Where—I mean, how did you get out? Where have you been?" asked Lucus.

Jo explained that the fishermen had thrown something at Robin, which knocked him out, so she had dragged him off the stage as the first explosion happened. She was near the rear exit, so she made her way through that.

"So, what happened to you?" asked Jo.

"I needed air and to find Robin. I thought he would be in the café. I didn't want him to go on stage so I was outside when the explosion happened. I rushed back to the club, but the doors were jammed."

Lucus started to cry. "I thought I would never see you again."

The three of them held on to each other tightly. Steph had been listening. She was pleased the three of them were safe. She got up, "Hey, where are you going?" asked Lucus.

"Lucus, I need to find my love. I'm pleased you have found yours."

"Hey, lady," said Jo. "You can't go out there. The fire is intense. It will be a miracle if anyone makes it now. I am sorry."

"He will have made it—I know it. I must find him," said Steph.

Jo grabbed her. "No, you can't. It's not safe, and if he made it, the emergency services would have picked him up. So, he will be in the hospital; maybe go there."

Steph could feel and see the fire. She knew Jo was right.

"Thank you. Maybe I'll go home. I'm not sure I can take much more today."

"You be OK?" asked Lucus.

"Yes, I will be OK. Thank you."

"Let us come with you; make sure you're okay," insisted Lucus.

"Look, we met through bad circumstances, and here we are again. I don't want to impact you anymore," said Steph.

Robin took hold of Steph's hand. "Look, you gave us money that really helped us. The least we can do is make sure you're OK tonight. So, come on, lady, lead the way."

"Well, if you are sure, the company would be nice!"

Chapter Forty-Three

WHAT HAPPENED NEXT

"Hey, pretty boy, you okay?"

"Yeah, you?"

"I'm hurting, man."

Rich dragged himself along the road to get to HEN. Sheets of metal had fallen on him, and his leg was badly damaged. Rich picked him up and tried to walk, but he was in too much pain.

"Sorry, man, I can't. I can't."

Rich collapsed next to HEN.

"¡AQUÍ, AQUÍ, RÁPIDO, RÁPIDO! ¡DOS VIVOS!" (Here, here! Quick, quick! Two alive!) shouted a guard.

Rich was aware he was being moved, but he had no energy to resist or speak.

Steph drove home in silence. All she could think of was Rich. Jo, Robin, and Lucus were unsure if this was a good idea until they arrived at the villa.

"Is this yours?" asked Lucus.

"Yes, it's mine."

"Wow! Wow! Wow! I mean, it's nice," whistled Lucus.

Steph did not know what to say to them, so she remained silent. Jo, Robin, and Lucus did not know what to say because they had never seen a villa as big and beautiful as this one. Steph watched them as they wandered around with their mouths open.

"Let me show you your rooms. You all have a bathroom, so help yourself to a bath or shower. As for food and drink, if it's in the house, you can have it. I'm tired. I'm off to bed. See you in the morning."

"What we gonna do?" asked Jo. "We can't stay here. What if he comes back? He'll kill us."

"Calm down," said Robin. "He was in the club. He'll be toast."

"But how about if he got out? He's an animal, Rob," insisted Jo.

"Look, if he comes home, he will be with her. He's not interested in us. Come on, let's rest. We need it. Just lock your door or something," said Robin.

Steph had made her way to their bedroom. She could smell his aftershave in the air. She climbed into bed, hugging his pillow.

Oh, Rich, please be safe. Don't leave me like this. I love you. I need you. We are good together.

She cried as she fell asleep, dreaming of him.

THE FOLLOWING DAY

The cleanup had begun. The club had almost burnt to the ground, taking with it some shops and cafés. The air was heavy, smoky, and dusty. Because the building was still smoldering in small pockets, a fire crew remained present at the site. An investigation into the cause of the blaze had started. The area was full of news reporters taking photos and doing TV broadcasts from the scene.

Cannary news

So far, we know that 77 people have died, according to the authorities. The authorities expect to find more. Authorities have confirmed that they took 121 people to the hospital with various degrees of burns or smoke inhalation. However, some had life-changing injuries. Investigations have begun into how the blaze started. The owners of the building have been informed that they confirmed they rented out the building. We do not have any further details on who actually rented it, but speaking with some locals, it was a young man known as Robin, apparently a lovely young man. He has not been seen since the explosion. We fear he may have been inside the club! We will, of course, bring you more news as it comes in, now on to other island news...

Steph turned off the TV and started to cry. The nightmare was real. Her Rich was missing, and how would they ever identify him? That's it, she thought. He's on the run. He's always running away. Maybe he was in the hospital and escaped because that's what he would do. He would hate the hospital. Maybe he is making his way home!

Steph caught her reflection. Best you tidy yourself up, girl, if you think he is on his way! One by one, her guests joined her.

"Here, help yourself to breakfast. How did you sleep?" asked Steph.

"Fantastic! Your beds are really comfy," replied Lucus.

Steph smiled. He reminded her of Terrance. When he was young, he was enthusiastic and forever hopeful, just like Lucus. Steph was not sure how or when Terrance turned into a lazy snob, but that's what he had become. Bless him. She missed him. She had high hopes for him, especially when Cindy came on the scene. She imagined grandchildren and being a glamorous granny, driving the Bentley to the beach with a few grandchildren in the back while the parents had a cheeky weekend away.

Steph sighed. Then it all changed. "Hey, you okay? You're miles away," said Lucus, waving his hands in front of her face.

"Oh, sorry. Yes, just thinking what to do next. I'm guessing you three will want a lift back to town?"

Robin's eyes welled up. "I don't know where to start," he wailed. "I feel so guilty. I handled the club, but I don't know what happened. I will be arrested. They will lock me up."

"Hey, come on," said Steph. "You don't know this. I will help you. I have money, whatever you need, okay? But in return, I want your silence. I don't want you discussing me, this villa, or my husband-to-be. Is that a deal?" asked Steph.

"What, you're gonna marry that bastard?" shouted Jo.

"Enough," snapped Robin.

Steph looked at the three of them. "It's okay. I know what you think. I don't care, but I am buying your silence. So is it a deal or not?"

The boys nodded. "NO! Not mine. You're not buying mine. He's an animal! I bet you're gonna tell me he didn't do that to your neck and your eye. I ain't stupid, lady," exclaimed Jo.

Steph touched her neck. She had forgotten about her injuries.

"Jo," said Robin, "we need to stick together. Who is more important, me or him?"

"You, of course. He's just a bag of shit," said Jo.

"Then, babe, do as she asks. For me, stay silent."

Jo sighed and nodded. "Okay, but I won't forget."

Lucus had been listening. He felt the intense sadness coming from Robin, the intense anger coming from Jo, and the intense despair coming from Steph. He liked Steph. She had something about her that reminded him of his mother. Not that he really knew his mother. His father had kicked her out when he was fou, but from what he could remember and from what his gran told him, Steph was like his mother.

"You okay, Lucus?" asked Steph.

"I also feel responsible. I'm lost and angry, and I don't know what to do," cried Lucus.

"Come on." Steph held out her arms. "Come on, we will get through this. You are all in shock."

Lucus let Steph hold him. He felt strangely safe in her arms.

"Come on, we need a plan," announced Steph. "Jo, get the coffee. Come on, gang, let's sit and plan. Robin, who owns the club? Do you have insurance?"

Robin looked up. "I don't know. I rented through an agent, and yes, I have content insurance and insurance for people, but not for the building."

"You need to speak with the agents, Robin. Jo, go with him. You're sensible, so listen to what they are saying. Robin lay it on thick. It was an old building, not maintained by the landlord, etc. Oh, and don't admit to anything, okay? Do you want to come back here tonight or go home?" asked Steph.

"Stay."

"Home?"

"Home."

"Home it is. I will drop you there, and then I am going to the hospital. I think that's where my love is," smiled Steph.

Lucus looked at her; she looked shattered. "How about I come with you? I can translate if you need."

Steph smiled at Lucus; he was a good boy. "Thank you. I would appreciate that." The hospital was busy. A special desk had been set up to deal with the major incident.

"Name?" said a rather abrupt guard.

"Stephanie Arlington."

"Problem?"

"I don't have one. I am looking for someone. I think they came in last night."

"Name?"

"Richard Luck."

"No, senora, no one of that name. Try missing persons."

Steph took a step back and burst into tears.

"Come on," said Lucus. "We need to go over there."

"Senora," said the man at missing persons.

"Do you speak English?" asked Steph.

"A little. Manchester United," he said, smiling.

"I am looking for someone. He was in the club last night, and now, well, we cannot find him. He must be here."

"Name?" asked the man.

"Richard Luck."

"No, no one identified as that, but we have many unidentified, so I think he is one. I put his name on the list," said the man at the desk.

"That's it then," said Lucus. "He's dead."

"No, no! It can't be! He would have got out. Ask her, ask her!" shouted Steph, pointing to a nurse.

Lucus ran over to the nurse and chatted in Spanish.

"Come on," said Lucus. "They have set up a ward for the injured."

The pair ran along the corridor and up one flight of stairs. "Here!" shouted Lucus. Steph rushed to the doors and started banging on the glass.

"Can I help you?"

The pair turned around to see a nurse. "We are looking for someone and were told he was on this ward."

The nurse looked at them. "I'm new here, so I don't know the patients. I was in the bank but got called in due to the incident. Now, what was the name?" asked the nurse.

"Richard Luck," said Steph, full of hope.

Mandy went cold as the name was said. Surely not. It can't be the same one.

"Wait here. I'll find out for you." Mandy made her way onto the ward and straight to the toilet. She felt sick and excited at the thought of him being on the ward. It can't be him, can it? And who are those people? Mandy informed them he was not on the ward. She actually did not know; this was her first shift. And just think, if it is him, this must be fate, and all her dreams have come true. And if it's not him, well, they are no worse off, thought Mandy.

Steph cried all the way back to the car. "I don't believe it. I feel he is still alive. Maybe he's injured somewhere. That's it! He's lying in the street somewhere. Come on, Lucus, help me find him." Lucus went along with her. He could see the desperation in her eyes and could feel the hope she had in her heart.

Steph and Lucus stood outside the burnt-out club. People had left flowers with beautiful messages. "He is not dead. He didn't die here. I know it," Steph wailed. "I must go in."

Lucus held her back. "You can't go in. Come on, let's get a coffee."

Lucus dragged her away. "He is not dead. I know it. We have a connection, and it's not broken. He's alive."

Steph was inconsolable. "So where is he?" asked Lucus. "Cause if he's hiding, this ain't fair."

Steph looked at Lucus. "You don't understand. He is not like most people. He runs away from things. Something overtakes him, and he runs until he can think straight. He means no harm." Lucus put his arm around Steph. Poor woman is deranged, he thought. "We will see, we will see. Come on, let's go get some coffee and find the others."

Jo and Robin had opened up the café. A few people sat having a drink, but the atmosphere was heavy. Everyone sat in silence.

"Hello, you two. How did you get on? Come sit down and tell me all," said Robin.

"He's dead," announced Lucus.

"No, no, he is not! I know it! They just put his name down on the register, but they didn't know," cried Steph.

"She is in denial," said Lucus.

"I'm still here," snapped Steph.

A group of men walked into the café.

"Can you provide us with some refreshments and some cake or something, please? We are working at the scene, and it's hard going."

"Yes, yes, of course. Take a seat," said Robin.

"Excuse me, señor," said Steph. "I couldn't help but overhear. You are working in the burnt-down club. Is that correct?"

"Yes, ma'am."

"Well, I am missing someone, and the last I saw of him, he was going into the club."

"I'm sorry, ma'am, for your loss," said the man.

"No, no, you don't understand! I know he's alive. I feel it."

"Ma'am, I'm sorry. No one would have survived. It was an inferno," said the man.

"But, sir, the club had a back door."

"I'm sorry, ma'am. Everything blew up. At this stage, I cannot say anymore."

Steph picked up her bag and walked out of the café, heading for the beach. She walked along the beach, remembering the last time she did this with Rich—how he held her, kissed her, and then they booked into a cheap hotel, pretending not to know each other. She smiled. She loved him so much. All she wanted was for him to come back to her. He could have anything he wanted. He could do anything he wanted. She would never challenge him again. She would never upset him again. He could be in control. She would even marry him if he asked her! I just need to feel your arms around me, she whispered. Feel your lips on mine. See you smile.

Steph made her way back to the car. "Now what? How do I find him? I know he is still alive." She drove back to the hospital and made her way toward the ward. It was where she got the strongest feeling.

"Oh, you again," said security. "We told you he is not here. Now, please go."

"No! I won't until I have looked myself. Let me on that bloody ward! I know he is in there!" screamed Steph.

"¡Alerta, alerta!" called the guard into his microphone as he tried to block Steph from going any further.

Soon, six additional guards appeared. "¡Cálmate, mamá! ¡Cálmate, mamá!" they shouted as they bundled Steph out of the hospital.

"So, what we gonna do tonight?" asked Lucus.

"Go home. Why?" replied Jo.

"What about Steph?"

"She will be alright. We have our own shit to deal with," said Jo.

"I know, but I like her, and she is really hurting," said Lucus.

"For fuck's sake, Lucus! She was living with a murderer—a monster. Did you see her neck? Good riddance, that's what I say. She will get over it. She's got money, so she can go anywhere she wants. She can buy what she wants and who she wants. So, no, I don't feel sorry for her," snapped Jo. "I feel sorry for us. We are on our arse."

"But she will help us," said Lucus. "She said--"

"Yeah, she will throw money at us, and we will be her little puppets. Yes, miss. No, miss. Three fuckin' bags full, miss. No, you're alright. I would rather starve," said Jo.

"Come on, Jo, we need help," said Robin.

"You two can do what you want. I'm going back to the flat. I need to sleep."

Robin and Lucus looked at each other, "Okay, we stay together. One for all and all for one, no matter what the circumstances," sighed Robin.

Chapter Forty-Four

MANDY'S STORY

Jessie had joined Mandy in New Zealand. Mandy's family fell in love with Jessie. Mandy got carried away with everyone's opinion of him, agreeing to marry him when he proposed at a family BBQ, much to the delight of her family. They married a few months later at a lovely mountaintop venue. Jessie adored Mandy. She was the woman of his dreams, and he would do anything for her.

Jessie desperately wanted children. Mandy wanted to travel before having kids, so Jessie agreed to travel to get it out of the way. They had been saving money and had been given quite a substantial sum by Mandy's grandfather. Jessie was keen to get on and find somewhere they could call home. Their travels had taken them to Singapore and Miami, then on to Rome and Venice, on to Lake Como and Madrid, on to Benidorm and Morocco, and now Gran Canaria.

They had allocated money for the travels, and this was now running low. "Mands, we need to pick some work up for a few months, enough to get back home and start our family," grinned Jessie one day.

Mandy found a job in the hospital as a junior nurse. Even though she was qualified, she could not practice until she had been on refresher courses. Mandy was okay with this. It was a bank job, but so far, every day they needed her, she worked—mostly on the ward for the elderly. Jessie got a job in a bar. They rented a flat, and suddenly, Gran Canaria began to feel like home.

"I like it here, Mands," said Jessie. "The people are friendly, and the tips are amazing," he joked. "You have finally got a day off work?" asked Jessie.

"Yes, well, until tonight. They want me to work on the trauma ward set up for the victims of the fire," explained Mandy.

"Oh, another night alone without my beautiful wife. Whatever will I do?" said Jessie.

"You'll manage."

"No, never! Not without you. Come here, show me how much you love your husband." Mandy knew what she had to do to get left alone. "You're a naughty boy," she said. "Now come here." Jessie crawled on his hands and knees toward her.

"You're a naughty boy. You have been a bad, bad boy. You know what happens to bad boys, don't you? Now, take your trousers off."

Jessie undid his trousers. "Now then, boy, take this!" Mandy got out the leather belt and slapped it across his arse.

"Please, please!" shouted Jessie.

"Take that, you naughty boy," Mandy said as she landed another slap, then another.

"That's it!" shouted Jessie. "I'm coming! Harder, harder!" Mandy continued to slap the belt across his arse until he was satisfied.

"Oh, my darling," said Jessie. "I love you so much. I want us to try for children, Mands. When can I, you know, do the dirty inside you?" asked Jessie.

Mandy looked at her husband. He was a good man—just not a sexy one. But this is what she had. "Come, let's have a sleep," said Mandy as she got into bed, feeling thoroughly fed up.

Mandy looked forward to going to work. Tonight would be different. She was making her way to the ward when she came across two people, one of them banging on the ward doors.

"Can I help you?" asked Mandy. It was at that moment life changed for Mandy. They were looking for Richard Luck—a name she was convinced she would never hear again. Of course, Mandy lied to them, dismissing them without even checking. And now, here she was, looking at him lying unconscious in a side room with no name above his bed. He was referred to as Side Room C. Mandy could hardly believe it. She checked his notes. He had no ID, and his unconscious state was a mystery.

"Nurse, what are you doing in here?" Mandy turned around. It was a senior nurse. "I—I cannot believe it. This is my brother! I never thought I would see him again. I am in shock."

"Are you sure?" asked the senior.

"Yes, yes, of course."

"In that case, you will need to complete the forms for us. What is his name?" asked the nurse.

"Name?"

"Yes, what is his name?"

"Oh, er... Cane. Mr. Cane. Richard Cane," said Mandy.

The nurse studied Mandy. "And you are sure this is your brother?"

"Yes, yes, of course. And I know I will have to look after him because he has no ID," said Mandy.

"How do you know this?" asked the senior.

"Oh, I'm guessing. My brother never carries an ID. He is what we call a gypsy," laughed Mandy.

"Well, okay. You must run along now. You are down to work on the other side," said the senior.

"Oh, I cannot leave my brother now that I have found him. If I have to work, then I need to stay on this side," insisted Mandy.

"Very well."

The shift was straightforward. Mandy popped in and out of Rich's room; he remained unconscious.

"Hey, nurse."

Mandy turned around. "Yes?"

"Is that my mate in there?"

"And who would that be, sir?"

"Rich. Richard."

"Oh yes, I mean… no," said Mandy, quickly closing the door.

"I think it is."

"No, no, sir. He died. It's another patient in this room, sorry. Now, you need to get to bed."

Hen looked down at the floor, tears welling in his eyes. My Rich is dead. Gone forever.

Mandy looked at Hen. "Whatever is wrong?" she asked.

"I have lost someone very special. Someone I loved and hated at the same time... but the love would always take over. It was so wrong and so right. Now I'm lost."

"I know what you mean," she said. "I had something similar with someone. He left me, and, well, I never thought I would see him again. But do you know what? Fate can sometimes be kind... although I'm not sure what I'm going to do. I'm married now, and this could blow it all up. Oh, listen to me, telling you my problems when you're the one crippled by a bomb and will never walk again," said Mandy.

"None taken," said Hen.

The girl gave him bad vibes. She reminded him of the stalker he had a few years ago. Now, she was strange—giving off the same energy as that one. Hen recalled the times with Daisy May, the stalker, and how Rich found it funny. But he was also one of the first to help.

Daisy May had become obsessed with Hen. She would turn up at his door, making up stories of rape or claiming she was being chased by a group of men. His security team would feel sorry for her and take her in. The next thing he knew, she'd be cooking in his kitchen. Hen smiled—it was quite funny now, although not at the time.

Rich had grabbed Hen and kissed him passionately in front of her. Rich made her believe Hen was gay and no good to her. She kicked off big time at Rich. Hen remembered him laughing at her, which only made it worse. Eventually, she got the message and disappeared. Rich said he had nothing to do with it—but you never know with Rich, thought Hen. And now he's gone.

"You okay?" asked Mandy.

"When did he die?" asked Hen.

"Who?"

"My friend."

"Sorry, who is your friend?"

"Well, the one in this room. You said he was dead. So, when?" demanded Hen.

"Look, love, I'm new. I'm sorry. I don't know the details. Anyway, I must go. Maybe I'll come back later, and we can chat. Now, off to bed."

Hen's senses kicked in—this woman was lying to him. Hen watched the nurse all night. She was in and out of the side room. She even put her chair across the doorway as if guarding it. Hen could sniff out dodgy, and this bird was dodgy.

Jessie was in bed when Mandy returned home. "Oh, my darling, come cuddle your old man." Mandy cuddled up to Jessie, but in her mind, it was Rich. She imagined she was holding him. Her hands roamed over Jessie's body, her breathing growing heavier.

"I want you," she whispered. "I want you."

Jessie rolled over. "Darling, Mr. Pickles isn't ready," he said.

"What?" she replied, suddenly realizing this wasn't Rich—it was her husband, Jessie.

Mandy rolled away. "Forget it. You're never fuckin' ready," she snapped.

"Hey, hey, come on, what's this about?" Jessie asked, stroking her hair. "Come on, you're emotional. Are you due on, darling? 'Cause if you are, we better track your cycle."

Jessie smiled at the thought of making a baby one day. Mandy recoiled in horror at the idea of having a baby with him. She wanted Rich in her bed. She just had to figure out a way to get him out of the hospital, and then they could be together forever. They could get married and Live where? She had nowhere to go. No spare money.

Tears fell from Mandy's eyes as she drifted off to sleep. Jessie had been watching her. He couldn't understand why she was so tense. She must be overworking, he thought. I can't have that; her health is more important than the money.

Jessie decided to call the hospital and inform them Mandy wouldn't be at work for the rest of the week due to a virus. She'll thank me later, he thought.

RICH

Rich began to wake. The bright lights hurt his eyes, and he immediately closed them again. His brain felt slow; he had no clue where he was. He could not hear anything, just a low buzzing sound.

Rich shouted, "Help," or at least he thought he did, as nothing came out of him. Suddenly, panic set in as he realized he could not hear or speak, and he had no clue where he was. He began banging his hands on the bed.

A nurse rushed in. "Hey, hey, hey! Señor, sh-sh-sh…" she said, reaching for the call bell and holding his hand to soothe him. A doctor came running in. Rich was thrashing about the bed. As the doctor tried to restrain him, Rich pushed him and the nurse. They both went tumbling to the floor, shouting for backup. HEN was wheeling himself down the corridor as the commotion started.

"Hey! English?" questioned a medic to HEN.

HEN nodded.

"Come." The medic asked HEN to come into the side room. He pointed to Rich. "English, English."

HEN looked up to see Rich, who was clearly distressed and thrashing about the bed.

"Hey, man! Pretty boy!" he shouted.

HEN moved the staff out of the way to grab Rich's hand. He started drawing with his finger a sign into his palm.

Rich immediately responded. He opened his eyes to see HEN holding his hand and a group of strange people around him. Rich looked at HEN. He could see his mouth moving, but Rich could hear nothing. Rich just stared at him.

"Man, you're okay. You're in the hospital. I thought you were dead. I came to find you, and now look at us. But we are gonna be alright. No more messin'. I found you. You can have everything I have, man. I just want to be with you. Will you… will you marry me?" asked HEN.

Rich looked at HEN. He could not hear a thing. He looked around the room as the people stared at him. HEN had tears in his eyes. Rich wondered what on earth was going on.

"Speak to me, man. Speak to me," said HEN.

Rich just stared at him.

"I don't think he can hear you," said the doctor. "Looks like the blast may have damaged his hearing. Can you write something down and see if he responds?"

HEN was given a pen and paper.

HEY, pretty boy, you okay? Can you hear?

Rich looked at the paper. He shook his head, then wrote:

No.

Okay, pretty BOY, the DOCTOR wants to send you for some tests. You okay with that?

Rich grabbed the pen. *Yeah, but get this fuckin' thing out of my arm and get me a drink and something to eat. And I want to go home. Okay?*

HEN smiled as he nodded and put a thumbs-up to Rich.

The tests confirmed Rich had damage to both ears, and his hearing recovery was uncertain. His speech was also affected, and the doctors were unsure if this resulted from his hearing loss or if he had lost the ability to speak. "Time will tell, time will tell," said the doctor. Fuckin' no good, thought HEN. I will get him back home and get the best, most expensive medical help for him.

Rich needed time to gather his thoughts and build his strength up. His hearing was gone, and his speech was strange. He decided not to say anything, as it felt strange. HEN had informed him it might or might not be permanent.

HEN seemed to oversee Rich's care. His senses had kicked in, and he knew when something was wrong. And he felt strongly that something was wrong—why was HEN here? He was good company. He sat with him throughout the day, and anything that Rich wanted, HEN got. They played cards and watched Spanish TV. Not that Rich could hear it, but he tried. And maybe he was imagining it, but he thought his hearing was improving—not that he would say anything.

HEN wrote: *Come on, mate, take me for a walk. You can push this wheelchair. The sun's shining.*

Rich looked at the note, smiled, and nodded.

"¡Hola, señor! ¡Deténgase, deténgase!" shouted the nurse.

HEN held his hand up for Rich to stop. The nurse came running to them, "Señor, no dejo salir a su hermana."

"English, English!" shouted HEN.

"Un momento, un momento," said the nurse as she ran to get someone.

Once she was out of sight, HEN raised his hand to Rich and beckoned him to go. They both laughed as Rich raced down the corridor, pushing HEN.

"Stop! Stop!" came the shouts, but Rich was oblivious to them, and HEN was having none of it. He had a van arranged, ready to pick them up. They had almost reached the doors when two security guards blocked the way. Rich stopped, unsure why they were doing this. The team of doctors and nurses soon caught up with them.

"Sir, sir, why do you do this?" asked the doctor to Rich.

"He can't hear you," answered HEN. "We were just going to the gardens. What's the deal? Why can't we get fresh air?"

"Sir, you can, but this gentleman, Mr. Cane, may not leave the hospital without his sister."

HEN looked at the doctor. "This is not Mr. Cane, and he does not have a sister. You have the wrong man."

The doctor looked puzzled. "No, no, sir. He is the brother of a nurse here in the hospital."

"No, I am telling you he does not have a sister, and he is not Mr. Cane. His name is Richard Luck," explained HEN.

The doctor shook his head as he explained to the team surrounding him in Spanish. Rich looked from one to the other, then to HEN. He sensed something was not right, and he sensed it had to do with him.

Rich grabbed some paper and wrote: *What the fuck?*

HEN smiled and wrote back: *Apparently, you have a sister, and your name is Mr. Cane.*

Fuck off, wrote Rich. <u>Tell 'em I don't have a fuckin' sister.</u>

I know.

Well, tell 'em.

I have.

Well, tell 'em again.

The doctor wrote: *What is your name, sir?*

Richard Luck.

What is your sister's name?

I don't have a sister.

The doctor looked puzzled.

Rich grabbed the paper again and wrote: *Call her. Tell her to come NOW.*

The doctor nodded. "Okay, we will do this if you come back to the ward so we can sort this out." HEN nodded, and back they went to the ward to wait.

Jessie thought he was doing the right thing when he squashed some sleeping pills into Mandy's orange juice. She had been sleeping for almost two days. She would wake up for the toilet, and Jessie would help her out of bed and back again. She would take a drink, and before he knew it, she was fast asleep again.

Jessie was getting annoyed by Mandy's phone constantly ringing. It was the hospital. He had informed them she was not fit for work, so why were they ringing?

"Hello," snapped Jessie as he answered the phone.

"Ah, señor, please, I need to speak to Miss Cane."

"Miss Cane?" questioned Jessie.

"Yes, sir."

"Do you mean my wife, Mandy?"

"Er, yes, sir."

"I have told you she is too ill to work."

"No, no, sir, it is her brother. He is trying to leave the hospital, and, well, she asked us not to allow it and to let her know."

Jessie felt quite confused. Mandy did not have a brother, and why did they have her maiden name?

"Ok, ok, I'll tell her," said Jessie.

Jessie looked at Mandy sleeping. She could go nowhere. It's best if I sort this out, thought Jessie.

Rich and HEN waited on the ward. HEN communicated with Rich on paper. Rich was sure he was hearing some things, but he remained silent. Eventually, Jessie arrived at the hospital. The senior staff would not allow him in. Luckily, Jessie had taken Mandy's passport, marriage certificate, and a letter from the hospital. Before allowing Jessie onto the ward, the senior staff engaged in a good hour of conversation.

Jessie was not prepared for what he was about to see. "What the fuck are you doing here?" he shouted as he looked at Rich. Then he saw HEN. "Well, well, well, I might have known—two fuckin' weirdos together. I can't believe this! You two in my fuckin' space again and getting my wife involved again. What were you gonna do this time to her?" he shouted at Rich.

Rich just looked at him. He knows me. And why is he throwing his arms around? He looks angry, thought Rich.

"He can't hear you, mate," said HEN.

Jessie stopped shouting.

"Come and sit down, man. You look exhausted," said HEN.

Jessie sat on the bed. "So, what's going on?" he asked HEN.

"Dunno. All I know is that bird of yours said she was his sister and that he wasn't allowed out of the hospital. Anyway, where is she?" asked HEN.

"Oh, sleeping. She's not too well."

"You still a copper?" asked HEN.

"No, mate, I work in a bar. I would report you both, but to be honest, I can't be bothered. I've moved on with my life. I don't care—just stay away from me and my wife."

"Well, can you tell these idiots he's not her brother and his name is not Mr. Cane?"

Jessie looked at HEN. "Well, I can confirm his name, but they need Mandy to say she made a mistake."

"Well, can you get her to do that?" asked HEN.

"Yeah, sure," said Jessie, unconvinced.

Rich watched on, trying to lip-read as HEN, the nurse, and now some bloke were very animated. He was sure he knew this dude talking to HEN, but he could not place him. *He wished he could hear.*

Rich grabbed some paper. *What the fuck's going on?* he wrote.

HEN looked at Jessie and shook his head. "Don't say anything—he'll go mad."

"Oh, still not controlled his temper then?" snarled Jessie.

"Well, it can't be that bad if your missus is willing to give it another go, so I would shut the fuck up, mate," replied HEN.

"What do you mean?"

"Well, it's fuckin' obvious—she said he was her brother so that she could take him home," said HEN.

"But I'm at home," said Jessie, puzzled.

HEN scoffed. "For now. Bet she was planning on getting rid of ya."

Jessie looked at the floor. *She did seem rather off with me, but it can't be. She wanted to have a baby with me as soon as possible,* he thought.

"Oi!" shouted HEN. "How does your missus know him?"

"He was the bastard that locked her up in a cottage, raped her most nights, and then left her to die," hissed Jessie.

"Oh," said HEN. "How do ya know it was him?"

"His DNA was all over it—and a few others. I should inform the police and get him put away, but you know what? I was a good copper, and they allowed some idiot to run the show. He was a lazy bastard, and he took all the credit for everything. So why should I help them out?"

"Good. I'm glad you feel like that. I thought I may have to get rough or get me chequebook out."

Jessie looked up. "Now you're talking. A few hundred thousand should keep me quiet."

"I do the deals," snapped HEN. "Get that wife to sign the papers, and we have a deal."

THE BAR

"You alright, mate?" asked Lucus.

"Living the fuckin' dream, mate, livin' the dream. Still, I'll be out of this shithole and this job soon," said Jessie.

"How come?" asked Lucus.

Jessie knew he should say nothing, but he was bursting to tell someone. It had been a week since his path had crossed with two of the scumbags from his past, but one of them had what he needed—money. And right now, Jessie would do anything for some big bucks. He was sure money would help bring his wife out of her current depression.

Mandy had admitted to making a mistake at the hospital, but since then, the hospital had not called her for work, and she blamed Jessie. She had taken to her bed and refused to get up. She would not speak to him, let alone let him anywhere near her. Jessie was glad he had this little job in the bar to get him out of the way and to earn some money. Lucus had only recently started working in the bar. Since the fire, things were really tough, so they all had to work harder to bring in some money. Lucus enjoyed working in bars, and this bar was busy enough for him, with a variety of people to chat with. Yes, he would like a day off, but at the moment, they could not afford to have a day off.

"So, you were saying, mate—you're out of here?"

"Yeah, yeah, let's just say some wealthy dude needs me to keep silent, so he's paying well. I won't have to work for a while," replied Jessie.

"Nice," said Lucus, instantly jealous. "Well, if he needs anything else, send him my way. I know people and how things work around here."

"Sure will. He may need a passport for the bastard he's taking with him."

Lucus looked at Jessie. "Sounds complicated."

"Yeah," laughed Jessie. "Sure is. Slimy bastard—like a cat with nine lives."

Lucus felt intrigued and wanted to know the details. This could be a great story to tell the others, and he needed money. Maybe this bloke would pay him to keep quiet, but he needed to know the details, and Jessie was talking in riddles.

Lucus thought about his situation as he cleaned the bar. He and Robin were happy together, but since the fire, Robin became stressed and worked day and night to bring in whatever money he could. Jo also worked as much as she could, but the money was just swallowed up by bills. Since Steph retreated to her villa, things had been difficult. Lucus knew she would help them, but Jo would have none of it.

"No! Just 'cus she got money doesn't make her a nice person. In fact, she's as bad as that bastard she wants to marry. He tried to kill me—leave me for dead—and she don't even care. No! Leave her!" Jo had screamed at them.

So the three of them struggled on. It was no fun. They worked day and night, seven days and nights a week, and still, they were no better off.

"Hey, mate, I was thinking—this friend of yours, you will tell him about me and how I can help with whatever he needs," said Lucus.

"Yeah, sure," said Jessie, wishing he had said nothing. All he wanted was his money and to be out of there. He dreamt of taking Mandy back home and starting a family—living by a river in a little cottage. He would go out to work, and Mandy would stay at home and look after the children. She would cook lovely meals for him, and they would be so in love. Life would be perfect. Jessie was convinced this would happen once he had enough money, and he was so close now to getting his dream.

Lucus smelled an opportunity a mile off. He also smelled a rat and thought Jessie had no intention of telling this bloke about him.

"Hey, man, fancy a drink after work?" asked Lucus.

"No, I need to get home," replied Jessie.

"Oh, she sure got you tied up," laughed Lucus.

Jessie looked at Lucus. He was right; Mandy treated him like a dog. He did everything for her, and now she wouldn't even speak to him.

"Why not, mate? Go on, let's have a drink after work." Fuck her, thought Jessie. Treat her mean—maybe then she'll want me.

The shift finished, and Jessie and Lucus stayed behind for a quiet drink. "Hey, man, sit down. Let me get the drinks." Lucus made sure Jessie's was a triple toffee vodka, and his own was a Coke with zero alcohol. It wasn't long before Jessie was wrecked.

"So, who's your wealthy friend then, mate?" asked Lucus.

"Well, actually, he's a criminal—shhhh, don't tell. I don't care. He can do what he wants. I could never fuckin' catch him anyway. Good riddance to him and his bastard mate. I don't care if they're a couple, just as long as he pays me, but don't tell anyone. Shhhh," laughed Jessie.

"Another little vodka, mate?" asked Lucus.

"Maybe just a small one. I must go to the wife. Well, some wife— she wanted to run off with the bastard, but oh no, I stopped her," Jessie laughed. "And now look, she won't speak to me."

Lucus was puzzled. Jessie wasn't making sense.

"So, who was your wife running away with?" asked Lucus.

"The same bastard that kept her locked away. I told ya, mate— shhhh," said Jessie, stumbling around.

"So, is he the rich man?"

"No, no, he's not got a penny to scratch his arse," laughed Jessie.

Lucus scratched his head. This made no sense.

"So, what's the rich man's name?" asked Lucus.

"Tom. Tom," laughed Jessie.

"Tom?"

"Yeah, Tom."

"Tom what?"

"Tom I-don't-fuckin'-know. Just Tom."

"And you say he has money?"

"Yeah, loads of it."

"How do you know?"

"'Cause he operates all the drug trafficking in and out of most cities."

"Oh."

"And the other bloke? What's his name?"

Lucus waited for the answer, but Jessie had collapsed in a heap.

Robin was out of his mind with worry. Lucus was always home by now.

"Something bad has happened," he said to Jo as he paced up and down the flat.

"No, the little shit is still working or…"

"Or what?" demanded Robin.

"Just still working," replied Jo.

"Oh, so you think he's with someone else, don't ya?"

"No, of course not. I mean, you two are solid. Just 'cause you're not married doesn't mean you don't love him, does it?" said Jo.

Robin looked at Jo. "That's not helpful."

Robin knew he had been neglecting Lucus lately. They had no quality time together; just work and more work. They needed a break. They needed money.

Robin suddenly had an awful thought. What if Lucus had gone back to being a *Ratboy* to earn more money? Just as he was about to ask Jo what she thought, Lucus came through the door, propping up another man.

"Where the fuck you been? I've been worried. And who is that?" asked Robin.

"Shh," laughed Jessie.

"It's okay, Robin. I'll explain. I couldn't leave him. He just needs to sleep it off. I thought he could stay on the couch," said Lucus.

"I'm off to bed now the little shit is back—and whatever this is," said Jo, pointing to Jessie.

"So compassionate as usual," snapped Lucus.

Robin made Jessie comfortable on the floor. "Come on, my love, to bed," said Robin, holding his hand out to Lucus.

Lucus smiled. "Thought you'd never ask."

"Fuckin' hell, Robin, where has this come from?"

"What?"

"All this passion."

"I realized I've been neglecting you. Will you marry me?"

"Kiss me."

"69 me."

"OMG, yes, yes, yes."

"Yes, yes, take me, have it all."

"Oh, Robin, yes, I will marry you."

Despite Lucus's attempts to explain everything to Robin, Robin remains confused about Jessie. However, he was aware of Lucus's ability to extract information from people and believed that if Lucus was right, it might solve some of their money issues.

"I have to go to work, darling. Be careful, and I'll see you tonight sometime. Love you," said Robin, kissing Lucus passionately.

Lucus smiled. "Leave it to me, baby."

Jessie was still fast asleep on the floor. It was early, but Lucus was impatient. He wanted to know more from Jessie.

"Oh, he's still here then," said Jo as she stumbled into the kitchen. "Want some coffee?"

"Yeah, please. Make one for our guest, will ya?"

Jo made the coffee and sat with Lucus. "So what's the story?"

Lucus explained what he knew.

"Sounds like this could be a waste of time. Just make sure you go to work today, Lucus, and don't waste your time chasing something that isn't yours," said Jo.

Lucus felt slight disappointment that Jo didn't believe he could get money through other means. *Working isn't the only way, Jo,* he thought.

"Hey, man, I made you coffee," said Lucus, shaking Jessie. "Hey, man, coffee."

Jessie started to stir, slowly opening his eyes. "Where am I? Oh, me back. Oh, me arm. Fuckin' hell, I'm sore all over. Who are you?"

Lucus laughed. "Bloody hell, man, you still pissed? I'm your work buddy. We're going to the hospital."

"We are? Why?" asked Jessie.

"'Cause you asked me to go with you to see Mr. Big," Lucus replied.

Jessie drank his coffee and tried to think. "What happened? Why am I here? And where *am* I?"

"You're in my place. You came back with me. We had a bit to drink, and, well, you didn't want to go home. You asked me to go to the hospital with you today 'cause you need to get your money."

It all began to come back to Jessie, although he didn't remember asking Lucus to come with him. "Oh, sorry, man, I must have been drunk. Ignore me. I can't take you."

"NO! You promised me an introduction. I had to listen to you all night talk about your fuckin' problems. Now the least you can do is introduce me, man!" shouted Lucus.

"Okay, okay. What time is it?"

"Nine. Why?"

"'Cause he said I had to meet him at ten. Or was it eleven?" said Jessie.

"Fucks sake, man, we better get going."

HEN was waiting for Jessie as arranged. "You're late. And who the fuck is this?" asked HEN.

"This is Lucus. I thought he might be useful for ya. He knows a lot of people, and you can trust him."

HEN looked at Lucus. "Fancy earning some money, do ya?"

"Yes, sir."

HEN turned to Jessie. "Here. It's all there. Nice doing business with ya. Now fuck off and say nothing about this to anyone. I might be in a wheelchair, but I will hunt you down if I hear a whisper."

Jessie checked the money. "My lips are sealed."

"Right, you come with me. You can push me back to the ward. We can chat," said HEN.

Lucus was happy to oblige.

HEN had secured a private room in the hospital. He was having physio and waiting for a new wheelchair. Apart from that, he was ready to leave.

Rich was also in a private room, undergoing physio. His hearing had not fully returned—not that he had said anything to anyone. He quite liked people thinking he couldn't hear. With the papers sorted, Rich was now ready for discharge. What Rich didn't understand was—where was Steph? He thought about her all the time. And why was HEN paying for the private room? Why was he in charge of everything? HEN hadn't mentioned Steph, and from what Rich could gather, HEN wanted to take him back home.

Rich had other ideas. He hadn't made the move to Spain just to be shipped back to England and become HEN's bitch. The problem was—he had no clue what to do. When the door opened and Lucus came in with HEN, Rich, deep in thought, felt like his prayers had been answered. Lucus looked at Rich and gasped.

"You know him?" demanded HEN.

"No, no, sir, I—I—"

HEN laughed. "Don't tell me you also fuckin' fancy him. Handsome, ain't he?"

Lucus said nothing. "It's okay. He can't hear you. The fucker's ears got damaged in the blast, so you can say anything to him," laughed HEN. "Watch."

HEN wheeled himself up to Rich. "You're a fuckin' handsome bastard that drives me crazy, and I can't wait to get you home and shag you 'cause you owe me big time. And I'm gonna have ya as me slave." HEN laughed. "See? He can't hear. He would've knocked me out if he had heard that."

Lucus wasn't convinced. He was watching Rich closely. Although Rich's face gave nothing away, his fists were clenched as if he were about to hit someone.

HEN was oblivious as he gave orders. "So, boy, if I put ya on the payroll, I expect full loyalty. I pay well for people to take the heat off me. I don't have many connections here, and the shit I supply is the best. I need a distributor, and that's now you."

Lucus was about to protest.

"It's worth five, maybe six grand a month. Maybe more, depends how well you do. I can give ya money in advance to keep ya interested. I supply the phones and codes. Questions?"

Lucus's mind was stuck on *five or six thousand a month.*

"No, no, sir. But I thought you needed help here today."

"No, do I shit? We're out of here soon. That's all done."

Lucus looked at Rich, who was staring at him.

"I'll think about it, sir, and let you know," said Lucus.

"What d'you mean, *I'll think about it*?" HEN mocked.

"Nothing to fuckin' think about. You're the man. You know too much now. So, you're either useful... or dead. Which is it?"

"I'm in, sir," said Lucus.

"Good. Now fuck off. Come back tomorrow, same time. I'll arrange for the team to call ya on that computer. We'll do the details then. You'll need to learn the codes we give ya. Apart from that, kid, you're gonna be well off."

Lucus left the room. Rich grabbed some paper. *What the fuck was that about? I don't trust him. I'm gonna follow him.*

HEN shrugged and nodded as Rich left the room. Ah, bless him. He's protecting me, thought HEN.

Rich caught up with Lucus.

"Oi, ya little fucker," he said, grabbing Lucus's arm. "In here."

Rich dragged Lucus into a consultation room.

"Sit."

Lucus sat and stared at Rich. "So what's this all about?" demanded Rich.

"Thought you couldn't hear," said Lucus.

"Well, you thought wrong. And if you tell anyone—"

"I won't, I won't! I said I didn't know you."

"Yeah? Why'd you do that?" asked Rich.

"Because I really like Steph, and she was broken when they told her you had been killed. But she didn't believe it—she just couldn't find you. So I figured she'd want to know you were alive… and she'd pay me. But now I'm involved in something else."

Rich suddenly softened toward Lucus at the mention of Steph. So that's why she hasn't been around. They told her I was dead.

"Who told her?" asked Rich.

"What?"

"You said *they* told her I was dead."

"Oh. Yeah, it was some dude on the door with a list. I was with her. She asked after you, and then your name went on a list of missing people. We managed to get to the ward, but it was locked. We asked a nurse if you were on the ward, but she said no. She was broken, man. Broken."

"So where is she now?" asked Rich.

"Dunno, man. I think at the villa. She wanted to be left alone, and the others wouldn't let me contact her."

"Others?"

"Yeah, I live with Robin and Jo. Jo is the woman you tried to kill when you left her on that boat."

Rich slipped to the floor.

"It follows me wherever I go," he muttered.

"What does?"

"Trouble. I'm not a bad person. I was off my face on drugs back then. I don't expect her to forgive me."

"She won't," said Lucus.

Rich nodded. "Anyway, man, you gonna help me or him?"

"Do I have a choice?"

"Yeah, man, you do. I'm not that person anymore. If you choose him, then fair enough, but I need you to keep quiet. If you choose me, well… we get out of here tomorrow when he's at physio."

"I dunno, man. I think I trust him more than you. But I like Steph a lot, and I'd like to see her happy… but I also like his offer."

"Well? You in or out?"

"Don't rush me, man. Why can't I do both?"

"Do ya think he'll do business with ya once I'm gone?" asked Rich.

Lucus wanted the deal from HEN. He liked the idea of regular money, and he liked the idea of being a drug lord—because that meant everyone would want him and respect him. Lucus had already dreamt of the money rolling in and the place he would buy for him and Robin.

"Well?" asked Rich impatiently.

"No, I'm not helping you. I'm sticking with Mr. Tom. I want the work, and I want the deal."

"You're a fool," said Rich as he walked away.

"Hey, if ya tell anyone we had this conversation, you'll be done."

"I know, I know. I'm not stupid," said Lucus.

Rich made his way back to his room. Hen was waiting.

WHERE YOU BEEN? WHAT HAPPENED? he wrote.

I don't fuckin' trust him. He went out to the bus stop, wrote Rich.

Hen laughed and wrote, *Thank you for looking out for me, my love. I know this is not the right time, but I wanna be with you all the time. Will you be my partner, Rich?*

Rich read the note over and over. He felt sick and scared as he tried to think of a way out of this.

Rich wrote, *Fuck off, man. Being in hospital made ya soft. Ya know me—I don't belong to anyone.*

Hen smiled, but he felt disappointed. He had imagined Rich throwing his arms around him, holding him in appreciation for saving him. But no—Rich was being his usual selfish bastard.

Thank God. I thought ya might say yes, wrote Hen.

Rich smiled, raised his thumb, and wondered how the hell he was getting out of here.

Lucus returned the following day to meet HEN. He stopped to see Rich first, passing him an envelope.

"Here. Money and instructions to get you to the villa. Best of luck."

Rich followed Lucus, but Hen was being wheeled down the corridor.

"Okay, nurse, thank you. He's my friend—he can take over."

Rich went to take over the pushing.

"No! Not you; him!" shouted Hen.

Rich looked at Hen.

"Oh, sorry, man, ya can't hear me, daft fucker," laughed Hen. "Just take over from him, push him out the way," said Hen to Lucus.

Hen got his notepad.

Fuck off, man. I have business with my friend, and it's none of yours.

Rich read the note, nodded his head, gave Hen the finger, and walked off.

Hen laughed. *Treat 'em mean; they stay keen.*

"Come on, you. We have business to discuss. Take me to the gardens, away from ears and eyes." Lucus pushed Hen toward the garden, all the while looking back at Rich walking away.

In the envelope were instructions on how to reach the villa by bus and then taxi. It also contained 30 euros in change. Rich smiled as he walked out of the hospital and toward the bus stop. Soon, he would be in her arms, and he was never leaving her side. She was the love of his life—the only woman who understood him and loved him for who he was. At last, he had learned that love was in the mind and not his dick. Rich felt so happy. He had survived the explosion and the fire, dodged the law, and now he was ready to settle. Then he realized that he needed to be on the opposite side of the road for the bus.

Leon had been driving oil tankers for years. He liked to think he was the best in the business, but today, he felt annoyed that they had assigned him the hospital run. It was a job given to novices, and when he got back, he was going to say something to that new boss—an unorganized twat.

The oil tanker seemed to come out of nowhere. Rich didn't see it coming as he stepped out.

Leon had just reached for his sandwich when he saw a bloke walking into the road. Swerving to avoid him, the tanker mounted the pavement, crashing through a concrete flower bed and hurtling toward the hospital grounds. Leon was trying to bring the tanker under control, but the beast was picking up speed, not slowing down. He banged the horn, shouting out of the window—he knew this was not good, and he would need a miracle to get out of this, as the tanker was not responding.

People were screaming, trying to get out of the way as the tanker plowed through parked cars, flower beds, and streetlights, flattening everything in its path as it made its way to the hospital grounds.

Hen had ordered Lucus to get them a drink. He was thirsty. He hated the sun and the heat. "Can't wait to get back home, get some rain. This fuckin' heat is crazy, man. Go get us some drink, man." Lucus dutifully went off as ordered—after all, this was his new boss.

Hen waited in the garden. He had found some shade by the wall under a lovely willow tree. It was nice and quiet. They had done some good business. Hen was pleased—little Lucus was happy to agree to his terms. Hen smiled. Dumb kid, he thought. But what did Hen care? He would make millions.

"Hen wouldn't have felt a thing. It would have been instant," said the doctor as he tried to console Lucus. Lucus was hysterical—not only had he lost the opportunity to make money, but a few more minutes either way and he would have been behind the wall. Of course, Lucus cried for Hen, but he cried for himself more.

Rich watched in horror as the tanker that had just missed him appeared out of control, making its way toward the hospital grounds. Suddenly, he remembered Hen had asked Lucus to take him to the garden. Fuck, thought Rich as he got onto the bus. Hope there's more than one garden. The bus driver was shouting in Spanish on his phone. He parked the bus and gestured for everyone to wait while he continued talking. Rich watched as the emergency services screamed around the corner.

Eventually, the bus driver returned, shaking his head. He looks sad, thought Rich. The driver spoke to the passengers, but he spoke so quickly that Rich struggled to understand. From the reaction of the women on the bus—some of whom started crying—Rich gathered it wasn't good news.

"Anyone speak English?" he asked.

"Señor, I do," said the woman behind him.

"Thank fuck—sorry, I mean, thank you. What's going on?"

"Ah, the, er, tanker... it, er, lost—how you say?—Control, and now in hospital grounds. Very sad. Killed twelve persons, most patients in hospital. It is a very sad day, sir," the woman said.

"Yeah, yeah, it is very sad," said Rich. "Do ya think the driver will be okay to drive us? He looks upset."

The woman shrugged. "I think yes, but maybe no. Spanish men are... how you say? Very, er, cry, very female... no, I do not know the word," she said.

Rich nodded. He knew what she meant.

"They're as soft as shit," he said.

The woman shrugged and nodded, not really wanting to continue a conversation with this English pig who clearly had no feelings. Rich got the feeling he had just stepped over the mark. Shut the fuck up, he told himself as he turned away from the woman.

THE VILLA

It was the day of Rich's funeral; not that anyone was coming, nor did she have a body, but it felt right to do something for the man she loved.

Steph had chosen the music. She had written some words and filled the place with flowers. She draped his clothes around the room and sprayed his aftershave on everything. Steph felt stronger today. The thought of never seeing Rich again was something she was coming to terms with. She had broken her heart over him. She had even hired a detective to find him, but that led nowhere, except to his name on a list of missing, presumed dead.

She missed him so much. He was so wrong, yet so right for her. They were a perfect match. Steph smiled as memories of Rich flooded her mind. The first time they met, the first time they made love, the time she watched him in the shower, how her body ached for him, how he made her feel. He was a real man—tough, manly, and she loved it.

She knew she was difficult to live with. She liked things her way. But Rich made her wait. He would never give in, and the arguments they had were off the scale. No one had ever talked to her in such a degrading way—and yet, here she was, missing those moments. It wasn't really the arguments she missed but the passion that followed when they made up.

Rich would be rough. She would pretend she didn't want him, and he would force himself on her. And she loved it. He was the kind of man she had read about in magazines and saucy novels, never believing such a man would be in her bed. But in her bed, he was.

Tears fell from her eyes as she realized she would never hold him again. The tears streamed down her face as she remembered her dear son. She felt guilty; she rarely thought about him. They had buried him with her late husband back in England. Perhaps this was karma, she thought, for not thinking about Terrance. Come on, pull yourself together. Stop feeling sorry for yourself. Get today over with and move on, woman, she told herself.

Steph lost herself in her thoughts and got lost in the music. She had thought about selling up, moving, starting all over again, but she loved this place. It was full of the best memories, all of them of him.

She recalled the first time Rich came to look at the villa. He had been like a child, walking around with his mouth open, not quite believing what he was seeing.

"I can't believe I'm gonna live here," he had told her. *"Rich Luck, living in a fuckin' mansion."*

"Not only live in it, darling, but you will own half of it. I will put your name down on the deeds. It will be yours, my darling."

Rich had grabbed her and kissed her with such passion she could still feel it. She wrapped her arms around herself, imagining it was Rich holding her tight. Swaying to the music, she was lost in the moment. And life, her only savior was gone. She had no one.

Yes, she had a beautiful villa in one of the most enviable locations on the island. She had land and businesses both here and in the UK. But they ticked over nicely; she didn't really need to do anything except spend the money they brought in. And she couldn't even do that quick enough—she had too much.

"Look at me."

She stopped dancing and looked at herself in the mirror—eyes bloodshot from crying, hair a mess. She wore another robe because it was easy. She couldn't recall the last time she did her nails or had a beauty treatment.

"You're just a sad old woman," she said to her reflection.

"Look at you, wallowing in self-pity, and you have all this. There are people out there with nothing. Pull yourself together, get yourself smartened up, and stop this. NOW!"

Steph raised her glass to her reflection. *"Cheers to that. And cheers to the new me. I start again."*

She picked up the pen and wrote.

To-do list

Clear his stuff out

Book a spa weekend

Call hairdresser

Book a holiday

New car

Call estate agent

Go see Lucus and Robin

Find someone to take care of the grounds and pool

Find a man!

There. That feels better already, she thought. I have a plan.

"Now, lady, get yourself smartened up, get out of this goddamn house, and start ticking off that list."

She smiled at her reflection as she headed for the bathroom.

Two Selfish

The bus seemed to be taking ages. Rich was convinced the driver was driving slowly on purpose. His mind wandered—what would he say? What would she say? He was definitely going to ask her to marry him. In fact, he was going to arrange it. No questions, no ifs or buts—they would be married. She was his, and he wanted no one else. He had been angry that she had never visited him, but…

To be continued…